The Cricket Cries, the Year Changes

The Cricket Cries, the Year Changes

By

Cynthia Harris-Allen

This book is dedicated to my parents, the late Robert Lee and Dorothea Lee Harris, who indulged my every whim.

In memoriam: To my brother
Armendez "Jerry" Harris
July 3, 1949——September 13, 2016

And, to my ancestors, if not for them........

ACKNOWLEDGEMENTS

To my children, Keith Allen, Brad Allen and Joy Allen Lawrence for their encouragement and active support throughout every endeavor I ever entered into.

My beta readers: Jewell and Ron Stewart, Michael Kevin McMahon, Rev. Dr. Cheviene Jones, Kevin Chapman and the Eastside Readers' Group, Molly Perry, Mimi Plevin-Foust, Mary Oluonye, Beverly Douglas-Weir, The Greater Cleveland Writers Group Meetup, Clara Gillow Clark, Carol Shaheed, Michael Kevin McMahon and Shirley Kilpatrick.

I am grateful to my aunt, Eudelia Harris Cummings who shared much information with me about her life growing up in rural Georgia. My late father, Robert Lee Harris was born in Monroe, Georgia which served as the fictional setting for my novel. I have visited Monroe and Macon, Georgia several times.

The red clay and tall Georgia pines are real. I acknowledge its presence and influence upon the many slaves who looked above and walked below.

I thank God who blessed me with a heightened sense of curiosity and perhaps the ability to piece together with words, what I felt when I walked upon those hallowed grounds.

"....the clay is vile beneath our, feet and long the mile..."

Paul Laurence Dunbar, *We Wear the Mask*

"The Cricket Cries, the Year Changes"
African Proverb

FOREWORD

In this set of slave narratives, Cynthia Harris-Allen creates stories rife with the untold history of the United States of America. Her portrayal of the sheer brutality of slavery as practiced on the Harris-Jones Plantation leaves the reader wondering how any human being survived such treatment. Slaveholders not only refused to recognize the humanity of enslaved Africans, but also employed ingenious forms of cruelty to see to it that blacks would not dare regard themselves as human.

But their tactics did not destroy the genial spirit deeply embedded in the African soul. The determination to be free was a centerpiece of their lives. They had the courage to run. The audacity to hope was part of their DNA. We all need to read these stories, identify with these beleaguered enslaved people, and understand how a people with not even a modicum of protection under the law managed to live and to make progress.

As African-Americans, we should be ever mindful of the details of their existence on the plantation, so that we can make ourselves into people who live lives worthy of such a legacy. It is our duty to fulfill their hopes and dreams.

Gail Rose
Life Member ASALH,

The Carter Woodson Foundation

FOREWORD

A quilt narrator measuring forty-eight inches wide, and five and a half feet long opens and closes this story, and like the pieces of fabric stitched together to make a quilt, so too are the lives of twenty slaves living on the Harris-Jones Plantation woven together to create a stunning masterpiece in Cynthia Harris-Allen's debut novel.

The story begins and ends with a slave named Kaffie. Using language that is vividly descriptive, reminiscent of Zora Neale Hurston, Harris-Allen tells the separate, yet interconnected lives of twenty slaves living on the same plantation over time. Unflinchingly depicted, and often in graphic detail, their lives are played out against the backdrop of unrelenting cruelty, violence, brutality, mental and physical torture, and inhumane conditions that slaves endured on a daily basis.

Harris-Allen does not gloss over details of the worst cruelties of slavery. While readers may abhor what is happening, they will also be riveted because they will have been drawn into the lives of the characters and understand their feelings, motivations, and come to know their friends, loves, enemies, as well as their relationships with other people, both black and white.

Readers will keep reading to find out what happens to them and to the people they care about. Numerous exacting details throughout the story gives insight into the amount of research involved in the writing of this book.

There is a flawless intricacy in the way that the life of each slave unfolds as a separate "mini-book" that contributes to the final completed book, much in the same way that the sections of a quilt contribute to the completed whole. Universal themes abound throughout the novel.

The Cricket Cries, the Year Changes is a poignant searing reminder of the horrors of slavery and a shameful period of American history, while shining a light on the men, women and children who struggled to survive in any way that they could under the circumstances in which they lived.

Mary N. Oluonye Reviewer, School Library Journal
Reviewer, Journal of African-American History

The Cricket Cries, the Year Changes

I am forty-eight inches wide, five and a half feet long, colorful, and three-dimensional. I've been told that I was a comforter to many people. My ancestors were the cotton plant on my mother's side and sometimes, a non-committing silkworm on my father's. I was plied through cards and spun into thread. My fluffy soft beginnings changed to off-white hanks of strong durable fabric.

Many melodies were sung over me——from my seedling start to my rows of snow-like harvest. Verses became lullabies born by the rhythms of the spinning wheels. They calmed my weavers while they moved me between bent fingers toward new beginnings. My family's merger with the palettes of indigo, madder, brown walnut and cochineal orchestrated my first communion. They showered me with rainbows of color that competed with intensity for attention.

In some instances, my basic body was block-stamped with symbols, imprinted with intricate designs or submerged in wax resists. I was boiled in huge cauldrons. The vigilant eyes of the dye makers anxiously awaited my lustrous hued debut. At times, I was vibrant and appealing; other times found me as a pale, melancholy, worn out piece. I could become a color-filled weave whose hidden symbols purposed the survival of many people. In all examples, I had the strength to cover and the genius to adorn.

I was known to appear rough and nubby. Many people luxuriated in my silky smoothness. I offered flannelled warmth as well as summer cool.

I am cotton, the Queen of the antebellum South. Cotton was the conscience of my many masters. I owned them. I am a cotton quilt. More pointedly, I am the African slave named Kaffie's, creation. Throughout her lifetime, Kaffie's tireless fingers pierced and placed my cotton remnants from the lives of certain slaves against a sorrow-filled background of soft needs and harsh realities. She chronicled their storied incidents through tear by salty tear as their intertwined testimonies formed the mosaic that is I.

Cynthia Harris-Allen

I can tell you each tale with circumstance and certainty as I clothed every member or visitor to, the Harris-Jones plantation as well as the outlying characters. They lay on top of me as they slept or made love. I would cover them when they sought warmth or rest. They shed their thoughts, motives, and dreams into me. I am both a witness for the prosecution and the defense.

As I hang from the exhibitors' clotheslines on this hot July day of yet another quilt fair, my competitors are swinging lively in the near-tropical breeze.

I, however, wish to remain motionless.

I have memories to share.

The Cricket Cries, the Year Changes

KAFFIE

Chapter 1

Snow flurries fell in Monroe Georgia? What a sight! It wisped through the air like tiny stray puffs of cotton as it circled silently toward the grounds of the Harris-Jones plantation. Sudden gusts of semi-frosty winds darted flakes in different danced directions before it settled onto the warm, red clay and onto the fields.

The wearied slaves up since dawn held their tattered and worn clothing closer to their bodies as they stood in the unseasonably cold weather. The din of the hoes, picks, and trowels gradually stopped while the workers witnessed this early morning miracle. Most had never seen snow before. They tried to catch the melting snow but soon lost it as it lessened in their calloused hands. Some of the black children opened their mouths with tongues extended to taste the snow. They squealed with wonder while this freak of nature entertained them.

Other slaves held their bare feet out from under thinning frocks and frayed pants to feel the white shavings fall upon them. It sharply contrasted with their coffee bean brown skins. Some showed fear not knowing or trusting this intrusion. They began to moan a unified song of uncertainty and doom.

The overseers, plus a handful of white indentured servants, stood transfixed among the Negroes. They marveled and reveled in the spectacle. This was a first experience for many of them as well. The owner of the plantation, Mr. Harris was awakened by the clamor that came from the central part of his large homestead. He realized the source of the uproar when he gazed out the window. The wintry mix greeted him.

He recalled a sudden snowfall as a child some fifty years ago growing up on his father's small farm in South Carolina. He sensed his own first delight. Harris dressed quickly and headed toward the fields upon his horse. The large assembly of huddled reapers had paused to witness the flurried light squall. It really did not feel that cold to Harris.

3

Cynthia Harris-Allen

Master Harris lifted his disheveled balding head to the sky; his squinting grey eyes followed the trail of a singular snowflake. It landed on the horse's mane. His freckled weathered face gave permission for a rare slight grin to form from his thin dry lips. He relinquished the nostalgic weakness and motioned to the overseers to order the slaves back to work. He feared it might get colder as the day progressed. The wrought-ironed rooster weather vane atop the barn showed no hard wind direction.

The slaves slowly returned to their field positions in the row after row of ripened crops. The grunts of hard labor normalized the farming routines on the Harris-Jones plantation.

Tillie Harris, the master's wife, walked toward the fields as she held the hand of their six-year-old daughter. She had hurriedly placed a coat over Luvinia's clothing as they came outdoors to view the snowflakes. With their hands held glove-to glove, Mrs. Harris walked toward her husband while he spoke to the overseers.

Luvinia's snaggled-tooth grin marveled at the white dots and soon loosened her mother's grip to chase them. Her mother warned her to stay close. Luvinia, with her hands high in the air, revealed crinoline petticoats, and knitted leggings underneath a calico dress. She twirled in a semi-circle as she playfully hummed a skittish tune. She crouched to the ground to peer as close as she could into the disappearing snowflakes seemingly to dare them to melt before she could finish gushing over their soft beauty.

Her mother turned her head away from her husband to gauge Luvinia's whereabouts and could not locate her. Slightly panicked, Tillie called out to her. Luvinia answered right away from her location. Her mother walked swiftly toward the voice and found Luvinia and a slave girl squatted together on the ground. They laughed as they studied the falling snow.

Tillie grabbed her daughter's hand and yanked her to a standing position. She scolded her for straying too far away from her. The startled little slave girl began to cry. Luvinia darted a peeved look toward her mother as she dragged her back towards the mansion. All the while, Luvinia ranted her need to continue to play with her new friend. Her reddened face blurred by the tears in her eyes gave several backward glances to the slave girl.

#

Two weeks later, on a more normal October sultry Georgia day, Luvinia and Tillie Harris strolled towards the fields accompanied by an overseer who rode on horseback not far behind them. Luvinia's ceaseless begging to let her play with her new friend, named "Kaffie," had brought them to the fields. Master Harris did not have a young slave girl with that name in his slave rolls. Luvinia had often pressed her parents for someone to play with. Now, she wanted this particular black girl.

This spoiled child cared for by a mammy, spent a lot of time alone with her dolls and her imagination. Her parents thought it was wild at work again as she had conjured up this "new friend." Just as her mother was about to give up the search among the slaves for a little girl named "Kaffie", Luvinia ran to a slightly built slave girl, pulled her from between the rows of corn, and hugged her as she claimed her prize. The girl responded by letting her arms fall limply at her sides. She dropped her gunnysack and stood still not knowing what to do next. Luvinia asked her mother if she could take her home with her. Tillie asked the scared mulatto her name. She softly responded "Kathy."

Tillie Harris agreed to let Kaffie come to play with Luvinia in the mansion yard just for that afternoon. She winced at the body odor of this girl. She shuddered when Luvinia grabbed both of Kathy's dirty hands with her own bare white hands.

Luvinia faced Kathy and walked backwards all the way back to the mansion path. She pulled the barefoot, reticent, tripping Kathy along. Luvinia talked incessantly about her dolls, her toys, her room, and her pony. She was glad to have them, but she was ecstatic to have her Kaffie even for one day. The slaves' roll revealed Kathy as an orphan who lived with a surrogate family in one of the row cabins. She was eight years old and had lived on the plantation since birth. Her birth date was the same as Luvinia's though Kathy was two years older than she.

Eventually within days, Mrs. Harris acceded to her daughter's unceasing appeals and brought the mulatto slave into the big house to live. Tillie had her inspected for sickness or disease by the mammy. The cook dunked Kathy into a worn wooden tub on the mansion back porch. Luvinia leaned on the large bucket the entire time teasing Kathy about the freckles all over her face. Luvinia's unbroken chatter did not stop until a coarse towel was used to dry Kathy off sealing her initiation.

The mammy had parted her soft, nutmeg brown hair and plaited two medium length braids. She told Luvinia to wait until she dressed Kaffie and then they could play outdoors. In the huge kitchen, the black cook, Mary, gazed upon Kathy cleaned and clothed. She offered her a piece of pound cake and some peach tea as she sat her at the small table. The cook understood how overwhelmed Kathy must have felt and extended her assuring and inviting arms to hug her. Kathy rushed into the smells of her apron as she released tears of questionable joy.

As she looked into her grey eyes the cook told her she could call her "Mary." Luvinia fidgeted by the door.

The arrangements made were that the two would play together under the watchful eye of the mammy during the day, but Kathy had to sleep in the attic in Mary's room. That suited Luvinia fine. She climbed the planked steps to the attic during the night and joined Kathy and Mammy in bed on several occasions.

The master officially changed the name of Kathy Harris-Jones to Kaffie Harris-Jones on the slave rolls. Wheaton Jones had been his partner for over twenty years and had died, leaving a huge debt due to his gambling. Harris assumed his obligations but had continued for business purposes to include the Jones name in the plantation slave rolls.

The Cricket Cries, the Year Changes

Chapter 2

Kaffie was educated while she grew up with Luvinia. It was against the law to do so, but she learned indirectly. Years later, her speech and reasoning measured equally or better, than most whites. Soon her skills as a seamstress became evident. She had an eye for detail as well as color. The mistress began outsourcing Kaffie's talents to other homesteads. Wagonloads of orders for southern ball gowns and northern heavy clothing came pouring in. Sometimes, Kaffie was driven to neighboring plantations to alter dresses or pants. The mistress was paid handsomely.

Kaffie decided to make quilts with the remnants of fabric left over from her work. One day, she presented Tillie Harris with a quilt that she had made for one of the guest rooms. It was hard for her to believe this slave, only eighteen years old could create such a piece without formal training. She praised her economy in using the waste fabric and the fact that she spent her own leisure time to construct the quilt.

Its workmanship was impeccable. The seams were straight, and the stitches were even. The patterned and solid colors were coordinated and complemented one another. Each piece in the quilt met the other in perfectly formed rows and angles in every direction. Mistress Harris decided to bring in slave girls and two indentured servant women who would learn the art of quilting at Kaffie's feet. This new enterprise could add to her burgeoning reputation and prestige.

\#

Luvinia, at sixteen, was introduced to southern society at a grand cotillion. She found little time now to be with Kaffie. She entertained prospective beaus and had grown-up tea parties with her girlfriends. She now considered Kaffie as part of the help and treated her with indifference. After all, one day she would be mistress of this plantation and their prior relationship would have to be severed.

Kaffie had the opportunity to commune with the slaves when she delivered their semi-annual allotment of two to three outfits each of clothing. The apparel was mass-produced throughout the seasons by Kaffie and the apprenticed help. The slaves greeted Kaffie warmly when she worked under a tent in the yards. She repaired and patched clothing that was not yet ready for the rag pile. She did not have daily access to them but welcomed their attention.

Under the tent she was informed of the events that occurred in the slave society. Other news came from the younger slave girls who sewed alone with her in the Big House. Additionally other details were exchanged by the house slaves as they whispered in the shadows. Kaffie joined her people with a standing invitation on many Sundays for cookouts and celebrations. She remembered from her childhood how to interpret the drum codes and whistled alarms used by the slaves. She would lift her head from her work to heed the messages.

Oftentimes Ngango, the witch doctor, sent her roots and herbs when he heard that she was ailing and desired slave healing.

Kaffie was sensitive about her place as a member in the Big House and regretted that her labor was not as arduous as the majority of the slaves. She was never whipped, punished or starved. Nevertheless, a slave did not have any privacy living in the Big House. One could be summoned at midnight or at dawn. Many days found Kaffie sleep deprived particularly during the height of the southern society party season.

She wept when slaves, especially the babies and children, died en masse from pneumonia, dysentery or hookworm. She sewed draw-stringed shrouds from the muslin she used for pattern pieces and slipped it to the grieving mothers.

Kaffie channeled the pain and shame when many slaves suffered at the whip as the passageway into her work. Respect for her genteel spirit, her willingness to keep them clothed and covered beyond what was expected enfolded Kaffie into their hearts. She was not emotionally equipped to process the protracted, layered atrocities that occurred on the Harris-Jones plantation. She found comfort in preserving the memories of some of the victims. The best way she knew how was through her quilting. My cotton remnants sedated her grief.

My quilt became their vagabond eulogy.

The Cricket Cries, the Year Changes

That is how I came to hang from this clothesline.

Cynthia Harris-Allen

ABIGAIL

Chapter 1

Abigail was black as onyx. Her face held huge lips at the base of her wide nose. She probably had the coarsest hair on the Harris-Jones plantation. It was hard as granite because she plaited it with mud as was the custom of her Watusi tribe. Abigail would crouch for hours in the hot sun on Sundays. She mixed water, palm oil, and red Georgia clay. She intertwined this concoction between the three-sectioned twists of her hair. It formed circular designs where it intersected. She piled it high upon her head. She held the strands in place with small smooth sticks that she had whittled. They kept the braids in place as the final assembly dried quickly in the sun. She protected the finished work with a turban.

Abigail was very tall, angular, and strong. She was a tireless worker. She harvested sugar cane along with the male slaves who treated her as one of them. They marveled at her strength. She could wield a machete better than most of them; her deftness with the huge knife impressed even the overseers as she held the cane stalks prisoner and swiped its leaves from the top. She simultaneously kicked them into a pile. She abruptly abandoned the shorn stalks on the ground as she trudged and reached for the taller uncut cane, some over thirteen feet high.

The shorter slower men labored to keep up with her while they retrieved the bamboo-like shafts to stack while the leaves were separated for fodder. Her movements with the machete formed a measured fluid pattern. Abigail sheared the leaves and stumped her feet to ward off the snakes that lay hidden. She controlled the arc of its downward swing to within an inch of her feet.

When Abigail chopped wood, she raised the axe high above her six-foot plus frame. The iron met the splintering wood pieces accompanied by her loud grunts. The pairing met with such fury that it instantly pulled it away from its barked shield fragmenting its former likeness. She held her breath when she hoisted the axe again and released rhythmic guttural sounds until all the pieces had surrendered. Her

10

large calloused hands revealed insect bites, burns, and the cuts of her labor. Her elongated fingers vexed by her ever-unraveling gauze turban accessorized her lengthy arms.

She had the neck of a gazelle that she adorned with a strand of beads; it symbolized her status as royalty from a faraway village. The brass beads with tiny inlaid carvings were given to her by her mother when she lived on the island of Jamaica where they were first enslaved. Abigail wore them in memoriam to her family now lost and gone forever. Her arresting medium-sized brown eyes charted the landscape of the plantation. She was very much in tune with her surroundings. She appeared to be always on guard for something——anything——that would unsettle her inward natural balance. She was a reliable worker and never exhibited any resistance or resentment to her enslavement. She did not talk much but when she did her words were measured, deliberate, but friendly.

Abigail's favorite color was red. Her turbans were made from the dyed gauze castoffs that Cecelia, the dye maker had given to her. She wore loose-fitting clothing of calico or muslin that harbored geranium red dots or splotches of crimson somewhere within its weave. Her skirts fell to her muscled mid-calves because her tall frame denied the hems access to her ankles. She tore off the sleeves of her blouses and shirts; they restricted her movement and were unable to sheathe her large upper arms in comfort.

The red dye washed away to a faded pink as Abigail pounded her clothes on the smooth gray rocks near the riverbanks on Sundays. She regrettably watched the cherry reds merge with the coarse lye soap as the duo slimed toward the high reeds that trapped the suds. She promised herself to petition Cecelia again for the coveted, cardinal pieces.

The overseers sat on their horses with whips and shotguns at the ready while they watched the slaves who washed their clothes, themselves or both. The slaves shed their tired coverings and with welcomed abandon plunged themselves into the cold refreshing waters of the river. They bobbed up and down. Adults and children alike played and splashed in the wet balm. Others just stood in the water with arms folded across their chests with eyes closed. Their bodies stood in silent repose.

Abigail immersed herself into the river fully clothed. She waded out into it until the cool waters met her neckline. She lowered her head into the water and held her breath for a very long time. The overseers thought at first that she had intended to drown herself. They soon dismissed this repeated practice as some ancestral ritualistic act. She emerged from the waters with her arms raised to the skies. She sent muddled shouts toward the sun.

Several white men aroused by the partial nakedness of the blacks, mocked with sneering remarks the physical attributes of the slaves especially the budding females. The men cursed them and desired them at the same time—— though the latter sentiment did not make its vocal rounds. Abigail made mental notes of their behavior particularly that of Joe Butler and Donnie Winbush.

The Cricket Cries, the Year Changes

Chapter 2

Newly purchased slaves to the plantation who had lived on the Sea Islands off the coast of Georgia were instantly reminded of their homeland when they saw Abigail. She called to their memory the Watusi tribespeople from the coastal villages of the motherland. They looked upon her with pride.

Abigail chose to sleep alone in the furthest cabin in the semi-circular area of the plantation. A choice granted to her by Harris. A few personal possessions littered the cabin. There were small charcoal drawings of Abigail created by Betsey that captured in detail Abigail's intricate braids and facial resolve. Cowrie shells once used as barter lay in a small pile in one corner. No longer a valid currency In America, it soon served a valuable purpose for the slave population.

Oval, orange trails, created by rusted chains flowed from empty holes in the stucco walls. Abigail had secured large nails from the blacksmith and pushed them into the holes. She hung her clothing high above the soiled and grimy floor rather than provide a muslin refuge for the night crawlers. The copper dirt floor held two hollowed out spaces to accommodate bowls and pots. A large woven mat constructed by Boway, the basket weaver, lay right under the one foot high, by half-foot wide window that faced southward. The portal enabled Abigail to see the comings and goings of the whites to the forward cabins under cover of night.

Abigail's observations of the treatment of female slaves included the scalding of those who had been impregnated by the whites. The results of these nocturnal invasions caused their dishonored and humiliated white women to react in anger. The black mothers became the surrogate punishment for their adulterous men. The mistresses and wives would burn the black females with hot lye or wax while they pretended to inspect their laundering of clothes or process of making candles.

The new black mothers, some as young as twelve, their after-birthed bodies still swollen with the sinful testimonies of recent mulatto births, bravely bore the onslaughts as they protected their newly born children. Mysterious, injurious, and sometime fatal events befell some of those white women who had participated in those heinous acts. Master Harris was unable to bring to justice the person or persons responsible for these retaliations. There were no witnesses.

On this plantation suspicious and vile acts were always attributed to Ngango, the witch doctor. The whites quickly surmised that if the slaves feared his powers, who were they to test it? Besides, Master Harris needed this dreaded, medicinal caretaker to preserve his property.

Abigail clenched her fists as she watched the treatment meted out to runaways re-captured and returned to the plantation. They would be chained together for not less than five days in the open yard for all to see. The guards whipped them fiercely. A barbaric solitary lash tore skin from several slaves at a time as it maimed ears, eyes, and noses. The leathery weapon thrashed loudly as it circled in the air. It was immediately drowned out by shrills and cries from the slaves. They took turns holding their breaths while fearful eyes followed the arc of the overseer's arm as it was raised again, and again.

They were shackled en masse as they slept. They lay in the knots they had created from the rusted iron circles. They struggled to gain a space to lay their heads. The male captives debased their chained female counterparts. The entire group was bound as they sought privacy to relieve themselves. The dragged group moved to a corner by the fence. The stench, the excrements, and the public shame that had trumped their private longings, morphed into a singular, miserable life in the hellish Georgia heat. The overseers kept the prisoners in the yard to teach a lesson but not to kill. They were not purchased for that long tortuous purpose. In some instances their levels of discipline outpaced their assumptions; several died in the restraints.

The captured runaways spied Abigail's red and white turban as it ambled toward them high above most of the other field hands. They were eager to see her and to feel her comforting hands. She calmed them down with a softening quiet. Sometimes, she brought more than consolation. Her deliberate long-legged stride was not altered by the weight of what she held on her head. Abigail carried multiple gourds of water and food sacks to quench thirsts and feed the shackled people. She darted looks of defiance to the guards and overseers who never challenged her presence or warded off her purpose.

She used a tool she borrowed from Scipio, the African blacksmith, to pry open the seams where one iron portion of the chains met the other. She inserted longer lengths of restraints that extended the space between the captured. She used the strength of her hands to reconnect the links. She rubbed palm oil on their unraveled bodies, saying nothing. Abigail had torn strips of Cecelia's discarded dyed cotton and dipped them in water from the well. She fashioned wet headbands for the males, and soaked turbans for the women to mitigate the incessant heat that bore down upon the yards. If runaways were caught during the cooler winter months, Abigail brought blankets to cover the common mound.

Master Harris appreciated her unsolicited care.

#

One day during the layby, the season between sowing and harvesting, Master Harris entertained his friends on the mansion porch. He proposed that he enter Abigail into a race. She was to compete against a horse in a four-furlong race. It would take place along a dusty road at the perimeter of his plantation. He bet his friends that if Abigail was given a head start of five hundred feet she could beat any horse to the finish line. A wagon would follow slowly, a good ways behind her, to monitor her progress toward the red flag. The five-hundred foot marker would hang high on a Georgia pine. The wager included a statement that the horse she would compete against could not be a thoroughbred. The bet was three thousand dollars.

A lone groomsman would follow behind the driven wagon while he paced the horse. He would slap its rear when Abigail reached the red-flagged pole. A simultaneous gunshot into the air would frighten the horse and inform Abigail that the race had begun. The men wagered heavily against Abigail.

Abigail told Master Harris that no onlookers could frame the sidelines. They would distract her. She jokingly said they could congregate at the finish line to celebrate her victory. Harris smiled. She checked out the route and found there were many swampy areas just to the right of that long road. She told Harris she needed to sweep the area for holes, twigs or debris that could dent her pace or cause her to trip. She insisted that future traffic on that area be detoured for she did not want to have to clean up the road again. For days leading up to the race she ran to the furthest part of the road and surveyed the larger landscape.

She then returned to the designated starting point. She placed her sweaty palms on her knees to catch her breath. She stood straight as an arrow with her arms rested on her hips. To the delight of Master Harris, Abigail sprinted twice daily, at dawn and at night. Each time she increased her speed and resolve as she mapped out the land. She reported to him that "day-clean" would be the ideal time for her to show her best skills. She would be rested and the air would be cooler. He agreed with her logic with a pat on her shoulder that offended her.

#

Upon hearing of Abigail's pending feat, the slaves celebrated in advance of the event. Many placed flowers on the path to her cabin and laid food at the door. Several small, carved wooden images that usually symbolized good fortune for a hunter or a warrior lay on the dirt floor. A woven bag filled with roots from Ngango was centered on her mat. These kind gestures three days before the race emboldened her.

Abigail had made frequent visits to the forge where Scipio worked in the past. She knew that they had something in common. Blacksmiths were considered royalty in Africa, and she was of majestic lineage though she never divulged her past. Scipio obliged her every request for any item or service. He had secured the blade of her machete to its handle by forging an iron band that was wider than most.

The day before the race Scipio welcomed Abigail. She stood at the door of the forge with a wry grin upon her face.

#

Abigail stood at the lead off point for the race. She had removed her turban. Like a crown, her intricate braids sat high upon her head. She wore no shoes and had chosen to wear men's pants and a loose-fitting muslin blouse with a red collar. The brass beads remained on her neck. She waited for the signal from the driver of the wagon to start running. She was intensely pensive and settled. Master Harris sat alongside the driver with Benjamin Wallace, the man who had bet

16

against him. Danny, the groomsman, pulled the bridled horse beside the wagon. Harris gave Abigail a confident smile. She nodded at him as she pursed her lips.

The chestnut brown American quarter horse, agitated by the bridled bit in its mouth so early in the morning, shifted its hooves. It bobbed its head to free itself from the reins. Master Harris warned Danny not to excite the horse or he would give him the whip. The horse sweated in the cool new-day sun. A frothy spew lined its mouth. Its listless and limp tail did not bother to defend the flies that had camped on its rear. Danny whispered into the horse's ear. He sought to calm him to escape a beating. The horse would have none of it.

Master Harris asked Abigail if she was ready to run. She nodded compliantly, stretched her back and neck, reached her arms toward the sky, and lowered them. With three daring, long, and deliberate steps, she took off. Her speed intensified with that immediate jolt. The cool dawn winds still enfolded in quiet were punctuated by her clenched fists that furiously tore into the air as she ran. Her strong feet felt the full brute force of her muscled calves as they catapulted her towards the red marker. Her soles parsed the hard clay with accompanying grunts that alternately traded places with her inhalations.

Abigail could not see or hear the horse yet. Her body blurred into the crimsoned dry ground. She created a swirling dusty cloud. The rising sun displaced the dew as it announced its pending summertime heat. She could not discern any other sounds but her own. She dared not glance behind her as any movement out of synch would offset her rhythm, her fate, and her future. She spied the red marker that hung spiritless on the branch. Abigail heard the lone gunshot that set the panicked horse free. She ran faster. Her brusque throaty sounds morphed into boisterous screams. They scattered the early morning awakenings of the forest denizens.

Her clothing bore the full measure of her sweat. Her braids had fallen onto her shoulders. Its dismantled designs had transformed into a twisted, tangled mane. Abigail detoured at the thickets. She ran at the same swift pace until late afternoon. Her spent body begged for reprieve and rest. She gradually lessened her pace to a trot and headed off toward the new trail at the farthest point, northeast of the plantation.

The Cricket Cries, the Year Changes

Chapter 3

Four years after her escape, Abigail sat on the rocks near the wetlands. She rubbed palm oil on her skin while she reflected on her passage to freedom. She had made it to the Savannah River community of runaway slaves, called Maroons. She had Totu, a slave from the Harris plantation place a canoe at the swamp that led to the Santee River of South Carolina.

During her practice runs she had buried clothing and other needed items that included her machete at different sites outside the perimeter of the plantation should her escape be complete. For weeks after the race she had stayed near the swamps. Many times, she stealthily sank her entire body beneath the scum to wait out the mouth of an alligator, the deadly bite of a diamondback snake or the bounty hunters who pursued her. With a hollowed reed in her mouth Abigail camouflaged her presence in the area. She became part of the murky greenish- brown waters. The exposed rod just the above water served as her lifeline.

Ngango had prepared a root-mix of ill-smelling potpourri that he advised Abigail to wear backwards around her neck to ward off the biting flies, stinging mosquitos, and blood-sucking insects. The anguished, bleating cries of the hound dogs lost her scent repeatedly and finally, completely.

The inhabitants of the community welcomed her as many of the people recognized her tribal features as African-born. Most of them were originally enslaved on the islands of Barbados and Jamaica. The purpose of these rogue villagers was to augment their clan with runaway slaves who vowed never to be held as chattel again. Abigail adapted to her new life. She used the first year of her escape as a time to heal her body and her spirit. With daily conversations, her knowledge of the world she now lived in was expanded by the tales and events relayed by the Maroons.

In the ensuing years, Abigail completely embraced her freedom. She fully understood its totality. Her extended ordinary life as a human being buried her past. Her softened gestures of communicating and shared knowledge of the planting processes endeared her to her new family. She became the hairdresser who created novel and unique styles for the women and men. She privately assumed her regal countenance. She now wore purple caftans absconded from raids on the ships carried out by the Maroons. The raiment restored her history. She gave her red turbans to a much younger woman.

There were not as many women in the swampy village as had populated the Harris plantation. The Maroons counted on young able-bodied males to protect and fortify their new society. These former slaves raided the plantations for foodstuffs. The Maroons brazenly traded openly with enslaved men on the wharves in Charleston for livestock that was unloaded from the ships. The fugitives masqueraded as slaves complete with the forged traveling papers and identification tags that hung from their necks. The state of South Carolina had mandated that all blacks wear the naming tags——slave or free.

The survival of the Maroons depended on such acts because the bogs were not suitable for planting staple crops. Rice became the major grain. The slaveholders did not seek to cultivate the marshy areas on their land. They could not maintain the back swamps. They feared its gun-wielding inhabitants. At times they enlisted the aid of other plantation vigilantes to assist them to protect their properties that included livestock, feed, and slaves from theft. The Maroon communities had given rise to a new type of bounty hunter——the black slaves who infiltrated their strongholds in search of the runaways that they harbored. They did it for the promise of their own freedom from their masters.

The Cricket Cries, the Year Changes

Chapter 4

Abigail lay bound in the open yard of the Harris-Jones Plantation in the very chains she had sought to extend when she cared for the returned runaways long ago. Her beaten inflated face refused to acknowledge the glazed-over glances of pity and remorse from the other slaves. A slave infiltrator accompanied by white bounty hunters had climbed a Cypress tree to view the Maroon marshlands and spied a woman wearing a red turban. Her physical attributes similarly matched a description of Abigail posted by Master Harris as his most sought out escapee.

The young black slave proudly relayed the information to authorities in Charleston with freedom on his mind. A band of mercenaries converged on the perimeter of the swamp and observed the women while they harvested the rice. They spotted a turbaned young woman. She held sacks to catch the rice yield from the other workers. The hunters kidnapped her and upon her convincing appeals soon realized that she was not Abigail. The woman offered them a valuable piece of information as a bargaining tool to regain her freedom. She agreed to take the six of them to find Abigail. Once in the area the young girl whistled a coded alarm.

Four of the six bounty hunters were killed by the rifled sentries who held their posts at the fringes of the swamp. Two of them purposely spared by the Maroons were allowed to leave provided they carried back the bloodied heads of the four men as proof of their militant resolve. Master Harris was enraged and emboldened when news of this atrocity reached him. He enlisted the help of an army captain whose unit he had allowed to bivouac in his fields. The platoon awaited Abigail's lone passage to her space of reflective solitude disclosed earlier by the young girl. Abigail sat unaware of the encroaching danger.

She fought bravely using the machete that she carried to ward off the swampy predators. She culled her father's chieftain strength when he pulled a much larger machete from a sheath made of bark and decorated with beads and shells. Abigail, drawing on her memory of harvesting cane swiftly decapitated one of the would-be captors. She managed to sever an arm of another soldier who filled her stomach with buckshot. She was subdued. The Maroons did not defend Abigail; they gave her up in lieu of an outnumbered bloodbath.

#

A huge net was thrown over her tattered purple caftan. It became her only cover for the long journey back to the Harris plantation. The heat, wind, and dust found its way through its openings, and she suffered. Abigail was allowed to relieve herself by the trees. The soldiers threw barrels of water from the streams to rid the wagon bed of the foul and nauseating smells she had created. She was kept barely alive during the return as ordered by Master Harris. He demanded that they maintain her condition long enough for him to see her——before he would have her killed. Abigail had made a laughing stock out of him. Word traveled extensively and fabled her successful escape that fed his expensive bravado.

Abigail sensed the smell of burnt molasses that evidenced the cane crop harvest. The odor of candle wax and pine tar drifted through the day air. The beefy scent of spit-fired animals heightened her awareness of where she was. As the wagon moved closer to the sounds of braying horses, squealing pigs and the busy clucks of chickens and hens, Abigail arrived at a plantation long forgotten. In the near distance Abigail heard songs of call and response by the slaves working in the fields. The downwind sifted the smell of their labor toward the wagon. The clamor of drumbeats heralded her infamous return. The evidence of her disarming arrival was crystallized as she felt the wagon make the sharp angular turn at the fence that long ago had inaugurated her trek from bondage.

The Cricket Cries, the Year Changes

Chapter 5

Many slaves avoided viewing the torture of Abigail in the yards. The cries of distress and anger at her treatment forced Master Harris to tone down the punishment for fear of an outright insurrection. The disconsolate slaves had placed flowers on the path to her abandoned cabin. Wooden carvings that normally welcomed a hero were placed on her mat.

Her blood-soaked and whipped body was dragged into her cabin by Joe Butler and Donnie Winbush. They struggled to lay her tall, chained body down. The lengthy chains added to the weight. Master Harris ordered them to stay with her at all times. Abigail, grateful to her gods to be able to lay her body in a different position, welcomed the onset of night. She settled on the mat on her right side.

Her shrinking eyes darted rebelliously to the two white men who crouched in opposite corners, one to her right and the other to her left. Most of the buckshot in her abdomen was removed by the doctor who Harris had sent for. It was not a benevolent gesture on his part; he wanted Abigail to die at his orders.

Abigail placed her hands on her stomach. She tried to squeeze the pain downward. She looked forward to her first real night of rest.

Scipio had walked cautiously toward Abigail's cabin late at night and peered into the tiny window. She lay under it as in times past. The moonlight had turned her purple caftan gray and its red bloodstains to brown. Her bruised unresponsive eyes gazed toward him. He cringed as they flittered that she was barely alive. Scipio longed for the opportunity to speak to her or to touch her. Her condition foretold that goodbyes were eminent. It was important for Abigail to receive assurance from him that her noble ancestors stood together ready to celebrate her homecoming. He had always known that she was of regal birth.

Winbush and Butler lay in a deep sleep exhausted from the ordeal of having to carry Abigail from the yard to the cabin. They lay besotted on the clay floor thanks to the emptying of a shared jug of rum that was a welcomed respite.

Cynthia Harris-Allen

He reached through the window with his massive arm and noiselessly placed a machete where Abigail could see it. Around it hung the tool she had borrowed from him to extend the chains of past runaways.

Scipio had expansive knowledge of horses. He knew that the strides and breeds of horses required different shoes that adjusted to the lengths, depths, and widths accordingly. Master Harris bragged that Scipio had paid his purchased price a thousand times over. However, Harris had accused Scipio of aiding Abigail's escape by disabling the horse. Scipio gently reminded Harris that the choice of shoes for the horse from among the ones that hung from the wall was indeed made by the driver of the wagon who verified Scipio's story and removed any doubt that he was complicit.

He had fashioned the horseshoes days before the race and had hung them in the usual place to be retrieved by anyone for the next horse in line to be shod. He plotted that the horse used for the race at dawn would be prepared the night before. He knew the horseshoes that he filled with iron shavings would render a pain-filled step. They would be the first set chosen by the groomsman.

He turned his eyes away from Abigail and wept openly.

The Cricket Cries, the Year Changes

Chapter 6

At dawn's first dove-gray light, the cabin's crime scene evidenced that Abigail had managed to wrap her chains around the neck of Donnie Winbush and choked him to death while she held his mouth shut. His putrid alcoholic breath was unable to render a sound. She lowered his urine-stained body silently to the mat and disturbed the piles of chain. The sound awakened Joe Butler.

She kicked Butler in the groin as he slovenly awoke to the clamor and tried to stand to defend himself. It disabled him for a moment. He lay bent over on the dirt floor. He cursed her as his body warped in pain. The numbing effect of rum was now absent. Abigail leaped high into the air and braced her palms upon the wall. She sent a backwards kick to Butler's head with such crushing force that he was killed instantly. She held her normal celebratory scream for a later, safer time.

Their bodies were not discovered until the light of a late airless afternoon exposed the horror. The smell of the blood-soaked victims combined with the vomitus odor of death, defeat, and defiance. The redness struggled to seep into the sweet grass mats as it distanced itself from the gore. Winbush's eyes bulged with evidence of lack of oxygen and plenty of fright. Butler's head hung loosely from his neck as he lay on his back. His rigor-mortised hands had formed a strange arc over his testicles.

Abigail was nowhere to be found.

She had hobbled away in her nakedness with only a gauze-bandaged stomach as her freedom dress during the moonlit night. She claimed the wooden carved pieces that had embellished her mat. A sack of provisions that included root medicines wrapped in purple cotton were mysteriously placed in her doorway. She limped along her too-familiar runaway path.

Abigail had memorized the landscape of the northward route in case she had to recall it in the dark. She remembered where she had buried other clothing in greased butcher paper. She carried her new machete and admired its heft. She gave a backwards smile to the forge as she gratefully thanked

Scipio. The instrument reflected the lunar rays. The lightning bugs clung to its blade. They impersonated the encased adornments of her father's sheathed saber. The machete assumed the dual duty of walking stick and wielding weapon.

The crickets' legs rubbed coded messages. The melodies warmed Abigail's heart.

#

Kaffie made a hopeless attempt to wash the dried blood from Abigail's faded purple caftan. She could not know Abigail's fate. She did not have that kind of fabric in her sewing room. She salvaged a part from the long hem.

Kaffie saved it in a trunk.

The Cricket Cries, the Year Changes

BOWAY

Chapter 1

As a young boy Boway was kidnapped from a village in Nigeria along with his parents. They were bound on separate ships for different seaports. Surprisingly, they reached the same holding forts close to the giant ocean. The reunion was brief. They were auctioned separately. Now thirty years old Master Harris was his third owner.

Boway walked through the forest with a large grain sack in tow. He filled it with slender branches of willow and oak. He gathered palm branches and sisal, bound them with string, and stood them up in the bag. On the way back to the barn he stopped at the riverbank to cut bulrushes. The tall dark green plants, some eight to ten feet tall leaned against one another with their brown chocolate thumb-like tips as they vied for his attention.

He was a basket weaver. In Sokoto, Nigeria, he learned the art of basket weaving and dyeing from his elders. He believed that they could see how blessed he was through his work to have been taught by the masters. Somehow, he knew that they often smiled proudly down at him. He felt their presence each time he submerged himself in this solitary endeavor.

His collection of materials could be as wide or as limited, as his imagination. He intertwined tan-colored sweet grass with darker strips of pine tree bark or palmetto leaves as he worked his weaves into circles or squares. He would lay out the branches and reeds to dry in the barn. Some are placed in the sun to bleach the color from them. He used tools such as shells, nails and even the flat end of metal spoons, made for him by Scipio, to fashion his baskets. Be they round, cylindrical or flat Boway embellished the baskets with color from the dye baths of Cecelia. He added cowrie shells and sometimes ribbon. For festivals, such as the cropover parties, he included feathers, beads and dried flowers.

His flat curved baskets were in huge demand in South Carolina. Many slaves carried rice from those fields in Boway's creations. His artisanship added to Master Harris' list of slaves that generated a lot of revenue. Boway lived in the barn with Lewis, the drum maker. They used nature's materials in their crafts.

Boway was about five feet ten inches tall. He pulled his long braided hair to the back with hemp. He wore printed shirts with inked symbols stamped upon them. He used halved apples or other dense fruits to render his designs. Sometimes, he used the pits of peaches to trail the inks onto one-of-a-kind applications for his wardrobe. The front of his button-less shirt was one solid piece. He crossed the long side shirttails over each other. He knotted them below his waist in the back. One wide deep pocket was sewn to the bottom front. It housed items that Boway picked at random from the plantation fields that could place unique impressions upon cloth.

He did not dress in the mass-produced allotments that most slaves wore on the plantation. His shirts topped a pair of off-white pants. They bore the stains of grass and red clay from Boway's gathering efforts upon the ground. He was grateful to Kaffie who took the time to sew his shirts to his liking. As thanks to her, he often created handkerchiefs for her from the remnants. He folded under a scant hem and bound it with an unusual stitch using corn silk threads. Boway gave her a huge basket each Christmas with a lid that was large enough to contain three to five of her lap quilts.

#

Kumaa and Panin, twin slave women, lived on the Harris-Jones plantation. No one could tell them apart, not even Master Harris. On the slave rolls at the auction their supposed origin was left blank; and so was their age. Harris only knew that they were fit for work. He ordered them to dress in distinctly different clothing. The overseer placed one twin in the cotton fields and the other among the rows of corn. They never knew when the young women switched places in positions in the field or not.

Both were in love with Boway. The twenty-some year-old twins loved to trick people. Sometimes it was in good fun and other times it was downright devious. Such was the case with Boway. Panin told him twins were special people in her native country whose name she could not recall. Kumaa said they possessed special powers of persuasion and influence. Boway asked if the two of them together were more powerful than Ngango, the witch doctor. They did not answer. Soon Boway was able to tell them apart; Kumaa's personality was a lot more aggressive than Panin. Panin begged Boway to choose her as his woman while Kumaa threatened him to do so or he would lose her affections for good if he did.

Boway slept with both of them. He pretended that he was interested in only one of them. The twins acted as if they did not know about the involvement of the other. As both began to have real feelings for him, that dynamic divided them. Boway soon pitted sister against sister. He made himself available to both. He did not care which one it was. They were both easy and accessible. One would meet him at night behind the barn when the candlelight was not sufficient for Boway to weave. The other set out to find him in the thickets and offer herself to him without even a "hello." To continue his ruse, Boway threatened to leave each one of them if a twin told the other that they had been together. The young women feigned adherence to his commands.

Boway made a herringbone bracelet from dried grass. He stained it with an indigo dye. When he met Kumaa at the riverbank one morning, he dampened it and placed it around her right ankle. He held it tightly to her skin as it tattooed a sideways "V" pattern. The dyed design circled her ankle. Now he would know which young woman he was with at all times especially when both chose to be silent and pliant. He gave Kumaa the still damp piece as a keepsake. She was thrilled at the prospect that soon Boway would choose her to be his wife.

Panin found the bracelet that Kumaa had dropped on the floor of their cabin. She re-activated the paler blue dye with water and placed the same marker on her right ankle. Panin had to remember to act as assertive as her sister did; otherwise, Boway would know of their conspiracy, she surmised. One afternoon Panin had followed Boway into the thickets. Boway kissed her deeply on the mouth. Kumaa suddenly stopped working in the cornfields, stood straight up and rested her arm on the hoe. She placed her hand over her mouth and felt the carnal urgings of her sister in her soul.

Weeks later, Kumaa sat on the riverbank on a Sunday night. She playfully splashed her feet in the cool water while she awaited Boway's footsteps. Panin, already asleep in the cabin, awakened to the sensation of wet feet. She noticed that her sister was absent. She quickly dressed and ran toward the river. She hoped to catch them together. Her sister had promised her that she did not desire Boway. The couple had left the river minutes before she arrived.

Boway's rough and wild lovemaking frightened them both. They stayed closed-mouthed to one another and did not offer details about their sexual encounters. They carefully concealed their mutual betrayal. Other slave women knew about this "side show'. They sucked their teeth and rolled their eyes at such a blatant display of promiscuity from Boway and the twins. The women would wager bean pies and hoe cakes as to who would win Boway over. It became the central piece of gossip among them for quite a while.

Some slaves from the Ivory Coast of Africa regarded twins as deity. To conspire to harm them would have serious consequences. They did not worship or revere Kumaa or Panin, but instead, held cautionary phobias toward their latent abilities. Each twin thought that Boway preferred her to the other. They wanted to have Boway's babies and then drop him like a hot, sweet potato. In their village, twins as divine beings only used males to procreate.

The Cricket Cries, the Year Changes

Chapter 2

Early morning cooking fires sent trails of smoke and scents throughout the plantation. The slaves tended to their own gardens; they pulled ripened vegetables and shucked corn. Harris gave small farm animals to the slaves. The overseers measured out tracts of dirt to sustain themselves. It removed the need to open the silos and slaughterhouses to feed them.

Harris had well over three hundred slaves on this vast homestead. He wanted the full yield of his cash crops and animals to be the source of his revenues. He did not intend to allot almost half of the products he owned to sustain a working slave force. The gardens were no more than twenty by twenty feet in size. Harris allowed them to grow whatever they wanted.

Beans and molasses accented the smell of the coveted bacon that wafted from the Big House. In contrast, corn bread, onions, and greens combined with the odorous fresh manure, when one stood downwind in the slave quarters. Young slaves cracked open pecans and peanuts that were called "monkey nuts" and playfully popped them into their mouths. Men fished at the river and brought to the fires catfish, trout, and bass. Ngango did not approve of eating a flounder fish. He told the slaves that anything with eyes that did not cooperate with one another would sway their spirits. He admonished those that ate them anyway.

It was Sunday.

A group of about five women walked from cabin to garden to fire and back as they introduced a new slave girl named Halima to the residents. A farmer in Macon, Georgia traded Halima for two of Master Harris' quarter horses. She looked ordinary but not plain. She had a gentle demeanor and smiled often.

The overseer had assigned her to the cotton fields to work. She had picked and carded cotton on the previous homestead. The women continued to escort her to the mainstays of the plantation. The group walked leisurely towards the fields of cotton, corn, peas, greens, and cane.

31

They pointed out the barns and named which activity took place in each one. The women held makeshift fans to shoo away the flies. Some wore their Sunday straw hats to ward off the pending noonday sun.

Halima stood at the entrances to the barns and tentatively peeked at the operations and equipment. She pretended that she understood what was going on. She was overwhelmed by the vastness of this plantation and the number of its slaves. The smell of the sugar mill intoxicated Halima. Fermenting molasses on its way to becoming a stiff drink of rum overpowered the apple vinegar and peach wine vats.

Lewis, the drum maker, brushed by her on his way out of the barn that he shared with Boway. He offered a quick "hello" to the women. Boway's back was to those who chattered away simultaneously. He was braiding long pieces of palm branches. One of the women, with one hand resting on her hips, cupped her other hand to Halima's ear and said something about Boway. The self-appointed welcoming crowd giggled with loud laughter and handclaps.

Boway turned his head to the doorway. He spied the diminutive young girl as she stood in the middle of the cackling women and cocked his head to the side. He stood up, brushed the straw and bark shavings from his shirt, walked towards Halima and extended his hand to her. One of the slave women slapped it down in mid-air and told Boway he need not bother to add her to his den. With that they all turned to leave. Boway's eyes followed Halima until her body became a wavy figure against the burning sunrays. Soon he lost sight of her within the crowd.

During the next few days, Boway pretended that he needed corn silk from the field to thread his baskets. He did not find Halima there. He already had over five pounds of bulrushes but he went to the riverbank anyway to see if Halima was part of the laundry detail. He walked over to the rice fields and hoped that Halima would not have to work there. It was the most dangerous, disease-ridden place for any human to have to work. He was thankful that he did not find her there.

The beige cotton fields were acres upon acres of rows. Boway was too tired to make that trek. What little area he surveyed while his hand shielded the sun from his eyes revealed nothing. He did not know that on that particular day, Halima was with Kaffie under the tent in the main yard. She received the usual fare of clothing and brogans, a coarse blanket to place on the bare cabin floor, and a square gauze cloth to protect her head from the sun. Kaffie also gave her a Sunday straw hat that was a bit oversize for the young girl's head.

Halima carried these items toward her assigned cabin. From the barn door Boway saw her as she traipsed down the crested hill from the Big House. He caught up with her and helped her to balance herself on the steep incline. He took her gunnysack and walked her toward the slave cabins. Along the way he introduced himself and proudly told Halima that he was originally from Nigeria. Halima stopped, smiled, and replied that so was she.

The courtship almost began in an instant. Saturday evenings and Sundays found the two of them almost inseparable. During the week, Boway would walk alongside Halima while she worked in the cotton fields. He disregarded the calls from the drivers to get back to the barn. The threats became a routine warning.

Halima worked alongside Kumaa——or Panin, if she stood in for her sister. Either twin harassed Halima the entire time they were in the field. One day, a hoe gashed Halima's big toe, though not inflicting permanent damage. The twin apologized for her "mistake". Their jealousies intensified towards Halima.
Boway gradually spurned their advances when either one of them found him alone. He had to know if Halima was going to be with him before he let the twins go altogether. He got his answer rather quickly.

#

Boway tried to keep the peace between the three women. He made coiled baskets for the twins. He hoped that the gesture of friendship would delay the widening rift between them. He presented an elaborately woven colorful container to Halima. She began to use it to port the carded cotton to the weavers as a daily favor for an elderly slave woman. She was seen by many when she pranced the crimson grounds, sporting the beautiful woven object. She took every opportunity to show off the basket. The slave women no longer placed wagers on the possibilities of a permanent relationship with Boway for either twin.

Embittered, the two did not give up that easily. Kumaa and Panin had their hair braided on a Sunday morning in intricate patterns that supposedly signified that a wedding or proposal was pending, they said. Other female slaves ridiculed the twins. They knew that the two were mere mortals and mocked them. They joked that Boway did not intend to marry either one of them.

The Cricket Cries, the Year Changes

Chapter 3

Halima and Boway learned that they were from the same village in Nigeria. They walked down many paths of nostalgia as they pieced together what they could recall of life in Sokoto. The conversations excited and bonded them. They both described the sacrament of scarification or cutting of the bodies, as a ritualistic art form among their villagers. They were taught at a very young age to create the patterns and interpret their meanings.

They met secretly on a Saturday evening in the barn and intricately inscribed symbols of love and unity upon each other's bodies. The artwork reached around to their opposite upper arms. When they held hands, the engraving merged as a continuous message of adoration between a man and a woman. Drops of blood splattered the floor in ranges of blotched circles. Neither cried out with pain from the incisions as two different knives cut deeply into their skins.

Boway and Halima lay partially naked in the morning Sunday heat to accelerate the healing process. The self-mutilations authenticated their love. Soon, many on the plantation marveled at the scarring designs. The twins, outraged at such a gory display of kinship by Halima and Boway, tainted the meat that Halima had placed in her basket. It did not cause a sickness unto death, but Halima had violent vomiting for two days. She lay in the "sick cabin," feverish, weak, and dehydrated. Boway warned the twins that these reprisals had to end. He stopped short of threatening harm.

The cuttings of Halima and Boway impressed Ngango. In his younger days he also partook in such a ritual. Cuts over his body were far more extensive than the two of them combined. He knew that they did not take anything to lessen the pain. They would not have known what was available on this plantation. He respected their courage and grit.

Ngango halfway acknowledged the twins' goddess-like status. He recalled that a baby from a set of twins on this plantation had died from malaria years ago. Its mother had Ngango carve a tiny wooden statue for her. The aggrieved mother carried the figurine wherever she went. She told him that it kept the surviving brother out of danger and kept him happy until the two reunited in death.

Kumaa and Panin curried Ngango's favor to devise potions or powder-filled bags that could remove Boway's love from Halima for good. The twins concocted ways to place the poison in Boway's water jug in the barn. Panin said she could carefully place a gauze-like bag inside Boway's big shirt pocket without him knowing. Ngango's powders were potent; all Boway had to do was touch them. Both elixirs were ineffective. At the most they made Boway nauseous but did not keep him from his basket weaving. He drew sympathy from Halima who said she thought that forces were trying to destroy them.

The twins were disappointed with Ngango. He was perplexed himself but promised he would increase the dosages. Another concoction meant to harm Boway morphed into an aphrodisiac instead of a spellbinder. The love he made with Halima was the best for the both of them——ever. Soon, Halima's baby bump was visible.

They twins were distressed that Boway would father a child with Halima, particularly when the both of them were already pregnant by him. A slave's job on the plantation continued regardless of pregnancy or sickness. Harris did not consider being with child a disability. All three of the women had to maintain their positions in the fields. The cash crops were growing. The slaves had a less difficult workload during the lay-by; all they had to do was weed and prune. The toil on this massive homestead continued from before sunrise to just after no visibility.

Boway had asked Master Harris to allow him to marry Halima. Harris regarded the slave without malice. He even attended the ceremony.

The weekend of the wedding Panin and Kumaa found Boway alone in the barn. They stunned him with the fact that both of them were pregnant by him as well. Boway knew he had not touched either one of them in two months. They countered his incredulous rant and insisted they were perhaps more than a month or two along than Halima was. They had bandaged their growing stomachs to give them support while they worked in the fields. They eagerly pulled their skirts high to show evidence. The twins happily over-talked each other and told him that they both conceived during the same full moon. Panin told Boway he had taken her early in the morning and her sister at night. They told Boway it was not necessary for him to wed Halima. Their love and commitment doubled hers.

Boway and Halima jumped the broom and moved into Boway's new cabin. The twins watched the ceremony with contempt. They simultaneously felt the first flitters of life within them. They secretly upped the ante. The twins ruined the food that Halima prepared for Boway. They put hainty dolls on the cabin mats to scare Halima to such limits that she feared that her pregnancy would not come to full term.

Kumaa poured red mud into Halima's large baskets of carded cotton. It rendered the batch useless. She had to work harder to make up for the loss. She left the standing cornfields and sat on the hard benches in the cotton barn. Boway had reached an agreement with Master Harris to produce one and a half times more baskets than usual per day. In exchange for that, his wife would not have to work the cornfields in her last months of pregnancy. The benefit would be twofold for Boway and Halima; it would shield her from the constant harassing by Panin and Kumaa.

Boway and Halima spent as much time as they could together. They expanded their family histories to assure that their first baby and many more would know their legacies. One late sultry evening the couple set on the stoop of their cabin. They separated the dried flattened branches and sorted them by length and strength for Boway's future baskets. They continued to talk about their family backgrounds and the environs of their common village in Nigeria. Boway placed his hands upon Halima's stomach and asked his unborn baby if it was listening to their stories. He joked that neither one of them wanted to repeat themselves once it set foot upon the ground.

Chapter 4

The twins visited Ngango and insisted he give them something to put in Halima's food to induce an early labor. They chastised him for not producing the results that they expected. Kumaa reminded him of their status as twins with chiding remarks that he disrespected them with his incompetence. Ngango studied the both of them silently and slightly moved his bottom lip. He reached under his mat and gave them something to use.

The twins had lined the wooden eating bowls with a poisonous liquid from Ngango. He instructed them to allow the moisture to dry completely. Its effect would be activated by stirring or mixing. The containers that Boway and Halima stored in the corner of their cabin were soaked with the solution by the twins when Halima was asleep and her husband was away. Soon after, she became sickly and weak.

#

Boway sat on a mat and lovingly fed Halima dinner late one night. He regretted the loss of time that he could have cared for her since he had increased his workload. His eyes messaged his longings for her. Her weak grin read his mind. At once, Halima gasped and grabbed her stomach. The two of them grew afraid for her health because the baby was not due for at least another three months or so. It needed every day to grow and survive.

Boway settled the crying and moaning Halima into the lone wooden chair in the cabin. He promised her he would return quickly. He summoned a slave midwife to come to the cabin. She examined Halima and confirmed that the baby was coming too soon. It moved sporadically. She said the baby could be born "downside up". The midwife placed a rusty piece of tin under Halima's mat to relieve the pain. She left and promised to come back in the early morning.

Meanwhile, the twins lay low on the outside of Boway's cabin at the opposite small window. They had spat upon leaves given to them by Ngango and, with his instruction, stealthily lined the perimeter of the cabin with them. They moved slowly with their own aching and birth-ready bodies upon their knees while their panted short breaths covered the ground.

The Cricket Cries, the Year Changes

Boway lay with his wife. He held her head in his lap and wiped the sweat from her face. He smoothed her hair while his fingers gently drew wide circles upon the now quieted mound. He began to sing Nigerian love songs to her though he failed at its full interpretation. He laughed between his mistakes to cheer and distract her. His eyes turned toward the cabin door. He heard sounds outside but credited them to the nightlife.

He began to soothe Halima with stories of his family. He described again his father's cuttings but this time, with detail. He demonstrated with a pointed finger as he followed the patterns from his collarbone to just above his neck. It was the same place where his father had carved his own symbols. Boway told her that the last design to his memory started from the top of his father's forehead and ended just above his eyebrows.

Boway said his grandfather had just died and his father had to add the scarring that signified that he was now the patriarch of the tribe. He described the cut circle around the skin of his father's neck where a shiny golden amulet of antelope horns hung. It belonged to his grandfather, he told her. Boway began to describe the ensuing ceremony. The baby moved violently. Halima screamed loudly.

Boway massaged the hurtful hump that the baby had formed on its mother's side. Boway apologized to Halima for his constant babbling; he just wanted to create a diversion for the distress that surrounded them, he offered. He then asked a weary Halima to pray with him to his father, Modozie Adebambo, and their gods, to usher in their son or daughter with no harm to mother and child. When he opened his eyes, Boway looked into Halima's face. It was ashen. Then her entire body shock.

She seized his strong arms and sharply dug her fingernails into them as she convulsed. Boway shrieked from the pain and grappled to loosen her grip. Halima had grabbed her hair so fiercely, that she pulled chunks of it out. The bleeding pieces of scalp joined the mangled mess and fell around her neck. She never verbalized the pain. She looked as if she was possessed. Her mouth opened but no sound came from it.

Cynthia Harris-Allen

Boway noticed that Halima struggled to catch her breath. He wanted to free himself to fetch the midwife but Halima had mustered enough strength to restrain him. It surprised even him. With a huge exhale Halima shrieked that Modozie Adebambo was her father, also! She belted to Boway that Adebambo had married her mother and fathered three girls. She spit out that she never knew of another family. She begged Boway to kill her. She shouted over and over to the ceiling that she had married her brother!

Halima cried that the pain in her stomach was because the gods were not pleased with her. She bellowed that they tormented her with mysterious sicknesses because of their incestuous deed. Exhausted, with tear-filled eyes, she finally commanded Boway to find the midwife to assist her in giving birth to the devil. She stood up and then she fell backwards and unconscious halfway into the wooden chair.

The midwife brought in rags, hot water, and some of the dyed branches from the porch for Halima to clench between her teeth. The ivy green dye stained her lips blue. The doula wiped the blood that had streamed down her face when she wrenched the hair from her scalp. Boway fainted. The midwife assumed that Boway did the normal thing most expectant fathers did at the birthing of their first child; but Boway was otherwise dumbstruck.

The baby boy was born with two heads and two penises. The midwife shielded her eyes with her apron and quickly found her way out of the cabin. The terrified sizeable woman ran all the way to the river, stripped herself naked, and plunged into the cold waters up to her neck to exorcise her body from the horror she just witnessed.

The spying, triumphant twins stood petrified at the scene and blessed Ngango with the outcome. It was more than what they had expected. They hugged each other tightly. Their backs began to ache.

Halima died. She never saw the child. Boway buried the baby deep into the ground. He beat the hard clay with his fists and feet so hard that they began to bleed. He surrendered it with cries of atonement and contrition to the underworld. He burned Halima's body where he collected his branches.

The Cricket Cries, the Year Changes

Chapter 5

Three days later in the middle of the night, an aggrieved Boway began to clean the cabin. There had been no drummed messages sent throughout the plantation about this tragedy. No slave wanted a part in spreading the news. Several of them feared retaliation from their ancestors if they shared or listened to the particulars. If asked, they acknowledged that Halima had died in childbirth along with her baby.

Boway picked up Halima's clothing along with the hand-dyed and decorated swaddling cloth he had made for his baby as a surprise for her. He had begun gingerly and tenderly to pick things up and then his rage took over. He snatched anything that reminded him of their life together which included most of the loose items in the cabin. He threw them into the blood-soaked birthing rags and hauled them to the barn. There, he gathered baskets——finished or unfinished and randomly threw them into a larger laundry basket.

He dragged these items to the deserted riverbank and sat down. As he cried, he took one item of Halima's and a similar possession of his own and placed them in the same basket. He set the reed transport in the water and pushed it toward the open river. He repeated this process several times until nothing was left to surrender to their yesterdays.

Emotionally spent, Boway returned to the cabin and sat on the lone mat. The single kerosene lamp yellowed the walls and turned the red clay floor amber. In the ghostly silence he crossed his arms over his heart and rocked himself to sleep. Come morning the plantation was awakened by the acrid scent of smoke that could only come from wood. Boway had burned down his cabin. Only a mysterious crusty perimeter of brown leaves squared the ashes where his home used to be. It prevented the flames from reaching the other quarters. Boway was gone.

Master Harris summoned his patrollers to find him, but not harm him. In two days' time Boway was captured and returned to the plantation. He was found in the thickets while he talked to himself. Harris sympathized with him and told him that he was going to give him time to come back to himself. He allowed Boway to return to the barn he shared with Lewis. He had to start from scratch to inventory the items he needed to resume his craft. His supplies had cured and would not bend.

He never looked for Panin and Kumaa though he often wondered if they had given birth to his babies.

#

Ngango spied Boway at the river one morning. He moved closer to him and sat down. They both looked at one another not saying a word. Ngango, first to speak, asked Boway if he would weave him two medium sized baskets and one large one. He wanted all three to be cylindrical and include the rooster feathers he extended to Boway within the weave.

Boway, still distant and apathetic, asked Ngango what he would give him in return. Ngango never bartered with any slave; It was beneath him; but he promised Boway that he would wipe all of his troubles away with a potion unlike any other once he delivered the baskets.

Boway consented.

#

On Monday, Kumaa fell to her knees in the cornfields in obvious labor. The driver lashed her face and told her to get back to work. About a half-acre from her sister, Panin suddenly grabbed her face while she picked cotton. She waddled quickly through the high grass toward her sister. She shouted her name to the top of her voice. Panin ignored the calls from the driver to return to her place. She cursed him and said her sister was going to have a baby in their cabin and he could whip her afterwards. The driver did not pursue her.

Two midwives accompanied Kumaa to the cabin. Their sable arms supported her as they inched along the dusty clay toward the quarters. She lay on the mats as Panin arrived breathless. She thanked them for helping her sister but told them that she, alone, was going to help her. The doulas with a collective hmmmpf left the premises. Panin readied the area for the baby's birth. Her snail-like moves hampered her efforts to carry small pails of water from the kettle on the porch. She set them by her sister. They held hands as they waited for the pain to increase.

The Cricket Cries, the Year Changes

Kumaa birthed a baby that was not complete in form. It was an undiscernible mass of tissue and blood fused together in a slimy, milky-white sac. Panin calmly placed the object in the corner of the cabin. She and Kumaa whimpered like dogs that were about to be put down. During the night Panin felt the onset of labor. She and her sister exchanged looks of an anticipated acceptance of what was about to unfold. A weakened and despondent Kumaa pulled an identical sphered wad from Panin. She held it up so her twin could see it. They both nodded their heads in guilty resignation and burned both objects in the fire.

Chapter 6

Boway remained distressed about his relationship with Halima. He was miserable and detached. His baskets still bore his signature artistry but their fabrication was more of a chore, than a labor of love. He grew impatient with the expectancy of his punishment from the gods for shaming himself and his ancestors. He felt that his father would never rest in the afterlife because of this vile act.

Boway walked deliberately in the lightning storms. His body welcomed its fiery, silver flash. By day he taunted and cursed the overseers and hoped his actions would cause him to meet the death whip; but they did not retaliate. They knew he was addle-brained. By night he stomped through the thickets. He craved the attack of a bear. Even his own body as a substitution in its place in the large traps would assuage his death wish. He smeared bacon grease over his shirt as a lure to any animal's heightened sense of smell. None of these repeated attempts to end his life came to fruition. They only increased his long-sufferings.

#

Ngango sat in his hut. His spirit troubled by the recent events. He knew what had happened to Halima and the twins. He still questioned why his potions had rendered opposite effects upon Boway. He had looked upon the scarifications of Boway and Halima and acknowledged that the both of them had to have come from royalty. He wondered how else they could have performed the secret ritual without something to kill the pain. Who had protected them?

Ngango admonished himself for silently accepting the rebukes from Kumaa and Panin as if they ruled over him. He cut his small toe off for humbling himself in front of two insubordinate women who usurped his authority and craft. He beat the severed member with a hammer. Though Panin and Kumaa smiled broadly each time they saw Ngango he was not pleased with the sight of them.

#

One night, Ngango placed two of the three cylindrical baskets made by Boway inside of the twins' cabin. He carried the larger one back to his hut. It was Sunday and he knew that they, like the other slaves, would arrive late after a long day of socializing. Upon their return, the twins were excited about the presents from Boway. At last, he had come to his senses and decided to be with them again. Such a sweet first gesture, they chortled. They simultaneously unlashed the woven covers and lowered them to the back of the baskets. Kumin and Panin reached in to see if Boway had inserted additional trinkets for them.

Two venomous snakes, kept in a larger basket to agitate them during the trek to their cabin bit two vanquished twins.

No one carved any wooden replicas as a memoriam.

#

Six months later, still shamed and haunted by his actions, Boway ran away again. This time, Master Harris put the full patrol with hound dogs, rifles, and chains on his trail. The dogs called, "coonhounds" bred specifically to hunt because of their ability to follow a limited scent. The short-legged, tan and black dogs hunted in packs. Their owners followed them on foot. The animals drooled excessively. They sounded out distinctive baying barks when the prey was at hand or the trail grew cold.

Boway had stripped naked and left his clothing at the feet of the high Georgia pines. The dogs discovered the pile and the hunt stalled. The runaway had traveled about twenty miles from the plantation perimeter with the amulet that Ngango had given him as his only cover. Cockles, thorny trees, and thistledown had lashed his body. The cuts superimposed themselves over the earlier artful designs.

Boway had randomly added deliberate cuts to his skin. He defaced his body even further. He sliced erratic lines of meaningless symbols over his legs, thighs, and arms. He bled for days. The open wounds attracted flies that laid eggs in them. This time that exercise proved to be quite painful. He did not mind. He continued to run northward with the muddy riverbank as his guide. At nightfall, he rested near the gurgling water. He was sleep-deprived. Boway prayed for divine or satanic interference to end the stabbing pains in his heart. He believed that he was doubly punished for being an adulterer and loving unabashedly his own sister.

When he first lost Halima, he tried to absolve himself of any guilt associated with her demise; he had no prior knowledge, he insisted to himself. He recalled the many times he regarded the harassments and vexations from Halima and Kumaa as personal attacks upon him and Halima. The gods had used them to run interference. Now he was certain he had disregarded the warnings and impediments from his dead guardians that would have paced his relationship with Halima. Their familial ties would have revealed themselves, if they had patiently measured out the time they had spent together.

He loved her, because she was his sister; she loved him, because he was her big brother.

\#

The next morning brought bright sunshine and blue skies. Boway cursed the gods for contrasting his black-as-ink agony with such illumination. Tired, hungry and chilled by the fresh air, Boway began to uproot reeds from the riverbanks. He piled them high on the shore. He added longer branches from the sugar maples nearby. He sat naked for hours on deer moss and used a sharp rock to remove the thin green bark.

He took breaks to drink short sips of water mixed with the contents of the powder from the witch doctor. He sat for a long time as he wove the pieces together. That same beautiful day yielded to a magnificent sunset. Dark orchid wisps, and slate blue vapor trails wrapped themselves around a crimson and amber sky. Flecks of yellow aligned with the horizon. The crickets were in abundance.

The peacefulness was blunted by a horde of bleating hounds fresh from rest and food. They lunged at Boway's body as it swung slightly from a tree hanged by his braided switches.

\#

Kaffie searched frantically for a piece of the hand-dyed cloth that Boway had created. Lewis found one for her in the barn. She decided to use fine corn silk weaving methods to bind his piece in a quilt. She buried her head in his shirt.

It smelled like green.

The Cricket Cries, the Year Changes

Chapter 1

Helder ceased tending to the beehives one spring morning and turned his eyes toward home. Though this land and his faraway land held the same sky, same sun and moon, and same red dirt, absent was the village life of Benguela, Angola. This season on the Harris plantation was an emotionally crippling one for Helder. It was springtime long ago when he and his family were captured.

As a young boy filled with excitement he awakened to the beauty of the new growth that hugged the land in his village. He explored the terrain, ran close to the riverbanks or paddled small boats to parts of the coast. With his young friends, Helder frolicked through deep dense foliage and dry savannahs. Visiting other villages with their families the Benguelans bartered for goods. They fished near the shoreline of the river Cuanza. Those occasions served the dual purpose of pleasure and provisioning.

Helder paid close attention to his father, Iddrisu's, actions during these trips. During subsequent hunts he would impress his father with his newfound knowledge. He was mesmerized by the rites of passage celebrations held for the twelve-year-old boys, who had crossed the threshold into manhood. They were readied to add their legacies to an ancestral eternity. They stood tall, erect, and silent with emotionless faces that glistened with pride. The priests and chiefs invoked the spirits to come and walk among them. Helder listened intently to the elders as they entreated the forefathers to prepare and protect those whose life stage had signaled their readiness to be men. Helder eagerly awaited his time of honor in his own ceremonial costume.

Iddrisu had remarked how tall his son would be. He promised his son that his strength, height, and muscle would surface soon enough to herald his participation into the solemn sacrament.

Despite the colorful embroidering of the Harris Plantation by the sprouting hues, the embedded memories of green mountains and the plains of his homeland caused Helder to pause. Springtime always used its potent advent to draw Helder into deeper and darker memories. She pulled him toward the powerful and greedy longings for his ancestral home of the storied Mbunda kingdom.

As a beekeeper on this plantation Helder's job was a solitary one. He had no previous knowledge of bees, their habits or their honey making. Harris had left Helder's fate up to an overseer who viewed his infirmity as too limited for fieldwork. Helder was insulted by the assignment. No one ever checked on his daily whereabouts.

The best part of his job was delivering the thick golden honey to Kaffie for her tea. She responded in kind by making him shirts with the left sleeve gathered at the bottom so it would not draw that much attention to his missing hand. Helder was grateful.

Harris had not known that Helder had become a sailor while enslaved in Charleston, South Carolina for eleven years. He was a shipbuilder first. He learned the diagonal method of placing wood at the foundation of the ship that added more strength to its structure. He became familiar with sailing terms, how to position sails for best performance but most importantly, how to use the stars as a navigational guide.

Helder could read charts. Regardless of the restricted use of his left arm, Helder learned how to tie knots that secured the masts of the ship's sails or knots that required a quick release. The captains were impressed with Helder's ability to sail a ship. Several challenged his knowledge and he proved himself worthy. Helder had sailed the Atlantic Ocean to ports like St. Augustine, Florida, the Beaufort and St. Helena Islands and many others where deliveries of goods and livestock were abundant.

He loved the smell of the ocean. He slept under the umbrella of thousands of stars. He learned to align the constellations to the seasons. When heavy fog made the oceans go silent and temporarily delayed their travel, Helder would think back to his first time on a big ship.

\#

Helder winced as he recalled the scourge, beatings, and suicides during the long trip across the biggest river he had ever seen; It had no ending. He and his people had heard too many stories about the traders and the traitors; our own people selling us like beads in a marketplace, Helder regretted bitterly. We had not let our guard down; there was just too many of them—just too many, he rued. The kidnappers had snatched us from the dense thicket. We heard the large, low-lying fronds of the jungle floor cut fiercely with machetes. Tongues unknown to us spoke with such urgency and pitch. We quickly sought refuge from our gathering of cowrie shells from the shore. We squatted, petrified, among the thorny and thick bush.

The group of us begged our jungle gods to protect us. We held onto tightened lips and breathed slowly and noiselessly through our nostrils. Our statue-like limbs had fallen asleep. The tingling sensations numbed us as we held those positions for a lifetime. The assembled were too afraid to swat the insects so we allowed the crawlers to bite and sting lest we be discovered. We were taken by surprise with the sudden appearance of Angolan blacks. They descended upon us from the immense tacula trees above. They aided the strange ones that had come on foot and dragged huge nets. They encircled the frightened masses.

The event triggered the heightened blaring sounds of the jungle inhabitants. Birds, monkeys, and even the slow crawlers, severed the sweaty silence of our hiding places, as they deserted their common refuge. The stampeding mixtures of animal colors blurred toward new shelter. "I begged them to take me along with my mother and sisters whom they had already taken. My family struggled to gain their footing as hands and feet fought the entanglement in the squares of braided rope," he remembered.

The calamitous movements formed a singular tumult of revolt. The conch pink sand and the freckled beige cowrie shells were lifted high as bare feet dug into both. It created temporary blizzards that blinded captors and captives alike. The thieves did not seem to want Helder. He could tell by the symbolic speech of their tongues. The blacks had said something about his scrawny, spindly size. "Did they not know that all warriors started out this way? Did they not know what I was destined to become? I was only eleven years old!" Helder screamed inside.

He had clung to his mother's woven dress. His arm had reached through the net that was thrown over her and his wailing sisters. She bravely sought to comfort them as she held in her own fear. She could only grapple the muddy braids of his sister, Bedri's, head to steady her. His other sister, Cheylah, had buried herself deep into her mother's breasts as if she wished to suffocate herself.

His mother did all of this as she tried to comfort Helder with her big brown eyes of tender mercies that readied themselves to bid him goodbye, forever. To keep from being separated from his mother's unrelenting grasp through the hemp- net rope, her colorful dress was held prisoner in a vise-like seizure with his small right hand. Helder's left arm thrashed the tropical breeze as he roared silently with bulging eyes. His mouth remained wide open. It inhaled panic, and exhaled horror.

One of the funny-looking men with red hair like the monkeys and ocean-blue eyes used a machete to cut his left hand off just above the wrist in an attempt to break his hold. As it happened, a black traitor quickly yanked a leather lash from his whip to wrap around his arm to stop the bleeding. He cursed the machete-wielding man with a glare and told him that this scrawny boy was part of the count that was required on the ship.

The African furthered that it was getting dark and they did not have time to find replacements to make up the number difference. The captor understood the tribal drumbeats that began to summon other villagers to the area. Word began to travel through whistles and birdcalls made by the ones who had gotten away. It was getting too risky, he hollered over the melee. His swagger as a traitor to his people betrayed his birthright.

Somehow, Helder did not scream out in pain when he lost his hand. The beet-red blood hurled itself onto the jungle fronds that in the end had offered them no protection. Other streams of the life fluid stained his clothing and fell for familiarity's sake on his bare left foot. When it began to dry quickly in the African heat, it matched the cinnamon color of the bark of the tall taculas trees that had hidden their kidnappers.

His mother and sisters wailed. Their shrieks and shrills, at the gory amputation joined other cries of horror. It curdled the air on an otherwise ordinary day. Helder did not cry. He was in shock. He was steeled by thinking of the rites of passage ceremony where he would never participate. He chose this moment to be brave for his women and strong for his ancestors. He exacted some much-needed pride from his father who was away on a hunt. There would be far greater torment than that for him to consider than just a bloody stump if his world was changed forever by the loss of his family.

Helder was first enslaved on the Macklin plantation in Charleston, South Carolina. He never saw his mother and sisters again. In the cotton fields at the age of twelve years old, he decided to carve out from his left arm the branded monogram of a slave trading company that had erased his identity on that ship. It created a deep uneven furrow in his skin. This was Helder's initiation.

He would belong to no one.

Cynthia Harris-Allen

Chapter 2

Helder spent three days in a holding cell in Charleston. The auctioneers awaited the arrival of the planters. Bad weather had delayed the event. Many slaves chained and huddled in the open cages grew restless and violent. After two and a half days the keepers decided to feed them and grease them down for the pending sale. In two rows of chained humans behind him Helder saw a woman who tried desperately to defend herself from assaults by the black men. When their eyes met she sent a silent soulful plea for help.

Helder, now well over six feet six inches tall, and twenty-three years old, dragged the entire chain of Africans that he was tethered to toward the area where the young slave woman was being accosted. His intimidating stare caused two of the men to cease their menacing. The rest of that same group was startled at the strength of this cripple who hauled eleven men with him to her defense. They did not bother the young woman after that. Helder was sold to a shipping company.

#

He visited ports of call and sailed many small rivers up and down the Carolina and Georgia coasts that spilled into the vast ocean. He had grown up on the sea. The waters had raised him. One rain-drenched morning the ship docked on the shores of Bluffton, South Carolina. Slaves had to wear their identification tags when they disembarked to unload and load cargo. Helder swore to himself that he would keep this item forever.

Helder saw a woman carrying sacks of rice in a basket on her head. She was moving toward the docks. She wore a printed dress with a wide emerald green sash that matched her headscarf. Her bare feet seemed to welcome the splash puddles, a warm and soothing balm for a constant pedestrian. She set the basket down quickly only to retrieve another one from the wagon a few feet away.

Helder lowered the boxes of freight onto the wharf. He stretched his giant frame and began to walk in the direction of the woman with the green sash. He blocked her path with a smile. She returned his. Helder tried to remember himself to her. She interrupted him and assured him that she already

52

knew who he was. It had been several years since the encounter in the holding cells. He had saved her long ago. She admitted that she had switched places with another slave woman so she could bring the rice baskets near him. They both laughed.

Helder wanted to know if she would be returning to the docks the next day. The woman, Beyla, answered that tomorrow was Sunday; it was free time on Four Oaks, the nearby plantation where she lived. Helder asked her if she would be able to visit the docks on Sunday. He told her the ship he worked on would not sail for three more days. Beyla said it was impossible. She had no one to bring her.

He asked her to point out the wagon that had brought her to the shore and he would follow the crowd toward the plantation. He asked her to tie her headscarf around a tree trunk after dusk on Sunday and he would find her there. Beyla was hesitant. Helder assured her he would protect her——just as he had done before.

Helder walked among the other slaves that followed the wagon back to Beyla's home. No one noticed him to be out of place. He hid his badge inside his cotton shirt. Over his back, he carried a small sack. Once he arrived at the small homestead Helder took shelter by the mill. He slept under a moonlit sky, happy that his lonesome life may begin anew.

He met Beyla by the green-strapped tree and hugged her for the first of many times to come. He told her he was going to take her with him to the plantation in Charleston where he lived. He told her there were many more slaves there and he would make sure that she blended in. In the small sack, Helder had brought clothes that the slave sailors wore. He had managed to pilfer a small size cap as well. He told Beyla to change into them. They buried her clothes under the brush. He was going to take her aboard ship with him disguised as a young boy.

Beyla presented Helder with a beaded green amulet, strung from a thin leather strap to wear around his neck. She told him that the color represented newness and spring.

\#

Cynthia Harris-Allen

The over one hundred mile trip up the coast from Bluffton to Charleston was harrowing for Beyla. She was not used to the sea and was frightened. Helder kept her close to him throughout the entire journey. During the daylight hours he showed her how to walk with the movement of the waves and not against them. Helder advised her not to talk because she could not lower her tone enough to sound like a male. He shared his food with her and sometimes gave her most of it. He made sure she had plenty of water to drink.

There were no overt signs of courtship; after all, she was a young man. No one approached her or questioned her presence onboard. There were too many slaves on this large ship for the white crew to have total recall. The last night before the ship reached Charleston, Helder and Beyla stayed on deck. He advised her to either lean up against the rails or walls of the ship or sit down. He smiled when he told her she had the stance of a newborn doe and would stand out if she did not do what he suggested. He sat next to her and said he would tell her about his life and then she could tell him about hers when they reached the plantation. He told Beyla of his family's capture from Africa——and how he lost his hand.

#

His mother and two sisters were taken toward the huge ship aboard large canoes that shuttled them back and forth in chained silence. It was a very long journey north up the Cuanza River to inside the belly of the merciless beast. The river spilled itself westward into the big sea to nowhere. Helder clung dearly to his family——even with one hand, he told her. The left hand was bound in rough gauze. It sent streams of physical pain that bested his mental anguish.

As captured peoples, we left our hearts and histories on the banks of the Cuanza River. Some of the villagers eluded bondage as they recklessly jumped into the river. With panic and doom in their eyes, they waded out up to their nostrils until the frothy, sun-kissed water chilled them in their last reality while it engulfed them. It acceded to their resolve by fashioning the sea into a common coffin.

Indifferent to what lie ahead, the others were consecutively chained by the necks and wrists. There was barely three feet of walking space between their shackled ankles. Our reluctance to die on the coast volleyed back and forth with the need to save and protect the women and children. Soon there was no longer a choice. We marched up the splintered plank with frozen stares ensconced in both fear and fright of the unknown.

Never had a captured soul returned home to our homeland, Bengula in the spirit or in the flesh to tell all what it was like to live "Below the Earth" as the unknown place was called, Helder told her. We were stolen and bartered as if we were maize or beans at the bazaars. Our bodies were branded. We were kidnapped with no mention of ransom he told her as he bit his lower lip. Beyla hid her tears. She likened it to her own similar experience.

Four years later, Helder was auctioned off to Harris-Jones. He and Beyla had had two children by then. Harris bought the entire family.

#

Now at thirty-seven years old, he was still tormented by that riotous mass abduction. As the buzzing bees began to swarm around Helder's head and ears, he opened his eyes and released sorrow-filled tears along with a single whimpered child-like cry. He was a grown man standing in a new spring; but he still questioned the skies as to the whereabouts of his father. He wiped his eyes with the half-empty sleeve from his left arm. He slid open the wooden doors of the hives that welcomed the bees return.

Beyla came to understand the haunting thoughts that plagued and debilitated Helder. She was very sympathetic toward him. Every year she prayed for an early summer.

Chapter 3

Helder restlessly shifted his body whenever he saw ships, barges, and sailboats. He would pause by the thickets near the beehives when he heard the blare of the ships' air horns. They were summoning him. He had lived on this homestead now for eight years.

Jelani, a half-Cherokee slave on the Harris plantation, taught Helder how to carve a canoe from an oak tree. He showed him how to hollow out the belly by slowly burning the wood, weakening it to ash, and then scraping it out. They used pine tar to seal the boat. Helder decorated it with symbols that he faintly recalled from his African village. He paddled the vessel on the inlet waters that eventually flowed into the mighty Oconee River. The smooth spruce oars parted the waters on both sides as the maiden voyage sailed forward toward nothing.

He was finally free! His muscled body guided the canoe for hours. At times, Helder allowed the tides to dance with the new water carriage in whatever direction it chose.

A copper streak of color formed behind the clouds. Soon a half-sun sank on the horizon. Helder thought about the time when this experience on endless open water had horrified him. Now he welcomed the peace and serenity. When he looked back in the direction of the plantation, Helder's assessment of his life's situation changed dramatically: Barn-red clay or silky gray-blue waters? Lemon-yellow bees or dolphin-blue oceans? Heated fields of almond cotton and jungle-green cane or the cool trade winds in his face? The stark comparisons urged him to change the course of his life——or die.

At nightfall Helder hid the canoe in the soft rushes near the river. It was a common place for canoes or other makeshift watercraft to be tethered. Slaves did a lot of fishing and trapping.

#

Helder turned to Beyla one morning and traced her face with his hand as she slept. Their two children barely grown, had jumped the broom and lived in separate cabins with their mates. Beyla had taken in an orphaned slave boy, Toby, who was now eight years old. He slept on the opposite side of the cabin on a mat. He was the apple of her eye.

With a heavy heart Helder removed the faded amulet that Beyla had given to him on the plantation in Bluffton and folded it into her hand. He knew that he would not return to her. He loved her but he loved the ocean more.

He quietly exited before dayclean.

#

Helder made the over two hundred plus mile trek on land from Monroe, Georgia to Savannah in just over two months. He made sure that he sought shelter among the slaves on the farms that dotted the landscape. At a certain homestead to get rest and a meal, Helder worked in the cane field. He hauled the cut six-foot shafts in huge bundles to the wagons. No one spoke about his missing hand. Many slaves had physical defects mostly due to occupational hazards.

As he prepared to sleep in one of the cabins he concluded that all the plantations were alike to him. The landowners, the slaves, the stench, the despair, the cruelty, and the hopelessness were fashioned from the same giant pattern. He saw the collective emptiness in the eyes of the blacks on large and small farms alike. It sickened him.

Arriving at the docks in Savannah on a hot Georgia day, Helder made sure that his South Carolina identification tag visibly hung from his neck. He blended in with the rest. In the beginning he loaded and unloaded the barges. After about two weeks he stowed away on a ship. The ship sailed with forty-three crewmembers, a captain, and fifty slaves. The cargo consisted of textiles, dried meats, woven mats, baskets, and tobacco bound for Miami, Florida, and slaves.

Helder soon established himself with the crew and captain as an able-bodied and knowledgeable sailor. His adeptness at tying knots was a sorely needed task aboard the ship. He sat on the upper deck as the crew looked on and used his left foot as a substitute for the missing left hand. He quickly constructed easy figure-eight knots and more complicated bowlines to tether the sails.

He could call out nautical terms like "point of sail" to denote the angle of the sails to the direction of the wind and "fore, aft, and starboard" as different locations on the ship. He knew the properties of the tides and the moon's effect on them and began to offer his advice to the captain. He predicted pending severe storms earlier than they could.

All was not well with the crewmembers. Many resented this black's acceptance as an equal by Captain Hilson. Hilson would speak to his men privately about how much of a benefit Helder was. Hilson said he was going to use Helder's knowledge to their advantage and they had better get used to it. He told the white crew they did not have to respect Helder, because he, himself did not. To him, Helder was just like any other field nigger——except he was on water, not land.

His crew was satisfied with his assessment.

#

Helder had been missing from the Harris-Jones plantation now for two years. Harris could not get a bead on when he actually fled because the overseers did not keep a daily watch on him. His job did not require supervision; and he was an invalid. Soon after the discovery, Harris had his drivers conduct almost daily whippings on Beyla. She swore repeatedly that she did not know when he left or where he was going.

Harris delegated a driver, named Fred Corswood, to extract information from Beyla any way he could. Corswood not only beat her, he raped her repeatedly and had her perform other sexual acts upon him. Convinced after three months of no change in her story, Harris had her broken body and spirit returned to the fields. Corswood continued his visits to her cabin.

The only family left to care for her was Toby. Her grown children and grandchildren were sold at the beginning of the second year of Helder's disappearance to get her to render a credible confession. Beyla was heartsick. She held on to Toby with dear life. She made sure he ate every day, sometimes foregoing her own food to keep him from going hungry. He, like the other children was used for any job on the plantation. Many times they worked longer than the adults in the furnace-like heat.

Beyla was depressed. She could not understand why Helder left her without explanation. She knew that his mental sufferings spiked in the spring. She blamed herself for not realizing how bad it had become for him. While still living on the homestead, his children were angry with him. They cursed his name and never forgave him for abandoning them and the ensuing harm he caused to their mother. One of the grandchildren was named after Helder. His mother changed his name when it seemed clear that their father was not coming back.

Harris developed a habit of selling an entire family. He had learned from other planters that sometimes it staved off runaways. He did not sell Beyla. He punished her for her runaway, crippled husband's disappearance.

As she washed her clothes at the riverbank on a Sunday, Beyla studied her face in the water. It was scarred and burned, thanks to the interrogation techniques of Corswood. Her right eye never fully opened anymore. Her arms and legs bore bruises, raised and welted wounds. She was sure that her back did not look any better. There were places in her scalp where hair no longer grew.

She and Toby would hold the ends of the clothes together and twist them in opposite directions to set the water free. During this process one morning, Beyla dropped the piece and ran quickly to the bushes and vomited. Startled, she placed her hand on her stomach and her baby responded to her touch.

Chapter 4

The trade routes of Captain Hilson's ship, *The Passage*, were permanently changed to the southwestern coast of Florida and the islands in the Gulf of Mexico. Trade had increased dramatically in that area once New Orleans became the premier southern seaport.

Helder continued his welcomed input to the captain and crew. He also transported cargo to and from the ship with the rest of the slaves. Several years into his disappearance from the plantation, he began to facilitate the escape of slaves who worked at the various docks and on the barges. He stowed them away below deck behind bales of hay and boxes on the southwestward trips of *The Passage*.

Once they reached Key West, Florida, the escapees with Helder's guidance made their way to the Yucatan Peninsula of Mexico. That country had abolished slavery and welcomed the fugitives. Plantation owners in the lower states issued the cursory runaway slave bulletins. The likelihood of recovering their property was slim at best. The numbers soon swelled to over two hundred or more slaves that Helder had helped. Helder was emboldened by his own daring.

Springtime no longer bothered him because he sensed that he was balancing the scales of atrocities from long ago.

In mid-August, at the height of hurricane season in the Gulf, *The Passage* sustained considerable damage as it struggled to stay upright. It was the worst hurricane the crew had ever encountered. The hero was Helder. He knew how to change the angles of the sails to sustain the least damage from the winds. He predicted the arrival of the pending eye of the hurricane. He challenged Captain Hilson to allow him to bring the boat to safety for a time in its peaceful circle.

During that time they could reassess the direction they could take to review the damage to the ship. They sailed into the eye of the hurricane. Cornflower-blue skies and sea gulls almost tricked the crew into thinking that the storm had passed.

Then the winds increased in velocity. Lightning, thunder, and hail were once again upon them. Kettle-black clouds sent painful horizontal slants of rain that doused the upper deck. The sails could not hold the wind and instead folded in on themselves in confusion. The ship began rocking toward its right side.

As they traveled westward toward Mexico they soon realized that they were way off course. The captain shouted above the calamity to his men to jettison the cargo below deck that apparently had moved from one side of the ship to the other. He knew that the ship was in danger of capsizing.

Helder followed the whites. The crew descended below deck where they discovered over eighty slaves huddled on the right side of the ship. The intended cargo was tossed overboard long ago. Before the sailors could alert the captain, Helder blocked the stairs and shouted above the wind to the blacks to seize them and kill them all. He told them to hurl them into the sea through the sole window in the hull now blown open three times larger than its normal size by the hurricane.

Forty-two of the crew of forty-three whites met their deaths in the high, foamy waves of the gulf. Nature's fury drowned out screams and calls for help. Only one sailor was able to escape to the upper deck to inform the captain. A stunned Hilson and that lone crewmember were powerless against Helder and the large group of slaves that came up from the belly of the ship. They had closed enough of the gaping hole below with remaining pieces of lumber from the ditched cargo to ward off flooding the boat. On deck, the slaves welcomed the water-filled deluge and the chance to breathe in the gusting winds.

It was nighttime now and Helder had to rely on his memory to guide the ship under the clouds. The two remaining white men became prisoners below deck. They were chained to poles in the filth created by the stowaways. Both remained silent and afraid. Sickened by the stench and muck, they began to heave.

Helder was able to navigate the ship toward Mexican shores though he could not be certain that it would be the Yucatan peninsula. However, it still was freedom, he grinned.

\#

The slaves fell onto the coral pink sands of the beach exhausted, but elated. They cheered Helder as he disembarked from the heavily damaged ship. Helder let them sleep until afternoon.

They then returned to the moored ship to bring the foodstuffs and water from the former crew area to sustain them until it could be determined where they were. Hilson and the lone sailor remained prisoners on the ship.

Through a telescope Helder saw several other ships on the horizon that seemed to be heading just to the west of them. He had not been that far off course after all, he surmised. He sent some slaves to retrieve the captain and the sailor from the ship. He chained the two of them to separate palm trees deep into the jungle with their mouths gagged.

Then Helder hid the runaways in the tropical forest. He left about thirty of them sitting on the sand in the open disguised as the ship's help.

He had them set fire to the large vessel to attract the attention of the other boats. The plan worked. An inky nightfall brought two skiffs to their rescue. Both vessels did not have the capacity to hold the "stranded" men. The rescuers promised to signal other ships in the area to come to this place to their aid. One of the captains asked where the captain of the ship was. Helder told him that he was lost at sea during the storm, along with the crew. He continued that they were spared because they were housed below deck.

The ships collectively left rations and plenty of clean water for the group. Helder asked the captain if he could board his ship for the return trip to the states. He told him he had been the captain's helpmate and possessed some navigational skills. He told him he really wanted to get to South Carolina to see his family. Helder showed him the verification tag as proof. The captain obliged him as he studied his infirmity. Helder told him that he would follow behind him soon to ride in the skiff back to the ship but first, he needed to say goodbye to the crewmates.

Helder's body was weakened by this last ordeal. It had numerous scars, some old, and some new. Most came from working on the ship and the docks. He had sustained an intimidatingly long gash over his eyebrows. That injury was caused by a ship's mast that had fallen on him. He wore a black patch over his right eye but it was a ruse. He had heard that pirates among the high seas wore them. He considered himself a pirate. He, too, stole treasure as he considered the slaves to be just that. Helder had placed a tiny pinprick in the piece of material, so he could still see with both eyes. He only wore it on certain occasions.

Over time, his mahogany colored skin had burned to onyx by the sun of the seas. The briny air had dried his skin considerably. He no longer bore the look of a young, strapping sailor.

He was tired——but proud.

Helder huddled with the forty or so blacks on the beach and smiled broadly at them when he said they were free men now. He cautioned them not to celebrate until the ships were far out into the ocean. He told them to take the rations, join the others hidden in the forest, and walk northward to Yucatan. They would be welcomed there. He told them to free Hilson and the sailor. Someone would rescue them or maybe not. He pointed out the North Star. He instructed them to "follow the Drinking Gourd."

Helder was moved by their gratitude. On the rescue ship, the black waters, flattered by a shimmering silver moon set him on course toward home.

Chapter 5

Helder's gnarled stump ran across the smooth birch fence at the perimeter of the Harris-Jones plantation. He placed one leg on the lower rung and sighed deeply. He studied the valleyed meadows and the expansive fields of crops. He had long forgotten how vast this homestead was. He had been gone for a long time.

He saw a wagon coming toward the fence and decided to hitch a ride down the long graveled drive. The black driver asked him if he was lost. Helder told him that he used to live on this farm. He asked the driver what day it was. He told him it was Sunday morning.

Soon Helder jumped from the wagon and walked toward the cabins. He did not recognize anyone he passed. The entire area was foreign to him. There were barns and silos that he did not remember. There were also many more cabins. A large house had been built close to the mansion. He thought one building looked like a jail. There were slaves everywhere! More than what he remembered on this one plantation. This was their rest day. Their spirits were elevated.

Helder's shoes hung tied together and strung over his shoulder. Though his gait was slower, it was still deliberate. The burnt sienna clay warmed his feet. After years at sea, he had to get used to the earthy side of life again. The land air smelled differently than the sea winds.

He finally entered what he thought was Beyla's cabin and was rudely dismissed by another family. He asked a young slave boy if he knew who Beyla was. The youth pointed him in another direction. Her cabin was the last one in a row of older cabins.

Helder stepped into the cabin and could not tell if it was Beyla's or not. He had forgotten her habits and ways. All of this was foreign to him. He second-guessed his return.

He sat in a corner on a mattress filled with Spanish moss and toyed with a stick. He was uncomfortable with the floor not moving with the sway of the ocean. He grew fidgety. He heard a noise from just outside of the cabin and moved toward it. The stench stung his nostrils.

The Cricket Cries, the Year Changes

It wafted from a skinny, ruddy white boy about nine years old who was tethered to a chain that was staked into the ground. The child had about ten feet of room to roam. There were two bowls, apparently one for food, and one for water. Both were empty. His clothes were soiled and there was a pile of dirty ones next to him. He had very red hair like the monkey in the jungle. His eyes were ocean-blue.

Helder's entire body jerked at the memory. He gasped. He startled the child that began to cry. An older woman came into Helder's view. She rushed to the boy to comfort him. She looked around to see what had scared him. Beyla came face-to-face with Helder. She knew who he was immediately. He did not recognize her at all. She was old, decrepit, gray, and toothless at the top of her mouth. They silently looked upon each other for a minute. Beyla wondered if the scars, wounds, and eye patch were the results of a life he chose or of one that he was forced to lead.

In silent unison their minds recalled better times. They searched each other faces for remnants of that long ago time. Unable to conjure up the reasons why he had loved her, Helder's voice broke the silence with two words: "I'm sorry." Beyla could not cry. There was no more emotion in her. Her husband had left her. She had no idea where her children lived. Toby had died with the influenza.

Tears? Ha-Ha, she teased herself. She had none for this deserter. She gave the boy a strap of sugar cane to quiet him. She walked into the cabin. Helder followed. She began to throw any heavy object at him. Her feeble pitches missed the mark several times. She cursed him. She jockeyed between anger and defeat. She told him of the hard life she had endured since he left her.

Beyla told him that she was beaten and whipped for months by a driver after his disappearance. She said none of them believed she knew nothing about where he had gone. She cried to him about the repeated rapes by Corswood, the overseer, and pointed with an evidencing, raging fist at the boy outside. She moaned she could not give him up. He was the only family she had. Beyla said she had kept him chained outside every day since he was two years old so no one could see his face while she worked in the fields. She continued when she brought him in at night, she could hardly see he was white. That was the only time he belonged to her. She told him his name was Sam.

She asked Helder why he had come back. Beyla said that she no longer loved him; she had not for a long time. Spitting through her missing teeth, she moaned that she wished she were strong enough to kill him now that she knew her wishes for him to be dead did not pan out. She ordered him out of her cabin and her life.

He went to see Master Harris.

#

Helder stood at the huge mansion door and knocked meekly. He asked the butler to see Master Harris. He told him to tell him that it was important. He had put his eyepatch back on. The butler, Meriday, told him to stay on the porch. He would see if Harris wanted to see him. He asked his name and Helder gave it to him. Harris, with two overseers armed with rifles, came out onto the porch accompanied by his dog. He looked at Helder with preening eyes and tried to discern if he really knew who he was.

Helder addressed him as "Suh," and told him he used to be the beekeeper on this land. He told him that one afternoon when he was standing in the fields with the bees, three white patrollers bound and gagged him and stole him away. He told Harris they told him that he was a runaway slave that matched the description on a poster. Helder told Harris he thought he was taken to another land. He did not understand the tongues, but they had slaves, too.

It was hot there like here in Georgia, but it had water all around it, he told Harris. He added it took a long, long, time to get wherever they took him in that boat. He said he was burned, whipped, and beaten almost every day. He raised his shirt to show him the welts on his torso.

Helder said when they saw he had only one hand they put a stick in it and made him tend the goats on the land. Then he pointed to the patch over his eye and recounted how the animal's horn had taken his right eye clear out.

He told Harris that after all these years, he was able to stow away on a ship all the way to Charleston and climb onto wagons to Monroe. Then he broke down and cried. Now he has learned that his whole family was sold down river. His wife does not even want him. He begged Harris to let him bee-keep again. He would not mind it if he had to sleep outside. Helder sobbed that he was just tired, worn out and ready to die.

All the time he spoke to Harris, he called him "Suh" or "Massa."

Harris restored Helder without prejudice.

#

Helder stayed away from Beyla. Their paths never crossed.

Once he spotted her as she sat on the riverbank on a Sunday. He was on his way to the perimeter of the farm to check the honeycombs. He had been making inquiries as to the identity of a driver with the last name Corswood. Many slaves knew him as a cruel man but did not know if he had a permanent place in the fields to oversee the slaves.

One day Helder used his one hand to scoop water from a trough to satisfy his thirst. As he did it a third time, a lash from a whip circled his neck. He screamed in pain while he gripped the whip's end with his wet right hand. He spun around to face an old white man with red hair and blue eyes. Corswood asked him what he was doing so far away from the rest of the niggers. He told Helder to tell him which field he worked in.

Helder walked over to Corswood still on his horse and told him he was the beekeeper. Corswood laughed and said that Master Harris would not have that kind of sissy job on his plantation. He tried to reign in his whip so he could strike the sass from Helder's mouth. Helder still held onto it. Corswood dismounted from his horse and stood in Helder's face. He was a man of short stature and breath. Helder let go of the whip and changed his demeanor. He told the panting driver that he could show him what he did and where the beehives were located. Helder apologized as a docile, head-bowing nigger was expected to do and asked Corswood to follow him.

Helder told him he had to go to his cabin which was on the way, to get his glove and head covering so the bees would not sting him. Corswood in his mind thought this black fool better be telling him the truth. They arrived at the last cabin in the row. Corswood looked confused as he dismounted and stood still. This was the nigger, Beyla's quarters, he determined. He had not taken her in years.

Helder went inside and purposely waited for Corswood to grow impatient with the amount of time he was taking. Corswood dismounted his horse with his whip in hand and entered the cabin. He saw Helder at the back door. He walked over to him and pushed him in the back with the handle of the whip. He told him to get a move on it. Helder seized the whip in an instant from Corswood's hand. He stood behind him and wrapped it around his neck as he walked him toward the outside. He forced Corswood's face toward the young boy that looked just like him.

Corswood's face showed a mixture of emotions. He thought to himself: "*Do I really have a son? Why, this boy is the whitest colored boy, I've ever seen! What's he doing out here? Is Beyla his mammy? Was he stolen?*"

Helder let Corswood stew in his own internal interrogations and then interrupted them by asking him if he knew who Beyla was. Corswood lurched forward at the sound of her name and tried to free himself. Helder then told him he was Beyla's husband, the one he had beaten, whipped, and maimed for information about his whereabouts. Helder yelled in Corswood's ear that he had raped his wife and cursed her with his own spitting image.

Corswood struggled to speak. Helder knocked him out with one hate-filled punch. He stabbed Corswood repeatedly in the heart with his own knife. He loosened the spike in the ground that held the baby boy. He smothered the stinking child to death with his big right hand. Helder placed him on the horse with Corswood already slung over the saddle. He took his time walking toward the deserted deeper part of the river as he led the horse with its perpendicular passengers.

Helder had remembered a sea-faring legend that said "the ocean never gave up its dead". He wondered if the same applied to a river. He chained the boy around Corswood's neck. He threw them both into the cold, pewter-gray water. As both descended into the deep, Helder whispered hoarsely, "Father and son."

The Cricket Cries, the Year Changes

Chapter 6

Harris sat in the Charleston City Market dining with friends. He was ready to cede some of his authority to Rockfield Stiles. He had a meeting with his attorney to prepare papers. Harris was getting more interested in politics and needed time to study the political landscape.

He read the menu and studied the day's offerings that were written in chalk on boards. The two-sided advertisement hung from beige hemp yokes around the little black kids' necks. They flitted from table to table, with bleach-white teeth flashing, but saying nothing. They turned around several times to display the day's offerings.

Eventually, Harris' lawyer joined him with another person. His lawyer introduced him as a retired ship captain, Purvis Hilson, a longtime friend of his. The lawyer asked Harris if he minded if he joined them to eat. They could take care of personal matters later. The men engaged in small talk at first. Harris then asked Hilson about his sailing career. Hilson elaborated about his earlier routes. Then he told him that he had retired soon after his trade route was permanently changed to the islands, and the Gulf of Mexico.

He said the defining moment to retire came when a slave commandeered his ship. Hilson said the slave had become a legend, but he knew first-hand he was real. He said he was the best sailor he had ever seen, despite having only one hand. His name was Helder. Hilson told them that this nigger stowed three to four hundred slaves to Mexico over a period of time. "He sure knew about ships and the sea," Hilson chuckled slightly.

Harris' feet tightened in his boots. He then asked Hilson to describe this Helder person in detail. Hilson defined Harris' own property to a tee.

He also asked Hilson how long this Helder person had worked on his ship. Hilson said about seven to nine years. Harris had to excuse himself. He had wet his pants.

\#

Harris had invited the planters to his plantation for a special event. He was particularly interested in the owners who leased slaves to work on the docks and barges along the Atlantic coastline and never returned to their masters.

Harris was going to have a hanging party. He repurchased Helder's family. His grown children and their children were uprooted from other farmsteads. Harris wanted Helder to see them all die.

He had Helder's face placed in a steel vice that was chained to a post embedded deeply into the ground. His strength could not move it. A metal brace was placed around his mouth and secured at the base of his neck, disabling his ability to talk. His entire body stood erect on the post, held by chains from his ankles to his chest. Harris had both of Helder's eyelids stitched open. The Georgia heat had begun to dry his eyes out. Soon, all Helder could make out were blurry images; but Harris made sure that he loudly identified Helder's children and grandchildren to him one at a time before he hung them all.

Beyla would suffer last.

Helder was in shock. His family members were paraded before him before they died. The whites cheered. They were drunk with peach wine. They ate fried chicken moistened with the spit of the black cooks repulsed by this abomination. As each stool was kicked out from under the screaming group, the levity grew more intense with each swing of a body. The limitless toasting of raised glasses highlighted the revelry.

Beyla, showed no emotion. She remained silent. She could not thank Helder more for the relief she was about to feel. He had damned their entire family with his selfishness and ego. When her slight body hung limp in the breeze, Helder remembered springtime again. A huge headache burst in his brain. His head fell to his chest and he died.

#

Kaffie chose the same ecru muslin that she had sewn Helder's draw-stringed shirts from long ago to add to her quilt.

He had freed so many slaves; he was unable to vindicate himself.

The Cricket Cries, the Year Changes

JELANI

Chapter 1

A frosty morning shrouded the forests on the perimeter of the Harris-Jones plantation. The heat from a cloud-shielded sun began to dispense the light fog and allowed a better view of the two deer that Jelani had killed the night before. The carcasses hung from ropes had bled out and created a pool of liquid red that rivaled the Georgia clay ground. Jelani peered through a slit in his makeshift tent and determined that there were no other large animals in the area. It was quiet. He exited the temporary shelter, stood outside, and stretched. He drew deep breaths from the new day air. His sudden movements disturbed the birds that had just begun their morning melodies, high in the pines,

He approached the deer and prepared himself for the heavy task of removing the internal organs. After that he would skin the animals, taking care not to leave hair in the meat that could render it inedible. He had already made the necessary incisions just below the necks that indicated where he would first pull the skin downward. Before that task began Jelani threw the tongues of the deer along with a piece of their meat into a fire as an offering to his ancestors.

Jelani was the son of a Cherokee Indian and an African slave mother. His father named him Jelani, meaning "mighty". His mother was renamed "Inda" which means "black fox". The tribe had purchased her from white traders in exchange for four painted horses. Like most of the other Cherokee women, Inda took care of the planting and harvesting duties while the men hunted.

The Indian and African ways of life complemented one another. Each worshiped multiple gods and lived co-dependent lives with Mother Nature. The exchange of ancestral methods of hunting, trapping and healing advanced their survival skills. Many of the slaves on this native land were treated as equal by them, though the Cherokee ownership trumped any disagreements.

Jelani had trekked as far north as Kentucky on many occasions as a young boy. The long hunts when food grew scarce in northern Georgia could last for months. The women stayed behind. Oftentimes, they spent many days digging for edible potatoes when this main crop was infested with fungus. When fierce frigid winters brought unseasonable snow and cold weather, the women as the sole overseers took shelter in the mountain caves with the children and elders. Many of them died defending their families from wolves, bears, and white men.

When Jelani was about twenty years old, Master Harris illegally annexed this potato farm to his plantation by paying a large sum to a politician that was a close ally of the president of the United States. Among his fellow planters, Harris cited eminent domain as his right to claim the land. The Cherokee people had to move west of the Mississippi as part of the relocation edict enforced by President Andrew Jackson. Soldiers were dispatched to evict this tribe, along with other natives found in central and southern Georgia, to Oklahoma territory.

Many of the Cherokee people resisted this declaration. Some even denounced their Cherokee lineage and insisted that they were of African descent. They longed to become enslaved so they could be near the sacred burial grounds of their forefathers. On the contrary, to gain their freedom from their owners, some blacks, who appeared to have Native American lineage, claimed to be Cherokee, Creek or Choctaw to escape bondage and join the tribal trek.

The ones that were children of African mothers and Cherokee fathers were considered slaves, due to the law of the South that stated that the race of the child followed the mother. Because of that proclamation, Jelani and his mother were branded with the Harris-Jones insignia of ownership when Harris seized the land. Jelani never saw his father from that day forward. The only memory he held from him was the brown fossil shark tooth that hung from a leather strap around his neck.

His mother, Inda now almost sixty years old, dumbstruck by the forcible removal from the sacred burial grounds, never spoke one word again up to the day she died. Her prized and only possession from her former home was a blanket woven by her sister-in-law. The wrap of many bold colors of blue, orange, and crimson, in triangular patterns

The Cricket Cries, the Year Changes

warmed her with fading memories on many nostalgic nights on the plantation.

Jelani had jumped the broom with a slave named Zumbi when he was twenty-five years old and she was twenty. They had three sons and a daughter. The oldest son they called "Waya" which meant "wolf." Jelani said this son's eyes seemed to pierce the night. The wolf was also a sacred animal of the Cherokee. The second was named "Unaduti", interpreted as "wooly head" because his hair looked just like his mother's.

They selected "Atsadi," meaning "fish" for the youngest boy. Jelani had caught the biggest trout of his life at the river the night that Zumbi gave birth. It fed the entire family in the morning as they celebrated his arrival. Their daughter, the youngest, was Ahyoka, the Cherokee saying for "she brought happiness." Ahyoka was able to summon a smile from her grandmother, Inda, as she held the newborn. She was her favorite grandchild until the "fluenzah" snuffed out Inda's light.

Now thirty-eight years old, Jelani was the principle trapper for the plantation. Many young slaves accompanied him on hunts. He and Scipio worked closely to design traps both large and small. Scipio became his only friend. The deer hunts took place three times a year, when its population grew to excessive proportions. At times the animals were considered as annoying and destructive as the diseases that affected the crops. The deer cut swaths through acres of corn and greens as they ravaged the fields in search of food.

The deer meat sustained the plantation. The hides were sold at market for coats and waterproof outerwear. The buckskin leather would be fashioned into gloves and coats. It was the reigning seasonal export.

Jelani and his wife adapted to the African slave plantation culture but retained their own tribal customs and beliefs. The daily acts of brutality and disrespect meted out to the slaves disturbed them. With his grown sons, Jelani hunted almost year round. Zumbi was a potter. These solitary tasks spared them from many of the punishments that occurred on the plantation.

When they were alone the family discussed how the lack of harmony in their surroundings left them unbalanced.

Cynthia Harris-Allen

Jelani repeatedly stressed to them that patience and resolve had to be the two things that greeted them every morning and put them to rest at night. He never felt at ease on this red ground even though the same sun, moon, and stars had followed him here years ago. Though his children were born on the plantation, they mirrored their father's angst and unrest and lived guarded and watchful lives.

The Cricket Cries, the Year Changes

Chapter 2

Jelani and his helpers used bows and arrows, spears and traps to capture animals. Harris would not allow such a large group of slaves to carry guns. Only the overseers who kept watch were armed with rifles. The hunters would position themselves with their long knives primed in the deer fields. They stealthily waited for the animals to pass through.

With an errant rifle shot from an overseer, several slaves would be killed or injured by deer during a sudden stampede. Jelani grew impatient with the random, inaccurate shots from the guards that scattered an entire herd in seconds. Though Jelani's English was not fluid, he relayed in irregular tenses to the overseers that he disapproved of their actions. The drivers totally disregarded his objections. They called him a "half-breed" or "the potato nigger."

One early morning, Jelani and his hunting troupe lie in wait for the herd. The deer had gathered at the riverbank and would soon make their way past them to forage on the fresh greenish-yellow sprouts of the shrubs. The men had covered themselves with mud, leaves or deer skins and leaned against trees or lay upon the ground——perfectly still. Some held blow darts in their hands at-the-ready. Others had pulled arrows from their quivers to be launched by their taut bows. The hunters had been waiting for hours. Their bodies were cold, stiff, and achy. The silent chilly vapors of breath intermittently disappeared into the frosty air.

The herd slowly walked past the stealthy troupe toward their morning breakfast. A loud clicking sound overtook the otherwise peaceful dawn. Seconds after, a rifle shot zinged a black hunter's ear and embedded buckshot into a tree. The startled deer herd bolted and scattered into the thickets. The white undersides of their tails dotted the landscape with warnings of danger. The birds flew away to higher trees. Smaller forest animals quickly sought shelter in nearby holes and under rocks.

Jelani cursed. He turned and walked toward the noise. With disgust Jelani pulled Evan Shaw, an overseer, from his horse for discharging the rifle that drove off the herd in all directions. It caused them to lose the hunt. Jelani damned him and mocked his irresponsibility as an onlooker. Jelani told him that no one invited him to participate in the hunt. He spat near him as he threw Shaw hard to the ground.

As he walked away from Shaw, he discerned that he had stood up. He heard him slap his chaps to rid them of the dirt he had fallen in. He called Jelani "a dead potato nigger." Jelani turned just in time to see Shaw ready his whip to strike him. The leather formed a semi-circle in the air. Shaw aimed its handle toward him from six feet away. With one backwards step, Jelani eluded the whip's forward progress. Shaw rewound the whip. Jelani rushed toward Shaw and grabbed him. He quickly flipped him around and held him by his neck with his own whip. Shaw was a portly man, with more stomach than muscle. The uneven struggle ended quickly as Jelani held Shaw in a chokehold.

The overseer's boots cut divots into the forest floor as he fought to remove himself from the lash that tightly bound his neck, discoloring it under the strain. He struggled to free himself from Jelani's grip; he sensed his own pending death. His face was florid and sweaty. His eyes bulged with undeniable fear and helplessness. Unable to speak or scream, his choppy pants for breath lessened with the force of Jelani's muscled arm around his neck.

Shaw was the only white man in the group. The hunters that included Jelani's sons stood and watched with mouths open and eyes big. They stood unaware of how this was going to end but even more surprised by Jelani's audacity. Jelani lifted Shaw off the ground as he continued to choke him. Pieces of cloth from Shaw's plaid shirt that were ripped by the tension from back-and-forth tussling took flight in the morning breeze and found new homes in the low shrubs and rocks. Jelani never spoke a word nor made a sound. His face had taken on a look of detachment.

The other slaves, who had accompanied him on many hunts, had never seen him like this before. He appeared to stare off into nothingness. He had disconnected himself from the present tense. When he knew that Shaw was dead, Jelani nonchalantly dropped him to the ground and stepped over him.

The overseer lay twisted on his face. Jelani removed his carving knife from his deerskin sheath, knelt and scalped Shaw. He held up the bloody mass and heaved shouts to the skies. His mouth was so wide open that one could see his tonsils. Jelani recalled the smell of blood and triumph when his tribe had engaged in battles in the lowlands. Decisive victories empowered the warriors and emboldened them for future acts of bravery. This was his initiation.

Jelani viewed the frozen stares from the hunting party. Their feet seemed nailed to the ground. He ordered them to begin to dig a grave. He instructed his sons, Waya and Unaditi to find and kill three muskrats and remove their glands. The secreted oils would hide the scent of the rotting body. He walked away from the crowd of about twenty men who had started to move closer to view the body.

As soon as Jelani was a distance away, they began to talk loudly about what they had just witnessed. With each pitched shovel full of red dirt, the slaves tried to best the other as each recounted their singular renditions of that one fatal swift move Jelani had made on Ole Fat Shaw.

By nightfall, with a day's preparation wasted, the hunters lit fires for warmth and cooking. Shaw's body had been lowered into the closely packed, unyielding clay. The grave was camouflaged with the elements of the forest. Shaw's personal belongings were buried with him. Musk oil was sprinkled between the dirt and the rocks before a final layer of brush would lie beneath the thicket's natural ground covering. Jelani removed the saddle from Shaw's horse. He faced the animal eastward and slapped its rear hard toward the open lands. He shredded the bridle and reins with his knife. The saddle was weighted down with rocks and thrown into the river.

Jelani did not speak to what he had done with the others. Instead, his normal tone returned when he told them to ready themselves for the same hunting exercise the next morning. He lay on the ground apart from the hunters to sleep with thoughts of returning home to his wife and children. He had been gone for almost two full moons and a half.

Chapter 3

With a payload of deer meat and skins, the hunting party readied their return to the Harris-Jones plantation, weary and tired. It had rained constantly during the final week of their passage. The unseasonable cold and chilling showers were felt down to the bones of the slaves. Many lay inside the wagons on the flat boards. They fashioned their blankets into makeshift tents. Soon the covers, soaked and weakened by the drenching waters, offered little protection from the inclement weather.

Several of them developed colds that escalated into pneumonia. At night, the constant coughing and vomiting increased. The stench of soiled clothing was rank. The trembling bodies sought warmth and relief as they traded dizzying fevers for the chills. Jelani, and two others, rode their horses back and forth among the five wagons while they administered food and water to the sick. Jelani rubbed turpentine and kerosene on their chests. He crushed the leaves of the peach tree, poured boiling water over them, and brewed it into a tea to warm them. He and others made heavy porridge from corn and added onions and wild carrots.

In some instances, these applications were effective; though he lost five slaves during the return trip. He burned the corpses and scattered the dust on the grounds. Jelani was taught, as a young child, that the gods of water and fire were the hunters' best blessings. His spirit was embittered that they manifested themselves as torrents of rain and funeral pyres.

#
At dusk the first wagon reached the slope of the hill that overlooked the plantation. It stopped. The travel-weary eyes beheld many bonfires. Jelani, who had stayed at the rear wagons with the infirmed, rode towards the front. He wondered what had made them stop the forward progress. Drums beat and bells constantly rang. Plumes of smoke blackened the skies, seemingly from every part of the homestead. Slaves carried makeshift cots with lifeless bodies

in them toward the outskirts of the plantation. Others just stood at attention with torches to light the way.

There were wails of sorrow and pain. Blacks had gathered in a circle near the entrance to the plantation. They sang a song to the top of their lungs in perfect harmony: *Heaven is my aim, let me be. I calls mysef a chile of God, heaven is my aim."*

Jelani roused his horse and quickly descended upon the area. The sound of pots and pans clanged along the side rails as the men in the wagons followed as fast as they could. Rusted wheel cogs begged for relief while they familiarized themselves with their Georgia home turf. The hunters who had not taken sick jumped from the wagons and ran barefoot toward their cabins. They frantically called out the names of their loved ones. They learned that the fever had enveloped the plantation soon after Jelani and the hunting party had departed.

Master Harris and his extended family as their usual custom had previously left for their northern vacation. Every year they would escape the most intense time of unrelenting heat in the South. They would be gone yet another month or so. He had left his drivers and overseers in charge. Many seized this opportunity to dole out unfettered acts of brutality and payback on slaves whom they felt had been insolent or "too uppity" toward them.

There was no Master to run to now. Even the chief overseer, Rockfield Stiles was up North with Harris. The epidemic thwarted most of their punishments; it claimed several drivers as well. The whites began to keep their distance from the coloreds. They sensed that the origin of the disease lay with the slaves: but they too, were part of the death count. In the Big House the slaves were not allowed to go outside lest they could never return to the inside. Many of the cooks, butlers, and cleaning people had relatives in the fields. Some deserted a safer place to care for family and friends. Ngango had prepared many potions and salves for the sick and had lost two of his prized apprentices in the process. Even the whites credited him for his assistance in containing what could have been an epidemic of greater loss.

Kaffie was cautioned by the overseers not to go under the tent to tend to the sick, particularly the stricken little children; there were so many of them. She ignored them and delivered on a daily basis, blankets, clean clothing and mournfully, shrouds for the dead. She supervised the cooking of peanut, chicken and corn soups.

Very little work was performed on the plantation. The crops, almost harvest-ready, had been neglected. Two thirds of the cane crop had black rot. Weeds, whose aggressive invasion was seen for miles, overran many of the vegetable fields. Add to that, the incessant heat caused by the hot winds pushed northeastward from South America. The entire plantation scene was nightmarish. The farm animals had fended and foraged for themselves since the outbreak of the fever. It was catch as catch can at feeding time. Many sheep roamed aimlessly with burdensome coats of wool. Cows had full udders and suffered for not having them emptied. Three foals lay dead in the barn unattended by the mares who were nowhere to be found.

Yellow fever had claimed the lives of forty-one slaves and thirteen whites. Zumbi was among them; Jelani and his sons were informed by an overseer. Atsadi and Ahyoka were also among the dead. Jelani asked to see them. They told him that his family was either burned or buried in a common grave with the rest of the dead in the Ole Field, the slaves' graveyard.

Waya and Unadati helped a dumbstruck Jelani up from the ground. They poured their own tears within his embrace. He walked on weakened legs to their cabin as the three of them locked arms together. They passed by slaves who were still sick with the fever. They lay in their own filth outside their cabin doors neglected and sought help.

Inside their cabin, Jelani immediately performed a Cherokee stomp dance. His sons looked on with respect and grief. The clay pots made by their mother were scattered about the cabin but not broken. Everything was in disarray. Jelani thought it was not his wife's habit to keep objects strewn about. Even if she were ill, she would have asked the children to help. Atsadi commented on how his mother kept her clay pots in the corner that faced the eastern skies as a sacred act. There were over twenty pots that were out of order, pattern and size. None had been broken.

Jelani used his hands to caution his sons to stand still. He walked over to the other side of the small cabin where

The Cricket Cries, the Year Changes

Ahyoka and Atsadi would sleep. Now in their late teens, they had their own collections of objects and finds from the forest that they enjoyed. His youngest son loved marbles and had collected quite a few. Jelani made sure he brought back shards of these glass treasures when he found them during his hunts.

On his woven mat, Atsadi had arranged the marbles that left a message for his father and brothers should they return. The taller, flat bottom pieces all faced northeast. The smaller ones surrounded them. Three flat pieces of marble are placed on top of some objects aside from the group. They were put in the northeast corner of the living quarters. Under one of the smaller orbs, a piece of Ahyoke's beaded headband lay nearby. Cloth from Zumbi's dress had long strands of her wavy hair folded inside of it. A pile of fish scales surrounded the last marble piece.

A frantic Jelani ran quickly to the open fields to find anyone to tell him the truth about his family. He finally found Scipio in the graveyard. He was placing iron symbols deep into the mass graves that held the newly deceased slaves. As he held the torchlight to his face, Scipio told Jelani that Shaw's horse had wandered back onto the plantation, with the "HJ" brand on his left rear end as the only identifier.

Scipio explained that he tried to hide the horse in the barn on the pretense of it needing new shoes so he could figure out what to do. An overseer had questioned Scipio. He had recognized that the horse had a marking between his eyes that resembled a white arrowhead. Most of the drivers knew Shaw's horse. Apparently, Shaw had named his horse "Arrow". Harris gave the animal to him seven years ago, Scipio told Jelani.

Shaw's wife, who was a cousin of Harris, had told one of the drivers that she had suspected foul play when she learned the horse had returned without her husband. She cried to him how much Shaw loved that horse. She cited numerous times when her husband told her he was afraid of Jelani, who always threatened him when they were away on hunts. In retaliation for Jelani being the prime suspect in the disappearance and probable murder of Evan Shaw, two overseers sold his entire family before the outbreak of Yellow Fever. Scipio told Jelani that his family was bound and chained on a wagon that was headed northeast. They were alive.

The Cricket Cries, the Year Changes

Chapter 4

Word spread quickly among the overseers and drivers that Jelani had returned with his two sons. The welcomed cargo of deer meat and skins was quickly unloaded from the wagons and used immediately.

Shiloh Tanner, one of the overseers took it upon himself to want to include Jelani, and his older sons in the same fate as Zumbi, Ahyoka and Atsadi. He also wanted them to be killed on the same trail the rest of his family was traveling. He insisted to the other men at a hastily called meeting that they keep Jelani alive until Harris returned. The group agreed with Tanner but asked him how he expected to pull this off. No one knew where Jelani and his sons were since being spotted two weeks back.

Tanner suggested that they search every slave's cabin until they found them. They knew that the slaves would give them information if forced to do so, but as in times past, even under the threat of the whip, they proved to be too willing, and too wrong.

Many of the men objected to entering the cabins. Though newer outbreaks were not reported, they were sure that some contamination still existed where the niggers lived. They shifted their attention to inventorying the entire homestead. They knew that Harris would be coming home soon. Most were sure that he knew nothing about the near total decimation of his properties. They might as well begin to assess the damages.

\#

Jelani and his two sons stirred quietly when the light of day cracked through the gables of the Big House. They lay on the planked floor on woven mats with folded quilts stacked high in front of them. At first glance the attic appeared as normal and usual as it always was——except this time Kaffie had company. Unknown to the whites, the three of them had slept in their own cabin the first night of their return. No one came looking for them during the calamitous events. Scipio's relationship with Kaffie allowed this family to sleep in her room in the large attic.

With the coded information that Atsadi left, corroborated by Scipio, Jelani decided they would travel northeast in search of the rest of his family. In order to do so, Jelani needed assistance. Scipio had agreed to supply three horses that were no longer in use. The drivers who owned them had died. He placed black soot over any white or tan markings on the horses and completely seared through the H-J brand on each animal. He told Jelani to get word to him when they were ready to depart; he would leave information about the pick-up point.

Kaffie had had limited access to Jelani because he was away from the homestead most of the time. However, she enjoyed a warm relationship with Zumbi and Ahyoka. She greeted them both under the tent for the many years she handed out the spring and winter allotment of clothing. Ahyoka had made Kaffie a cornhusk doll with clay-colored beads for hair at Christmas years ago. It was about eighteen inches high and sat in the middle of all the pillows made from quilt scraps on Kaffie's bed.

Ahyoka teasingly asked Kaffie each time she saw her if she could count her freckles. Zumbi had given Kaffie moccasins made by Jelani out of deerskin. Atsadi would often tell her that her grey eyes reminded him of his marbles.

Kaffie knew that Jelani's family had been sold. Grafton and Meriday, the day and evening butlers had also heard the entire dinner conversations about that situation. They were able to gather a lot of information about their fate. It was not difficult to get them into the attic. Most of the resident whites were up north with Master. The house slaves were a close-knit group; most of them had been raised inside.

Jelani, Unaduti and Atsadi were grateful for the sanctuary. Two days and nights of rain was the melodious balm that sang them to sleep. Far from the drenching chills that claimed many lives, the three were calmed by the same source. Several saucers and flat pans that caught the raindrops that seeped into one corner ticked like a long case clock. It offered the tranquil setting that gave rest and renewal to the tired hunters.

When they awoke, they ate heartily. Days later on a Sunday when the slaves normally had their rest day, the fields were crowded with the weakened workers. They cleaned up, weeded, and harvested fruits from the crops that could be

The Cricket Cries, the Year Changes

salvaged. Jelani sensed this busyness made for an opportune time to escape. He and his sons would not stand out. They were no longer dressed like hunters. The night before, Jelani had shaved his head with a small piece of flint, leaving only enough hair in the middle braided down his back. Kaffie swept up the long shavings and concealed them old newspapers to throw away.

She placed Jelani's discarded shirt under her bed. She burned the rest of the clothing that the three of them had previously worn. She outfitted them with several replacements from the allotment that now overflowed. She offered brogans for their feet but Jelani kindly refused explaining that they could not feel the earth beneath their feet in such thick shoes. Scipio had rolled other essentials into three separate thick blankets and tied them with a leather cord. Jelani's blanket held a rifle and ammunition. Several knives of different lengths, sharpened and sheathed were also included for each of them.

The three men left the plantation unnoticed early Sunday morning. They rode northeastward for thirty hours. By nightfall they camped near the riverbank. Before a big hunt Jelani remembered that his tribe performed a ritual. He and his sons honored that tradition as they stood in the water and chanted prayers to the gods of the environment for protection and success. After eating a meal, they extinguished the fire and smeared the ashes on their chests.

Jelani stood before his oldest son, Waya and removed the shark-toothed amulet from his own neck. He placed his fist on his son's shoulder and pounded it three times in a solemn gesture of a rite of passage. Waya felt the cold fossil piece against his chest. It warmed his heart.

Chapter 5

With over one hundred miles between them and the Harris-Jones plantation, Jelani and his sons slowed the pace of the journey and began to look for signs left behind by his family. They decided to spread out but search in the same direction. Waya became the designated bird caller. He would use his throated shrills to message danger or summon his father and brother to him.

He scaled a Cypress tree to get a better vantage point. He used a wide leather strap wrapped around both wrists to secure his body as he grabbed the branches. His moccasins gripped limb by limb. When he could no longer support himself on the smaller extensions near the top, he chose the elbow of a thick bough to sit upon. In the near distance, he saw a train of about ten wagons that ambled southwest. To get a better view, he stood up and leaned against a weaker branch. He jerked and almost lost his balance. The fraying leather strap broke apart from his neck and silently sailed to the ground. It landed on the spikes of a young pine tree.

Waya spied a wagon with a red canopy covering. He recognized it as Tillie Harris'. He cleared his throat and twice signaled an alert to Jelani and Unaduti. The two followed the sound until they all stood at the base of the Cypress. Waya short of breath told them what was headed in their direction. He was certain that it was the Harris entourage. The slow traveling parties would soon be upon them.

They quickly hid the horses in the thickest part of the forest. They removed the saddles, bridles, and knapsacks and hid them elsewhere. They knew that the road did not come close to the riverbank but pedestrians could seek rest and water if they chose. The three took refuge in the high branches. They had already sprinkled pepper on the ground should hound dogs have accompanied the group. They used the brush of the forest to erase their tracks. They waited.

The wagons stopped. Harris jumped from the third wagon in the line. Rockfield Stiles followed him. The hunters could not make out what was being said between the two of them but their gestures concluded that Harris, after stretching his legs and wiping the sweat from the inside of his hatband, had won the argument. He climbed back into the wagon.

Seven men with three black boys loaded with canteens and buckets came to the riverbank and filled up the receptacles. Some relieved themselves in the bushes. Two bay hounds began to walk around in circles near the peppered area. They were shooed away by Harris' men, anxious to return to the cool of the canopied wagons. One of the boys spied the shark-tooth necklace in the bushes. He walked backwards into the shrub and grabbed the broken strap with the dangling piece on it. He quickly placed it into his pocket.

Jelani's and his sons' eyes were fixed on the wagons. Some of the women stepped from the parked coaches and stood behind blankets that were held up for them to dress in much lighter clothing. The Georgia heat reminded them that they were almost home. Some poured the fresh, cool river waters over towels and placed them around their necks.

The waggoneers continued their journey. Many of the drivers lit kerosene lamps that hung along the sides. The wicks were held low. It was not yet night.

#

Harris and his party were in utter dismay over the condition of the plantation. The scent of death, the scorched and rotting fields, the loss of lives and livestock sent Harris into a tailspin. He got drunk that night. He met for four days with the people whom he had left in charge to reflect on all matters, not just the Yellow Fever outbreak. His employees had recorded the number of lives lost among black and white alike.

Because there was only a scant labor force they attributed the outbreak of the fever to the ensuing events that ruined the harvests and animal production. The few that could have worked tended to their sick families; others tried to benefit from the situation by running away. Harris would deal with that situation later. He knew that he had enough money saved to survive the months before spring but that was not the point.

Harris met with Evan Shaw's wife. She told him she knew that her husband was dead. She blamed Harris for not having more than one overseer to watch over all those bad niggers and that one crazy savage. She told Harris she wanted the rest of his family caught, killed or sold "down river". On the fourth day he ordered the overseers to accompany him on a ride throughout the entire plantation. He wanted to be up-to-date on its every nook and cranny. As they rode toward the slave cabins, Harris noticed many slaves with injuries, welts, and maimed faces. He asked the drivers to explain what had happened to them; yellow fever could not inflict such damage. The drivers did not answer the rhetorical question.

A young slave boy propped on a birch fence, overheard Harris' question. He told him one of the drivers had beat and whipped his momma for nothing. He had put out one of her eyes. Harris demanded the boy bring his mother out of the cabin. The young slave woman tentatively walked onto the porch stoop and stood in front of Harris. He told her to remove the bandage from around her eye. He asked her what did she do to deserve the whip; he cautioned her to tell the truth or he would have her beaten again. She said a driver done it. She pointed to Shiloh Tanner as the man who beat her after he raped her.

Just as Harris turned on his saddle to look at Tanner, another young boy who had accompanied Harris on the northern trip came out of the same cabin. He stood next to his mother and placed a protective arm around her waist. That move exposed the item strung from his neck. Harris knew that the shark toothed piece belonged to Jelani. He asked the boy where he got it. The boy, unafraid, answered that he had found it in a bush at the river when the wagon stopped just before home.

Harris knew that Jelani was now tracking his family. The drivers had not seen him since he brought home the spoils from the last hunt. Tanner told Harris he thought Jelani believed him when he told him his family had died from the fever. Harris put Tanner in the jail on the plantation—— for two reasons.

Harris borrowed a Cherokee trapper from his friend Elias Tucker who lived in Macon, Georgia. He charged him with finding Jelani's entire family. He wanted them killed and their bodies brought back to the plantation. He told the trapper he would pay him handsomely. Harris knew that that tactic could possibly lure Jelani back. A savage tracking a savage, he mused. Once done, he could avenge Shaw's death.

Chapter 6

Father and sons continued their quest to find their family members. They had deciphered many markings left behind by Atsadi that proved that he, his mother, and sister had headed eastward. Atsadi continued to use fragments of marble that he had stuck into the bark of trees as their pointy clues. The three came to the foot of the mountains and decided to climb them to search inside the caves where even they had taken shelter on previous hunts.

As they ascended they sighted small, bloodied pieces of cloth that stuck to crevices that overlooked the forest grounds. They recognized the fragments as Inda's blanket that Zumbi wore after she had died. More scrap pieces loomed larger and larger as the higher elevation currents began to swirl them toward the cragged edges of the cliff.

The stench of death hung in the downwind and stung their nostrils. The three men did not speak one word but continued to climb the rocks toward the opening of a cave. Their soft and careful moccasin steps barely made sounds save for a twig or two that snapped pending heartbreaks. Their measured breaths countered the silence as one by one three worlds were being shattered.

Inside, they found Zumbi's decomposed body along with three other white men. Judging the size of the open wounds and scattered half-eaten body parts, they concluded that all had been attacked and eaten by bears. Waya and Unaduti built a fire outside the cave and burned Zumbi's body. Jelani ate some of her ashes. Waya placed a bloodied blanket remnant in his pants waistband. Unaduti beat his head against the cave wall. Now they had to find Ahyoka and Atsadi.

#

The trapper hired by Harris had closed in on the two young children. He had spied them one evening in front of a small fire. The brother was comforting his sister as he sang a Cherokee love song to her. Atsadi encouraged her to eat part of the fish he had caught earlier in the day; but she was despondent to the core. The trapper was impressed with this half-breed; Jelani had maintained his half- Cherokee traditions despite the fact that his black children had been born on a plantation. He waited until it was very dark and supposed that they were asleep, came upon them.

Atsadi did not drift off to sleep. He had spied the man out of the corner of his eye when he doused the fire. The rising crackling embers had reflected a shadow upon his knife when he knelt. Atsadi lay next to his sister. He whispered to her that when he threw a big rock to the ground she should quickly run toward the waterfall. Ahyoka's eyes grew large with fear. Atsadi hushed her with his fingers. The rock hit the ground with a thud and Ahyoka jumped up and dashed as fast as she could toward the falls. She screamed for her brother to follow her.

The trapper chased Atsadi for a while, but he was too swift and nimble to catch. He wanted to divert him away from his sister. The hunter turned in the direction that Ahyoka had fled. She had sought refuge in a small opening into a cave. When she made one small step to the ledge to peer into the night sky to find some sign of her brother the trapper hovered atop the cave opening. He pounced upon the ground in front of her and grabbed her. Ahyoka hollered as loud as she could. She bit the trapper's arm and loosened his grip with the sharp pain. She ran down the cliff sideways and straight.

The cuts from the rocks broke the skin on her legs and feet. Bristled bushes slowed her speed down; its spiked thorns slit her arms and trapped her long black hair. She pulled a sharp knife from the sheath and sawed her entangled hair free. She continued to holler helplessly for her brother to rescue her. Atsadi chased the sound of her voice. He came closer and closer and then heard nothing more. He cupped his hands to his mouth and shouted her name again, and again. She did not answer.

Ahyoka had hidden on rocks behind the falls. The deafening roar of the water cascaded over her as it stung her open wounds. She pressed her back against the slippery back walls and tried desperately to dig her feet into the slimy green crevices of the scum-covered rocks. The fury of the water fell just inches from her body. It was a pitch black liquid in the dark night. It found its home in the tides of the river and heaved huge back splashes onto the slick sleek stones where Ahyoka stood precariously in shaking silence.

Atsadi jumped into the river and dove deeply into it to find his sister. He hoped that he would not be successful. While he was under the water, one bare foot of the trapper paddled the water just ahead of him. The other weighted Ahyoka's head down to the depths. She had slipped into the falls. Atsadi pulled his knife from his pants and placed it between clenched teeth. He swiftly swam to the top. His head emerged within inches of the trapper.

They began to fight. Atsadi cut a deep slice into the trapper's stomach but the trapper did not lunge for him. He stayed in his spot as he lured Atsadi to him. He was drowning his sister upon an underwater rock. The painful, piercing bubbles that merged with his blood accented her urgent final struggle for air.

#

Jelani and his two sons came upon a marker on the ground and were confounded. Atsadi had made the initials "H-J" with smooth white pebbles in the red clay. Above it was a pointy-ended piece of marble embedded in the dirt that signaled a southwestward direction.

Waya concluded that his two younger siblings were on their way back to the Harris-Jones plantation. They had lost their mother and the party that was taking them eastward had died along with her. They had no protection. Exasperated and exhausted by this ordeal, Jelani wept openly. They began the trip that would return them to the homestead.

#

The trapper had to transport the bodies back to Harris to ensure payment for his work. His stomach wound had infested and he was weak from loss of blood. He had taken the bodies from the river and placed them in one of several canoes that he had hidden in the bulrushes. He rowed close to the riverbank towards the plantation boundary as a rope towed the dead weight bodies in the second canoe.

Days later on land, he constructed a gurney out of long birch branches. He used the children's blanket from their campfire and secured it to the poles with dried willow stalks. He fashioned triangular pieces of wood to the top and stabilized it with hemp. He wrapped his arms around the top and dragged the bodies behind him over the clay roads toward the plantation. Soon his right side was not able to sustain the pain of movement from the open, gangrenous wound in his stomach. His left arm swelled up as it bore the weight of the makeshift hearse.

One hard-rain morning, Waya, Jelani and Unaduti had sought shelter in the high thick Cypress trees in the near thickets of the Harris-Jones plantation. The night before they discussed with heavy hearts how they would enter the fields to find Ahyoke and Atsadi.

Through the wailing wind-blown water they heard a rhythmic grunting sound from below. They quietly moved their bodies to the opposite sides of the trees. The rain lashed their faces. The wet clothing, saturated by the deluge, caused them to tremble in the cold. Their hands and feet were numbed and wrinkled. The group spied a lone Indian who pulled a load with great stress. He stopped several times to regain a foothold in the muddy puddles. As he trudged under an opening in the tree, the three of them recoiled when they beheld the bodies of their loved ones.

Atsadi's and Ahyoka's matted black hair almost covered their entire faces. Their swollen grayish bodies with bloated stomachs lay side by side. Rain fell in shivering angled sheets.

With each stuttering step the man took, the hands of the dead siblings touched each other and then released when he stopped to catch his breath. The trapper's moccasins splashed red mud onto their half-naked bodies. The three watched in sickened horror as the man took at least ten steps that were even more laborious. He lost his grip on the gurney and fell heavily upon his face into the mud, dead.

\#

A grief-stricken Kaffie was sick to her soul. She stood in the barn with many other slaves who had come to see the bodies recovered by the drivers who were returning to the homestead. As she made her way toward them, the crowd parted to let her through. She knelt and took Ahyoka's river-filled hand, held it to her own cheek and began to count her freckles to her. Her tear-filled grey eyes bid good-bye to Atsadi, the brave.

Later, in the attic, Kaffie would sleep with the cornhusk doll that Ahyoka had made for her, until the day she died. She retrieved Jelani's shirt from the box under her bed.

Tomorrow, she would wash it and store it for her quilt.

ABRAHAM

Chapter 1

Abraham was a captured slave from Mali, an interior country of Africa. African slave traders led the kidnapped on a seven-month trek to Ghana. They were held for several months until canoes took them to the big ships that waited out in the Ocean of No Return.

In his youth, he was enslaved on the island of Barbados; as a man, Mr. Harris purchased him at an auction in Savannah, Georgia. The previous slaveholder had written on his papers that he had "innate abilities to create; he was of good demeanor, in good health and an excellent broom maker". What the slave bill did not advertise was that Abraham could read and write. Slaveholders could not buy educated Negroes. He fetched a high price due to his youth and physicality.

During the ship's voyage to a port in Savannah, Abraham harbored, with trepidation, the prospects of a more brutal treatment of the slaves in the southern states. He had read that slaves were their number one import——vital to their economic growth and survival. The enforcement of many laws and codes that suppressed uprisings, escapes, and acts of insolence were strict and unyielding——far more than what he had experienced in Barbados.

One morning, during the dreaded voyage, the ship dropped anchor in the vast blue-gray ocean. As was the routine, Abraham, along with the other males, was moved topside every four days. The captain had to follow the mandates of cargo preservation that stipulated that no more than two percent of the ship's manifest could be lost at sea for whatever reason.

To that end, the crew threw buckets of brackish seawater onto the stinking bodies. The drenching added to the dizzying movements of the ship. Standing upright from lying on their sides without interruption augmented their

The Cricket Cries, the Year Changes

seasickness and caused most of them to vomit. The crew hurled slabs of rancid meat and rotted fruit at the slaves. That action created a frenzied food fight as the strongest of them yanked the linked chains in their favor. The crew used whips and sticks to settle the melee.

The heat of the sun on the deck of the ship sharply contrasted with the dank darkness of the hull below and caused the eyes of the slaves to squint in pain. That day, they caught sight of another trade ship that passed them as it headed west as well. As their eyes adjusted to the glaring sunlight, slaves on both passing ships exchanged surreal retrograde glances with their shackled counterparts. The anchored ship appeared to move backwards. The eyes messaged the common inconsolable grief and woeful defiance one to the other; then heads hung down in mutual dismay and defeat. Abraham catalogued the vision of that incident and was able to recall on demand the mirror image of the diaspora that defined those times.

Abraham made whiskbrooms out of straw on this plantation. It was yet another one of Master Harris' enterprises. Harris was a huge supplier of these items to overseas markets as well as local plantations. He managed to secure a huge purchase order for the straw products from Great Britain that was to be dropped-shipped in increments. The schedule of this order kept Abraham and his apprentices very busy especially at harvest when so much straw was available.

Many trees were felled during the "lay-by," to produce the wooden handles for both the straw sweepers and whisk brooms. Abraham would grind, sand, shape, and varnish the various handles that would hold the bristles. He oversaw the gleaning of the hairs from the pigskins that made the sharpest bristles for shaving brushes.

He created his own daily diversions that included sweeping clean the mansion's expansive plank board veranda. He would rid the passenger wagons of dirt and mud. He cleared the long white stone pathway that led to the mansion entrance as he removed its dirt and debris. He was always testing the durability of his brooms. He was not restricted from any parts of the plantation as most slaves were. The clay dirt formed clouds of red haze as Abraham rhythmically swept it aside on hot dry days.

The heavy rains would create cinnamon rivulets while the heavier and wider brooms worked hard to keep the mud at bay. Abraham loved to sweep while barefoot. The mundane exercise took his mind to other places. He wished that the red clay of Georgia could magically restore his presence onto the disembodied red clay villages of Mali or Ghana.

When he finished fighting the blowback of the dirt by the breeze, he would walk among the slaves in the fields or saunter through the cooking grounds with his brooms on his shoulder. He offered stories to the slaves, some old, some new. He cheered them up until he found himself back at the barn.

He always whistled.

Abraham soothed and comforted many slave children who were sick or just plain tired, sexually abused or beaten. He temporarily distracted them from the barbarity and hopelessness of a slave's life. He offered his wonderful stories as an illustration of healing and encouragement. His entourage included many adult slaves who sought him out on their free day, Sunday, for some type of comedic relief or general counsel.

Kids too small, frail or sickly for hard labor, followed behind their parents in the fields as they held seed packets or small cultivating tools. They looked forward to hearing Abraham's booming voice over those of the overseers. His whistles served as a bellwether of his pending arrival to certain sections of the fields.

During the spring planting, he captivated them with tales of fantasy and folklore that he intertwined with coded messages for the adult slave population. The cryptic words indicated what mood the overseers and drivers were in, the names of slaves who could not be trusted and any other information to keep them safe and on guard.

Other times, his stories contained jokes about the white men and their women. The barbs were dispatched from field to field. Often, the overseers witnessed a groundswell of laughter among the slaves that seemed to ebb and flow as Abraham's humor made its rounds. He showed the little ones how to make short brooms out of the castoff wood and the unevenly cut golden straw. He encouraged them to whistle while they kept their cabins clean.

The Cricket Cries, the Year Changes

He recited many fables about Anansi, the spider, the great trickster of the Ashanti people from Ghana. Abraham taught the children to memorize a famous African proverb: "When spider webs unite, they can tie up a lion."

Chapter 2

Abraham always wore corduroy pants. He knew they absorbed moisture away from his skin. He learned that fact while enslaved in the tropics of Barbados. He paired them with dull white ill-fitting shirts to deflect the sun as he pulled strands of straw together with wire.

Kaffie and Abraham would talk privately about current events in secret and developed a very close relationship. Abraham had been on this plantation now for twenty years and had learned of her arrival to the Big House from the fields as a young girl. He was glad that she lived in the mansion; she was much too genteel, and kind, and soft to endure a slave girl's life. God had blessed him with her friendship.

He debated many long hours with Grafton, the apprenticed butler during late nights in the barn. Grafton hid among the supplies and shouted whispered rebuttals to Abraham's thoughts and opinions. Sometimes he paced back and forth behind the cover of haystacks. Grafton thrashed his arms in the air to make his point. He thought this old man was out of touch with contemporary thought.

Grafton shared with Abraham a lot of abolitionist literature that the slave Betsey had given to him. Abraham feigned that he had heard conversations about different people named Henry Clay, Frederick Douglass, and John C. Calhoun when he was driven to other plantations to make deliveries. Most of the plantation whites took his ramblings as that of an aging Negro who was full of himself or a great mimic.

He warned the whites one day, with Master Harris among them, that the wind was changing direction on the slave "question." That was the first time that Abraham was struck hard in the face by Master Harris. Though Harris immediately regretted doing so, he blamed the message, not Abraham himself for his reaction. He did not apologize.

\#

Abraham tended many of the sick when malaria, cholera, and other diseases raced through the plantation. Many slaves refused the medicinal ministering of the white doctors and were willing to die first rather than receive treatment from foreign and untrusted methods. They relied heavily on the witch doctor, Ngango when traditional medicines recommended by the white doctors were rendered ineffective. Tonics in vials and gauze bags filled with roots and herbs were worn around the neck of the sick and the healthy as preventative care.

Ngango supplied the treatments to them. Ointments rubbed on chests and backs were used frequently to cure the sickened slaves without interference from Mr. Harris. Sometimes the elixirs that were ingested caused immediate vomiting and thereby shortened the recovery periods.

Abraham often thought about the Abraham he had read about in the bible. He sensed a kinship with him. His own wife, Nema had become pregnant when she was fifty-five years old and he was sixty-one. He compared her to the Sarah of the bible, though Nema died in labor. He had had the letter "N" for "Nema" branded over his heart by Scipio as a tribute to his wife soon after the baby was born. He vowed that nothing could hurt him as long as he could remember the strength and endurance she showed as she bestowed their only son, Isaac.

Isaac, now seventeen, tended to his father's needs. He fashioned crutches and canes out of the pinewood that his father had used to form broomsticks. Abraham had fallen and injured his knee. It was shattered through and through. It would not mend. Gangrene had set in. Abraham suffered endlessly with the daily pain until his pride was overrun with common sense. The left limb was amputated in the slaughterhouse just above the knee. Isaac made his father a hollow wooden replacement leg that attached with leather straps to his lower thigh.

Now aged, idled, and infirmed, Abraham was no longer in charge of making brooms but still oversaw the processes. He began to speak secretly about freedom to the slaves. He provided them with maps stolen from the master's office that showed routes for the steamboats and river barges to the North. He spoke to them about the islands off the South Carolina coast where free blacks lived. He circled Tybee Island on the map. It was just off the coast of Savannah, Georgia. He had passed Tybee while on that long ago ship that docked near it, he told them. He said he had heard that slaves were treated a lot better there.

Abraham drew lines in the hard clay representing the southern route to Mexico where slavery was outlawed. He provided information about the state of Florida and how the natives had married blacks and formed a powerful militia group called the "Black Seminoles".

He became more belligerent and intimidating in his old age. He spoke openly about rebellion and insurrection and the need for it to present itself as the only alternative to freedom. Abraham began to challenge the younger white planters. Once he warned them that cutting down trees during a full moon would weaken the wood over time. They gave him three lashes for giving them unsolicited advice.

Saddled with idle time, he created small native symbols out of kindling and glued them atop walking sticks for the bent and decrepit field hands. From his timbered chair without arms or back rails, Abraham leisurely carved spoons from discarded and smoothed dried gourds and gave them to the black cooks.

He hid cowrie shells in his peg leg. He would give one each to a slave and explained its significance. The item when sewn into the undersides of their clothing served as an identifier to abolitionists and other runaways that the wearer was not a bounty hunter. Whites paid many Negroes to infiltrate these groups. When spies were discovered among the ranks, the future placement of the shell in the clothing would be switched by the slaves. The would-be informants were often killed or seriously maimed for their treachery.

The Cricket Cries, the Year Changes

Chapter 3

On an early Friday evening after it had rained steadily all day long, Charlie, an overseer conducted his usual rounds of slave cabins and the grounds. Most slaves had doused the indoor embers. They lay sleeping on the worn blue ticking mattresses that were stuffed with whatever they could find. The exhausted bodies, sore and stiff, welcomed the early retirement with competing snores sent into the hot humid air.

He neared the straw barn and heard voices. He inched his body slowly to the window and peered through it. He heard something drop loudly onto the barn floor but it did not disrupt the conversation. Abraham was talking hurriedly to Grafton. He spoke loudly and excitedly about a planned escape of over twenty-five slaves from the plantation this very night. They were going to take cover in the northwest thicket by seven o'clock.

Charlie only heard one person speak for he knew Grafton was a mute. As Grafton turned expressionless towards the door to leave, the overseer stealthily removed himself from the barn area to inform Master Harris of the pending plan.

Harris allowed the plot to develop. He knew that many plantation slaves attempted to escape on Fridays. Their owners would not be able to post bills that offered rewards for their capture until Monday when the presses would be available to ink the information and distribute it. By six-thirty, Harris had positioned thirty-one men within the thicket at the fringe of the plantation. The group consisted of overseers, drivers, and planters. With fully loaded rifles and extra ammunition, they crouched in the prickly brush. They awaited the assembly of the would-be runaway slaves.

Master Harris sent Danny, the black groomsman to summon Stiles to come to the mansion immediately. He was somewhere on the vast plantation.

Abraham had intended for Charlie to hear about the plan. He was alerted to Charlie's nightly spying routine by one of his apprentices who slept in the loft of the barn. The apprentice Jawan was to give Abraham a signal that Charlie

101

was in the vicinity by throwing one of the shaving brushes hard to the hay floor.

Abraham found Stiles and told him matter-of-factly about the pending escape. Abraham expressed his concern to him; he said many slaves would be leaving their children behind and those little babies' lives were bad enough already without having to add more orphans to Master Harris' rolls. Abraham looked him dead in the eyes and with certainty added that he knew Stiles understood what he meant about leaving kids without a daddy.

Stiles took it upon himself to hastily rustle up at least twenty white men and arm them with rifles, hatchets, and knives. He would order them to enter the thicket that bordered the marshlands by seven o'clock based on the information given to him by Abraham. He was able to gather only twenty indentured farm hands some never having fired a rifle in their lives.

Exasperated that he could not find the men he needed, he was angered that they were not at their assigned posts. He would have to deal with them later; there was hardly enough time for him to ride to the mansion to give Harris the news and apologize to him for the hastily assembled rag-tailed militia. The rain had stopped.

On that cloud-filled night, about forty-one of the two groups of white men ended up killing one another. They could not know the race of the men in the thicket or discern their dialect. The confrontation was too quick and deliberate. The men could only defend themselves from the rustlings of shadows and sudden movements. It was total darkness. The carnage was illumined by the red shots from the rifles. Brief plumes of gray-blue smoke from the discharging gunpowder heightened the battle.

The screams and shouts continued from the brush as the whites insisted that their names be recognized. The din of the attack snuffed their urgent pleas. No one stopped to listen; the melee had morphed into a showdown. When the yelling was reduced with each fallen man and almost all of the ammunition spent, they beheld with lit torches the grim and gory scene.

The Cricket Cries, the Year Changes

Charlie, mortally wounded, shouted to the others: "It's that nigger Abraham done this! Kill the son of a bitch!"

The remaining men, some of whom suffered crippling injuries and gunshot wounds soon realized the ruse. With an adrenalin rush the abled, angry crowd ran toward the slave cabins at the back of the plantation. They murdered ten children and Isaac as their accusatory retribution.

Abraham had seen the intermittent flashes of gunfire when the massacre unfolded in the thicket from afar. He hid himself between the hanging wet cotton sheets of Cecelia's dye work. They sheltered him. The dark night erased his shadow. He was proud of what he had done.

However, when he saw the gang of wounded and limping whites with rifles, ropes and torches that hastened toward the slave quarters, a panicked Abraham tried to whistle one of the coded songs to alert the slaves of pending danger. His lungs would not grant him the strength. The exhausted blacks asleep in the cabins could not be aroused. The mortal wounds visited upon them by the angered whites and the horrifying screams from the terrified blacks owned the night.

Abraham sank to the ground in anguish, ripping his wooden leg from the straps that held it. The clotheslines, now shaken from its foundations, engulfed him in reds, yellows, and blues.

#

On Saturday morning, the remaining militia, planters, Stiles and Master Harris convened in the mansion to fully reconstruct and recount the consequences of the plan solely drawn up by Abraham. The slaveholder was enraged that the men who worked for him would kill his property of innocent, future workers. They had not posed any threat to them as they lay in their cabins. Eventually, he indentured these men to work off the debt amounting to what he had paid for the collective body of dead slaves.

The whites were totally outmaneuvered and duped by whom they referred to as this old, peg-legged nigger. Abraham's exacting exhibition and execution of treachery and trickery baffled and inflamed them even more. They would not hold Grafton responsible. Witnesses said he was tending to his sick mother at the time of the massacre and besides, he was a deaf mute.

The men had removed the torn bodies from the thicket; most of them were pieced back together and lay covered with Cecelia's sheets on the dewy grass. Their women ran to the scene, their billowing skirts soaked up the morning mist. They prayed for their loved ones not to be among the dead. The wounded men were treated in different quarters; their conditions and identities were not yet confirmed.

Master Harris asked the men where was Abraham. They did not have a chance to answer him. Abraham suddenly appeared in the midst of their startling revelations. He stood erect in the beveled oak foyer of the mansion without the assistance of a cane. His wooden leg was missing. He balanced his thin, wiry body without quivering. His cane lay on the porch.

He stretched his arms upward in glorious surrender with a smile that stretched all the way back to the straw barn and hoarsely whispered, "Anansi." Master Harris walked toward him and with clenched fists, cleared his throat heavily to extract as much phlegm as he could, and violently spat in Abraham's face.

Chapter 4

The men seized Abraham and took him to the back of the plantation. They tied him up, chained his one foot to the ground, and whipped him until sunset. They were baffled that this old coon, in the face of his waning strength did not cry out once during his torture. Tears of pain cascaded from his eyes but Abraham never screamed. Each time he was scourged, he would gaze downward towards the letter "N" emblazoned over his heart. His skin was splintered, bloody, and welted by the whips. His shirt was shredded and trapped in the blood. The brand was almost invisible; but the knowledge that the loving monogram existed gave him comfort and relief.

He believed that like the Abraham in the bible, God had endowed him with the mantle of being a father to many generations, though with Isaac's death, he had no progeny to continue his true bloodline. Abraham had adopted all the enslaved from the past; hoped his courageous act would fortify their resolve and edify their future generations. He semi-consciously aligned his freedom wishes with theirs. He knew in his heart that their journey of bondage would be a long and tortuous one.

"*But those that wait upon the Lord shall renew their strength; they shall mount up with wings as eagles; they shall run, and not be weary; they shall walk and not faint,*" he recalled verbatim from the Old Testament book of Isaiah.

The drivers overheard the beleaguered slaves speak of Abraham's longsuffering. They learned through them of the true meaning of the insignia on his chest and informed Master Harris. He ordered that Abraham's heart be cut out along with what was left of the letter "N." He mandated that the entire slave plantation attend the event. Harris wanted the torture to emphasize that the exact fate awaited those who chose to walk the same rebellious path as Abraham had.

\#

Cynthia Harris-Allen

It was Sunday; some slaves were dressed in their perceived best already. They had bible stories told to them by Luge, a black priest. Others joined the rituals of the witch doctor and asked for exorcisms, prayer, and incantations. They had not expected to witness an execution.

Ngango danced in his nakedness with a red clay plaster all over his body, and chicken feathers pasted upon his head. He was celebrating the pending death of a new ancestor. Some cried in groups while they recalled personal experiences of Abraham's benevolent deeds.

Kaffie and Grafton stood in silence on the back plantation porch of the mansion away from the crowd. They saw Abraham chained to a giant rock set before a fire. He kneeled one leg on the ground with his arms tied behind him. The new barn served as his backdrop. The two tried to steady one another. A tsunami of tears offset Grafton's usual stoic demeanor. He privately resolved that he could not just throw verbal rocks at this institution of slavery any longer. It could not be killed; it was not human. Kaffie was numbed by the calamity. At one point, she could not sense her own breathing.

As Abraham lay dying, his fading eyesight caught the crying and terrified faces of many of the children and adults who had gathered. His stories over the years had often lifted them to a short-lived ethereal normalcy. He was now ready to enter it for good, certain that it held no pain nor prospects, no tumults nor truths——only beauty and peace. His ears received the grand requiem of the funereal slave song as it swelled with the burgeoning crowd. It was more magnificent than Abraham ever thought it would be. He knew that this tribute ensured safe passage over the horizon; He grinned.

He really wished that he could whistle.

With deliberate steps the chief overseer Stiles, his eyes ablaze with contempt approached Abraham. He wielded a freshly sharpened long-bladed slaughterhouse knife. It reflected the peach glow of the fire and the looming orange sunset. As he grew nearer, Abraham's last inhale was a long one. His screams finally came from eternity; his exhale was but a whimper.

His heart was cut from his chest and thrown into the flames. The startled coals darted wayward flecks of orange-red into the sky. As if on cue the dirge stopped abruptly. There was complete silence but for the sound of the whippoorwills and the crackling fire that had received the excised heart. The barn that had been built with Abraham's warnings about the chopped trees that were felled during that full moon creaked and bowed to the ground.

On Monday morning, Abraham's body was prepared for burial by his people. Ngango had cremated Abraham's son, Isaac, and spread his ashes into his casket. Blacks carried the thin wooden case overhead. The huge multitude of slaves thinned the grass as their bare feet trod towards the slave cemetery. The Ole Field, as it is called, was located on a remote part of the plantation.

The mourners threw foodstuffs that consisted of bean cakes and bits of corn inside Abraham's open coffin to ensure he would have enough to eat on his journey. They jumped and twirled in colorful outfits that created a color-filled prism of a celebration that changed with each body movement. At the cemetery the ten muslin-shrouded bodies of the murdered black children were readied to share a common grave with Abraham at the request of their families. They outlined the perimeter of the huge red hole that had been shoveled out to receive them.

Master Harris granted the slave community the day off; he did it out of respect for the dead children. At the gravesite, six large men held Abraham's coffin high in the air and with precision rotated it so his head could face in all four directions to ensure that he would find his afterlife home.

The crestfallen crowd that was Abraham's generations, dispersed slowly. Some children started to whistle and soon others joined in. The slaves returned to their quarters and as was their custom, sprinkled water to the left and right of the cabin entrances so their sorrows could be washed from their souls before they entered.

Scipio soon forged a black wrought iron marker for Abraham's grave.

It was a large letter "N" and beneath it, a small "X," that symbolized the Roman numeral for ten.

Kaffie cut a swatch from Abraham's corduroy pants that Grafton had brought to her from the barn.

Cynthia Harris-Allen

She rubbed her fingers over the wales of the cloth as she hoped to sense his presence when she placed it in her quilt.

The Cricket Cries, the Year Changes

Chapter 1

Lewis was a maker of stringed instruments. He was a drum maker at heart. He strung banjos as well. He was an expert at creating these items from memory to finished product. When Lewis was purchased, certain aspects of his origin were kept secret to complete the sale that might not have happened had full disclosure been given about him.

He was first ported to the island of Jamaica. Lewis was a Cormanti, the name that the British gave to the Akan slaves taken from Ghana. Lewis had come from the Ashanti descendant of the Cormanti. This group of warriors was very militaristic and lived primarily in the Caribbean islands. The Akans were the largest African cultural influence in Jamaica. They carried out numerous slave rebellions on that island. Despite their reputation as strong workers, they had a very violent nature; so fierce, that the white plantation owners wanted legislative restrictions enacted that would ban the further importation of them to the States.

Lewis studied daily the art of self-defense and weaponry from his father and brothers until he was captured at fifteen years old. Chained in a ship and bound for the unknown, Lewis never saw his family again. He was raised in Spanish Town, Jamaica as one of their own; He was adopted into the Akan clan. He became an apprentice to a drum maker named Cudjoe, who appealed to Lewis's creative side. Cudjoe told Lewis many stories about the patched lives of their ancestors. He vacillated between stories of triumph, trickery, death, and defeat. Lewis never forgot how mesmerized and enraptured he was by this griot. Many of Cudjoe's proverbs and precepts never left his memory.

Lewis was a massive dark brown man. His molded physique was intimidating. Despite his well over six-and-a-half feet height, he chose to make instruments. Thick fingers on big hands misrepresented the intricate work of a true artisan.

Cynthia Harris-Allen

Master Harris and the overseers stepped lightly when they dealt with Lewis, without really knowing why. He presented himself as a quiet but purposeful artisan.

When most of the drivers and overseers spoke to Lewis, they realized that he completely erased their shadows when they stood face to face; most of them had to look up to him. It was something about their perception of Lewis's demeanor behind that wide crooked grin that unsettled them.

Lewis engaged in conversations with everyone. He was kind and considerate. He was also a very responsible worker. He guarded his feelings. He was not much of a joiner. The slaves loved him not just because of his generosity towards them, but because they knew he cared for them, too. He helped them out whenever he could. Hoisting the children to higher branches of the Rome apple trees to get the best fruit for themselves was a usual Sunday morning feat. His large frame and height intimidated them when he perceived that they intended to do harm to a slave. He silently stood close to the drivers until most withdrew their whips, sheathed their knives or holstered their guns.

Lewis favored animals more than people. He would talk to the goats and whisper to the horses. Much of his limited free time was spent in the cow or pig barn where he paid a great deal of attention to their habits and mannerisms.

The Harris-Jones plantation had many enterprises that made Master Harris very wealthy. He knew how to establish a continuum of work output in goods that rivaled any other planation in Georgia, and beyond. He made sure that the unique, innate talents that some of his Negroes possessed were taught to younger slaves, men and women, boys and girls. To that end, Harris initiated apprenticeship platforms for them to learn from the journeymen. He knew that this practice was vital to the sustaining revenues he enjoyed.

Harris took greater care of these blacks than what he termed his "ordinary field niggers". He dispatched doctors to heal them and arranged marriages if the slave requested that he allow them to "jump the broom." He acceded to their request for more help or materials without question. The skilled laborers enjoyed a lot of autonomy and free space to produce.

The Cricket Cries, the Year Changes

The drivers and overseers resented this specialized group; they could not whip or cause any physical harm to them upon strict orders from Harris. One slave driver named Tom, chafed at the idea of having to walk on eggs around these "chosen niggers".

Lewis made beautiful drums that emitted soulful haunting sounds. He knew which woods cut from certain trees created the varied pitches when covered on top with stretched goat or sheepskin hides. Some drums like the Gumbi, could be as long as six feet. The sub-tropical climate allowed palm trees to flourish in Georgia. Lewis used empty coconut shells with dried beans and seeds placed inside of it to fashion an instrument called a calabash. He had made many of them in Jamaica.

He produced a Sanku harp lute, native to his country, that featured catgut strung from a board to a long stick. It could have as many as fourteen strings which could be plucked or strummed. It was one of Harris' bestsellers second only to the banjo that fetched the best price.

Lewis supplied the plantation elites with instruments played by orchestras or in small venues. Intermittent orders were for singular use by farmhands, cattle drivers or as presents for children. He also made instruments of African origin that were important to the slaves for use in their religious ceremonies or celebrations.

The slaves were often summoned to entertain their masters on certain holidays and cookouts. Many brought instruments that Lewis had made. Even the messaged drum codes that served as the unifying communicator to the slaves were dispatched upon Lewis' work.

Chapter 2

Lewis made "house calls" accompanied by a driver to tune pianos, violins and other stringed instruments. Sometimes drum repair or replacement was on the work order as well. On one of those trips to a very small plantation whose only crop was corn, Lewis saw Wani in the rain.

Wani's drying laundry was caught off guard in the rain. What had started as a mild drizzle, turned into a steady, heavy downpour. Panicked and exasperated, she began to run between the five clotheslines of freshly laundered clothing. She hurriedly yanked many of the large sheets from the confines of the pins and gathered them in her arms.

Lewis became her hero.

When the wagon entered the plantation by the thickets, he spied her as she frantically tried to salvage the entire day's laundry. All he could see was a blue skirt with a white full apron as it zigzagged between the ropes. He jumped from the passenger seat and asked the driver to wait for him. The wagonneer replied he would give him no more than ten minutes. He reined in the two horses, pulled his umbrella out from under the floorboard, and waited for Lewis to return.

Lewis ran about thirty yards through the cloudburst towards Wani. He lifted her up into his arms and ran to the barn entrance. He deposited her muddy and water-soaked body on the corn-shucked floor. He returned to her work area and quickly removed the remaining saturated sheets from the lines. He balled them up into a giant cotton wad. Smaller hanging items like pants and shirts were handled easily by him.

He took all of them to the shelter of the nearby barn freed from the torrents of rain, wind, and the liquefying red dust. His clothes were soaked through to his skin and molded to his body. He had lost his hat in the storm. Wani retrieved it later and slept next to it.

Wani meekly peered out from the entrance to the barn and stared with astonishment at her deliverer.

Lewis had ran back towards the wagon. He turned his face to her with his crooked grin, and shouted over the wind that he would see her again.

Wani formed the words "Thank you," with her lips and clasped her hands to her chest.

The Cricket Cries, the Year Changes

She held the disfigured hand to the inside of her apron pocket.

At the age of ten, Wani was sold away from her family that lived on a plantation in Florida. She was now twenty-three. She had no tangible memory of her mother or siblings; the separation was so traumatic. She was the laundress on this small plantation. The backbreaking task kept her busy all day and well into the evening. Well water was constantly emptied into the five boiling cauldrons that set on rock-filled pallets.

Wani dissolved the lye and candle soap before she immersed the soiled clothing. Sometimes she had help from the children who were not needed in the cornfields at certain periods of the day. They helped her wring the water from the big sheets and heavy pants of the plantation household. The kids held onto the long pieces of wash while she twisted them. Many times the suds-filled fabrics demanded to be rinsed or soaked again. Wani encouraged them to sing along with her to lighten the monotonous burden.

Most of the time, she carried the water from the well by herself. It was at least thirty feet away. Paprika-red clay trails of worn out grass evidenced the path that Wani took to the well and back. The depth of the furrows called attention to the weight of the dragged buckets ported two by two.

Wani beseeched the overseer to relocate her washing duties nearer to the well. She was whipped and admonished for doing so. The overseer knew that the well was very close to the mass thicket that was on this property. It boasted hundreds of Acacia trees; some were more than fifty feet high. Many plantations in Georgia had fringed perimeters of trees and low-growing wild plants. Some served as property markers; most served as hiding places.

This driver was not willing to move her closer to an escape route. An overseer was killed there two years ago, when he entered the thicket to investigate an unusual sound. His murder remained unsolved. The master of this small plantation of twenty-nine slaves had none to spare to incarcerate or punish.

Many children would play hide and seek in the brush. Both slave and free used that thicket to have sex. Some entered on their own accord; others had to be dragged there. As a habit, slaves would hide in the upper branches to take a nap or catch their breath under the shade. Most of them hid in the dense forestation from the incessant heat and the ceaseless whip. Even on a sunny day, one could not see far into the thicket.

Wani had burns on the right side of her face that traversed downward to the side of her neck and shoulder, then just above her fingers. She had tripped one morning, when she tried to rearrange two boiling buckets of water that were filled to the brim. She had hoped to shorten her workload by placing them closer together.

She was ashamed of the disfigurement. She kept to herself. Her markings were not mocked by any of the other slaves. Her "good side," as she called it, revealed the face of a pretty girl. Her thin body was loose-limbed. She walked with the grace of a gazelle——albeit with a backward-leaning gait. She could hold a basket of freshly dried clothes on her head as if it were a crown.

On a daily basis, Wani walked purposely along the clothes-filled lines. She inspected each piece for cleanliness. She hummed to herself as she released the sun-kissed items from the clothespins and filled the wicker baskets.

The Cricket Cries, the Year Changes

Chapter 3

Lewis and Wani began a friendship.

Wani talked about her life and exchanged what little information she remembered about her family. The small talk was irrelevant. She just wanted to be with Lewis. She was more forthcoming than Lewis was for reasons of his own. He told her that he lived south of her, nothing more.

He substituted his life story with folktales that Cudjoe had told him repeatedly long ago. He admitted that he had not shared them with anyone. Lewis recited his favorite story about a changed spirit. Cudjoe had told him that all life had two sides. He said we could be humans that changed into animals or animals that had human characteristics. We could hate like the evil one who lived underground or love like the gods that were found everywhere above the earth. We could be creative or destructive, Lewis added. After all, we used the same hands to do both, he told Wani.

Cudjoe had told Lewis he was only a slave if he took on slave-like qualities of hopelessness and anger. He impressed to Lewis that no man's soul was ever born enslaved; therefore, a man could never die as one.

Wani listened with genuine trusting interest to his every word. Lewis' love for her was soon wrapped like a Christmas present. He made sure that he cracked the bridge on a violin or left an instrument obviously out of tune on several homesteads that ensured a steady return to her arms. Master Harris now allowed Lewis to travel alone. He trusted him to return.

At another visit, Lewis presented Wani with a baby goat with black and white markings true to its lineage. He told her he knew the kid's mother well and he suspected that this goat would behave properly in her care. Wani was elated. No one had ever given her anything. She named the animal "Thundastorm".

Wani's heart was suspended in disbelief that such a kind, strong man had told her how beautiful and desirable she was to him. Lewis' visits included carrying the water to her laundry tubs. The two of them would sit and stare at one another. The noise from the boiling, bubbling pots eavesdropped on the golden silence. They were locked in the grip of gazing eyes. Many words were spoken without a sound. Separately, they hoped their feelings towards one another ran far enough beneath the surface to understand its depth.

In far less serious times, Lewis carried the huge, black cauldrons filled with water from the well and set them on the rocks to boil. Wani would follow his steps back and forth while she touched his strong back with both urgency and tenderness. While the lye penetrated the clothes he kissed her calloused hands and brushed his lips against what she termed, "the bad side" of her face.

His muscular arms wrung the soapy water from the laundry and heaped them high in a pile in the cold-water cauldrons. He jumped barefoot inside the tubs and stomped the clothes downward to free the suds while he sang a silly song while beating a pretend drum. His actions elicited her excited child-like laughter.

He then pulled out the pieces and wrung the water out. His strong hands rendered them almost dry. There was more sweat on his brow and his massive chest than water in the clothes. He then challenged Wani to run to the clotheslines to hang the sheets on the ropes suspended by poles.

The playful relay began. Wani's stained apron pockets held clothespins that were very familiar with her touch; they fit perfectly in her tiny fingers. They rattled against one another and joined in the revelry while she ran. She snatched them out to meet Lewis's playful command to hang the clothes high.

The sunny fly-filled afternoons teemed with laughter. Private thoughts danced around personal longings. They rested on the grass. He held her and rubbed her tired feet and her bending back. He fed Wani the lunch that he had packed for the trip. He surprised her with bean cake and dried yams. After they ate, Lewis plucked a low soft tune on a real small fiddle.

Wani fell asleep exhausted and snored loudly.

Finally with the last set of laundry done, Lewis knew it was soon time to head back to the plantation before nightfall. Lewis awakened Wani with a hard kiss on the mouth and a soft one on her cheek. Her hand sought his and intertwined her fingers. They disappeared inside of his.

The Cricket Cries, the Year Changes

Silently they walked to his wagon. The early fireflies lit their path. Thundastorm ambled behind the two of them. A fading rose red sunset had drawn just one line across the horizon. As what had become their custom, Lewis gently removed each of Wani's reluctant petitioning fingers that grasped his hand until they no longer held on to him. Somber grins sealed the benediction of their rendezvous. Lewis walked toward the wagon and dared not offer a backward glance to the heaven he had to abandon with each goodbye.

Wani returned to her solitary work. She put out the cauldron fires. She sat with a thud on the grassy clay-mixed soil and cried between the sheets with the scent of Lewis on her body. She felt the movement of his child.

Lewis sat in the wagon for a while then gave a sigh-filled click-of-the-teeth sound to the old mare. The noise of the shod feet drowned out the rhythmic pulse of an empty heart. He steered the wagon towards the one-hour ride home. Lewis would never petition his master to buy Wani because he knew that it could be used as an advantage by the overseers once she came to live with him. Harris would come to know his weakness. It was a known fact that Master Harris never believed that slaves had feelings of lasting love. He felt that their turns in the hay represented their random bouts of pagan lust.

Chapter 4

Lewis arrived at the plantation before the thick darkness of a moonless night enveloped the grounds. He walked to the cabin that he shared with a family found his corner, and lay down. He was grateful that Marie, the mother with the five children who slept there, had stuffed his coarse blanket with new shucks from the corn. The sweet smell of the grain still embedded in its leaves reminded him of Wani.

In the morning, Lewis went to his workstation in a barn that he once shared with Boway, the basket weaver. The place had been ransacked. Drums had been shattered; its mixed woods were strewn all over the floor. Animal skins that Lewis had pinned tautly on stretchers to dry were slit into pieces. Lewis noticed that the fallen scraps had jagged-edged cuts.

The stains that he used to color the drums and the palm oil polishes and resins had both been spilled upon the dirt floor. The drying catgut strings that hung from nails on a wooden board were cut to less than three useless inches each. Lewis's area was damaged severely. The new basket maker's twisted and braided sticks and works-in-progress were left unharmed. Master Harris was incensed at the display of destruction. He was bent on ferreting out the ransackers—— probably some young slave boys. Lewis did not believe that for a minute. Vandals did not discriminate with their mayhem. This was personal, he thought.

Lewis's schedule of production was set back by four months at least. The woods from the trees that he used had passed the optimum time to be cut down and hollowed out. Harris would not allow even a small slaughter of cows, goats, and sheep to supply the hides needed to cover the drums and fabricate the strings. Most of these animals would not be mature enough to be sold as edible meats.

Lewis had no materials to build new instruments. It was almost October and he had tuned and repaired most of the instruments in the surrounding areas. Most homesteads had already completed their entertainment venues. They had scheduled early retrofits for him. He no longer had a reason to leave the plantation to see Wani.

Master Harris decided to use Lewis on the various construction projects that were in progress on the plantation. Harris was completing the building of a jail to house the slaves and indentured servants instead of leaving them chained outside in the yards. He was also erecting a smaller mansion as lodging for guests or travelers. Many roads led to Atlanta from the northeastern part of the south, especially from South Carolina through Monroe. Lewis was upset about his new duties but took them on with the confidence that he would soon return to his craft. He was emboldened by Cudjoe's words of wisdom and patience. He often visited the goat that had given birth to Thundastorm with hopes of feeling an emotional connection to Wani.

#

As the late summer heatwave gripped the estate, the slaves moved sluggishly in preparation for the harvest. Many were beaten or whipped for resisting work in the unremitting heat. Some suffered sunstrokes while others begged for more water to hydrate themselves.

Mosquitos had begun to swarm in large numbers around stagnant lime green watering holes unfit to drink by man or beast. Small animals such as squirrels and moles sought cooler shelter in between rocks and shade trees. The leaves had begun to change colors. The heat curled them up and dried them within several hours once they fell to the russet clay. Only the pines held onto their needles.

Thousands of cicadas filled the thick, humid night air with their loud continuous screeching sounds. They informed the world that they had left their underground homes for the vertical shelter in the trees to shed their skins and further annoy the masses.

The excessive heat and the circumstances of Lewis's new job began to vex him. He was angered by the whipping and beating of slaves by the drivers and overseers; they too, were irritated and agitated by the elements. Tempers grew shorter between both groups.

Master Harris decided that the slaves needed to arise just before dawn to take advantage of cooler mornings. He told the drivers that if they set a two-hour lead with the maximum amount of workers at their stations it would increase production. He said nothing about reducing the back-end time because of the earlier start. The slaves continued to work well into the night.

Soon everyone was cross, tired, on edge and feisty. Intermittent skirmishes between slaves started up among the harvesting rows. Whites got into arguments with one another when it was time to be relieved at their posts. Tension was high; some of them fought.

At an early sunrise, Lewis sat on an empty barrel that was turned upside down. He took the scrap of rag from his head and wiped the sweat that had pooled on his chest. Dawn be damned, he thought to himself. It was just as sweltering and sultry as the rest of the day would promise.

A knife cut into his huge bicep accompanied by a boisterous command from Tom, one of the drivers. He ordered Lewis to get off his lazy black ass and haul the lumber to the building site.

Lewis, taken aback by the boldness of this man to slice through his shirt with a knife when there was no provocation, stood up and grabbed Tom by the neck with one hand. It appeared to encompass it in its entirety.

The slightly built driver's legs dangled and twisted in the air. He painfully struggled to disentangle himself from Lewis's grip. Lewis raised Tom's head above his own and slammed it downward into the barrel. The force of the impact splintered the container. Tom lay on the ground knocked out. His body lay centered in the middle of the sixteen slats of the barrel that encircled him in a perfect pattern.

Lewis examined the superficial cut on his bicep. He removed his shirt. Upon examination, the shirt had sustained more damage than Lewis's arm. Lewis kicked Tom lightly to see if he was still unconscious. He was. Then he walked over to the knife on the ground and picked it up. It had an eight inch curved blade that was serrated. Lewis turned himself toward the rising sunlight and further examined the knife.

He walked over to where his shirt lay on the ground, picked it up, and parted the cut made by the knife with his fingers. It formed jagged edges. Lewis went to the barn first to change his shirt and saw the bloodied carcass of a goat upon his assembly table. Lewis dropped to the floor. His breath had temporarily been cut short.

He sought out Harris on the far side of the plantation. He told Harris of the assault by Tom that morning and how he had defended himself. He asked Lewis what shape was Tom in. Lewis replied that he had knocked him unconscious. He added that a bucket of water thrown over him was all he would need to come around. Lewis showed Harris the jagged cuts on his shirt and compared them with the pieces of goat and sheepskins from the barn that also bore the same type of patterned incisions. Harris knew it was not a coincidence. In the past, he had to shut Tom's belligerent mouth down on more than one occasion, particularly when he set the rules for the treatment of his skilled black laborers. He assured Lewis that he would deal with the situation.

Chapter 5

Tom was killed by the blow to his head inflicted by Lewis. Though Harris knew that the driver was responsible for his own demise, he did not want to send the wrong message to the hundreds of slaves that he owned. He was not going to sanction future random acts of killing whites by blacks. However, he did not punish Lewis. Harris' employees were up in arms with him; they sensed that he had believed Lewis's account without question.

Harris snapped that he owed no one an explanation about any decision he made.

The slaves, who already respected and looked up to Lewis, were glad that Tom was dead. In fact, they danced about it on Sunday. The celebration gave rise to the overseers to be even angrier about the master's decision to leave Lewis be.

#

For the first time in five months, Lewis had to take a trip to repair banjos for a quintet that was to perform in Macon, Georgia. The destination was just passed the plantation where Wani lived. It was Mr. Wilkerson's homestead. Lewis was familiar with it. He had made a banjo and two drums for him. Harris did not allow Lewis to travel by himself since the incident. He feared Lewis might want to escape in light of the continued disgruntled murmurings from his men. Lewis did not care if someone accompanied him. He remembered Cudjoe's stories and opted to be the better man.

Harris sent the oldest driver he had to ride with Lewis. The bent-over decrepit man named Luke, had seen his last slave-driving days. Harris kept him on because he had been with him for years and he had no family.

The aged driver wanted to keep a conversation going with Lewis for the entire trip. Lewis did not want to hear about the "good ole days". He just wanted to relive the moments he shared with Wani until he saw her face again. They traveled over graveled or dirt-filled roads. The trip took a little over a day and a half. They stopped three times to rest, refresh, and relieve themselves. It was still hot but not as humid as it had been in past weeks. It was a stress-free trip for Lewis. He began to hum inside.

The Cricket Cries, the Year Changes

Lewis repaired the banjos in a period of two days. He tuned them and replaced strings. Only one of them needed a new backing. Wilkerson who had ordered the work was very pleased with the job he did. In fact he paid a ten-percent increase over the invoiced amount. He gave Lewis four dollars, unbeknownst to the elderly driver.

The two decided to stay the night before they returned home early in the next day. Luke preferred to sleep in the wagon. Lewis took shelter in one of the slave's cabin. In the morning, Lewis found the old man stiff as a board in the back of the wagon. His eyes were closed. His mouth was open. He was very much a pale, dead man. He had drunk a mug of rum. The empty vessel rested on his sunken stomach. Lewis covered him with a blanket just as Wilkerson reached him with a basket of rolls, cheese, and jerked meat for the return trip. Lewis had already filled his water jugs.

He lied about Luke's condition when he said he was going to let him rest for a while in the bottom of the wagon while he drove back most of the way. Luke's body stunk of alcohol and urine. Wilkerson praised Lewis's compassion for the old fellow. He added that the best thing for the drunken man to do was to sleep it off. Lewis agreed. Wilkerson wished him God speed.

After a half-day's journey towards home, Lewis turned the cart into the plantation path where Wani lived. He hitched the horses to a pole behind the barn where she did the laundry and went to find her. He had covered the dead man with a blanket. It was dusk.

He sneaked up from behind her and picked her up. He hugged her tightly. With his eyes closed, he gave thanks to the gods. The woman screamed. She was not Wani.

Chapter 6

Wani had died the month before. She had given birth to a stillborn girl. The oldest woman on the plantation an enslaved midwife told Lewis that she had gotten terribly sick. She just wasted away. She told him that Wani struggled to deliver the baby before her time to die, to give it more air but she was unable to do so. The doula told Lewis that she knew who he was without question when she first laid eyes on him. She said Wani had often wondered what had happened to him; she did not know what homestead he was slaving on and could not get word to him about their baby.

Lewis's life ended that moment. He had already planned to ditch the white man's body and burn the wagon and spend the rest of his life on the run to freedom with Wani. The midwife took Lewis to Wani's gravesite. She left Lewis alone with her. The slave's graveyard was located near the end of the plantation. It had markers made of shells, cloths aged by the weather and bells and stones piled high in different configurations atop makeshift tombstones.

Wani's shallow grave was a clumped mound of dry red dirt. A lone flower lay withered on its side in the middle of the small hill, its petals dried inward. Lewis buried his head into the dirt. His indistinguishable words sank into the clay. His huge hands picked up pieces of dirt and ate it. He was temporarily blinded by his sorrow. The well of tears drenched his shirt. His heart was heavier than anything that he had ever carried. He longed for Cudjoe to comfort him; he wanted his Wani back.

As evening fell, Lewis stirred in the graveyard. His grief had lulled him unconscious. He decided to dig a deeper grave for Wani and his child before the sunset. Earlier he had noticed animal tracks around the too-soon grave. He retrieved a shovel from the wagon. By nightfall, Lewis had relocated Wani to a different place in the graveyard.

He lifted the light stiff body that was wrapped in sheets from the hole. It had a tinier piece of cloth tucked into it that held his daughter. He found his rotting straw hat among her remains. He placed both gently into the deeper ground. He faced Wani's head towards the thickets on the plantation where they first sealed their love, but not often enough.

As he paced his steps to the wagon, a tiny bell rang rhythmically behind him. He turned to see Thundastorm much larger than he remembered. He hugged the goat, looked into its eyes, used his arms to snap his neck and killed it. He slit its chest, tore out its heart and ate the entire organ. He cut the leather-strapped bell from its neck and placed it in his pocket.

The Cricket Cries, the Year Changes

#

Lewis arrived at the Harris-Jones plantation. He left the old, rigor-mortised Luke in the wagon and headed toward his cabin. In the morning, Harris summoned Lewis to his porch where he sat with his white help. He wanted a full explanation as to what had happened to the driver that drove him to Macon. Lewis remained standing as he told him that Luke had insisted on sleeping outdoors after he refused Wilkerson's lodging offer. He said he found him drunk and dead the next morning. He challenged Harris to ask Wilkerson if he had told the truth.

Lewis angrily threw the four dollars that the man had given to him for his work toward Harris' face. He barked to him that money meant nothing to him. Master Harris questioned if the money was actually intended for Luke. Lewis fearlessly asked Harris what did the drunk do to deserve it.

At that moment, Lewis vowed to Harris that he would never make or repair an instrument ever again. He strengthened that threat and said that the last tree he hollowed out was indeed the last tree that he hollowed out. He surprised all of them with a voice they had never heard with anger unmatched by anything they had seen.

Harris fed up with this high-sounding nigger, struck him with his walking stick and broke it. Lewis never flinched. He then ordered the overseers to have him whipped and jailed for insolence, insubordination, and possibly robbery.

The overseers reluctantly beat Lewis, even though they were glad to do so with safety in their numbers. They were afraid to make eye contact with this massive man as their whips and chains tore his flesh. Lewis made no sound. He did not even wince. He still refused to make instruments and told Harris to go to hell. The master then threatened him with amputation of his hands. Lewis, in his defiant grief, extended them to him and dared Harris to do so. The master set dawn as the time that Lewis would lose his hands.

Harris felt that this act would even the score over Tom's killing in his employees' eyesight. It would reduce the strife between the two communities on the plantation. Since Lewis's attitude indicated that he was no longer going to be of any use to him, Harris thought that he could afford to mutilate him. Lewis could continue to teach the young black apprentices his craft as a maimed man. Harris knew he could break him.

#

A chilly Sunday morning found Lewis kneeled against a large tree stump. His hands faced upwards and his head faced downward. The goat bell hung from his neck. Bloodied pants were his only attire. His back had so many lashes inflicted upon it that they overlapped each other in chevron welts. His eyes were slits and his swollen head bore large gashes from the farming tools that were used to beat him.

Lewis's large arms and chest were peppered with cuts and slashes. Several of his teeth were missing. Only a few slaves huddled together to watch Lewis that morning. The masses decided that they could not bear to witness the pending horrible act to one of their best friends.

The overseer raised the axe while his backup stood behind Lewis with a rifle. They were the only two white people present; Lewis was no longer a threat to them. It had begun to rain. The assembled slaves turned to run back to the cabins as the axe reached its zenith. Lewis, with chained wrists, managed to grab the descending handle in mid-air. He decapitated the overseer, turned swiftly and sliced the other one from the middle of his chest downward to his groin.

Lewis hobbled to the graveyard of the whites and peed on Tom's grave. He cursed him for being born. Lewis cried to his god of grief that he owed him an explanation for the turn of events in his life. Scores of whites on horseback spotted Lewis as he walked erratically around the plantation. He talked to himself. He ranted and fumed as he rubbed the white men's' blood from his chest. He fought the air with massive fists and kicked the red earth with muscled legs.

Slaves stood frozen and afraid. The overseers surrounded him. This time Lewis was lassoed with five different ropes. He was placed in the jail that he had helped to build. Master Harris learned of this while he was at an auction. He could not fathom the strength of this nigger as relayed by his men. He had never seen one like him before. He asked that Lewis not be harmed until he got home. He had plans to breed him and produce more offspring like him. He could charge huge stud fees to his colleagues on other homesteads.

During that week, most of the overseers took turns and whipped Lewis as he was bound in chains. They tortured him with shovels and picks through the jail bars. It was their cowardly retaliation to a man that they knew could not be suppressed. Some of them mentioned Tom's name with each strike of their weapon. Harris returned and discovered that Lewis had been hung from a tree horizontally by his ribs despite his orders. He went to the site and previewed the behemoth in a stage that was too late to cut him down to see if he could heal properly.

It took six men to put him on the wagon to stand him up, Harris learned. The overseers could not balance him onto a horse or a wagon. He was dead weight. They finally used a scaffold from the barn and hoisted him upwards. Lewis, almost lifeless at that point offered no resistance. He had been chained in this position for seven days.

Kaffie had visited Lewis while he still swung by his ribs from the massive tree branch. She stood under him and cried. She whispered his name only once. Lewis's body was bloated and distended. Flies were all over the place. Buzzards awaited their turn at the feast of rotting flesh. They roosted in the nearby trees; their large, black bodies swayed in impatient posts as they awaited their reservations to be filled.

Despite the stench, Kaffie stretched to touch the hands that no longer held Harris' interest. Her index finger briefly made contact with his thumb. That sudden, subtle, soft gesture jerked Lewis's flittering one eye into a downward glance. Blood, guts and excrements had leaked to the ground. His shredded, soiled clothing corroborated the animalistic savagery of his beatings. The tiny bell around his neck rang out faint uneven tones.

The sound of insects that had gathered on his skin was louder than his faint breathing. That lone orb showed Kaffie his inner suffering and despair. She prayed for the ending.

Kaffie was visibly distraught.

She had revered Lewis because of the joy that he had brought to the plantation. With his music and drums he had connected many of the slaves both old and newly purchased to faraway memories. Kaffie knew that his gifts allowed the slaves to get through each day with songs that were sometimes hummed in unison in the fields or whined in private.

In spite of her prayers, that strong body took four more days to die.

The slaves held one of the largest memorials to one of their dead that the plantation had ever seen, second only to Abraham's homegoing. Harris allowed the assembly; he did not want any insurrection or uprising to be seeded by what had happened to Lewis.

The slaves played instruments as a tribute to their friend and Musician. The drums accompanied the harmony of the too-familiar songs of sorrow and loss that gripped the plantation slaves. Kaffie requested that the slaves cremate Lewis so he could still hear his drumbeats above the ground. He was never a slave, she assured herself; she would not commit him to the ground.

She scattered his remains throughout the plantation, especially near the groves where the trees were his lifeline to his craft.

The next morning did not bring busyness as usual. Code words delivered repeatedly by a drummed message from the witch doctor, Ngango interpreted: "A good man has gone over from us. The time for deliverance is at hand."

For well over two months, the behavior of the slaves was outwardly subdued and inwardly angry. The Master and his employees were cautioned by the eerie bold silence among the slaves as they toiled in the fields. Hoes dug deeper, axes cut harder; cotton was pulled defiantly from the bolls. Their demeanors insinuated an uneasy foreboding. Master Harris, his planters, and overseers grew uneasy. He instructed them to remain vigilant and on guard.

Kaffie cut a swatch from Lewis's favorite shirt that Wani laundered for him each time they met. She never knew the true significance of that piece of clothing. She would use it in her quilt. The bell from his neck was placed on her dresser.

Cynthia Harris-Allen

BETSEY

Chapter 1

Betsey was the love of Daniel Oakley's life. She was a slave. Oakley, a white man was an artist originally from Ohio. He was raised on a farm in Chillicothe. His father discouraged him from pursuing his passions because he spent too much time woolgathering and drawing. The family was dirt poor and sorely needed Oakley's labor. He beat Daniel often when he failed to complete his chores. Oakley ran away at the age of seventeen and never looked back. He came to the South to escape the biting Ohio winters.

When he was thirty-six years old, he met Master Harris at a slave auction in Atlanta. Oakley had set up an easel in the town square. His India ink drawings depicted the auctions of slaves. He sold them to newspapers up North. His talent was undeniable. Soon, Harris commissioned Oakley to draw oil portraits of himself, his wife Tillie, and his daughter Luvinia. The project expanded to include Harris' horse and his dog.

Oakley asked Harris to compensate him with his own separate living quarters on the plantation as payment for his artwork. Any additional work that he created for sale would be sold at a fifty-fifty split between him and Harris.

Betsey was a Nigerian. Her straight ivory teeth starkly contrasted with her obsidian skin. The artist compared her face to a piano——musical, lively but sometimes morose. He appreciated her blackness; he said it reminded him daily of a mystery, a secret or a closed book.

Their relationship was not hidden. She lived openly with him in a separate cabin near the slave quarters. It was well furnished. One end of this larger cabin was devoted to Oakley's oil painting pursuits. It was replete with easels, canvases and rough sketches strewn on the floor or taped to the walls. Brushes, rags, and turpentine lined the wooden shelves.

Oakley painted nude portraits of Betsey. He used her as his model in all of his work but he completed the portraits as that of a white woman. He sold many of these one-of-a-

The Cricket Cries, the Year Changes

kind illustrations throughout the counties in northern Georgia. Because of the nature of this type of art, most of them would hang from walls of saloons or private clubs.

Oakley held Betsey's head toward the light with his two fingers when he posed her for his rough drafts. He softly propped up her chin to catch the sunshine when he sketched her face. Sometimes the paint on the brushes would almost dry; he could not help but stop to behold her beauty. He marveled to himself how much in love he was with his midnight black possession. Betsey's face returned a different kind of love to Oakley. She coveted other things: freedom and reconciliation with her ancestors.

Many derisive comments were made about Betsey to her face or otherwise in the fields, by the slaves, particularly the men. They called this Yoruban woman "dapo" (promiscuous) or "agbere" (whore) in her own language. Betsey would threaten to have them whipped ("na legba") If they did not cease the torment.

She was haughty and self-absorbed; those traits were developed with a price.

During a slave sale at a racetrack, her entire family was sold to what might as well been the four corners of the earth. She was seven years old when she arrived at the Harris Plantation with no siblings. She never allied with a surrogate family. Harris did not remember purchasing Betsey. Supposedly, she was hustled into the wagons with other slaves whom he had actually purchased. When they arrived at the huge plantation Betsey was the only one that did not have the Harris-Jones brand on her shoulder. Harris kept her anyway. He casually named her Betsey when he recorded his ownership in his slave rolls. She insisted that her name was "Ludie."

As a young girl Betsey would steal away by herself to sketch with small pieces of black coal hidden in her pockets. She drew on brown meatpacking paper, newspapers and sometimes, upon her own clothing. She illustrated flowers, trees, and cascading waters, but her best works were those of birds. Betsey sketched them with larger than normal wings and hardened stares of defiance in their eyes. As a young girl she would give her completed drawings to the slaves as she sought inclusion or acceptance from them.

Betsey did not have a stationary cabin to sleep in as she grew up. Oftentimes she was banned from sleeping in some of them because there was no room for her. Other times it was because she was becoming a beautiful young woman; some of the slave women were intimidated. She carried coal to the Big House every morning. She gladly swept the cinders from the fireplaces in the various rooms. From the ashes she was able to cull slivers of black sticks that she used for her artwork.

She gave several pieces of her work to Kaffie when she carried coal to the attic. Each one was of a different bird. The two developed a relationship over time. Kaffie complimented her talent as she accepted the drawings. She displayed them prominently in her sewing room. Her walls were papered with Betsey's work.

Kaffie knew of Betsey's orphaned story and was filled with a similar compassion. She was in awe of Betsey's work. She witnessed the evolution of her sketches from the crude, elementary drawings that marked her budding capability to the impressive work she now produced. She secretly schooled Betsey.

At seventeen, Betsey drew the attention of Oakley, who was then thirty-nine years old. Oakley had visited Kaffie to be fitted for his spring clothing allotment and spied the drawings on the wall. He walked closer to them to examine the detail. He touched the single letter in the corner of each picture and asked Kaffie about the artist.

Kaffie told him that Betsey, the young woman who ported coal to the mansion each morning made the sketches. She told Oakley that Betsey's real name was "Ludie", hence the "L" on the artwork.

One afternoon, Oakley found Betsey near the perimeter of the plantation thickets. Betsey enjoyed unfettered supervision. No one ever came looking for her.

The only audible sounds were the insects and the birds. A gentle breeze flapped Betsey's papers while rocks held them down. She studied her rough outlines. She sat on the ground with her back to him with her long spindly legs crossed. Betsey gently massaged the brown paper with a wet finger to soften the black shadings of a bird's feather. She was lost in her work.

Oakley's presence startled her.

Betsey jerked then covered her mouth to catch her breath. She recognized this man and was no longer afraid. Oakley sat next to her on his knees and introduced himself. He complimented her work-in-progress and told her how he was so impressed by the drawings displayed on Kaffie's walls. She bit her lip and sighed that she drew some of them when she was quite young.

Betsey continued her secret schooling with Kaffie during the day after her early morning chores. Soon by night she began to sleep with Daniel Oakley, in the midst of the essence of an artist's hopes, and a slave's dreams.

Chapter 2

Betsey tried her hand at rendering portraits of Master Harris, the old butler named Meriday, and Sue Anne, the cook. The pieces captured the informal expressions of their faces. Master Harris won over by her work, asked for more. In the beginning, he would have Betsey present at dinners and cookouts with the sole purpose of entertaining his guests with free portraits. Later, however, he charged them a fee.

Betsey learned portraiture from Oakley, who welcomed the opportunity to touch her during the day. He guided her wrists and arms with his own while he instructed her on form and composition. Their blossoming love combined on the canvases, and fulfilled a mutual need to belong.

As she walked the grounds toward her cabin, she was certain she would be confronted and cursed by some slaves. That day was no exception. Slave women threw rotten eggs at her and called her a fallen woman. They harassed her and said she was no freer than they were. Some jeered and taunted that she was still that stinky orphan girl that carried coal that was as dirty as she was. One woman defiantly blocked her path and spat in her face. She told her that she was far too black to act as if she was white. Betsey was used to this treatment though she grew tired of the harassment.

In the cabin that evening, she showed Oakley her soiled dress and recounted what the women had said and done to her. Oakley, exhausted from painting all day. held Betsey to comfort her. He told her he would speak to Harris about it. Then Oakley on a whim told her to pack a suitcase. He was taking her to Ohio again in the morning; he needed art supplies.

Betsey felt good. Oakley had taken her to Ripley, Ohio, just southeast of Cincinnati on many occasions especially during the summer lay-by.

\#

Betsey always packed her favorite red and white dress that Kaffie had made to wear on the promenade. The quality of the tailoring and attention to detail drew a lot of attention and compliments. Betsey liked that. The dress had a white background with tiny red fleur de lis all over. It had a full skirt; the back hem was drawn up at the center to meet at the waist and exposed a solid red underskirt.

She was Oakley's mistress. She was a free person in Ohio, a non-slave holding state. She would lean her head dangerously over the railings of the steamboat. She felt the mist from the lacy trails of the parting waters divided evenly by its paddles. She loved the steamboat trips. She inhaled the free winds on the river and wished that one day she could become water. She took mental pictures in her mind of the river scene. The barges were filled with slaves heading south. Other passenger boats that passed them with all different types of people on board seeded a vision of a montage in her head.

Betsey was conscious of the looks she received from the gentry. She was a black woman accompanied by a white man on the deck of a steamboat and not in chains. She would link her arms in Oakley's and intentionally display publicly her affection for him. She ran her fingers through his hair or whispered reddened phrases in his ear. She garnered even more attention from the disdainful passengers who were also traveling north. She further provoked their ire when she made sure that they were aware that the two had booked a first class crossing.

In Ripley, they would dine, shop, and be entertained by black-faced minstrels. The minstrels offended Oakley; it made no difference to Betsey. She and Daniel Oakley lodged in the only hotel in town. Now well-educated and well-read thanks to Kaffie, she noticed that Ripley had many abolitionists among its citizenry. One man in particular lived in a house called "Liberty Hill." He was the richest and most influential man in Ripley. He owned a news press.

She spied him surrounded by people at a recital held at the hotel. She stole away to the interior part of the hall and spoke to one of his associates. He told her about the Underground Railroad and the rich man's staunch support of abolition of slavery. The two agreed for a price that he would supply Betsey with newsletters and columns from newspapers like the *National Anti-Slavery Standard*, the *Anti-slavery Bugle*, *The Liberator,* and others each time she visited Ripley.

Betsey covertly used the papers to wrap the perfume, glass, and clothing she purchased during subsequent trips. In secret, she would distribute the leaflets and editorials to the educated slaves on the plantation. If any information could enable her to escape without ever being captured its use would benefit her as well, she concluded. She loved no one but herself. Her survival was her sole instinct.

#

Oakley was now approaching fifty-one years old. Betsey had come to love him in her own way. She surmised that hearts of artists could always find peace with one another. He had rescued her itinerant life from the dirty cabin floors and given her a sense of belonging. However, belonging was not freedom, in her mind. She knew she was very much a slave. At twenty-nine years old, Betsey knew she had a lot of life to live and it was not going to continue as chattel.

That night before boarding the boat for the return trip, Oakley gave Betsey a necklace. It bore a hewn silver artist's palette about the size of a two-bit coin with semi-precious stones of six colors. It hung from a sterling chain with a double clasp. Betsey gasped. She bowed her head to receive the shiny object around her neck. She made Oakley laugh. She joked that silver could be the types of chains that she could learn to live with.

Soon it became the only thing that she wore to bed.

The Cricket Cries, the Year Changes

Chapter 3

Oakley impregnated Betsey when she was thirty years old. She went to Ngango for the potion known among the slaves that could terminate a pregnancy. She would not be misshaped or burdened with a child. Ngango informed her that she would have to stay with him for a while in order to heal properly.

Betsey knew that Oakley had business away that would be about an eight to ten day round trip. She told him that she would be going by the Sycamores at the fringes of the plantation to sketch her montage while he was away. She said she wanted to be able to concentrate in the open area. Oakley arranged to have easels and materials moved to that area. He included a comfortable, armless chair.

Betsey loved the chintz-covered seat. It was heavily padded. Red roses flooded the ecru background fabric while green leaves and tendrils held them at bay. The back of the chair settled just below her shoulders. It offered a suitable position to draw for hours. It was the first thing that Oakley had purchased for her in Ripley. He placed a closed parasol next to the chair in case the heat from the sun became unbearable. As usual, Oakley left a love note for Betsey; this time he placed it inside of the umbrella.

#

While Betsey was sedated from the procedure, Ngango erased the skin color from her breasts, back and lower torso with a pure lye paste. He wanted Oakley to be as repulsed by her altered outward appearance as her African family was by her blatant inner one. Ngango meted out the collective retaliation for her reckless ignoble abandonment of her culture and traditions——all for a white man.

Ngango kept Betsey on opiates for five days. His assistants raked the burned and scabbing skin loose with lard and softened it with palm oil. Soon her skin began to heal. It was smooth but colorless in many areas and extremely raw to the touch. When Betsey finally came around she discovered what Ngango had done to her. Before she could shriek, he covered her mouth with his leathery, large, dirty fingers. With bulbous yellow eyes, and raspy cutting whispers, Ngango threatened her very life if she told anyone what he had done to her.

He strengthened his warning by telling her he could get word to Oakley that she came to him to get rid of his child. Ngango then yanked out clumps of her matted hair. Betsey screamed this time.

He placed a hex on the straggly bleeding roots as he used unintelligible words that sealed the spell. He held the dripping pieces high above her head and breathed slowly upon them. He told Betsey that he would torment her head forever as a reminder of the bed of nails upon which she slept. Ngango bragged to her that he had also given her another treatment that only time would reveal.

Betsey considered the life-altering consequences from both sides. The warnings from Ngango and his reaction, if her secret was revealed to Oakley gave her no choice but to obey him. She could not offer a rebuke to the medicine man as she was wont to do with the rest of the slaves.

A week later, slave drums coded what had happened to Betsey. That Sunday many slaves rejoiced with dancing and singing. Many of the men wore red and white headbands to simulate Betsey's favorite dress. They were ecstatic that retribution had finally come to this harlot who had been an outsider from the very beginning. They burned the circled cloths at sunset. The slave women clicked their teeth and clapped in rhythm as they shouted praises to Ngango.

Kaffie learned when she was under the tent what had happened to Betsey. She was heartbroken for her friend. She tried to be neutral on the subject when slaves approached her with the news and sought a response from her.

When Betsey was able to deliver coal to the sewing room, she dropped the bucket unable to repress her bitterness at the disfiguration and wailed. Kaffie quickly protected the open fabrics and dresses in progress from the plumes of black coal dust that had filled the air. This was the first time Betsey's emotions had unraveled since the assault.

Also, her voice strained as she told Kaffie the full story which included why she went to Ngango in the first place. Her trembling hands twisted Kaffie's dress for support as the emerging details were spilled. Kaffie comforted Betsey but also admonished her about the brash and haughty manner she treated other slaves when she herself was one. She reminded

The Cricket Cries, the Year Changes

Betsey that her life was not the only one punctured by tragedy. She had previously told Betsey about her life as an orphan on the plantation. She, too, never knew her mother or father.

Kaffie suggested that Betsey soften her approach to the slave population. Maybe then she would not be so reviled. She told Betsey as long as she flaunted her relationship with Oakley not much would be done about how the other slaves regarded her. Under the tent the Blacks talked about Betsey's duties as a coal porter and mockingly viewed it as being lightweight work for a slave Kaffie said. Most importantly, Kaffie told Betsey no other black woman on the entire plantation lived openly in a white man's cabin.

Upon Oakley's return, he became selfishly embittered and angered by what had happened to Betsey. She lied to him that her skirts had caught fire when she rustled through the embers to collect the pieces for her drawings. Luckily, some field hands had put the flames out; but not before the unsightly damage would burn her torso, she fabricated. Betsey knew that white people could not interpret the drummed messages. She felt safe to render her own version of what had happened without question.

She leaned into his arms and cried not with sorrow but with anger and a secret vow to avenge. Quickly, Betsey recoiled at this involuntary show of frailty. She immediately loosened Oakley's arms from around her. Soon, a debilitating headache gripped her body for hours.

Oakley continued to paint his nude white women but with the inclusion of the new colors of black, brown and white skin. The smiles that once graced the faces in his infamous paintings were now replaced with solemn, slight grins. The sparkling eyes he so deftly captured in the past looked back at him with a distant pang of longing and isolation. His hands trembled at each insertion of these substitutions. The stark modifications to Betsey's canvassed flesh pained him. The new squatters in these pictures had pilfered his gold mine. They were stronger than Oakley's slight paintbrush weaponry that failed miserably to remember the past.

139

Chapter 4

Betsey, now thirty-five years old, winced at her leprous appearance as she stood naked in the full-length mirror one morning. The night before, she had sought help from some strong slave men to capture and drown Ngango. She felt that the river could engulf him and pull his satanic spells to its depths along with him. To kill Ngango and bury him on land would somehow empower him to rise again. He would own the air that she breathed, she feared. His death would remove the spell that Ngango had placed upon her head years ago.

The black men refused. They called her a traitor, a harlot, and an outcast. They told her they felt no kinship with her. Her bribes of money were useless to them.

Betsey trudged the ground back to her cabin. Her head began to ache. Often the pain was so agonizing and tortuous that she felt that her eyelashes had turned into giant cascading boulders. Each time she blinked the earth quaked. The suffering compelled her body to remain deathly still to stave off any movement lest it invite more distress. She had to cover the windows to keep out the light that forced her eyes shut because of its intensity.

Betsey decided to kill Nagano herself.

#

With the enticement of a piece of metal fashioned into a palette, Betsey bribed a slave girl that she did not know.

The young girl ground roots into powder. She hid the poisonous substances for Ngango in a quiver slung over her back. Ngango painted fresh designs on this girl's face and arms at the beginning of each week. Upon her back, he etched symbols with wet red clay that warned the slaves of pending dangers throughout the plantation.

The girl would slowly walk the plantation grounds while the working slaves would pause to read her back like a telegraph. Some of the cautions included which watering holes were not safe to drink. Others named white men who carried sexual diseases that the female slaves should resist at all cost.

Ngango allowed the griot, Amidou, to insert a messaged symbol upon the girl's back from time to time. His signs of hope, strength, and courage stained the slave girl's skin until the sun or rain faded its dispatch.

The girl, named Star, was Ngango's daughter. She was conceived under a stellar canopy one evening fifteen years ago. Her mother, a voodoo priestess slave from Haiti, lived on a nearby plantation in Macon. Ngango had spotted her a long way from her master near the banks of the Oconee River one night. She and Ngango soon operated at cross-purposes. She surrendered Star to him. He arranged for her to disappear.

Betsey wanted this girl to give her a potion that could kill a man——instantly. The young girl agreed to give her a liquid encased in a dart in exchange for the shiny bauble.

She held the three-inch long toxic spear in her hand as she headed back to her cabin. Though her headache was intense, her heart raced with anticipation.

She figured she would wear her favorite red and white dress that she normally wore on trips to Ripley on the night she planned to kill Ngango. She changed her mind and opted for something more slave-like.

#

Ngango had planned a ceremony for those slaves who wished to purify their evil thoughts and deeds. As the Sunday sun set, many of them congregated around the bonfires. They sang, bleated, and danced. They entreated their gods for mercy and forgiveness. Many of them imbibed the hallucinogens that polluted the distilled water prepared by him. His assistants administered it to the crowd.

The torch-lit frenzy around several fires went on for hours. The witch doctor conducted a call-and-response chant with the slaves. Ngango threw gunpowder into the heat-filled heaps of wood. It exploded, sent orange sparks into the opaque skies and disappeared almost as soon as they were created.

The bonfires illumined the eyes of the intoxicated. It confirmed the transfixed, zombie-like poses of the exhausted participants. Their movements slowed and their bodies grew loose and limp. Many collapsed upon the clay ground and were dragged away from the inner circle. Their departures were highlighted by the heightened enthusiasms of the fresh, overexcited replacements. The younger slaves free of burdening thoughts of guilt watched as they sat and enjoyed every moment. Some of them would stand and dance as well, while others clapped to the changing cadence of the drumbeats.

High-pitched drum sounds merged with their fellow low bass partners. The collaborative rhythms accented the spellbound steps of the costumed slaves. The revelers were dressed in their traditional celebratory garb that included loincloths, feathers, and beaded masks. Ankle bracelets made from hollowed nuts and cowrie shells emphasized their movements. Many wore animal-toothed neckwear and snakeskin headbands. They shook metal clappers in their hands; others rang cowbells.

Master Harris did not allow any displays of nudity.

Betsey viewed this ritual from afar and decided that this was the night where she would feign remorse for her deeds and attitudes towards these savages. She hoped that they would not bar her from joining in. She wanted to get close enough to Ngango with the poisonous dart bribed from the young slave girl who now wore the small silver palette around her neck.

A short time ago, a black male had informed Ngango of Betsey's petition to help her to kill him. Ngango had also learned of Betsey's request from Star when he recognized the foreign piece of jewelry. He gently coerced her to reveal her benefactor. Upon admission, her father did not harm her.

\#

Betsey walked back to her cabin to bathe in the wooden tub that Oakley had built near the back door. She no longer washed herself in privacy at the river. She was ashamed of her partially bleached body. She hummed as she used the perfumed soaps that Oakley had purchased in Ripley to lather her body. Betsey leaned back in the tub and thought how she would take those vindictive slaves down a notch by killing their witch doctor.

That sorcerer would get what he deserved from her. He was a fake, she joked to herself. He could not even tell if she was pregnant or not when she first consulted him, she thought haughtily. After he burned her skin off, she never had a monthly again. She stepped out of the tub and wrapped a heavy cotton towel around herself. She stopped suddenly and pressed the towel towards her womb. Were her years of infertility induced by Ngango? Was that the "extra treatment," he had teased to her when he took away her skin? Betsey was horrified at the prospects of her own thoughts.

Tonight, this voodoo son of a bitch was going to die, she promised herself.

Betsey stepped inside the cabin to dress. She loved her home. The oil paints, the coal slivers in jars, and the smell of primed, stretched canvases comforted her. Her sketches, along with Oakley's oil paintings, complemented the walls of the cabin and gave temporary worth to their lives. Streams of vertical light from the high lofted ceiling windows fell upon pictures and portraits.

She dressed in all white. She did it to symbolize her fake communion with Ngango and her people. An off-shouldered, pocketed gauze garment flared at the bottom. It fell to her calves as she wanted it to. The red mud and dirt at the revival would be upon her feet and not the hem of this dress. She hated walking barefooted. It was so primitive. Betsey decided to carry her shoes just in case. She might have to run for her life when this potion killed Ngango instantly, she considered. She dabbed Eau de Cologne on a piece of cotton and placed it in her cleavage.

She missed Oakley. He was away delivering the commissioned portraits. He had been traveling for almost three weeks now. Before his departure, he encouraged her to finish the mural and noted that he had set up her usual spot by the Sycamores.

Betsey observed herself as she twirled in the white dress in front of the Cheval mirror. As she spun around, her eyes caught a large canvas covered with a sheet in the corner. She had not realized that Oakley had started another portrait. She wondered why he had not finished this one in time for his trip.

She walked over to the easel and lifted the covering and viewed a painting of a black woman in a white off-shouldered gown. In her right hand, she held a pail of coal; in her left hand, she gripped a bleeding heart that had stained one side of the dress. Perched on her shoulder was a large bird. The woman was barefoot. Around her neck was a chain without an ornament strung from it. Her lips were halved; each one occupied the space where the ears should have been. Flames erupted from a black hole of a mouth. The eye sockets held the misplaced ears. On the head of this woman was a huge gray rock.

Betsey was disturbed by Oakley's work. "Who was this woman?" she fretted. Betsey pondered the portrait for a moment. She continued to step backwards from it until she reached the bed. She sat upon it and continued to study the work that looked even more disturbing from a distance. She did not have any more time to think about this, she thought. She would ask Oakley about it upon his return.

The sun had set and the evening's festivities were in full swing. Her head began to ache.

The Cricket Cries, the Year Changes

Chapter 5

Betsey removed her shoes and gently lifted the bottom of her dress. She walked with counterfeit fearlessness toward the fire; she ambled nonchalantly towards the drumming noise. She gingerly navigated the ground as she avoided rocks and twigs. Her head was wracked by the motion.

Many slaves gathered at the ceremony. Betsey's delusional impressions sensed that the crowd had swelled because word had spread somehow that she had planned to attend. She breathed a long sigh of contentment satisfied that tomorrow would herald her new beginnings.

Ngango welcomed Betsey into the inner sanctum of the penitents who had already imbibed the liquids. As he walked towards her he threw open his arms and urged the other slaves to join him to receive her atoning heart into their ranks. Betsey had brought her own container to stave off participating in the circled drinking. She wanted no part of the unsanitary communal shells that the slaves shared.

When he embraced Betsey, Ngango filled her gourd with water. Betsey, offended by his rank odor, refused the drink he had offered. She told Ngango that she preferred to watch the ceremonial dances for a while before she took part in them. Ngango obliged her. He then told her he would hold onto her cup until she was ready to repent. When Betsey was distracted by the revelry, Ngango was able to slip a poisonous ground powder from the castor seeds into her open drinking gourd. He stirred it with his finger.

Betsey walked over to a group of reveling slave women and found a place to stand among them. The fires reflected on her white dress and colored it amber. She did not know how long she could bear the stench of these females. Some of them bared toothless grins. Other bodies evidenced the perils of hard labor with cuts, burns, and disfigurements. Some slave women genuinely offered friendship and kindness to Betsey. Betsey was caught off guard by her own inward equal reaction to their gestures.

The slaves that had danced in the first round for what seemed to have been hours soon found rest away from the fires. Many of them were exhausted and drugged. A fresh crowd of male and female slaves entered the circle to partake of Ngango's potions and begin their spirited purge. Betsey decided to join them. She signaled to Ngango that she was ready to repent and change her evil ways. The two of them exchanged superior but suspicious glances as they neared one another. She hoped that the elixir would numb her head. Ngango extended the gourd to Betsey. He raised his cup to hers in solidarity.

Betsey enthusiastically drank the cinnamon-smelling intoxicant in seconds to assure Ngango of her intentions and to bring him within her reach. Ngango hovered over her as he awaited her reaction. She pulled the poisonous dart from the pocket of her dress. The blazes from the mandarin orange fires grew higher as added kindling fanned them toward the night sky. She was sidetracked by the sudden bursts of brilliant flames.

She began to feel the effects of the drink. In her disorientation, she stabbed a slave who was not Ngango. The man circled the fire once. He grabbed his neck with the dart still inserted and fell dead to the ground joining the others who had merely passed out. Betsey's bare feet grew unsteady and reached out to anyone or anything for support. The crowd withdrew from her and left her to fend for herself. She fell to her knees. She felt the effect of the brew that all the slaves had experienced. It was horrifyingly wonderful. Her mind now straddled two worlds.

In her head, Betsey saw her montage come to life. The sights and sounds of Ripley were amplified over the shouts of the slaves. She had killed Ngango! She envisioned herself levitating while she held his bloodied decapitated head against her white dress. Her falsetto laughter drifted downward towards the stunned crowd as they welcomed the victorious whore. She heard Oakley's voice but could not find his face. Their artwork started to float toward the ceiling in the cabin.

As the effects of the drug began to lessen, Betsey heard Ngango call her a bitch, a tart, and a "dapo." Betsey realized, for one brief moment that the painful scorching of her throat had signaled her own demise. Upon the ground she began to feel her insides burn just as her outsides did from the lye. The ricin ran its course throughout her veins and then navigated them once more. Her body convulsed and twitched on the clay. The clamor of the celebration continued without interruption.

The Cricket Cries, the Year Changes

Betsey's explosive vomiting soiled her dress and feet. Her dimming sight held the face of Ngango. He peered into her eyes, and grinned while he repeated, "amin, amin" (amen) to your ashes." Betsey was slowly dying. Her panicked, pain-filled pants and darting eyes marked her for death. Her last lucid thought was that she had not collected her thoughts on how she would meet it.

Ngango had the expiring body moved to the site where Oakley had set up the easels. The slaves removed the red field dust from her feet and laced up the shoes she had left upon the ground. They placed Betsey in the cushioned chair under the giant Sycamore tree.

It was midnight.

#

Daniel Oakley found Betsey on the margins of death. The flies had already swirled around her charred mouth. She had been out there for several days. He held her rank body closer until her scant last wisp of life provided a different liberation than she had longed for.

She never knew he was there. She never made a sound.

The slaves did not lament her passing. No mention of what happened to her went beyond the barbed wire fences of the plantation. The drummed reports that beat the next morning alerted the uninformed field workers of Betsey's demise.

Oakley had her body cremated. He burned her in the clothes she wore when he found her dying in the chintz chair. The ember-filled funeral pyre unified its dual purpose as her Muse, and her mortician. The sterling chained necklace that he had given her survived the heat. The tiny artist palette charm was not attached.

Oakley knew that Betsey had committed suicide. He had had glimpses of her deteriorating, dolorous state. Each time he left for days on end her melancholy would begin. Betsey hated being alone. She owned him. She had told him so many times. In his mind he knew that she had harbored that twisted thought. He owned <u>her</u>.

Cynthia Harris-Allen

He was destroyed in his grief. Inside the cabin, he unveiled the covered self-portrait in the corner that Betsey had painted whenever she was beset by those crippling headaches. Deprived of the strength to survive the tortuous bands which she claimed held her head in a vice, Betsey attempted to paint in oils. She drank rum until the intensity of the pain and her drunken stupor showed her the floor. Oakley studied the bizarre painting once more and then burned it. He walked back to the Sycamore tree to retrieve the chintz chair. It was of no good use. Betsey's bodily fluids had ruined it. The umbrella was gone.

He spied his last love note to Betsey caught high in a slender branch. It challenged the breeze to set it free. Oakley had written his routine professions of love to his "Ludie".

Oakley took her remains aboard the steamboat for her last passage towards Ripley, Ohio. At the stern of the steamboat, he splayed them into the Ohio River. He watched as the paddles churned her ashes into the ages.

Soon his new oil portrait characterized a female figure with a black face with no details within it but for a pair of eyes that gazed downward. She sat on a mahogany chair dressed in a red and white dress with vacant palms held opened in her lap. Her obscure eyes appealed to the elongated silver tear to seek refuge in her waiting hands. Oakley kept this painting for himself well into his eighties.

Kaffie was glad to find a sample cloth of the red and white dress she had made for Betsey. Her death was so unnecessary.

Another piece to add to the pending inlaid work.

The Cricket Cries, the Year Changes

DILSHAD and MATHILDE

Chapter 1

Dilshad loved his family. He, his wife, Matilde, and their two sons and two daughters were auctioned as a complete package. They were known to possess superior planting skills. Their proven expansive knowledge of flowers, trees, and roots was a convincing selling point to Master Harris. They were second-generation Ghanaian slaves on southern American soil. They held fast to their traditions of earth, wind, and sky worship and knowledge of natural plant life.

They were brought to the Harris-Jones plantation by one of the master's slave traders who had traveled to the Gullah islands for an auction. He arranged for the purchase. He was impressed by what he read in their bill of sale. As the owner of a three thousand acre plantation that produced cotton, cane, corn, peanuts and wheat, Master Harris heralded this family as a viable and valuable addition. He concluded that if he owned an entire family, it would reinforce their commitment to one another and reduce the probabilities of any one member running away on his own.

Soon after their arrival, the Master allowed Dilshad and his family lots of free time to survey the crops and examine the soil. Harris sought his suggestions to reclaim the areas where seeds refused to take root after years of planting in the same Georgia red clay.

The slaves thought it uncommon for an entire family to be presented intact to a farmstead straight from a selling block. They were eager to learn why this group was so special. As time passed, no one second-guessed their abilities. The other slaves came to respect them. The information they dispelled to them in the fields was useful and oftentimes reduced their workload. Dilshad advised them to mix ground, dried moss with the shucked corn dust to soften the soil as they tilled; over time that suggestion straightened many bent backs.

Cynthia Harris-Allen

Those who feared the Dilshad Group as they came to be called were the whites; Even Master Harris had his doubts. The family isolated themselves from the rest of the slaves. They often gave the "evil eye" to the overseers and planters. Because of that gesture, the drivers sought to punish the clan but heeded Harris' warnings against it.

Dilshad and his family wanted to be left to themselves while they worked. They dispensed sage advice during the planting, pruning and harvesting seasons. They collected many plants and herbs that only grew in the thickets and the bogs. They dug roots, and cared for the flowers at the entrance of the mansion. They created a beautiful landscape of color at the master's door.

The Cricket Cries, the Year Changes

Chapter 2

Master Harris isolated Dilshad's family in a cabin far away from the others so the overseers could listen to their chants and incantations. He wanted them to figure out what they were doing. The family frightened the whites with the strange calls they made through the night. The odious smells that came from the cabin combined incense and sulfur, pine needles and dandelion greens, to name a few.

Due to the somewhat strange behavior of this family, the master and overseers believed that they could possibly possess magical powers. The master expanded the work detail for the family to lessen the opportunities for them to have enough strength to conduct their midnight rituals. He had heard from his fellow planter that some of these niggers could indeed rouse spirits to cast spells upon the whites. Harris had their cabin searched frequently to ferret out powders, roots, amulets, and any other magical apparatus. To their limited knowledge, they never found anything unusual.

The two young men, Kwadz and Yawo followed their father wherever he walked; but they also kept watchful eyes on their sisters Abena and Esi and their mother, Mathilde. Each family member continued to give any white person that lecherous look that soon became legend. The whites, including the master, deliberately avoided lengthy looks with them. They forestalled any punishment even if any one of them did something that warranted it.

Harris did not like the feelings they unveiled to him. He told the overseers that they gave him the haunts. He decided to chain this family at the ankles and wrists in their cabin at night to allay the nocturnal sacraments complete with the wild and flailing gestures.

Others would watch Dilshad's family celebrations during the "free time" beginning on Saturday evenings that continued through Sunday. They had never seen anything like this before. Through strong oral traditions slaves conducted rituals that celebrated births, named babies, mourned deaths and welcomed the changing seasons. They feted the rites of passage and called on spiritual interventions to end their plights in their own ways. The slaves never judged the distinct rituals of any other African. They did not fear this family at all.

Dilshad's family offered no objection to the chains; they still chanted and danced in the cabin, though with limited movement. They continued to commune separately on Sundays and in secret during the workdays. Most slave owners and their overseers did not care about the cultural, ritual, religious or social dynamics of any slave; but this self-contained group unnerved them.

Slaves outnumbered whites twenty-five to one on this homestead; the drivers knew best not to interfere if the nature of their singular actions were not menacing. Their words, codes or gestures often placed the whites at a serious disadvantage. They did not trust the mindsets of their slaves. On the other hand, the slaves knew the characters of the whites as well as they knew the fields.

#

Dilshad and Matilde grew small herbs and tubers in the fields hidden by the vegetation. The growth escaped detection by the overseers. They thought it was some annoying weed or low-growing ground cover that did not interfere with the crop. The two would harvest Angels' trumpet, a beautiful tree that bore purple, red, orange, and variegated blooms. The flowers hung like bells. These trees would grow to fifteen feet tall and made great decorative backdrops to any garden. All parts of this tree contained dangerous levels of poison. The seedpods could grow to be three to six inches long and carried the most concentrated levels of toxicity. Tillie Harris praised Dilshad as she welcomed the pretty trees.

The family added White Snakeroot, a shrub that grew to about three feet tall. The dark chocolate foliage served as a background against the contrasting floral peaks. The root when mixed as a tea drink, treated diarrhea and fever. The plant if consumed directly by cattle contaminated the animals' beef and milk. It also caused "milk sickness," a contagious type of near-death illness when consumed by humans. Tillie Harris would place her irises and tulips in front of this dark background. It created such a beautiful contrast, she boasted.

Many more roots and special plants were cultivated on this plantation by this family; its beautiful floral beginnings belied its portending poisonous endings.

The Cricket Cries, the Year Changes

One day, the master finally had Dilshad punished. He had slapped an overseer who had put his hands on Matilde. Under normal circumstances this act by a slave would have resulted in a severe inch-of-your-life beating or even a hanging. The master cautioned this new overseer not to exact revenge on this man. He later recounted to him the history of this slave family and said its worth to his plantation had cross-purposes. He could not even sell them. Their witch-like reputation of bizarre practices had overshadowed their planting skills. They were fabled throughout Georgia, Tennessee, and South Carolina.

The minor punishment for Dilshad was to be chained to a tree and not fed for two days. He was only allowed water. His older son, Yawo gave the master the evil eye. Within four days, many of the master's cattle had gotten sick. Yawo had administered White Snakeroot the day his father was partnered with a tree. Yawo did this under the screen of a moonless night.

He also knew to give a lot of water to the cattle within two days. That hydration would allow them to live but they could no longer produce drinkable milk; nor could they be slaughtered and sold as edible beef.

The only use the animals had now was to draw the plows. The master had the blacksmith, Scipio brand them with a double "XX" so they could be separated once they grazed among the other cattle. Harris suspected that the Dilshad family had something to do with this but he could not prove it. The veterinarian arrived after a seven-day trip. Traces of the poison in the cattle's systems had disappeared.

\#

A month later on a sultry, sweltering, breezeless Sunday afternoon Master Harris walked among the slaves as they sang, danced, cooked, and played. He spied Matilde and her family. They sat along the perimeter of the riverbank and viewed the activities with indifference. They talked among themselves. Matilde caught his glance and fixed a spear-like stare upon him. She then turned to her girls and said something. The three of them cackled a secreted laugh. The master quickened his gait toward the plantation porch.

153

Cynthia Harris-Allen

Dark clouds began to lower themselves.

The early Monday morning brought a mammoth tornado that cut a jig-sawed swath of shattered windows, splintered trees, and mowed down cane fields. The powerful winds left only the red clay mud-filled floor of an auxiliary barn in its wake. It had lifted the entire structure and its contents of hay, farming equipment, soil, and lumber and emptied the debris in the next county. The twister had produced over three to four inches of rain as it loosed plants from the soil and beat cotton rows to the ground.

Dead fowl lay among the yards. Pigs were blown into the thorny bushes; most of them were dead. Large trees were felled on mansion and cabin roofs alike. Many horses had bolted from their tethers in the stalls. They were rounded up from the faraway fields at the outskirts of the plantation.

Some slaves had run to Dilshad's cabin for safety when the long, high wind did not stop. Some had never witnessed a tornado. Dilshad and his family assured the screaming, frantic slaves that the brief but strong path of the tornado would pass quickly. They had witnessed both hurricanes and tornadoes in the past.

At the orange-pink daybreak promise of yet another hot and humid day, the master ruefully surveyed the ruins. The slaves meandered in groups as they clicked their teeth while they took stock of the damage. Harris knew he had to suspend the normal schedule for weeks to repair the damages to the buildings, salvage the crops, and replace an entire barn. His eyes continued to take in the results of the catastrophe.

He caught sight of Dilshad. He saw him crouched on his knees in the mud barefooted. He was attempting to preserve some of the flowers from the Angel Trumpet trees that had splintered near the porch of the mansion. He tenderly examined them as he spoke softened words in his native tongue to the broken petals. His actions disturbed Master Harris. Dilshad sensed the shadowed movement of someone near him and turned toward Harris with a stare of thinly veiled disdain. Harris tried to avert his glance but could not. Dilshad stood up. He touched his heart as a gesture of thanks to the heavens and blew a kiss toward the sky. He softly patted one bare foot on the ground three times.

The Cricket Cries, the Year Changes

Master Harris shuddered with the thought that this demonic black could also possess the power to curry favor with Mother Nature.

Chapter 3

Tillie Harris grew prized hydrangeas. She had established a reputation for the hybrid white clusters throughout the northern Georgia counties of Walton, Fulton, Oglethorpe, and others. She even commissioned a huge oil painting of them stretched out in a sky blue vase that hung from the massive fireplace in the dining room.

One day, Esi and Abena dug among the Monkshood bushes. The Monkshood was a deadly lavender plant. Its regal spires of white, purple or bi-colors bloomed in late summer to early fall. The young women knew to plant them beneath the giant trees that served as a sunshade to the east and west of the huge planked plantation porch.

They looked forward to the perennial blooms' ability to paint the landscape when the spring and summer offerings had begun their color-drained exit. The two and a half foot plant disguised its pestilence with graceful long stems that sprouted fans of color.

Tillie Harris saw the girls rake the dirt too close to the hydrangeas and thought they would harm her prized plants. She shrieked a "shoo-fly" command and the startled girls bolted. Mrs. Harris summoned her husband and informed him of the insurrection. Mr. Harris stood by and supervised as each girl took three very light lashes from an overseer. The girls cried and reported this incident to Dilshad.

Infuriated that any white man dare touch his girls, Dilshad walked straight to the overseer. Harris was in the vicinity. Dilshad stood within inches of the overseer's face for what seemed an eternity. Both struggled to gain control of the grip on the whip the overseer held. Each said nothing; their combined non-verbal exchanges consisted of glaring eyes and flaring nostrils. Harris had given a signal to his overseer and the other drivers that had converged onto the scene to lay back.

The red-faced overseer angrily spat on the ground near Dilshad. Dilshad released the whip and stalked away with a backwards menacing glance to all. Around midnight he skulked around the area of the hydrangea gardens. He sprinkled a powder containing lime with a liquid potion from the witch doctor at the root base of the bushes. Days and weeks passed. The master was perplexed. He had waited anxiously for some sort of vodoo reprisal from these family members; but nothing happened.

#

Spring ushered in the full bloom of plant life that had lay beneath the ground. The flowers did not need an engraved invitation to nature's dance. Flora had pierced the loose and warmer soil with budding stalks that sealed their initiation by the sun.

Tillie Harris watched as her prized hydrangea bushes began their perennial reach to beauty. The stems had been cut to ground level in the fall, yet she never tired of the process that brought them to full height. They yielded great globular blooms. As the buds began to open, the woman of the house discovered a horrible aspect of her blooms. They were no longer white! They were different hues of a dismal blue and dull pink; others were a mottled purple.

She was distraught and demanded that her husband do something to Dilshad and his family members. She was certain that his daughters had poisoned her bushes when she had caught them digging around them last season. Master Harris went to Kaffie and ordered her to make shirts and blouses of the same yellow material for the Dilshad group. He demanded that the females wear head wraps also of the same color fabric. He wanted that family to be seen no matter where they were on the grounds.

No other slaves were permitted to wear this calico color. He wanted it bright yellow. Any other slave who wore even a similar color had to discard that piece of clothing never to wear it again or face the whip. Kaffie summoned Cecelia, the dye maker, to stain the cotton hanks a marigold yellow as none that fit the master's description was available. This was the first time in her memory that she could recall that custom clothing had been ordered for slaves.

The Master created a rolling twenty-four hour schedule for each overseer to watch this family. Most of them reluctantly accepted their shifts; all of them averted their gazes.

Dilshad had passed on a lot of his root culture to his sons and daughters. As they reached adulthood, they cared for many of the other slaves that had taken sick in tandem with Ngango. They applied their endowed West African traditions as they used natural ingredients for medicinal use. Dilshad's family never took sick; it was as if an invisible wall of grace protected them.

Their children blessed Dilshad and Matilde with grandchildren who were taught at an early age to intimidate others with "the stare" in order to protect themselves. Their grandfather commanded them to follow the dictates of Mother Nature.

Dilshad was the first to die in his family from natural causes. Scipio continued his tradition as he fashioned personalized wrought iron pieces into the grounds of the graves of slaves. This time he forged a black magnolia marker replete with tendrils and roots; Mathilde humbly accepted it.

Despite Dilshad's death, Master Harris did not relax his rules of observation for that extended family. There were over fifteen additional members to his family. Dilshad's descendants continued to work the plantation in marigold clothing. Additional cabins were assigned to the growing family. The slaveholder relocated others who lived nearby; he wanted all the "Dilshads" in the same space.

#

A year and a half later, Dilshad's two sons, Yawo and Kwadz poisoned the night overseer assigned to watch them by placing the juice from Doll's Eyes a white fruit from the baneberry tree into his drinking gourd. The guard had groped three of Dilshad's granddaughters by the well. The berries contained toxins that had an immediate sedating effect on the heart muscle tissue. It was so named because each white berry contained a black circle in its center; it resembled the ceramic eyes that were placed in doll's faces. The overseer became disoriented as he secured the accused males with chains. He went into a deep sleep and died.

The two brothers escaped to northwestern Georgia to the Oconee River that spilled into the Tennessee River. The two had overheard the song that some slaves sang repeatedly that contained the code to find the Ohio River. The song was called "Wade in the Water". They never wore the color yellow again once they reached Ripley, Ohio. The master did not issue a fugitive slave warrant for either one of them.

The Cricket Cries, the Year Changes

Dilshad's two daughters, now grown women with children of their own, counseled the new generation of planters and tillers. They continued the covert retaliations initiated by their father to keep the aging Master and his staff at bay. The group never neglected their duties as they tended to the plants and shrubs around the plantation. The manicured plantation grounds were famous for their beauty and attracted many tourists on their way to Savannah. To that end Harris had a second smaller mansion built to accommodate the visitors for a price.

Master Harris did not fear Dilshad's second generation of children as much as he had the first. A few years ago he had decided to blunt the characteristics of Dilshad's future offspring. He seized the opportunity to give his approval for Esi, one of Dilshad's daughters, to marry a free Cherokee Indian from another plantation. Harris wanted to break the cycle of a long succession of strong-willed quasi magicians. The welcomed suggestion was given to him by a horse breeder.

Harris had not considered that the Cherokee lived as close to the earth as their African counterparts. The cross-breeding resulted in a shared knowledge that augmented their skills as planters and hunters. The Cherokee-African merger of Dilshad's family brought forth children with tremendous strength and resolve. Their long, wavy hair was blacker than they were. They all loved, revered, and cherished their dear, "Mum-Mum", Matilde.

Chapter 4

Matilde sat in her rocking chair made for her long ago by Abraham, the broomstick maker. She held two of her great- grandchildren in her arms as she sang to them. She gently swiped away the flies that buzzed around their sleeping faces. She was no longer required to work in the planting fields. Her grown children strongly objected to their kids being held or cared for by any other slaves. After all these years and many unexplained incidences the slaveholder was still hesitant to rebuke them. Master Harris thought it best that she babysat her offspring to allow their parents to tend to their duties.

Matilde had slouched into a different person since Dilshad slipped away into that long ago night, his arms around her as they always slept. She missed her sons Yawo and Kwadz. She had not heard anything about them for about thirteen years now. She was glad that they had been taught to read and write in secret by their father long ago. Their father told them it would be their protection one day.

Mathllde and the girls would sing loudly and dance while they beat tambourines late into the mornings. These night rituals that disturbed everyone had covered the English lessons from their father. The young girls not directly involved in the reading exercises, actively listened and learned to speak well at the foot of their father in their far away cabin.

Under the tent in the yard one summer Kaffie had noticed that Dilshad could read. She had wrapped the marigold clothing in newspaper to separate it from the others and she followed his eyes and fingers as he silently read the words. From that moment on, Kaffie inserted pages that covered the bolted fabric in the sew barn into their yearly allotment of clothing. She folded the papers into very small pieces and placed them into the pockets of the shirts. This routine went undetected for years.

Dilshad acknowledged that transaction only once when he placed his thumb upon her forehead, stared into her eyes, and winked.

#

On what became a very humid morning Matilde learned that the mistress of the house, Tillie Harris, had called several women from the fields into the kitchen of the mansion to help to prepare lunch for some children of the slaves. Matilde was wary of this gesture. She suspected that all was not well given this mean-spirited shrew never wasted an ounce of her energies to show kindness to the slave population.

She placed her slumbering great-grandchildren on the red clay ground. She fashioned a lean-to tent from Dilshad's yellow gauze shirt. It turned their brown faces to soft orange as it deflected the hot sun's rays. She ambled toward the grounds; her cane steadied her pace. As she walked, she heard the noonday bell ring that signified lunchtime for the children.

Three long troughs that were used to feed the pigs were placed in the yard. They were low to the ground, about twelve feet long each, foul smelling, and greasy. The children had never eaten food this way before. Usually there were several large bowls filled with food. The kids used mussel shells to scoop whatever was prepared while they squatted in circles on the ground.

The little black children squealed with delight as they ran to the area but stopped abruptly. They looked upon the hot lumpy steaming grits that were poured into the troughs by the indentured servants who had carried the huge pots from the kitchen. Not knowing how to eat it without the scooping shells, the children hesitated. Tillie Harris stood nearby and with a threatening scowl ordered the children to eat it with their hands or face the whip.

With big brown trusting eyes, the kids dove into the hot beige grits with their still dirt-filled hands. They screamed in tortuous pain. The grits turned a murky brown with the invasion of the field dirt. The hominy lava scalded and skinned their tiny hands. The glove-liked grits trapped the searing heat onto their fingers and arms.

Matilde reversed her steps and quickened her aged pace towards her cabin. The slave mothers heard the screams and dropped their planting hoes over the objections of the overseers who fired warning shots into the air as they defiantly ran towards the yard.

Mathilde had gathered palm oil, lard, brown flour, and yellow gauze remnants from her cabin. She returned to the site as she dragged the items in a stringed gunnysack. The angry mothers cursed in their native tongues and in English. Their crying eyes struggled to disbelieve the sights before them. As Matilde disbursed the healing oils and powdered remedies, many mothers tore off their own head wraps to continue the application of the oils to the arms, hands, and elbows of their precious babies. They sat disheartened, appalled, and helpless in the heat on the ground. They rocked and comforted their shocked and suffering children.

The witch doctor stood far off and looked upon the victims. He had gotten an eyeful of the clamorous event. He watched Tillie Harris walk victoriously toward the mansion as she prevented the hem of her dress from touching the ground. His body was plastered all over with white clay. He had placed his right foot on top of his left knee and held his hands palm-to-palm at his chest as if in prayer. He clicked his teeth three times. The slave drums messaged to the rest of the plantation that trouble was nigh.

In the still hot night air, the slaves could hear the Master from their cabins as he screamed angrily at the Mistress about what she had done. They determined by his tone that he was not pleased at all with her actions. He admonished her for disabling their future workers and perhaps inciting a swift retaliation from the slave population that sorely outnumbered them. He threatened to send her back to Savannah to live with her mother.

A few slaves had stealthily positioned themselves at the back of the mansion wall and listened to the exchange from the windows. In their quarters, they mimicked scenes of how Miss Tillie had cried for mercy.

She screamed that she was scared to death of the slaves who worked in the house and the fields especially when Master and most of the men were away for long periods at a time. She argued that each time he returned with new slaves, they were a more frightening and resistant bunch than the last. She did not trust the white indentured servants, either. They resented being treated like the niggers and did all sorts of things to sabotage or ruin everything she wanted them to do.

Harris calmed down as he empathized with his wife's pleadings.

The Cricket Cries, the Year Changes

Two days later, Master Harris' dog Luke, his favorite horse, Red, his two cousins, Lizzy and Marina, and the newest overseer, Clifton Bobbett were all poisoned to death. Tillie hysterically elevated her fears of the slaves continued avenging acts. She now had her husband convinced that something had to be done. She wanted Dilshad's family removed from the plantation immediately——gone before the funerals——in fact gone before noon.

Cynthia Harris-Allen

Chapter 5

Master Harris had the overseers and drivers round up the yellow-clad clan to meet him in the yard. He informed them that he was ordering them off his property never to return. He pointed to the readied paddy wagons and told them they only had a half an hour to gather their things. They were going to be driven to the edge of the plantation and set loose.

Dilshad's daughters asked Harris how they could be able to travel without papers from him that allowed them to move about safely. He dismissively replied that it was not his concern; they would have to fend for themselves. He shouted that he knew all along that their voodoo practices of scaring people with their evil eyes and poisoning both human and plant life would be his plantation's ruination. He raged that an eviction was way overdue. His added that even friends and family were afraid to attend the funerals of Lizzy and Marina.

Not fearing the whip one more time before the eviction, the emboldened male slaves of Dilshad's part Cherokee and part African clan demanded that Harris provide proof that they had done these deeds. Harris scorned them as he cracked his whip high into the air. He ranted that he did not have to give them anything. Everyone knew it was them who did all of this——and he was still the damn master of this damned plantation!

The daughters pleaded for their mother Matilde who had sat in a worn wicker chair and listened to all that was said but remained silent. Her mind could not process what Harris had said. She silently prayed with her yellowing aging eyes open to her Dilshad. She asked that he protect her family from hurt, harm or danger. Her heart sank.

The family begged for mercy. They insisted that their mother was not fit to travel due to her age and frailty. Harris told them he could attempt to sell her as a mammy to another plantation though with her family's reputation it was not likely to happen. If he could not sell her within thirty days he would put her out in the thicket on her own.

Whistled sounds and birdcalls, coupled with drumbeats on washboards and fence posts, catalogued the news of the day and sent it winding throughout the plantation.

164

The Cricket Cries, the Year Changes

On the twenty-ninth day since the families' departure, Matilde sat short of breath on her rocker in the ninety-degree heat. She grieved the total loss of her family. Her salty tears mingled with droplets of sweat as the brackish duo found refuge on her dirty marigold cotton dress. She had not heard of any bad news about her family. The days since their absence trudged slowly as she languished in her cabin.

She envisioned bygone days with Dilshad. Throughout their lives this clannish family's plant gatherings were dried, burned, and powdered for the sole benefit of their fruitful illustrious planting processes. The only thing that superseded those acts was the pride they took in their work. A smaller portion of the poisonous roots and herbs that they stealthily grew and gathered were at the behest of the witch doctor from Haiti who compensated them with poisons upon request.

Matilde still had some of the small sacks Ngango had made for them long ago. It housed the many mixtures they had grown for him. She placed several of them in a grimy feed sack and slowly and unbalanced, pulled the stringed contents behind her each morning as she made her way to the porch. She placed the now impotent mixtures onto her chest every day; its healing powers, now moot, rehabilitated only her memories. The contents could only recall the smells of the earth after a soft rain. She feebly swished the flies and no-see-ums away from her space. She wondered when the gods would summon her to rest. The cicadas and crickets were her only day and night visitors respectively.

Meanwhile in the mansion, Tillie Harris kept up her insistence to her husband that Matilde be sold or gotten rid of by the end of the thirty days. She stated that Mathilde had outlived her usefulness and too many devilish things still occurred on the plantation. Someone had stolen her silver thimble and her amber-handled hair comb. Through pursed lips she boldly hinted to him that lack of action on his part could weaken his authority over other slaves throughout the plantation and beyond.

Master Harris tried to dodge the issue while he still mourned the loss of his horse and his dog. He decided on this day to take his wife to Conyers, Georgia to shop, dine, and see a minstrel show. He told her to get gussied up for the occasion. Harris would see to it that a slave would fit the wagon with a canopy to ward off the day's heat or the yet unfulfilled promise of pending rain. The cook would pack a light lunch of sandwiches.

Tillie was uplifted by the invitation. She accepted it cheerfully as his reconciling gesture of forgiveness for what she had done to those slave children long ago. Many were maimed and traumatized by that event.

Dismissing those thoughts, she rang the bell to summon the cook to bring her a cup of peach tea with a piece of cake as a quick bite before she dressed. Master Harris insisted that he make her tea; he called it just the renewal of his pampered acts toward her.

She sat at the dining room table and looked out the window at her new hydrangea bushes. Their root bases were doused with water every hour by a slave boy. She smiled at their pending progress and hoped that these new, white, five-pointed clusters would restore the status that she coveted at the upcoming floral fair in Macon.

Harris brought in her tea and cake. He said he would give her a few minutes to get dressed. He then left to check if his brown boots were polished. He placed a shallow kiss upon her forehead.

Standing while studying the dresses she had placed on the bed, Tillie gently blew into the tea in the Blue Willow cup. She held it on the saucer with her thin, pale, blue-green veined fingers. Her smallest digit extended outward. She enjoyed the smooth hot peachy taste as it soothed her throat. She bit into a tiny morsel of the moist pound cake and turned her thoughts to what she would wear to Conyers. She felt calm for the first time in a long time, thanks to Master Harris. She sipped the amber beverage.

The china cup and the silver spoon fell to the floor. Tillie's hand clutched the starched yellowing lace tablecloth in agony. She sank the other trembling hand deep into her stomach hoping to relieve the suffering. The blue and white shards of china extracted pinpricked dots of blood as they lay trapped under her cotton gown. Her last act of ringing the silver servant's bell fell upon deaf ears. Her body banged the floor poisoned and dying. Raindrops began to fall.

The Cricket Cries, the Year Changes

At the very same time, an overseer lurked behind Matilde's cabin and spotted her as she sat in the rocker chair on the porch. Her white coarse hair was matted and unkempt under the yellow turban that lay askew upon her head. She had refused to bathe and oftentimes had soiled her clothing.

No one had come to see about her since her family was forced from the plantation. She fended for herself as best she could, unable to draw water from the well by herself. She softly sang a prayerful song: "Befoe, I die, Good Lord, 'foe I die, give me a cool drink of water, Lord, 'foe I die."

As the rain quickened, the curved blade of an overseer's knife came from behind her and deeply slit her throat. It cut short the smile of relief that had just begun to fill her face. Her dry chapped lips fought to pull the cooling drops from above into her mouth. The gash sent a cascade of warm ruby-red blood that streamed downward and formed a pool in the faded yellow uniform that had defined her family.

It rained on Matilde for three days and two nights. She would not be discovered until the blood had turned to a muddied brown crusty paste in her lap. Her rigor-mortised fingers gripped the rails of the rocker. Her eyes were shut. Her head hung low. The odor of death had taken up residence on the porch of the cabin at the end of the row.

Kaffie slowly washed the faded yellow wrap taken from Matilde's head to use in her quilt. As her hands plied the sudsy water, she reflected on the entire family. She was pleased that Dilshad and Matilde were buried in a color made special for a slave.

Cynthia Harris-Allen

CECELIA

Chapter 1

Cecelia clasped her hands together behind her back as she ambled down the hill toward the barn. She stopped to secure the poles that held the clotheslines into the ground. It was just before sunrise and the cool still morning hung over the hushed grounds as it awaited the noise of life. She stood by the huge black cauldrons, eight in all, that housed the many dye baths that she created. She had painted small symbols on the bellies of each one. The Gambian glyphs represented the colors she created.

Cecelia would often sit upon the red ground as she guarded her boiling pots. She waited for the dye recipes to marinate before they met the off-white hanks of cotton. She sought comfort through this daily ritual because she did not want to be a slave. This routine dressed her to face each day. If she did not have to the chance to reflect, she would somehow trip and fall as if her soul was out of balance.

Cecelia worked in a huge barn with a very high windowed-loft that let in a lot of light down upon her work area. She had other slaves that worked with her. She had trained them to grind roots of plants, nuts, and dried insects. She placed them separately into small woven bags. From the black walnut, she gleaned the full spectrum of the color brown. The cochineal insects that the overseer bought from the drug store produced a beautiful crimson when used at full strength.

The flowers from the Osage trees could be ground to a yellow-orange pigment. Her prized color was Indigo blue. It was first cultivated in the Caribbean by colonial planters, when brought to the Americas by African slaves. It eventually thrived in South Carolina. At one time this crop was second only to cotton as a chief export to Europe.

Cecelia loved the smell of the barn. The red clay floor spotted by various drops of dried dye dots maintained its smell of the earth. Many baskets woven by Boway lined the barn floor. It held hanks of various dyed hues that she had experimented with. The odor of the plaited sweet grass seemed to renew itself each day when the morning's coolness summoned it back to life.

The Cricket Cries, the Year Changes

Long metal mixing spoons hung from leather straps by the door as they musically moved in the breeze. Their flat iron bottoms struck each other with their off-key tones. Piles of wood and pine needles lay at the entrance to be carted to the boiling pots. Cecelia made a mental note to herself to place new screens on top of the pots to ward off unwanted objects and insects that had fallen into her mixtures.

Cecelia was both a dye maker and a weaver. She understood the hand of the cloth. Trial and error gave way to what dye strengths were best suited to its different weaves. She was a third generation Gambian, whose ancestors were enslaved on the same plantation in Jamaica. Many of the natural resources of her native country were also present on this island. Likewise, the similar land composition of Georgia supported her craft. She transitioned easily to her new habitat.

Cecelia had an area of land cordoned off to grow most of the plants and flowers she used to produce different stains. One could view rows upon rows of endless color in one stretch of the valley. The hemp-stringed sheets of cotton billowed in the breezes as it highlighted its kaleidoscopic palette.

The Master's relationship with Cecelia as well as his other artisans was a good one. It was imperative to allow them autonomy to create, he thought; mostly because they knew more than he did about the jobs they performed. It made him a lot of money. He was the wealthiest plantation owner in all of northern Georgia.

Kaffie took pride in Cecelia's dyed fabrics returned to her for sewing. She always left a running mark at the ends of the bolts that only she and Kaffie could discern. The master ordered Cecelia to tell one of the overseers what her mixes contained so that he could write them down for future reference. She resented the fact that some foreigner wanted to record the knowledge that she had acquired from her ancestors and pass it on as theirs. She would not betray her foremothers. She gave Harris full but incomplete disclosure.

Chapter 2

Cecelia was in love with Jonah Stansfield, a free black that negotiated trading, leasing or renting slaves between plantations. He visited several farms to scout the field hands, housemaids, and artisans; then he would parley their worth to other planters who might have long or short-term needs. They met one morning when she caught his glance as the overseer drove him passed her dye operations toward the cane fields. On his way back, he hopped from the wagon to ask her name. Stansfield told her what he did for a living. Cecelia resented his business purposes.

As his trade visits increased, they engaged in long and lingering conversations while she stirred her dyes in the boiling cauldrons. She told him he was as indifferent as the white men were toward slaves like herself. He divided families and separated mothers from children and children from their siblings. She recalled her own personal Jamaican experience as evidence. She said he was responsible for killing some of them when he traded them up north. She had heard of places like New York where extreme cold resulted in many deaths.

Stansfield replied that he looked upon it as a business, nothing more. He told her that the slaveholders believed that using him in this capacity because he was black and literate, engendered some sort of trust. It really made no difference to the slaves who shipped them "down river" he scoffed. He held her close to him and said that he could not be a sympathetic businessman. Then he asked her how she expected him to buy her freedom, if he could not make money.

Cecelia found hope and promise in that question.

She learned that Stansfield was from Boston. His family was free people. Stansfield was seventeen years old when the elder man died. He had purchased nine slaves that he immediately freed as part of his abolitionist's views. They lived in a large house with him and his wife. The lot included his parents, two siblings and four unrelated others.

They all worked in Stansfield's Printing Shoppe, except for his mother and a cook. His mother was the laundress. They were taught to read and write by the master's wife. He told Cecelia that he had observed the negotiating skills of Stansfield who printed campaign posters for politicians, store trade papers and some fledgling abolitionist newsletters. His business increased when he started to print runaway slave bulletins for distribution up North.

Cecelia loved to hear the tales of his travels that excluded information about trading his own people. She thought him worldly, ambitious, and confident. Stansfield was smart, well dressed, handsome, and smitten with Cecelia. Her eyes darted with the images she formed in her mind of the kind of life he lived as opposed to her own. Stansfield sensed her uneasiness and pulled her close to comfort her.

Often, they made love in the barn after the apprentices had retired for the night. Cecelia grew accustomed to Stansfield's practice of withdrawing from her and spilling his seed upon the ground. She did not want to raise a child on her own; the act did not trouble her. Master Harris thought Stansfield had bunked in the visitor's cabin during his increased calls to the homestead.

Stansfield teased Cecelia constantly about the many times she would trip over virtually nothing and fall to the ground. He chided that it must be her ancestors trying to get her attention. Cecelia offered no explanation to him, but she knew that it was a sign of her troubled spirit. Their love could possibly last a long time, but Stansfield as a peripatetic partner cast a lot of doubt on their relationship. In addition, his "lack of sympathy," statement, about trading his own people jarred her.

#

A storm in the mid-Atlantic ocean had sunk a ship destined for a Charleston, South Carolina port. The bulk of its jettisoned cargo was for the Harris-Jones' plantation harvesting season. The master was facing huge losses. A visit from Stansfield suggested that he consign some of his artisan slaves to other plantations as temporary trade for their field hands. The output of a skilled slave could be several times the value of field hands, Stansfield offered. Harris could get ten to fifteen field hands for every skilled slave he owned. The master's only monetary matter would be his fee.

Stansfield closed the deal with little effort. Harris was desperate for help. He knew that additional slave labor could replace the equipment lost at sea until the insurance claim settlement was paid. His shrewd business sense prompted him to summon his attorney to draft a contract that ensured that his slaves' return would be at his will.

Cecelia fetched the highest ratio, twelve slaves to one.

Stansfield was caught off guard. His cunning business sense had unawares trumped the love he had for her. Cecelia's heart was laid to waste.

#

On the Thomason plantation in Jacksonville, Florida, Cecelia was put in the fields to harvest potatoes by a driver who did not know who she was, nor where she came from. Many planters put unknown slaves to work on their plantation without question——especially able-bodied ones that did not cost anything.

Cecelia resented the fieldwork that was assigned to her. She felt that it demeaned her. She had never worked on her knees. Her back had never been bent over from before sunrise to an exhaustive sunset or beyond. She became very arrogant and resentful and often feigned illness to get out of work. She demanded to see the owner to explain the error; she was whipped for her insolence.

Cecelia was shocked and pained by the brutality. She lay on her stomach in a cabin filled with sixteen other people. The open stinging welts on her back were exposed in the darkness. She was afraid to go to sleep yet afraid to stay awake. She did not want to think about Jonah Stansfield during the day or the night. She felt herself slipping away.

Mr. Thomason had written a letter to Mr. Harris asking where the dyemaker was. He had posted it a month ago and had not yet received an answer. He finished the letter by pointing out that his field hands were already working for him——where was his slave that did the skilled labor? Thomason post-scripted that he had confidence that the business relationship between the two of them would remain fair.

Later, Thomason learned her identity from his wife. She began talking with Cecelia when the doctor had come to tend to the sick. The slave, feverish, weary, and spent had broken down and cried. She identified herself as the chief dye maker from the Harris-Jones plantation. Soon, Thomason assigned an area to Cecelia to begin the craft that had brought such notoriety and monies to her former master.

She did not like the barn nor the people he had assembled to assist her. She told him that the trees and roots that she used were not available to her knowledge in Jacksonville and she knew of no other substitutes. She complained that the cotton bolts he supplied were of poor quality with a very loose weave that could not withstand the boiling that set the dyes. Cecelia used these boundless pretexts to stall time until she could return home. Thomason grew tired of her obvious excuse-riddled resistance and had her whipped by the overseers. He told her he would put her to work in the onion fields if she did not comply.

Cecelia half-heartedly relented and soon began to work but gave false information and flawed details of her dye making processes. The owner did not like the resulting effects of the   dyes. He accused her of "gold-bricking", a term many owners used that signified a non-compliant slave. He continued the beatings that eventually escalated into savagery.

When Cecelia was able to walk between the drying sheets colored by her understudies during her healing, she disdainfully touched them with her swollen, aching hands that had defended her against the whip. She was gladdened by the lackluster inconsistent tones. Her cracked hands began to bleed again. Cecelia had inadvertently left tracks of blood on the still-wet sheets. She quickly jerked her fingers away not willing to allow the stains to serve as her new running marker.

It seemed an incredibly long walk back to her cabin, Cecelia thought. She had already tripped and fallen twice. An overseer had been watching her. He was waiting to bind her to the cabin walls upon her return for her continued impudence. Thomason had advised him to let her walk for a while to see if she was steady enough to get back to work. Cecelia willingly laid into the chains.

Chapter 3

Thomason received mail from Master Harris that inquired about the health and welfare of his slave. Receipt of Thomson's own letter was not mentioned. Thomason read of Cecelia's personal relationship with the black slave trader Jonah Stansfield who negotiated the exchange of slaves. Harris wanted to know if Stansfield had visited Cecelia in Jacksonville. Thomason wrote back that he had not seen him but asked for his assistance to summon Stansfield to his plantation. He wanted him to use his influence to talk with this woman about holding up their bargain. He wanted her dyeing techniques written down.

Harris received his letter weeks later and made no effort to contact Thomason. The contract stipulated that Cecelia was leased to him. Harris did not agree that she make known her trade secrets. She still belonged to him.

Cecelia continued to rebuff Thomason's demands. Chained in solitary confinement, she was fed very little. She began to lose weight; at times, she was disoriented. Upon seeing how emaciated she had become, Thomason reinstated her normal feeding times. He could not afford to pay her worth should she die on his watch. He was still waiting on Stansfield to come now that he knew of their relationship.

#

In Georgia, Stansfield had met with acrimony from the white slave traders. They felt he thought he had become their equal. Many described him as self-absorbed and arrogant. One hot afternoon, several of them, including Stansfield, rode on horseback toward a small plantation. The men diverted from the red clay trail and rode towards the shade trees.

Welcoming the opportunity to rest, Stansfield was ordered to stay seated on his horse. A hangman's rope was slipped around his neck. He was struck and spat upon and threatened within a slap on his horse's rear end that would have him swinging in the wind. They commanded him to cease from this line of business and leave the state never to return——or be killed. If they even smelled him crossing the Georgia line they would have him quartered.

The Cricket Cries, the Year Changes

Stansfield had wet his pants; vomit rose in his mouth from this near-death experience. They took his horse from him. They rummaged through his knapsack finding nothing of value. They robbed him of his horse and good clothing and kicked him as he lay on the ground petrified. Two of the men stood over him and peed on him while they laughed that that gesture was the last time he was going to get something for nothing from them. They left him to his own devices.

Later, Stansfield stood up bloodied and angered. Dumbstruck, he recovered from his fright while he clutched his ribs. He leaned against the side of a tree to steady himself. He surveyed the open fields of grass and was not sure of his location. He considered sleeping in the open at night. At least he had a blanket, water, and some jerky in his bag. The only weapon he had for protection was a small derringer hidden in his boot. He knew a small bullet could not kill a bear and sensed his own danger. Four dollars were concealed in the other boot along with his freedom papers.

He prayed for a starlit sky that would determine north from south by the placement of the Drinking Gourd, the constellation that the whites called "The Big Dipper" that contained the North Star. Stansfield considered whether he could continue to trade slaves in another state. He was a free man after all. He decided to visit the landowner, Thomason, in Florida.

After a month-long arduous journey, he finally arrived in Jacksonville. He had found work on a barge from Charleston to Savannah. He had never done hard labor before in his life. To him it was demeaning and belittling. When the Atlantic Ocean waves reached the St. John's River, Stansfield showed papers that proved that he was a free man and sailed west in steerage toward Jacksonville.

On land, he paid a white wagonneer his last four dollars to hitch a ride in the back of his buckboard to the small homestead of Thomason. The driver took him to within fifty miles outside of the plantation. Stansfield walked along well-worn roads and found ways to sleep in the slaves' cabins on various small farms. Most thought that he was just a new arrival.

His clothing, now tattered, worn, and dirty, did not give away his past life. His matted hair, a full slightly graying beard, and tired worrisome eyes offered him protection from being recognized as a man of former means. He wore the stench of a field worker. Stansfield was given food and a cast-off tattered jacket by a slave. Refreshed, he slipped away into the night, going from farm to farm. He stole or accepted anything that could sustain him. Thirty-four days after entering Florida, he arrived on the Thomason plantation.

Stansfield met with the landowner who angrily summed up Cecelia's situation. She was not worth the trade, he barked. He also commented on Stansfield's appearance and made sure that he stood downwind from the smell. Stansfield lied that he had been robbed at gunpoint and his horse was stolen just outside of Jacksonville.

Thomason, with a flip of his wrist, dismissed Stansfield's escapade as not as important as his own circumstances while he argued that he traded twelve slaves for Cecelia solely to gain from her craft that Stansfield had negotiated. Stansfield consented to see her after he cleaned himself up and had eaten. Thomason urged him to talk some sense into her; she still had seven months left on his plantation.

\#

Stansfield was taken to see Cecelia in the last cabin by an overseer. Mutual hostility walked between them. No words were exchanged between the two. They entered the door-less cabin by moving the worn greased butcher paper to gain access. Cecelia was chained to the wall, malnourished, and blank-stared. The buoyancy and joy that once claimed his heart was gone. She was broken and so was he at the sight of her. He caught his breath in disbelief and held it to ward off her smell.

He directed the overseer to unlock her chains. The guard, taken aback by a command from a black person recoiled and approached Stansfield as he raised his whip. Stansfield pretended to kneel down but drew his derringer from his boot and dared the man to make a choice. The overseer removed the chains. Stansfield replaced the derringer.

The Cricket Cries, the Year Changes

Cecelia cried out in pain as Stansfield picked her up and carried her out into the early evening air. He laid her on a blanket and held her head up to allow her to drink water from a gourd. He then muffled his cries into the foul odor of her dress as more water flowed freely between them. Later, he carried her to the well, washed her body and replaced her stinking garments with coarse but fresh cotton ones. He saw the crisscrossed welts from the whip on her body, some healed and others still open. Tears stung his eyes. He contemplated murder-suicide.

Stansfield stayed on the plantation for six weeks to care for Cecelia. Her previous gaunt appearance was showing signs of added weight and lifted spirits. Cecelia told him that she would never forgive him for what had happened to her; the entire experience had altered her life. She said she no longer knew who she was. She screamed hoarsely that she was abandoned by him and left unprotected by her ancestors.

She was mad at the heart that kept on beating and prolonged her hell. She wanted it to stop. She wept she still loved him, but did not like him at all. Cecelia said she was as lonely and invisible as the wind. Stansfield countered that never in life did he think Harris would barter her skills; there were so many others that he could have chosen from.

He thought to himself that he should not have come to Jacksonville. Vivid memories of her liveliness would have remained in his heart. His past actions now placed her life in peril and their love in jeopardy.

Chapter 4

Stansfield stayed in the visitor's cabin at first. Soon after, his living arrangement with Cecelia was approved by Thomason with the caveat that Stansfield persuade Cecelia to resume her duties. Often, Thomason invited Stansfield into the small mansion to dine with him when his wife was away. She did not cotton to blacks eating at her table. Thomason wanted to talk about other slaves that he could get his hands on.

His daughter, Dinah, took a liking to this handsome mulatto. She joined her father for dinner whenever she learned that Stansfield would be present. She met with disapproval from both her father and the few black house slaves as she threw herself at Stansfield with the full gamut of flittering eyelids, horse-like grins and squeaky, coquettish laughter.

One evening, Stansfield gave a detailed account to Thomason about his near-death experience not far from the Harris-Jones plantation. He expressed concern about not being able to work as a trader——the only skill he had. Dinah's eyes darted back and forth between Stansfield's lips and her father's face. She listened attentively to his story. Stansfield did not yet know what to make of her.

One day in the yards, Cecelia overheard a conversation between Thomason and his wife. They made derogatory comments about Dinah and Stansfield's budding relationship. The crude jokes about his race and Dinah's unrestrained promiscuity stung Cecelia deeply.

#

Dinah followed behind Stansfield one night as he trailed the dry red clay ground towards Cecelia's cabin. Cecelia and Stansfield still slept together though her feelings for him vacillated with the changing hours. Dinah slipped her arm into his and pulled him behind a vacant cabin and raised her skirt. She hungrily kissed him while she fumbled with his pants. She told him that if he made love to her she would petition her father to have his trading papers repurposed.

The Cricket Cries, the Year Changes

Dinah bragged that Thomason had influence with the northern bankers who factored the southern planter's crops. She was sure she could persuade him to do something for him She coyly added that she was sure she could persuade Stansfield to do something to her also. Of course, Stansfield took her. Of course, he withdrew from her as he ejaculated on the ground. Of course, Cecelia witnessed the entire scene.

\#

Eventually, new papers from the banks were sent to several southern plantations that included Harris-Jones that re-introduced Jonah Stansfield as a slave trader. The banks pointedly asked for their cooperation and consideration.

Dinah lay naked in the visitor's cabin. She happily trailed the papers along Stansfield's bare back. He lay on his stomach, partially clothed. He was dumbfounded and ecstatic. New possibilities danced in his head. He fantasized. His head was turned away from Dinah who continued her incessant chatter. He thought to himself how much he hated a white southern drawl.

He dressed quickly, put the papers in his coat pocket and walked to the slave's cabin. He awoke the next morning in the cabin with Cecelia next to him. He studied her face. The softness that first stirred his heart had partially returned. The deep vertical furrows that rested in the middle of her forehead above her eyebrows had almost disappeared.

He could feel the numerous, blackened, scar-tissued welts on her back through her thin muslin gown. Her rough hands and arms still discolored by the dye stains signaled that she was returning to normalcy. Privately, he cursed the day that Harris fed his own greed with her worth. They were partners in her demise.

Cecelia lay still, awake but with her eyes closed. Stansfield had brought Dinah's overpowering perfume into their bed.

That afternoon as they sat on the ground by the bubbling pots, he decided to tell her it was time for him to leave. He was returning to Boston. He felt safer there. Cecelia said that she only had but a few months left until she could go home and it did not matter to her what he did. Stansfield was put off by her reaction.

She told Stansfield she had known about Dinah from the beginning. His impassioned response was that it was only business. He had shown Cecelia the letters from the banks that credentialed him as a trader as soon as he received them. He explained that he could not ignore what Dinah wanted in return for aiding him. If he had rebuked her he felt he would face a hanging. He told Cecelia that he had his life back now. She could not expect him to hang around a slave plantation not doing anything but helping her to recover and be well. He needed money to buy her freedom. He needed money to restore his position.

Cecelia was dejected.

That morning their lovemaking, fervent and feverish, arrested the angst that had hung over them since Stansfield's arrival. It was new again, like the first day of spring. They urgently connected to the yesterday they longed for before they parted. They longed to live inside each other's love rather than die outside of it. Cecelia cried like the abandoned child she once was. Stansfield sighed deeply, unable to release himself from her in ecstasy.

\#

Stansfield saddled a horse, lent to him by Thomason, as he stood in the stables. He would ride the horse to the train station and leave it at the livery to be returned to the farm. Dinah rushed into the barn. Her rustling taffeta skirts announced her intrusion. Her perfume doused the smells of hay and horse manure. She begged Stansfield to take her north with him where she felt they had a better chance of being together more frequently. Stansfield told her she had to travel by a separate and later scheduled railway.

He thought of his experience in the fields near Monroe and knew that he was already taking a chance to travel on the Georgia rails towards the north. No way was he going to risk his life for this tramp. Dinah happily agreed to meet him in Boston, his hometown. Stansfield hurriedly wrote the place and the time in the margin of a newspaper.

The Cricket Cries, the Year Changes

Stansfield did not keep the rendezvous as Dinah had hoped he would. Dinah was so excited about the northern life that she gave no thought to locating Stansfield. She had monies to live on from her father. Despite her mother's concerns with Dinah traveling alone, Thomason was glad to have her out of the mansion along with her nigger-loving ways. One of Thomason's banker colleagues had written him that Dinah had really immersed herself into New England society. Many thought that her southern drawl was so endearing. The colleague did not mention Stansfield.

Chapter 5

Three months later, Stansfield returned to the Thomason homestead. He appeared restored and confident. Cecelia was happy to see him. He changed into worn out clothing and immediately began to help Cecelia with her work.

As she sat awkwardly on the ground while he carried water and wood, Stansfield noticed that Cecelia was pregnant. A wave of paternalistic joy and expectation came over Stansfield. He hugged her hard. He ran to Thomason and told him that he and Cecelia were getting married. Thomason was hesitant to allow that to happen, but in the end saw no reason why it should not. Hell, Harris knew Stansfield and he owned Cecelia. Thomason was fine with it; Dinah was out of the picture.

The slaves celebrated that evening when Cecelia and Jonah jumped the broom. They had made hoecakes that consisted of corn meal and molasses shaped into a patty. They were baked on the blade of a hoe in the blazing hot sun. Other dishes included yams, okra stew, roasted corn and dried groundnuts. They sang and danced around a bonfire well into the night.

Stansfield and a very tired Cecelia returned to their cabin. The jasmine and peach blossom garlands made by the slaves hung from their doorway. Cecelia broke the news to Stansfield that Master Harris had added another four months to her stay. Thomason's field hands were not finished with the construction of the guest mansion. She said she knew she would go out of her mind if she had to stay one day longer. Now that he was with her as her husband, her renewed spirit had given her heart rest, she said softly.

Stansfield gave Cecelia a gift. It was wrapped in a piece of gauze. Cecelia's eyes gleamed while she held the rounded object in her hands as she speculated its identity. She was delighted to hold one of her own clay pots from the Harris-Jones plantation. Stansfield had taken one of her pots when he first learned of that fated trade. Cecelia pressed it upon her stomach and told her baby that the symbol on the pot meant "home".

The Cricket Cries, the Year Changes

#

Dinah returned home in late fall with her fiancé, Prudhomme Delacourte. She had met him in a saloon. He told her his job was playing poker with his inheritance. She told her parents he was a banker. His proud look and mastery of French and English imbued a hint of his nobility to her family. Her mother was overcome with joy that her daughter was home again——this time with one of their own. How tall and dapper her future son-in-law appeared! Dinah may have redeemed herself, she thought.

Mrs. Thomason was effusive. She had a wedding to plan and wanted to attend to every detail. She would order Cecelia to produce pea-green and lemon yellow cloths so she could have dresses made for the bridal party and matching cummerbunds for the grooms. She insisted to Dinah that the ceremony be held on the grounds. With a passive nonchalant shrug, Dinah told her to do whatever she wished.

Later, Thomason invited Delacourte to ride with him for a brandy at the lodge near the center of town. He wanted to become acquainted with Delacorte as was the custom for men of means.

Dinah was not bothered at all by the news that Stansfield and Cecelia had married, though it probably was not even legal, she mused.

#

One oppressively hot afternoon, Dinah walked barefoot among the drying dyed sheets on the clotheslines. She inspected the shades of green and yellow that Cecelia had produced. She lifted the cloth as if she had an eye for such a thing, Cecelia thought negatively. She had eyed Dinah from another row of dyed, drying cloth.

Dinah took off her overdress to remove a corset that had bound her tightly. With a great sigh of relief, Dinah leaned against a sawhorse, wiped her brow, and began to fan herself with her hand. She shouted out a "Whew" as she exclaimed what a relief it was to let it all hang loose. She sat upon the wooden stand and lifted her skirts up and down to ward off the heat and the bugs. Then she unbuttoned her blouse, excited about the sudden freedom it granted.

Cecelia, not knowing what she meant, looked closely at Dinah and saw her huge stomach. Dinah was pregnant! The

X's of the corset's knotted trail had left a reddened pattern from her navel to just under her huge breasts. She suddenly appeared to Cecelia as bloated and definitely unattractive. Her too-red lipstick was even more garish than before.

Dinah, surprised by her sudden appearance, assured Cecelia that she had nothing to worry about; this baby was definitely Prudhomme's, she bragged.

Cecelia walked away and tried to count backwards. She placed her hand over her own swollen expectancy to calm herself. Could Stansfield have fathered Dinah's child? She struggled with the thought because she could not accurately pinpoint any dates or months. She was crestfallen the rest of the day.

By nightfall, she fretted.

Her baby moved.

She heard the ceaseless hooting of an owl.

#

The inconsequential wedding was over. Dinah's pregnancy, now in its final trimester had fooled none of the guests even though she wore a billowing white empire-waist gown. The sun shone through the inexpensive cotton and revealed the maternal silhouette. Her father escorted her down the yellow sheets that lay upon the grass. Dinah moved awkwardly toward the waiting Delacourte.

Dinah gave birth to a black baby boy.

Her husband, with rage, killed her with a pistol before the horrified black midwife could clean up the afterbirth. Mrs. Thomason present at the scene was overcome with grief and shame. Delacorte was arrested and taken to the town jail though conventional wisdom would free him based on the circumstances. Dinah had violated the Slave Codes by sleeping with Stansfield, a black man.

Stansfield entreated Cecelia to believe that Dinah's baby was not his. He told her she was a whore and he only lay with her twice——once to get the credentials he coveted, and when she had actually given him the letters of introduction. He stressed to Cecelia how he routinely withdrew himself even when they made love. He told Cecelia that she was the only woman in the world who had caught his seed.

The Cricket Cries, the Year Changes

Stansfield was jailed for breaking the Slave Codes that applied to free black men as well. He asserted his innocence and demanded a lawyer.

Cecelia went into a free fall.

She was not sure what to believe. She had learned through recently overheard conversations that Dinah had followed Stansfield to Boston.

\#

At the funeral, Cecelia spied Mrs. Thomason holding the dark baby against her white skin with her eyes toward heaven. Her freckled red chest, laden with grief, heaved back and forth.

Cecelia hid behind a tree and peered into the face of the baby that cried that familiar newborn cry. It did not bear any resemblance to Stansfield. The child's hair was too straight and his tiny hands were almost dainty looking.

Just then, Delacourte, escorted by two sheriffs, joined the services. He was nattily dressed and not handcuffed, and had a distant look in his eyes. He appeared to be inconvenienced. Rumors alleged that he would not be charged with Dinah's murder. It would be ruled as justifiable.

When she saw him, Mrs. Thomason screamed. She was consumed by his audacity. The baby fell to the ground when she flung her arms into the air with revulsion. Thomason glared at Delacorte for a split second. Then he rushed to his wife's side. She lay sprawled on the ground frozen and twisted. She had stretched her arms toward the shrieking baby. Thomason noticed her mouth was askew and her eyes were glazed over. Later that evening, most learned that she had suffered a stroke.

Delacorte left town.

Chapter 6

Thomason allowed Cecelia to visit Stansfield at the small jailhouse because she promised to give him her authentic dye recipes. Stansfield remained adamant about his brief relationship with Dinah. Cecelia shared her thoughts about the baby not bearing any of his features. She asked Stansfield to give her the name of a banker who could verify who Delacorte really was. She would get someone to inquire, if Stansfield penned the request. Unbeknownst to her and Stansfield, Mr. Thomason had launched his own inquiry.

Thomason soon redirected his grief toward Cecelia, because Stansfield, her cheating husband, was responsible for the loss of his wife and his strumpet daughter. Perhaps if she finally faced Stansfield's betrayal, Cecelia could turn against him and Harris and stay on with him, he schemed.

Cecelia, very distressed, waited nervously for any news to come back that could free Stansfield. She sank into a dysfunctional depression. She was over-burdened by all of the tumultuous events. Cecelia put off the dyeing of the cotton. She remained in the cabin all day. She tripped and fell on the grounds by night. She constantly drew imaginary circles around her stomach with her fingers. Her ear piercing screams summoned rings of protection from her ancestors for Stansfield and their child.

The overseer, who had the altercation with Stansfield when he was first taken to see Cecelia, reported to Thomason that his dyemaker was now a maniac. Thomason had her beaten severely, despite her eighth month pregnancy.

Weeks later, word reached Stansfield in jail about the condition of his wife. She had gone into premature labor and had given birth to a stillborn baby girl. No one assisted her with the delivery. Thomason would not permit it. An aggrieved Stansfield banged his head against the bars until he passed out.

Cecelia had cremated the tiny bundle and poured its ashes into the small clay pot that Stansfield had brought to her. She was determined to take her baby back home with her.

The Cricket Cries, the Year Changes

#

Stansfield bargained with a black slave to assume his identity with his papers that would make him a free man. In exchange, the slave allowed Stansfield to be released on bond to his master in his stead. Stansfield had brought the papers with him when he was arrested. He had hoped the contents would give him credibility. The man readily agreed to switch places. To the guards, all niggers looked alike to them. Stansfield easily escaped to the Thomason place.

Cynthia Harris-Allen

#

Stansfield arrived at the Thomason plantation at night. His head was wrapped in a now dried bloodied piece of rag. One of his eyes was but a slit and his nose was broken. The injuries were the summation of the anger he had vented upon the wrought iron jailhouse bars. He had a massive headache.

As he entered the cabin, he saw Cecelia bent over in a pile of grief. He gingerly lifted her as if she was a cloud not wanting to place his arms through her lest she would completely evaporate. He whispered in her ear that he was home. Cecelia jerked in his arms at the recognition of his voice and opened her eyes. When she began to wail, he covered her mouth with his hand to quiet her and not disturb the night. He rocked her in his arms as he used to do.

Stansfield privately cursed the fragmented pieces of their lives now lost forever. He wanted to know which one was the dream. Which was the nightmare? He questioned if they were one in the same.

At nightfall, slaves assisted him in hiding Cecelia in the back of a wagon that was already loaded for a mill stop. He would take her back to the Harris-Jones plantation, setting aside the threats upon his life by his former associates.

During the journey, Stansfield attempted to nourish Cecelia and build up her strength. His headaches had subsided but his head banging had blurred the vision in his right eye. The long trek did not show much improvement in her condition. The arrowheads of physical, mental, and emotional anguish had pierced her too-long-waiting and wounded heart. Stansfield was never accosted on the road. Those that passed him by noticed a wagonload of dried corn with a very tired Negro at the reins.

#

A drunken Thomason sat on his porch and sipped more scotch from a flask. He was contemplating selling the plantation and moving north. His health was failing. His little black grandson was given to a slave on another plantation with the stipulation that he never have to see him again. His Thomason birthright was stricken from all records.

The Cricket Cries, the Year Changes

He uncrossed his legs to watch a garter snake climb over his other shoe. Just then, one of his indentured servants brought the mail to him. He was not expecting anything of any consequence. He had ceased his active business negotiations after he had to pay Harris the price for the loss of Cecelia. Stansfield had stolen her. Because he violated the contract, Thomason also had to relinquish his ownership of the slaves that he had lent to Harris. Harris had made sure that a double indemnity clause was written into their contract.

He was still receiving notes of condolences from family, friends, and former business associates. A thick envelope, with the return address of the bank that he had requested to reinstate Stansfield, was at the bottom of the pile. He opened the letter to learn that Prudhomme Delacourte was an itinerant poker player of no means wanted in Boston for not making good on a huge gambling debt.

More importantly, to Thomason's astonishment, Delacorte was a runaway Creole slave from a New Orleans cane-producing plantation! He was used as a breeder. He had fathered over twenty children of various hues in his first five years as a stud.

The letter enclosed a tattered slave bill that was posted when he ran away to the North twenty years ago. It bore the youthful description of the man that had ruined Thomason's life. The yellowed, fading notice had been inked long ago by M. Stansfield Print Shoppe of Boston, Massachusetts.

Chapter 7

The wagon passed under the arched entrance with the wrought iron initials "H-J" perched high above the trellis. The tired horse rounded the long path toward the spacious plantation,

With the corn haul long gone, Stansfield coaxed a backwards smile towards Cecelia. "Welcome home, my love" he sighed, tenderly.

Cecelia lay still on her side atop blankets covered with the empty sacks that once held the corn. She could scarcely hear Stansfield's voice. It was a gray dawn, chilly——but peaceful. The soft wind whispered as it repeatedly sent the vapor trails from the horse's mouth into the void.

Cecelia opened her weak, red eyes to her very own Jonah. She mimed through chapped cracked lips a soft "Thank you" and died.

The earth stopped moving for Stansfield. He sat frozen to her image. He stared blankly into the red clays of their beginning. He leaned back and touched Cecelia's still warm body. His hand traced the round cold vessel that held his little girl.

Stansfield pulled his derringer from his boot. He jumped from the slowing wagon. His pins-and-needled legs guided him towards the thicket at the fringe of the entrance. Hot tears stung his eyes as he ran toward his ending.

The weary horse sluggishly plodded the worn pathway towards Cecelia's home. The driverless cart, once a sanctuary was now a servant's hearse. It stopped about two miles from the mansion and stayed there for two days in the rain until a visitor came upon it.

Kaffie personally oversaw the burial of Cecelia along with the clay pot that had to be pried from her stiff, steeled hand. She made sure she was buried in her own hand-dyed cotton fabrics. Cecelia was wrapped like a mummy that had suddenly tripped over a rainbow. The small vessel was placed next to her face. It would receive her first kiss from her mother in the afterlife.

The Cricket Cries, the Year Changes

Kaffie, in her numbed reaction to her friend's death, could not remember how she got through the ordeal. She took part of the indigo-pieced remnant that wrapped Cecelia's head at the funeral to use in her quilt.

Cynthia Harris-Allen

BARBURY

Chapter 1

A white indentured milkmaid named Lottie loved Barbury, a Senegalese slave. Barbury did not appreciate her advances. He avoided her whenever he could; but when they did cross paths, he would control their conversations with short trite chatter. He was in love with his wife, Chenzy.

Lottie had many opportunities to be near Barbury because the milk cows were located in the barn, just a stone's throw away from where he worked. She toiled alongside the younger slave girls. They rose before dawn to relieve the cows of their white bounty. Rows and rows of empty metal pails stood at the ready each morning to be filled with the creamy beige liquid. The milkmaids sat face-to-udder on wooden stools. They made sure that warm hands made their first touch to the teat.

There was little talk among the milking group—except for Lottie. She maintained a daily level of friction with the black female slaves. Her false claims always within their earshot of having gone often "into the bushes" with Barbury was getting on their nerves. She boasted that he preferred her kind to his own and that he came looking for her every day. Occasionally, she would slip into another Barbury "story," so-called by the slave women, as she spilled lies about their sexual encounters. The slaves chuckled and clicked their teeth in disbelief while they sneered, "the po' white gurl" with their rolling eyes.

Lottie prattled endlessly about leaving the plantation when her time was done and "marrying up". She said she would not have to work hard ever again like a slave had to until the day they died. She curled her lips and scoffed that they did not even have a life. They might as well be worker bees or worker ants or worker "somethins", she would jeer.

Often, the slaves avenged her ridicule and sarcasm by putting dirt into her milk-filled pails. They "accidently" tilted one or two of them over at the very instant the driver would come in to count the number of units produced per person. Lottie's sub-performance was punished with an increase in the number of buckets of milk she had to provide the next morning.

The Cricket Cries, the Year Changes

Barbury worked in the slaughterhouse. He processed the animals for market by killing them first in the pens, stalls, and stockades. He singlehandedly carried a hog or dragged dead-weight cows to the barn. He disjointed them and salvaged the separated bodies for optimum use. Young slave children rushed to the pens when they heard that Barbury was going to kill pigs. They gleefully watched him as he chased, caught, and roped the plump pinkish porkers.

Barbury was a huge African, whose upper torso was shaped like the letter "V". A full expansive chest and musclebound arms assisted the mammoth hands that wielded the large knives. He did not wear a shirt when he worked. Instead, a long leather apron hung from his neck to below his knees. A double layer of pants shielded his legs from the droppings of animal entrails and blood on his skin.

He received an allotment of four pair of brogans a year due to the wear and tear from the beasts, blood, and bones. Barbury wore huge colorful kerchiefs tied around his head. His wife, Chenzy, made sure he wore a fresh one each day. Her ritual was to beat the fabric pieces upon the rocks down by the riverside. She rinsed away the remnants of his day's labor. It was her last chore before she retired for the night. Chenzy worked in the fields where she planted beans and watermelon. She never saw Barbury until nightfall. Inside their cabin, she greeted him with her body and a fresh clean head kerchief.

\#

Barbury did not kill many animals at once. Storage of the meats had to be a consideration. One method of drying it called "jerking," was the most expeditious way to prolong its shelf life. Other methods used were salting and smoking the beef and pork, a process mostly done by the slave women. Barbury oversaw the rendering of the fat from the animals. Huge pots that boiled the animal tissue at extremely high heat all day long were positioned just outside of the slaughterhouse.

Young slave kids stockpiled wood near the kettles that stood over five feet high from the ground. The blacks stood on weathered wooden stools and stirred the hot fatty contents in the pots. One of them was Barbury's son, Charlie. The cauldrons were placed atop wrought ironed grates. The kindling wood was shoved beneath it. The exhausted fires cooled to copper-colored embers. The mixture hardened throughout the night. In the morning, the solidified fat floated to the surface. It was removed and mixed with lye for soap or candle making.

#

Oftentimes, Barbury accompanied a driver to meat auctions in various nearby towns. The slaves herded the animals on foot. The owners rented stalls for the weekend to carry out this method of slaughter-and-sale to fetch the highest prices. Lottie asked to ride along on occasion. She sat in the front of the wagon and turned her head repeatedly to look at Barbury. She pretended that the forward-blowing Georgia clay dust had irritated her eyes.

Cannon Bowles was the driver on one of those trips. He warned Lottie to keep her gaze forward or he would put her out of the wagon. He glanced backwards with a menacing scowl only to find Barbury fast asleep.

Lottie's was in servitude because she committed robberies at a homestead in Macon, Georgia where she helped the cooks. She stole jewelry from the mistress of the house. Guests who had lodged there, found their trunks broken into while they were away socializing or sight-seeing. On occasion, money was taken from the inside pockets of clothing that belonged to the visitors by Lottie under the pretense of having to launder them.

When questioned by the slaveholder, Dane Johnson, Lottie denied any involvement and directed blame toward the slaves who lived there as the real thieves. Johnson knew that money was worthless to a slave. Where could they spend it and when? It would arouse suspicion if any slave showed up at a general store with money without a list from their master and no traveling papers. He had thirty slaves, most of whom he had owned for years. He had maintained a good relationship with them. He did not allow any physical punishment.

In this relatively peaceful environment Johnson knew that Lottie was the individual that had committed the robberies. They had not occurred until she had arrived, due to a court order, to do time as an unpaid servant. Johnson petitioned the judge, his brother-in-law, to move this thief elsewhere. Harris, unaware of Lottie's past, did the judge a favor.

Chapter 2

Cannon Bowles shifted Lottie's attention away from Barbury. As a homely young woman, she was flattered by Bowles' tokens of candy, cheap jewelry, and short strands of silk ribbon that he exchanged for sex. Bowles only wanted to weaken and wrest her pining away from Barbury. He just wanted her not to like niggers. To him, she was just another flat back on the ground.

Lottie soon realized that neither man was attracted to her. She took revenge by creating lies that Barbury and Bowles hated each other because they both vied for her attention. She hatched the rumor that Barbury had used negative descriptive terms about Bowles' small private parts. It became a common traveling joke among the slaves that soon fell upon his ears.

Early one morning, accompanied by three huge white men, Bowles waited until Barbury went into the slaughterhouse. They entered and tied his wrists to hooks that normally held slabs of meat and whipped him. Surprised and severely pained by the altercation, Barbury fell to the animal blood-soaked straw floor and gasped for air.

Lottie heard the melee and ran towards the slaughterhouse as she knocked over three milk-filled pails. She entered the area. Barbury was on his knees and struggled to get the leather ties loosed from his wrists. Lottie used one of the many knives to free him. She was remorseful that she had caused Barbury real pain; she reached out to help him to stand up. Barbury cursed her and pushed her hard toward the swinging knives. One of the blades cut a deep angled gash near her right temple. Lottie screamed. He yelled at her that he knew why he was beaten because Bowles in his fury had mentioned what lies she had spread. Barbury told Lottie to stay away from him or he would kill her.

Bowles spied Lottie as she ran from the barn. To him, she looked as if the lovers had had a tiff when she tried to sop off the blood from Barbury's bullwhipped back and arms. Bowles smirked. He decided to pay a visit to Barbury's wife.

\#

The Cricket Cries, the Year Changes

Chenzy sang softly to herself in her place in the rows. Over thirty other field hands in that section of the plantation surrounded her. She walked to a fully ripened watermelon, stooped to inspect the lower bottom that touched the ground and assured by its yellow coloring, separated it from its vine. Young slave boys pulled wagons between the watermelon patches and placed the chosen ones onto the carts. The stronger youth opted to carry two or three of the green-striped ovals upon wide shoulders and placed them at the end of the rows.

A hot, harvesting sun had born down on the fields all day long. The monotonous sound of the hoes, picks and grunts would often be interrupted by a driver's whip. It cracked the air and hurried the already frenetic pace of the reapers. Chenzy stopped briefly to wipe the salty dripping sweat from her eyes. She was very tired. The sun had begun to set. She motioned to the water bearer to allow her a drink from the gourd.

She shielded her eyes to regain her place in the row of watermelons. As she resumed her bent over position, the sting of a whip laced her lower back. Chenzy hollered. The overseer, Bowles ordered her to step outside of the row. She painfully moved into the open. He chastised her for holding up the pace of the harvest and for not asking for permission to get a drink of water. Other slaves continued to work with picks down—— but eyes up.

Chenzy explained that she was thirsty and she never had been "whupped befoe." She implored the overseer to excuse her. She then moved back into her place in the row and resumed her work. That gesture incensed Bowles. He thought that she was just as bold in her manner as her husband was. He dismounted from his horse, formed a slipknot with his whip and wrapped it around her neck. He towed her to the back of a barn as the lash tightened with each step.

Bowles raped the tripping and defiant body that was petrified with fright. Chenzy did not resist nor respond, but instead, stared directly into Bowles's eyes. As he pulled on his drawstring pants he warned her to tell her husband to stay away from Lottie the milkmaid. He held his boot on her thigh and whipped her again——this time with more lashes than one. He kicked Chenzy in the ribs and ordered her to return to her spot in the rows.

Her legs were weak. Her thighs bore bruises that showed Bowles's hands had restrained them towards the ground like two opposing dinner bells. The back of her dress smelled of cow manure. Bowles had thrown her onto the pile after he had slapped her face. As she walked back towards the fields, a driver blew the bugle that signaled that work was over for that evening. It had grown too dark to continue.

Chenzy then turned her weakened body toward the river to wash Barbury's head kerchiefs. When she reached the semi-deserted bank, she knelt, placed her head under the water, and screamed. She released giant bubbles of rage and humiliation into the dark.

The Cricket Cries, the Year Changes

Chapter 3

Chenzy looked upon Barbury with a different eye ever since the incident. She had ceased her fabric-beating ritual for three months now. She did not want to believe what Bowles had told her. She did consider her husband's unfaithfulness a possibility because Lottie worked near him. However, their son, Charlie, was around his father all day.

She countered her own inner thoughts on whether to trust Barbury or not. She knew her husband kept his feelings to himself. She sometimes would watch him as he sat in deep thought without any outward displays of emotion. She asked herself if tricks of the mind always weakened trust in the heart.

Barbury worked well into the nights; he was too tired to consider the change in his wife's behavior. Soon, that did not remain the larger issue.

Chenzy visited Ngango on a Sunday. She entered his raised mud hut and sat on the straw floor. Master Harris had allowed Ngango to erect this structure in the middle of the slave quarters. He knew that this practitioner was trusted and revered by the majority of the slaves——even those from other plantations. Ngango cured the sick, both physical and mental. His potions, libations, amulets, charms, and balm were steeped in ancestral ministerial traditions. Harris let him be.

Chenzy asked Ngango for something to kill the baby inside of her. She told him of the rape by Bowles and insisted that she had just finished her "moon time" two weeks before it happened. She interjected that she had not slept with Barbury since the incident and she was positive the child was not his. She relayed the warning Bowles gave her about Barbury and Lottie.

Ngango asked Chenzy if she had told Barbury about the rape. She replied that she had not. The all-knowing Ngango pressed a root bag into the palm of her hand. Chenzy thanked him and left. Ngango grunted.

#

On an unusually chilly morning, slave children shivered as they stockpiled wood near the cauldrons. Their

199

vaporous breaths temporarily dotted the air. They had to wait for the wagons to port the solid fat chunks to the soap house and replace emptied kettles atop the grates. As was their routine, the young boys hoisted themselves onto the rims of the heavy pots to peer inside. The boys would use sticks to gouge out portions of fat and give it to their parents to cook with or to make soap.

One of them straddled Charlie's shoulders to peek inside the vat. He screamed like a girl. He jumped from his temporary perch and ran towards the fields. Charlie fetched a stool and asked another slave boy to hold his hand so he could look into the cauldron without falling in.

The head of a white girl leaned on its side; it was stuck in solid animal fat and stared blankly into nothingness. The skin had been partially removed by the searing heat of the grease. The straw-colored hair lay in snaggy patches on the head. Blue and white gingham fabric was draped in the lard-like layers. A huge gash on her face was filled with the sinewy dotted residuals of the melted fat.

Charlie was speechless. He sprung back and stepped slowly off the stool. Some of the boys viewed the gore and laughed while the sight frightened others. They climbed the stool in turns to cast brief looks upon the truncated piece. Soon, crowds of slaves had gathered at the slaughterhouse. The milkmaids had just finished their duties and converged on the site.

The incoming wagon was about twenty feet away. The crowd of slaves had blocked its normal pathway with their curiosity. The driver drew his whip and popped it twice into the air and commanded the pedestrians to disperse. He then fired his rifle into the air to signal that help was needed in the area. Overseers quickly responded as they rode on horseback to retrieve the slaves who were not at their field posts and to investigate the commotion.

Barbury had just arrived at the butchery. His leather apron was still draped over his shoulder. He made his way through the noisy crowd. Some were familiar with the rumors about him and Lottie. They began to grow silent as Barbury approached the cauldron. He towered over the pot. His over six-foot six-inch frame loomed closer with his hands clasped behind his back. He knew instantly that the head belonged to Lottie.

The Cricket Cries, the Year Changes

With no reaction, he silently walked towards the slaughterhouse to begin his work. His son, Charlie followed him.

Inside, they exchanged questioning glances of "what the hell?"

Cynthia Harris-Allen

Chapter 4

Lottie's body lay sunken into the solid fat. Master Harris was riled at such a brutal act set upon a human being by another. He considered how his own reputation as a slave owner and custodian to indentured servants would be impugned by such a horrific deed. He had Lottie's remains cremated. Her room in the white servant's quarters was purged of any personal items. It bore no trace that she had ever lived there.

Harris convened a meeting with his drivers and overseers to determine what led up to Lottie's death. While they ate, Cannon Bowles was the first to speak to Harris. He recounted that Barbury was accosting Lottie. He said Lottie had confided in him that she was afraid of the black butcher. He said she told him many times she was left alone in the milking barn to make up for the pails of milk that the slave workers had knocked over on purpose. Barbury conveniently raped her repeatedly, he said.

It is quite possible that during that time, Barbury could have had access to her, Bowles guessed. He then apologized to Master Harris for not protecting Lottie. The house slaves continued to serve dinner to the men in attendance. They exchanged knowing glances with one another as they acknowledged the ridiculous yarn that was spun by Bowles.

Master Harris warned the men not to react to this event on their own. He would handle Barbury himself. He insisted that news of this murder stay contained on his land. He intended to talk with Barbury after his return from a two-week vacation up north with his wife, Tillie and daughter, Luvinia.

#

A week later, Bowles went to see Barbury in the slaughterhouse. He entered and stood near the knife racks and said nothing. The smell of fresh animal blood, mixed with manure and rotted pieces of stray animal flesh, invaded his nostrils. The barn floor was filled with bones both large and small that lay in various piles.

Barbury's tools included iron mallets, paring knives, bone saws, and the large, square-shaped blades of the cleavers. Most of the instruments were forged and sharpened by Scipio. Barbury had heard from the house slaves what Bowles had said about him and Lottie. He struggled to keep his composure while he beheaded a hog in one fell swoop. He threw the head toward the pile of pieced carcasses that would be gleaned for whatever purpose, in Bowles's direction. The large animal with its eyes still in their sockets stared up at Bowles as blood and tissue began to seep onto the floor.

Barbury stood still and glared at Bowles. He hoped that the gesture would signal to him that the same thing that had happened to Lottie could also happen to him. Barbury rammed the bloody cleaver into the butcher's block and walked toward Bowles. The handle of the tool still quivered from the force. He was considerably taller than the overseer was. He stopped within two feet of him and folded his arms over his leather apron; his chest heaved under the soiled slimy sanguine wrap. Bowles tightened his hand on the grip of the whip and wished he had not come there alone.

Charlie entered the butchery, with three squealing pigs in his arms. He informed his father that the cook, Sue Anne, needed them slaughtered right away. Bowles seized the opportunity to walk backwards as he exited the barn. Each slow boot step searched for a clear unobstructed exit as he and Barbury continued to message with their eyes a mutual contempt.

#

Within three days, Bowles had to take Barbury to town to slaughter and sell cattle at the behest of Master Harris. Bowles brought along five other men; four that included himself sat in the flatbed wagon as they surrounded Barbury. The cattle were herded to the city a week ago. Barbury slept most of the way atop his bag of knives. Bowles was vexed by the overt silent signals of naked hatred that Barbury often bared towards him. He soon realized that this nigger did not fear him at all. He anxiously waited for the time that Barbury would attempt to avenge his attack on Chenzy. Then he would have a chance to kill him in self-defense.

Master Harris had stressed to Bowles that there was not going to be any confrontation of any kind with his slave——on the plantation or away from it. Nevertheless, Bowles chafed at the bit. The slaughter was conducted without incident.

On the return trip from the sale, it began to rain. In fact, a severe thunderstorm had already cracked trees and flooded the clay roadways. The wagon had slowed considerably, unable to traverse the mud-filled furrows. A huge tree branch had fallen across the road. Bowles ordered everyone out of the wagon and told Barbury to remove the object that had blocked their path. Barbury reluctantly tried; he did not use his full body strength on purpose.

Bowles, sopping wet, yelled to Barbury that he would whip him well into next week if he did not do what he was told. Barbury, tired from that day's slaughter, shouted over the wind and rain to Bowles to have his "protection detail" help; he could only do what he could by himself. Bowles knew that whipping Barbury in the rain would not affect him at all. He also recalled Harris' warning to him to do no harm. Bowles stood down. He demanded that the five white men move the log. The men cursed at Bowles. They taunted him and asked him who was actually in charge.

Barbury stood and watched.

After the road was cleared and all were back in the wagon, the rain began to pelt the group. Lightning blazed the fields, lit the darkening skies, and frightened the team of four horses. Large hail stung the men as they cowered in the open carriage. Bowles was angered that he could not seize an opportunity to hurt Barbury. He could not make sure which body was his in the dark under the mounds of coarse blankets.

Silence prevailed during the remainder of the trip. It was early evening. The wind and rain had slackened. When the wagon turned that ninety-degree angle onto the plantation entrance, Barbury jumped from it with his tool sack in tow. He splashed mud up to his knees. He walked toward the slave cabins. The rain had subsided and left the humid, muggy air as its R.S.V.P. Birds and insect life, that had taken shelter from the all-day storm chose this small opportunity to feed or be fed upon.

Bowles sat next to the driver of the wagon. He hollered hoarsely to Barbury to ask his wife who was the real boss. He tossed an empty jug of rum from the wagon to the ground. Barbury stopped to consider why Bowles would say such a thing. His heart quickened. He would ask Chenzy what this white man meant.

Chapter 5

It was Sunday and the slaves had their free day off. Some attended the white church services that preached servitude as their God-given duty. Others showed reverence to their own gods. People socialized in the fields and fashioned quick picnics on the spacious grounds. Ngango meted out ointments and bandages to the weary and field-wounded workers. Children were entertained by stories reenacted by the griot, Amidou.

This was the day of rest. It temporarily blotted out the previous six days of toil, trouble, and torment. The slaves used every inch of every second of Sundays to reconcile themselves to humanity. There was a relieved sense of calm as always on that day. The slaves were virtually free from hard labor for twenty-four hours. Many of them gathered at the river to refresh themselves in the waters.

It was a perfect morning——not a cloud in the sky. The sun seemed to shine with a grace that was foreign to them. Usually, Ole Sol would bring incessant heat to bear when they planted or harvested or rested, but this day was a cool azure blue.

There were only two guards at opposite ends of the river. They nonchalantly oversaw the activities. They sat relaxed atop their horses. Occasionally, the men shifted positions to have a panoramic view of the plantation activities. They engaged in idle conversation with some of the slaves. They gave little children black scrap, the shards from hardened molasses as treats. The slaves' day off was the guards' day off as well. Even the horses they sat upon had one eye closed refusing to swat flies with their lazy tails.

Without warning, a band of patrollers who had hidden in the thickets unnoticed overnight, charged toward the fifty or so slaves at the riverbank.

They jumped from their horses while others ran on foot toward the shocked blacks. They positioned themselves between them and the two overseers. They shot and killed the guards. Soon slaves that included those who could not swim were randomly heaved into the deeper parts of the river. Smaller children were held under the water until their heads bobbed listlessly. Their gasping-mouthed bodies collided with others whose eyes were frozen open with hysteria.

The river was filled with blood from the banged heads and limbs that had hit craggy rocks when they were hurled aimlessly into the once placid liquid. Family members screamed and scrambled to attempt to rescue their loved ones.

The invaders tied ropes around the necks of seven older slave men who were immersed in their Sunday cowrie shell game. The assailants hoisted the frail necks upon nearby tree branches. Young slave men who were fishing from the banks ran toward the elderly. They got on all fours and used their backs for the weak and highly frantic men to stand upon to keep from being choked to death. Some of the old blacks kicked the step-stooled help out of the way. They preferred to die, unable to fight for their people.

The attackers moved on to other targets. They dragged slave women by any limb that they could grab, over rocks and hard ground toward the stockades. They gathered the huddled shrieking females together and threw lamp oil onto their clothing and into their hair. In solidarity, the women joined hands and arms and sealed their fate with a show of unity and resolve. With lit torches near the hems of their clothing, the raiders demanded to see Barbury else they would incinerate them. None came forward. Soon the screams ceased.

Negroes, who had quickly armed themselves with broomsticks, hoes, shovels and even chains, began to fight with the white men. Though they outnumbered the patrollers, their weapons were no match to gunpowder, knives, and barbarism. Many slaves were killed; but some had managed to murder a few of the whites that had breached the Sunday peace. Ten of the women in the pens were burned to death. Others suffered severe burns.

The entire scene was punctuated by the agonizing yells from the dying or wounded. The sporadic gunfire that muted the power of the harvesting tools was set against the frenzied drumbeats that alarmed the entire plantation. The sun no longer shined.

Barbury was away at another slaughter.

Cynthia Harris-Allen

\#

Master Harris and his family were within sight of their home that same evening. He could see smoke that appeared to rise from unfamiliar places. He heard the urgent drum communiques of his slaves as he had never heard before. The slaves beat boards, sticks or rocks to message the melee. Some of them had whipped their own bodies with any object that could produce a sound.

Harris ordered the driver of the covered wagon to speed up. When he grew impatient with the pace of the horses he halted the wagon. He removed one of the horses from the team and rode it bareback toward his plantation. It was dead calm until he reached the river.

As he reigned in the horse, he saw slaves bent over their dead loved ones whose faces were covered with ragged cloths supplied by the crying mothers who had ripped their skirts in agony. His eyes darted toward the trees just by the river. Torches, lanterns, and tears bore witness to the seven elderly slaves who were hanged. Their bodies in frayed, ill-fitting clothing moved with the earth.

Harris drew his pistol and shot it five times into the air. He startled the horse and caused it to bolt. The horse threw Harris to the muddied and bloodied ground and ran off. He shot the gun once again. He relieved the chamber of its last bullet to summon his drivers, overseers——anyone to the sound of the gun and his wailing cries. His shock tripled with the gory sight of his slave girls and women. Some lay on the ground partially burned and in excruciating pain. Others lay dead and unrecognizable. Their clothing had melted into blackened skins. They lay contorted in the yards.

Harris' eyes stung with briny tears of anger and inconsolable woe.

The Cricket Cries, the Year Changes

Chapter 6

To his alarm, Master Harris learned the next morning that there were quite a few unaccounted slaves. He suspended the fieldwork and immediately oversaw the counting of his slaves that also included the hanged, drowned and burned. Come evening, it was revealed to him that about forty-three slaves had run off during the pandemonium. All totaled, ninety-six slaves had been lost. Master Harris did not know the names of the missing yet. He decided to allow the slaves to bury their loved ones so the healing process could begin before he launched a full inquiry.

The slaves held a singular funeral for all the lost. The griot wept for the drowned children that had listened to his stories. He tried in vain to comfort their parents, whose swollen eyes and hearts silently spoke of the enormous grief within that awaited its calamitous release. Slaves toiled in the Ole Field; they dug deep holes to accommodate members of entire families.

Ngango stood in the midst of the circled bonfires and threw red dust over the remains. Some slaves had their loved ones cremated. They wanted the ashes returned to the river. He stood motionless wearing only a loincloth. He had not accessorized his body with henna tattoos, feathers or masks, as was his custom in the past when he mourned. Instead, he had cut deep symbols with a knife into his chest, thighs, and arms that only he knew the meaning. Ngango moved closer to the fires and coaxed it to sear the raw open wounds that were patterned in angled lines all over his body. He never spoke a word nor uttered a sound. The slaves were afraid to approach him. They had never seen him in this state before.

There was no celebratory homegoing with dancing and singing and dining. There was too much grief and not enough comfort to go around.

Master Harris attempted to get to the root cause of the siege. He wanted to know why there were no sentries posted at the perimeters of the plantation, and why they were asking specifically for Barbury. He learned from one of the five men who had accompanied Cannon Bowles to the slaughter auction with Barbury that recently the two had had harsh words on the way back to Monroe. The man told Harris that Bowles had made a derogatory statement to Barbury about his wife. Harris had an overseer bring Chenzy to him.

#

As they sat on the porch of the mansion, Harris assured Chenzy that he was only trying to find out what had caused the violent acts three days ago. She told him that she was whipped and raped by Bowles, in retaliation for her husband having feelings for Lottie. She said Lottie had lied that she slept with her husband; it just was not possible.

Stunned by these new accounts, he asked her if she knew of any direct confrontation between Barbury and Bowles. She responded that after Barbury returned from the last trip, he had asked her if Bowles had touched her in any way. Chenzy assured Master Harris she did not tell her husband Bowles had raped her but somehow or in some way, he had found out. She wept that Barbury knew it had happened because her tears had betrayed her when he questioned her.

Harris pieced this ongoing feud together as he interwove these new slim details with what had been told to him earlier. He had no clue that the hatred between the two had cut this deeply. Privately, he cursed himself for allowing Bowles to drive Barbury to the slaughtering auctions. It had to be a true test of endurance for the both of them as they sat within striking distance of one another for miles on end, he thought.

He dismissed Chenzy and told her to gather her belongings and her son, Charlie. He was sending them to Sumatra, Florida to work on another plantation. He said it was for her safety and the well-being of his other slaves. They were to leave the next day. Chenzy, numbed by the immediate relocation, nodded and excused herself. Her body trembled as she walked to her cabin.

Months later, Harris learned that several of the thirty missing slaves had escaped to Mexico. This country had abolished slavery not too long ago. It had become a not-so-distant safe harbor for runaway southern slaves. He could do nothing about it at this time.

The Cricket Cries, the Year Changes

Master Harris allowed Barbury to stay on the plantation. He had returned from slaughtering a week after Chenzy and Charlie were sold to another plantation. The aggrieved butcher pleaded with Harris to let him join his family. He was dumbfounded to hear what had happened in his absence. He told Harris he had nothing to do with Lottie's death.

He lamented those lost in the carnage; but he was relieved that his family was still alive though now many miles from his safe embrace. Harris promised Barbury if he showed other slaves and whites his slaughterhouse methods in true form he would let him join his wife and son in Florida.

Three years went by. Harris' prolonged, protracted promises to Barbury went unfulfilled. Barbury had only received word twice about the welfare of his wife and son. He had co-operated and taught others to master the skills of a butcher. He overheard that Harris was more than satisfied with the results. Barbury grew bitter and distant because of Harris' broken pledge.

Rockfield Stiles convinced Harris to allow Barbury to leave.

\#

Sue Anne, the house cook, drew up Barbury's travel papers. She had had a relationship with Cannon Bowles long before Harris had him arrested, convicted, and jailed for the murders of his property.

Harris concluded that Bowles planned the raid and Lottie's death presumably to frame Barbury. Bowles had given the sentries that fateful Sunday off with pay with money apparently stolen from the sale of meat at the slaughters. This information came from those who explained to Harris why they were not at their posts. The identities of the few whites who had been killed during the raid revealed that they were Bowles' poker partners from outside the plantation.

Sue Anne vengefully stale-dated the papers for Barbury's departure. The contrived error would have Barbury off the plantation unauthorized as soon as he left its boundaries.

The Cricket Cries, the Year Changes

Chapter 7

Barbury traveled southward by wagon and on foot with some of his tools in a sack. He jumped onto a barge and quickly showed his prowess. He butchered the animals that were transported along the Atlantic coast. He continued this type of work for four months as he inched towards Florida.

One morning Barbury was approached as he walked a dirt road near the Florida-Georgia line by patrollers who demanded to see his papers. He gladly retrieved them from his shirt and offered them as proof that he was allowed to travel to Sumatra, Florida. He bragged that Master Harris was one of the richest landowners in northern Georgia. He hoped that they would not sense his false allegiance.

The paperwork, however, indicated that Barbury should have been back on the Harris-Jones plantation months ago. Fearing retaliation from the long reach of Harris if they harmed this slave, the bounty hunters returned Barbury to the plantation. Harris was angered and refused to pay a bounty to the three men. He claimed that Barbury was not a runaway and a mistake was made in the papers.

Harris allowed a frustrated and exasperated Barbury to leave the plantation again after two days' rest. This time, Harris made sure that everything was in order. Kaffie had given Barbury two extra flannel shirts made from blue and gray plaid fabric, along with a new blanket. The patrollers had thrown his knapsack in the river when they arrested him. She wished him safe passage. She reminded him to give her love to his family.

Barbury left at sunrise with brand new butchering tools and never looked back.

#

C.H., a troublesome slave, on the Harris-Jones plantation, had to be whipped for resistance, insolence, and robbery. He spent a lot of time in the jailhouse that Harris had erected on the plantation. Harris told him this was the last time he would whip him and place him in jail. He warned C.H., that when he did the next slightest wrong thing, he would "put him in his pocket," which meant that the slave would be sold probably, "down river". C.H managed to escape that very night.

Harris' runaway bill described the slave as tall and thin, clothed in Russia sheeting trousers, mismatched shoes and a head kerchief. He was last seen wearing a blue and white plaid flannel shirt, far too big for his frame. Harris placed a larger than normal reward for C.H.'s capture, dead or alive. In fact, he made it a point to himself if he was returned alive he planned to have him lynched at the Hanging Day picnic at the Dunne plantation.

Hanging Day picnics served as a reminder to all would-be or repeat runaways what fate awaited them. Slaveholders had collectively held back about fifteen to twenty recaptured runaways to hang during this annual event.

#

Bounty hunters came upon Barbury as he sat in a wagon in front of a general store. The driver had gone in to purchase supplies. The men, four altogether, surrounded the wagon and shouted to Barbury to produce papers or die. Barbury nervously showed the papers. The driver came out of the store to attest to its authenticity. He told the men that he was paid to drive this man to Florida by Master Harris. He added that they had just left the plantation five days ago.

They pointed shotguns at the driver and threatened his life if he continued to rebuke them. They shoved a runaway bill in the driver's face that proved they had the right nigger— —clothes, height and all. The slightly built driver withheld the fact that "C.H." was not Barbury's name but he did not want to advance the altercation. The men took Barbury northward. He protested and was tied to a tree and whipped.

They relieved Barbury of his knives and camped overnight during the long transport. The four men agreed that his escape would be highly unlikely because if he put up a fight the fugitive warrant for C.H contained the words: "dead or alive". If they had to kill him, the bounty would not be jeopardized. They kept watch over him in shifts.

The guards began to grumble after several days. The bounty was too much trouble to watch and feed. It was still a good ways back to the Harris-Jones plantation. They grew tired of Barbury. To them, he had become more trouble than what he was worth for them to have to split it four ways. They decided not to tie him up anymore and make Barbury consider that he could escape; then they could kill him and just haul him back like a dead animal.

Barbury had overheard the plan.

#

One night, Barbury lay on the ground, his head butted against his knapsack. A bounty hunter whittled sticks until darkness threatened to steal a finger. Barbury fought off mosquitoes and night crawlers. He twisted his body to shake the annoyance away. Each time he made a sudden movement the guard on duty would draw his pistol.

He assured the man that he was not going anywhere and asked him if the bugs were biting him as well. The man responded that indeed they were but mockingly said to him they loved nigger meat more than his. He cautioned Barbury that he was keeping his eye on him anyway.

Barbury rolled over onto his back, put his hands behind his head and examined the astral skies. He chose a star from the millions and wished upon it. He wanted safety and happiness for Chenzy and Charlie. He longed for Chenzy to know that he did truly love her at all times. He whispered to Charlie that he missed him so. He hoped that someday soon his son would be a free man.

Barbury had never made peace between himself and the carnage that was visited upon the slaves in his name by Bowles. Flashbacks of the stories of the slaughtered that included some of the young boys who stood watch over his kettles haunted him. They would never reach his age.

The elderly men who had died by the rope, had collectively labored on the Harris-Jones plantation for over three-hundred and twelve years. Barbury personally knew three of the women who were burned to death. He measured the anguish of the widowers against his own emptiness for want of Chenzy; it was no contest.

#

The guard lay snoring. Drool ran down the corner of his mouth. The fire was extinguished. The other three men were fast asleep. Barbury's new peaceful spirit was entertained by animal noises and vexed by the continued bites from mosquitoes. He traded glances with the eyes of several unknown creatures in the sylvan thicket. The bodies were camouflaged in the darkness. The orbs appeared suspended in mid-air. The wildlife blinked on occasion and then disappeared. They silently bid goodnight to Barbury. Neither man nor beast sensed any harm from the other.

Barbury's reunion with his family was stolen away again, this time by the telltale blue and white plaid flannel cloth. He gingerly sat up. He opened his knapsack and retrieved another shirt to wear. He felt for the only head kerchief he had in his pocket and searched it for Chenzy's scent. Not finding any trace of it, he regretfully balled it up in his hand.

He took out his new leather apron from the sack and achingly stood up. His legs wobbled from lack of motion and snapped twigs as he struggled to support himself. The guard shifted his position but never stirred.

The inside folds of the long bib had hidden his longest knife from detection. He ambled over to a Cypress trees and found a hole in the thick trunk that was wide enough to support the handle of his favorite cutting tool. He positioned it into the tree at chest height, ran his fingers over its sleek long blade and staggered backwards about five yards.

Barbury had placed the head kerchief between his clenched teeth. He pressed down on it with all the love that he held for his family and all the sadness he had triggered for so many others. Each contended for first place in his thoughts.

He breathed a bottomless sigh of relief. The night air offered a refreshing coolness among the hanging branches that seemed to beckon his advance toward relief. Filled with expectation for where he knew he was going, Barbury ran with full force as he leaned his body into the direction of the blade. His large brogans trudged the ground and crushed leaves. His body, slightly off center, charged into the long cutting tool that excised the pang of a heavy conscience, shamed by guilt and self-condemnation.

The Cricket Cries, the Year Changes

It entered his heart and exited through his muscled back. He never made a sound. Only the deserving had the right to scream in agony, he concluded.

The guards discovered him in the morning. Barbury stood with his huge palms placed flat upon the tree that had obliged this butcher's wish to carve out his pain. The head kerchief lay upon the bloody opening of his heart.

A frozen broad grin validated his desire to be free.

#

Scipio forged a wrought ironed symbol of a knife as Barbury's grave marker. On each anniversary of Barbury's death, Scipio tied a head kerchief around the blade to replace the ones that had rotted with the seasons.

Kaffie was devastated that in haste she had supplied the same patterned shirt to Barbury that C.H. wore. She never ordered that fabric again.

Grafton brought Kaffie one of Barbury's shirts from the slaughterhouse floor.

A piece of it would be stitched among the others.

Cynthia Harris-Allen

KALULU

Chapter 1

Kalulu came to the Harris-Jones plantation at the wiry age of fifteen by way of a slave auction in Savannah. He was originally orphaned on Tybee Island, one of the Sea Islands off the coast of Georgia. The sale of his parents and six siblings splintered in all directions. He never saw them again. Now, at the age of fifteen, he did not belong to any slave family. He took shelter in various cabins of those who invited him in.

Others begrudgingly allowed him to exercise a squatter's right though they had no basis to evict him. He slept in the doorways when the insides held no room for him.

He was becoming a man. His muscles had begun to shape his upper arms. He was a runner. That skill sealed his usefulness to retrieve needed or forgotten tools for the planters and to get the mail posted at the perimeter fences. He would run and frolic in games and races on Sundays with the older men and boys. He won most of the time. Many people watched in amazement at how his fleet-footed abilities quickly distanced his image as he ran toward the forbidden thickets and back. His budding maturity opposed the mischievous smile that quickly elicited trust and belief from whomever he spoke to.

He made friends among the slaves with his gregarious nature. He always grinned, teased, and played tricks. He had nicknames for the slave children based on their body parts. He teasingly called them "Big head," "Giant Belly" and "Feet of an Elephant and Ears, Too". Soon they adopted his nicknames and even referred to themselves using the names he had given them. This was an old custom in his village and some of the Gambian slaves were reminded of it. They would pause for a second when they heard Kalulu's names for them before they decided to laugh or cry.

He heeded the words of the Griot, who repeated stories about the scrub hare from Gambia named *Kalulu* who always managed to get out of every situation. He listened with rueful

218

pride to the griot's tales of this rabbit. His own father had told him why he had given him the same name. His father had held and comforted him as they lay chained together in darkness on that massive ship.

Kalulu spied on the slaves and soon established himself among the planters and overseers as a credible source of information that would otherwise be unknown to them. Though they never gave him anything for the different reports, he had positioned himself for personal gain.

His dark side revealed that he was a thief. He would steal the slaves' clothing to impersonate its original owners and not return their scant wardrobes to them. He made time to mimic them as he stood in their exact field location to plant, harvest or mend. He was adept at mirroring their gestures, sighs, gaits, and callouts to the gods that caused much laughter among the slaves on Sundays.

He chose to wear shirts with big pockets to hold his bounty. He had asked Kaffie to sew two more pockets on the inside of his shirts on each side. He pilfered food from the crop storage areas. The shards of hardened pieces of molasses, that had fallen unnoticed to the wooden sticky floors of the sugar press, were his prized items.

Kalulu would sometimes secretly place into the hands of the waiting slaves this coveted slivered treat if he felt the information revealed about the goings-on at the plantation was useful. The slaves were eager to summon the confection from the pockets of his large ill-fitting shirts. Kalulu used his stolen cache mostly of foodstuffs to bargain with the slaves for beads, trinkets, and small tools that he would stash below the loosening floorboards of the abandoned barn where Abraham, the old slave had made brooms.

For hours or sometimes days at a time, Kalulu was never missed from the plantation. His manner of dress blended with all the other male workers. Some were tall and wore large yellowing shirts along with drawstring pants. Others carried planting or harvesting hoes in hand, ported freshly chopped wood or bales of wired straw to the barn—— all done in various shades of black skins.

Kalulu would increasingly stretch his absences from the plantation. He tested the wits of the overseers until he determined that he could be gone as long as three days without being missed. On Sundays, with free time allotted to the slaves, he spent a lot of time convincing the slaves that he knew every inch of the plantation. He boasted that no white man paid any attention to his movements.

He talked of the great thicket at the outlying parts of the land. He knew which fences were mended, what trees had been felled, and what roads the wagons traveled to take crops to the market. Kalulu knew which river docks were used to load products onto the barges and what times of day were the busiest. He bragged that he overheard many conversations while he sat outside under the parlor windows of the mansion. He knew there was talk of freedom for them.

He continued that once the mute slave, Grafton had spied him as he crouched behind the hydrangeas. He did not give away his presence but he warned him with his eyes to leave. Kalulu recounted the time that he wore clean white clothing and entered the mansion's dining room from the kitchen. He assumed the position of a fan boy. He pulled the lever that waved the damasked fabric overhead and focused on every conversation. No one noticed him.

He cautioned the slaves that he had heard Master Harris talk about bringing in a mission man to talk to the slaves about their gods and this man was going to bring just one god to replace all of theirs.

Upon hearing this, many slaves became upset and worried that they would not be able to continue their homeland traditions should this happen. Some broke instantly into a song of abandonment and loss. Later in the evening, their coded drumbeats signaled doom as word spread of his reports. Ngango, present at one of Kalulu's testimonials, assured his people that that would never happen.

Sometimes Kalulu impersonated Master Harris, complete with the black hat and the gimpy walk as he relayed their owner's spoken words. He crowed that he knew of the routes toward the northern places that harbored slave runaways. Stationed bounty hunters, some even Cherokee, lurked in the marshlands and thickets waited to capture them. He said he could identify the posts where they camped. He even knew where the bounty hunters hid canoes in case runaways would use the riverbanks as their routes to freedom.

The Cricket Cries, the Year Changes

Many slaves clicked their teeth as they questioned his ability to know all things. To that challenge, Kalulu told him he would leave on Monday morning and not come back until evening on Wednesday and no one would come looking for him. He urged the slaves to look for him at the sugar press at dawn the next morning where he would wave "goodbye" and then look for him again by the broom barn by Wednesday evening. He promised that he would raise his hand "hello" wearing the same big shirt and drawstring faded brown pants with the navy blue patch that he had retreated in. Kalulu told his fellow slaves that if any one of them heard the hunting dogs or the Goodbye Bell ring (as the slaves called the runaway alert) during the time he was gone, he would give them anything they wished if he could get his hands on it.

Most of them agreed to keep watch for him. That Monday at dayclean, most of the slaves had readied themselves to go into the fields. Whispered and whistled notifications and messaging with their eyes proved that Kalulu had stood behind the sway-backed horse at the sugar press. When he felt he had garnered enough attention, he smiled a mile-long grin and walked slowly but deliberately north toward the fences.

Chapter 2

When the Monday sunrise plastered the expanse of grass with light, dispensing the dew as if it had never had a purpose, Kalulu knew he would be at the border posts long before a planter or overseer could see him in the open. They were too busy assigning the adult slaves to the planting rows as they passed out the seed pockets worn around the necks of the children. Others made sure that the water bearers had arose before anyone else to fill their gourds and walk among the tillers.

As his toes rode over the top of his makeshift basket woven sandals, Kalulu decided to take them off and leave them by the fence. He had tripped several times in the high grass before he decided to ditch the worn and too-small footwear. The noises from the awakening morning fields were drowned out by the demons that had once again convened the memories of Kalulu's family——especially his father.

Kalulu's long shuddering sighs bore witness to their haunts. He was powerless in keeping them at bay. When alone, his entire facial expressions dismissed the mask of gaiety and naiveté. It was replaced with a dark brooding fixation that tilted his head towards the ground. Kalulu's large black eyes shut as the lids shielded the light in a feigned sleep. Recurring sights and sounds, that he should never have had to witness as a young boy, pounced upon him.

#

Kalulu had stood next to his father in the canoe. Chained together, each tried to steal a last glimpse of their native shore. They queued up like ants on the planks as they waited with heavy sighs their first footprints on board a ship that immediately reshaped their family futures as irredeemable.

Scores of worrying and wandering eyes searched the lines for their women and their children before stacked below on the huge vessel. The desperate enslaved families shouted names of the captured relatives and friends high into the air. Each voice sought to overpower the other in degrees of urgency. The deafening roars and cries of torment from above and below the deck diminished the boisterous noise from the ship's tattered sails; it struggled to take full advantage of the ocean winds.

The men lay chained in the ship's hull. The rise and fall of the sea waves served as a rhythmic recoil upon their chafed left arms that were pinned under their bodies. The slaves rocked on their sides. They lay on splintering, wet, shit-filled and vomitus floors below deck. The rattling of the common lengthy chains that were forced through metal loops shackled to ankles that routed to waists. They leveled off at the necks of male slaves and kept the base beat with the course of the ocean waves.

From the beginning of the journey, slaves writhed violently from the mass incarceration. An ebb and flow reaction of their movements affected entire rows of men and boys who exhorted the others to lie still. The blacks felt the full freight of their weight upon them. The chains scraped and wore down their skin. It became more sensitive with raw, open, bleeding wounds caused by the slightest motion or movement on a calm or tumultuous sea. The winds stood still or howled and whistled.

Kalulu's father, Ogu, of the Kunda's of Gambia, used his body to brace for the impact the chain reaction would have on his son. He clasped his teeth during this repetitive act until most slaves were too weak to resist. We learned that the women and children were held above us, Kalulu remembered. We heard cries from the women, girls, and even some boys, accosted by their captors.

They often hauled us to the top of the boat to feed us. Our eyes, pained by the glaring sunlight, eventually made sense of what was before us. They washed us with salt water. It intensified our open wounds with its briny onslaught. Some of us were forced to eat. During the long voyage those who had willed themselves to die of starvation had their mouths wired open to accept food and drink. Many who relentlessly cried their agonies out into the air had their mouths wired shut.

The tired and worn-out crewmembers would deliriously delight themselves as they whipped us into submission to sing or dance for them. How could our traditional acts of known celebration be forced upon us to perform when our dignity, worth, and happiness were not part of this kidnapping? They made us hoist and repair the sails, clean the decks and perform any tasks necessary. We even maintained our own deathbeds. We prolonged the tasks above deck. It was a relief from the hell below.

Kalulu paused in his thinking to eat. He had brought along a gourd of water. Its warm and almost slimy taste quenched a thirst he did not know he had until he had stopped to rest. He realized that he had traveled quite a distance. The plains were far behind him. The drone of the brook that inched toward the streams would soon lose its identity in the river. That assured Kalulu that he was halfway toward his northern route before having to turn back.

He munched upon a softened baked yam that he had retrieved from the floorboards in the barn. Along with that was a piece of flat bread and some dried beans to sustain this short trip. He sat under the high Georgia pine trees for shade. The pairing of the sun and the water heightened its scent. He fanned the big shirt to loosen its grip from his sweaty body. As he continued his trek, Kalulu resisted in vain the thoughts of the horrible journey.

Along the route there were deadly diseases that we did not know about that tossed many of us overboard. The resistant stench could not be rinsed away. It combined dysentery, bodily excrements, and rotten food. The dead that lay in their own waste were given to the sea once death was certain.

The drunken sweaty kidnappers reeked of bad breath. Their body smells, palm wine and rum-stained clothing added yet another layer to the odious air. At times, they appeared to be just as afraid of us as we were of them. We certainly outnumbered them but our chains became their equalizers.

Kalulu reflected on the suicides and the planned unsuccessful mutinies, revolts, and insubordinations by the slaves that warranted punishments worse than the whip. Some slaves were singled out for punishment. To that end, that slave had to be loosened from the others. He or she was tied to a sail mast or to the hooks on the small boats that held the barrels of rotting food. When that exact moment presented itself to a slave, they jumped overboard. The sailors stopped that practice of unchaining them and subsequently whipped the insurgent still chained to others. If the strap caught an innocent, so be it.

When his father held him at night, he whispered stories to him about the scrub hare named *Kalulu* whose character was a part of their oral traditions. This animal's fabled life was one of survival. It showed how to get along with others if ever you found yourself lost and alone. Ogu would tell his son to "Go to the villages and seek out a family. Let them see how helpful you can be to them and they will feed you." That thought made him shiver. He felt his father had foretold his fate when he burdened him with this name at the birth ritual. He was indeed alone and lost.

Soon we neared the land in the distance. We were fed more food and washed more often, Kalulu recalled. A full day was dedicated to branding all of us with a hot iron. It signified a new tribe of people gathered from what seemed to be every village of my mind. This new common symbol held no meaning to us. The burned flesh was a bitter initiation. When the ship dropped anchor near land, palm oil was generously shellacked on the stiff, and the broken. They allowed the women to wash their hair. Their mangled coarse thicknesses met with wooden combs that were ill prepared to navigate a straight line.

At the sale, we were marched from the ship to the makeshift forts on that island that would hold us until the auction. We were chained together. We shined like first-day-of-spring new. Many were sick and weak. We set foot on this new land dejected, defiant, displaced, and dizzy. All were confused by the presence of red clay all around us. The hot breeze and the burning sun were like our homeland. Had we sailed back to our villages? I believed it to be a dream.

They sold us with something called the "inch of the candle" rule. Fast burning, ruled tapers were used. Loud and raucous bids were accepted until exactly one inch of the candle had burned down. The sellers accepted the last bid. The barterers hastened to sell the rest of us, each at the same price before dark of night rendered individual inspections moot. It soon became a buyer's paradise when the earsplitting stampede to round up the fit ones among us was likened to a bazaar.

Black men, women, and children were groped, probed and picked through. Dirty white hands opened mouths of the freight in their quest to divide the herd. The buyers shamed us while they used those same noxious fingers to inspect our genitals.

Kalulu could not locate his father. He never saw him again.

The Cricket Cries, the Year Changes

Chapter 3

Kalulu returned to the plantation on Wednesday evening as promised, to the smiling faces of the slaves who had known of his escapade. The young boys beamed with pride for their hero. In his absence, word had spread by drum of his looming adventure and now announced his arrival. His caper remained secret; he had established himself. Soon, grown slaves approached Kalulu to discuss how to run away to the north or to the free Sea Islands of the Atlantic Ocean. These groups maintained smiles on their faces and sometimes laughed aloud to mask the underlying "freedom" conversations.

Tayweo, a slave of considerable height and indignant repose, engaged Kalulu on several occasions. Kalulu informed one of the planters that five slaves that included Tayweo, who was their leader had planned to run away and had sought his help. The planter gave Kalulu a copper half-cent for the information and promised another one if he would agree to pretend to lead the toilers to freedom and reveal the proposed route to him using signs of broken brush and other markings.

Kalulu agreed not knowing the real value of his deceit. He admired the coin as it grew warm when he pressed his newest possession tightly into his oversized palm. He excitedly ran to Kaffie and asked her to sew the half-cent into his shirt so he would never lose it. Kaffie promised to do so if he swore that the money was not stolen. Kalulu declared with a big wide grin that it was not. He said he had earned it while helping a planter get a wagon wheel out of a ditch.

This is Tayweo's tale:
"We lie in wait in the moonlit night. We had run non-stop for six hours. Kalulu, the younger slave, had less stamina and cannot keep up with the five of us. I feared that we might have to leave him behind. I was surprised that Kalulu's storytelling of his willful travels on the plantation did not match the strength required to run more than three hundred miles. He appeared to be unfit.

"He was too young to stand any torture if he was caught and would surely tell the hunters about our route. They would want to know what conversations Kalulu had overheard and who else had collaborated in aiding our escape. If by morning, he is still too fatigued to catch up and lags too far behind us, we may have to kill him and throw his body into the creek. Maybe we will bury him. I remain uncertain about his fate.

"The sounds of the night were familiar but much more pronounced. We never had time before to absorb the noises of the mockingbirds and owls. The leaves would suddenly rustle below our feet and reveal that a trail of a lizard or a snake was making its way north—-like we were. We became expectant of these sounds. They regulated us and calmed our fears.

"I spied a bear, albeit a cub about one hundred yards to the left of us. Its mother had to be nearby. I quietly motioned to the group to quicken their steps and maintain silence. I had to quiet the two frightened women who accompanied us. We assured them of our protection from harm. The group agreed to ditch anything that would hold our progress back. We discarded the extra clothing we had brought except for the uniforms that the boat help wore. We expected to climb aboard one of the docked ships at the Tennessee River and mingle in with the rest of the slaves as they loaded wares headed north.

"We could not burn our clothing. The source of the fire would attract bounty hunters. To bury them was not a good idea, either. The hounds could sniff out our scent. So we threw them high into the pines until they were snagged by the branches. I took Kalulu's sack of clothes and extracted a pair of pants and a frayed-sleeved shirt that was far too big for him. I lightened his load when I placed these two items in my burlap bag.

"As the pink sunrise gave way to a pending cloudy day, we arose from our three-hour rest and continued along the banks of the Oconee River. Kalulu was still asleep and did not want to rise just yet. He told me how tired he was. I looked into his big black sad eyes and saw both the pity I felt for him and the obvious impediment to our escape he had become. I reached for him and snatched him to a standing position. It frightened him. The quandary was no longer to kill him, but when and how.

"His youth held the expectation of a brighter future than ours did—-but did it? He seemed very different from what we remembered of him. Gone were the engaging conversations, exaggerated stories, and swift running. His faraway glances signaled to me a distant melancholy. I yanked him close to my chest by his long arms and scolded him into compliance. I lifted him from the ground. Either he keeps up or we would leave him.

"We ate dried fruit and nuts, drank water sparingly and then disappeared again into the thicket. We broke twigs and moved rocks on purpose to mislead the trackers. The markers meant absolutely nothing. We placed cowrie shells and castor beads under certain rocks. We pushed nuts into the openings of the bark of trees in different formations, mainly an "X" or a circle. The other runaways would know what these meant.

"Our deliberate fugitive steps plodded the ground beneath our bare feet. We did not need shoes; they were a hindrance. Bare feet allowed us to feel the ground, which gave us a lot of information as to where we were; but the warm crimson clay signified that we were still in Georgia. As the dawning sun's warmth removed the clouds, we affirmed our direction to be northeastward toward the Tennessee River. We ran, renewed from the brief respite and buoyed by the hope that we were not yet caught. We knew that several slaves acted as decoys for bounty hunters and infiltrated groups of us who would run away.

"We only trusted the ones who had cowrie shells sewn into the right pant leg of the males and the left hem of the skirts of the women. Our elders prompted us not to trust anyone so quickly who wished to join us. I had changed many of the routes on this journey that met with a lot of resistance and argument from Kalulu. The discussions finally ended by the third day when I strongly suggested to Kalulu that he run back to the plantation because I was not going to take further instructions from a child.

"One of the runaways commented that when we had walked single file on our trek through the woods with Kalulu in second-to-last position, he caught him marking trees and large stones with strange symbols. He did not make anything of it at the time. He thought that Kalulu was trying to impress us. He was known to be a show-off. None of us knew him well. We did not know who his people were.

"We were startled by the sudden onslaught of three large bears that barreled down on us. The cold morning air accented the breaths that escaped from their nostrils and gaping mouths. The bears' hungry grunts and growls vaulted our frightened escape into a naked, terror-stricken panic. We muffled our screams. The quick breaths and raised heartbeats were the only noises we could not suppress. Our eyes bulged with fear. Cold streams of sweat poured out from our bodies. We tramped through the biting damp grass.

"The rhythm of our running was timed by how our pant legs swished against each other; the skirts of the women were held high and hurled left to right. Feet hit the ground hard. Sharp rocks, fallen twigs, and nutshells assaulted our soles. We slid and slipped in the muddy areas as we grabbed the huge fronds of the ferns for balance.

"Moving closer to the trees to steady ourselves, we strained to stretch our hands out behind us to secure any part of the women to drag them along with us lest they fall behind. None of us looked around for Kalulu. Soon his loud agonizing screams pinpointed that he was a good two hundred feet behind the rest of us. We made no effort to rescue him. We had come to a singular silent conclusion that Kalulu was more like chains to us than the ones that shackled us on the plantation. In addition, the bears had stopped their pursuit of us, apparently satisfied for now, with the one that did not get away.

"Our run slowed down to a standstill when we realized that we were no longer in danger. We paused to catch our breaths as tightened chests begged for relief. We tended to the wounds on our legs and arms. Our faces evidenced bloody slices from branches that had impeded our run to safety. The cuts and the prickly spines of some bushes embedded in our blood-soaked feet would have to wait for another recess. It would be useless to tend to them now; those wounds would surely repeat themselves before we reached the Tennessee River. We were so far off our route that we had to rest and consider where we were."

#

By nightfall, the group stopped to eat after three days of being on the run. They decided to bathe in the brook and discard more clothing in the branches. They felt for Kalulu's shirt and pants that he had placed in his bag and found the coin sewn inside the pocket. The group peered at the copper half-cent with a jarring revelation. They did not find a cowrie shell sewn into his extra pair of pants, either. They resolved to double the amount of time needed to run towards the river to place even more space between them and the soon oncoming patrollers.

Unlike the scrub hare, Kalulu never proved his usefulness to anyone.

Chapter 4

On the Harris-Jones plantation, the Goodbye Bell had rung on a long ago Saturday morning. It shattered the pre-dawn sleep of all who had to rise to repeat yesterday's toil and till. The overseers had discovered five slaves missing. With Kalulu's betrayal in hand, they secretly covered the fact that they knew where the runaways were headed. Weeks later, the bounty hunters returned to the plantation with word that they had found Kalulu's body but found no trace of the other runaways. Even the dogs could not pick up a scent.

The drummed codes sent by the slaves messaged Kalulu's fate. It said he was eaten by an animal--possibly a bear due to the size of the open wounds on his torso. His left arm was missing. The hunters had found him among thorny weeds in a coagulated pool of brown sticky blood. Kalulu lay on his back. His eyes bulged in a horrific stare; he was open-mouthed and exposed bloodied and missing teeth. He was maggot-filled.

The hunters also reported that only a few yards from him lay a medium-sized dead bear. Upon examination they could not discern a gunshot or knife wound in the animal. Its neck appeared to have been broken. They carted the animal home next to Kalulu's body to salvage the skin.

Even hares can kill a bear when they are hungry enough—hungry enough for freedom, friend, father, and family.

Maybe Kalulu's demons killed the wild animal. Perhaps they claimed his haunts as their own personal effects and private property.

#

A young slave boy who hoped someday to run as fast as Kalulu had, found Kalulu's sandals at the outer fences. He decided to run in them as he turned back toward the cotton fields.

Kaffie learned of Kalulu's demise and cut a remnant of yellowing cotton from a random shirt brought to her for repair. It resembled the big shirts that Kalulu wore; never to reach the size he had hoped to be.

She stored it for her quilt.

The Cricket Cries, the Year Changes

TANDY

Chapter 1

Tandy pulled the frightened baby from its screaming mother's womb and held it into the air. The slimy little creature flailed its sticky arms and legs as Tandy offered the mother her first glimpse of her new baby girl. *"Funny how the mothers' incessant screams of pain change instantly to cries of joy when they see that little thing held just within their reach"*, Tandy thought. She cut the umbilical cord down to almost a nub and applied a dark powder to the remainder to dry it quickly. To honor this new black mother's culture, a ceremony to ritualize the placenta was necessary.

Tandy had two other babies to deliver and called on the doulas to assist in the rites. She motioned to the younger girls to sweep up the waste that had been absorbed by the sawdust from the dirt floor. Other helpers stacked clean torn up sheets and coarse fabric discards at-the-ready.

She removed the rusty piece of tin from under the mattress of the new mother and placed it beneath a woman who was in the first stages of labor. It eased the contractions. Tandy was a midwife on the Harris-Jones plantation. Harris bought her when she was forty years old for fifteen hundred dollars. She was highly recommended to him by a colleague who knew that Harris trusted his judgment. Slaves of that age did not fetch high dollar amounts; but Tandy possessed a unique gift of midwifery. Harris had tired of the many slaves who told him that they knew how to "pull babies out".

Tandy was a slave on the island of Haiti when she was five years old. She performed a litany of chores until she was a teen. Orphaned, she lived with the Catholic missionaries in a commune in Port-au-Prince. They taught her to read and write in both English and French. Many Africans in Haiti accepted portions of the Catholic messaging and merged it in their own practices. That dual education produced a young woman who had gleaned precepts from both.

She remained in Port-au-Prince until she was twenty-five years old. Then she was auctioned to Jekyll Island, off the Savannah, Georgia coastline. She lived there for approximately fifteen years and was sold again in Savannah. Harris did not know that Tandy could read and write very well. He was surprised at the level of intelligence in her speech and communication and attributed it to her growing up among missionaries.

Tandy appeared young for her age. She was fit and strong. She was dark as burnt molasses. She shaved her hair close to her head in the warmer months and embellished her scalp with razor-cut designs. When she experienced the cooler northern Georgia temperatures, she let her hair grow out and plaited it in a crown of spikey braids interwoven with clay beads. When she walked the plantation fields, the sound of the beads that rattled against one another was heard before she arrived.

Tandy's eyes were huge and brown. She had a keen nose and full lips. Her cheeks appeared to have had two Rome Beauty apples implanted in them. She had a wide ivory grin that highlighted huge teeth. Her muscled arms and legs spoke to her years of navigating between laboring mothers around the clock. She ate only vegetables, fruits, nuts, and cheese.

Tandy asked Harris to build a bigger birthing cabin. His slave population was increasing by the hour, she joked. The new cabin contained two fireplaces, a leveled gravel floor and open windows set higher than normal for privacy. There were tiny cribs made from remnants of wood from the lumber mill.

The shelves on the walls held Tandy's medicines and potions. Others were stacked with colorful cotton remnants that Kaffie supplied to wrap the newborns. There were osnaburg drawstring bags that would hold the corpses of the stillborn stored on a lower shelf in the corner. Cots with mattresses filled with corn shucks or Spanish moss and old blankets, served as the beds for the new mothers. Just outside the front door were wrought-iron racks that Miss Luvinia discarded. They held the chopped wood.

Large black cauldrons for water stood in reserve on the iron grates. Pots and pans were staged near the other fireplace for cooking. Fruits and vegetables were strung from pegs on the walls. Tandy dried them for the women who were in labor to eat.

Tandy had talked Harris into giving her two goats. She used the goat's milk for the newborns. It made them less colicky. The animals lived in a pen just beyond the back door.

The Cricket Cries, the Year Changes

Tandy gave young children treats when they milked and grazed them from time to time. When the animal was slaughtered Tandy asked for the skin. She knew how to tan the leather. She used it to waterproof the tiny cribs. The dead goats were replaced with young kids.

Once a month, she asked the slaves that sheared the sheep to give her at the least one bundle of freshly cut greasy wool. Tandy applied the oil from it to the skins of the newborn babies. She had the softest hands of any slave worker.

Tandy had a separate room that was divided by a wall. She referred to it as her "crèche," French for "nursery." It also served as her living quarters. She shared it with two young women. A rocking chair that had belonged to the slave Abraham was in the center of the room. Tandy did not like it because it moved around the floor a lot when she calmed the little babies. If she held a baby in her lap and faced the east, by the time it had fallen asleep, the baby's head faced west.

In Haiti, she learned that it was bad luck to leave a chair rocking once you rose from it. She vowed to fix that before she sat on it again. Additionally, Tandy did not like animals to roam free near the cabin. Her Haitian beliefs supported many of her fears. She told her helpers that if a rooster stood on the doorsteps and crowed, it was a death omen.

Tandy wore a brass bracelet on her upper arm. The item was used for currency in her native land. It was given to her by a youth who had pickpocketed it from a trader in Haiti. She misplaced it many times as it was too big for her arm. She always managed to find it in the birthing cabin or near the door. It was becoming more trouble to find than to keep.

#

It was December, one month before the cane harvest. The crop had fully matured in its eighteen months growth. In terms of yield, it was Harris' most profitable crop. The sugar mill was readied. Scipio had forged new machetes, sharpened long knives, and hammered ladles. The coopers had produced over three hundred hogsheads barrels that would hold the raw, dark sugar for shipment to Great Britain to be refined. Coal and wood were stacked in bins ready to fuel the boiling water in the steam pipes.

Cynthia Harris-Allen

As was his custom, Harris held a huge party before the cane harvest began. This event was for the plantation residents only. It started on a Saturday night and would end before Sunday evening. Come Monday morning, Harris ceremoniously cut the first stalk of cane. Tandy chose Saturday to attend the party. She had never attended one before. Her life was the birthing house and the nursery. There were three women in labor already. Two of the doulas stayed behind to tend to them.

It was dawn. Male slaves walked four by two as they carried the freshly slaughtered animals toward the fires. Carcasses of cattle and hogs were bound and hung upside down with their feet tied to long thick branches. The posts rested on the shoulders of the men. Their black bodies were silhouetted against the semi-circled sun as it rose above the horizon. The slaves were colorfully dressed and happy to have left their field clothes behind. The array of hues competed with the meadow flora at its highest peak. The temporary respite from the labor and the whip lifted spirits and gave way to swells of jubilation and song.

Tandy greeted slaves that she knew. She hugged little babies that she had delivered and marveled at their growth. Pregnant women asked her to touch their emergent bellies for good luck. She did not lament the fact that she was childless. The Catholics had placed so much guilt in her about chastity and virtue. That part of her spirit had kept any carnal thoughts at bay for a long time until she saw him.

Hampton was a slave that Harris had placed as the foreman over the cane production. He had worked in those fields since a young boy. Harris was confident that no one knew more about the processes of sugar boiling than Hampton. Hamp was around forty-four years old. He was a bold and strapping figure well over six feet tall and muscular. He was a serious-minded no-nonsense man. He was responsible and respected by all who worked for him.

As he made his way through the crowd, some of the males patted him on the shoulders out of respect or joked with him. Tandy watched from nearby and waited for the boys to walk away from him. She walked up behind him and stood on tipped toes to tap him on his shoulder. Hamp turned toward the prettiest smile he had ever seen. She smiled like the sunrise, he thought. Tandy motioned to him to come and sit under a tree out of the heat and away from the crowd. He followed her.

She shook his hand and introduced herself as the midwife for the slaves. She joked that all she saw day in and day out were women and babies. She laughed that perhaps she had forgotten what a real man looked like. Hamp was light-skinned enough to blush.

He described his duties on the plantation. He, too, admitted that he worked hard for eighteen months straight while he oversaw the growing of the cane. For the next three months, he would be the head sugar boiler. He told her that over the years, he only had eyes for the cane. Tandy pointed out to Hamp where the crèche was located and asked him to visit when he had the chance. With a grin, he showed her the chimneys of the sugar mill that rose high into the sky.

The drums summoned the people to the huge porch area to eat. The two of them began to walk together toward the mansion in silence. Tandy exhaled deeply; Hamp even *smelled* like molasses. Just then he turned to her and smiled with his own private thoughts.

CHAPTER 2

Tandy walked up to the Big House to pick up more cotton remnants from Kaffie. She was glad to get away even if for a short while from the birthing cabins where fifteen mothers-to-be were in various stages of labor. Tandy had plenty of help but she still had to oversee the actual birthing process should something go wrong. Receipt of more cloth from Kaffie was a blessed diversion.

She knocked on the door and one of the young houseboys answered it and recognized Tandy. She told him that Kaffie had left a package for her. He told her to wait, he knew where it was. Soon, he eagerly brought the box outside. Tandy thanked him for it then asked him if he could do her a favor.

The boy listened. Tandy told him about the trouble with her rocking chair. She wondered if he could think of anything she could use as a stop piece to place under the rockers. The boy's eyes grew big as he thought quickly. He told Tandy he would be right back. He returned with two books from the library. He gave the leather-bound reads to Tandy and told her no one looked at books in this house. It was just for show. If she needed more books, just ask him. There were tons of them, he said.

Tandy gladly accepted *the* possible solution to her problem. She tossed him a trinket and scurried back to the cabin. She turned to remind him to thank Kaffie for her.

#

Tandy arrived at the birthing house to deliver one baby and a set of twins. She marked three lines on the door that indicated the number of babies born so far. Harris would send an indentured servant at the end of each day to count the lines on the door that indicated how many live births he could add to his slave rolls.

Tandy performed a ritual over the placenta from a twin birth. She greased the freshly washed bodies with lanolin from the wool bundles. She instructed the doulas to watch over the new mothers for any signs or effects. She suggested that they make tea from chestnut leaves in case any one of them had a fever.

The Cricket Cries, the Year Changes

A young slave boy rushed into the cabin. Breathless, he told Tandy that Ibina was giving birth in the cornfields. Tandy grabbed her sack that included knives, clean cloths, and root medicines and followed him to the location.

Ibina lay on the red clay as she writhed in pain among the three-foot high shafts of lime green. Her hands grounded her to the bottom of the plants in search of some relief. The twisting motion yanked some roots to the surface. A driver arrived from three rows over to investigate the work stoppage. Slaves were trying to calm Ibina until help arrived. Calling them "niggers", he cracked his whip several times into the muggy air and ordered the slaves back to work, including Ibina.

Ibina looked at him with unbelieving eyes and tried to stand up. She held her bulging stomach with both hands. She tried to take a step forward but fell to the ground as the stabbing pains of labor accelerated. The driver's whip tore through the back of Ibina's blouse. She yelled more from the contractions than she did from the scourge. The slaves dropped their hoes and gathered around the driver, still on his horse. Some cursed him; others threatened him to leave the birthing mother alone. The driver feared for his own safety and pulled a rifle from the sheath and cocked it.

By this time, Tandy had arrived. She rushed over to Ibina and propped her up on her butt as she comforted her. She asked the slave women to use their top skirts to form a private, protective covering while she prepared to deliver the baby. They raised their dirty clothing, muddied by the field dirt and filled with cockles and burrs at the hems. With their calloused and dirty hands, they formed a close circle around Ibina.

The overseer demanded that the women return to their places in the fields or there would be more trouble than they could imagine. One slave woman turned toward him and spat on the ground. He then placed the rifle over his lap and raised his whip. The lash cut the face of the impudent woman. It added a diagonal wound across her face. The woman did not shriek. She only winced and continued to hold her skirt up.

The overseer, inflamed by her impudence, wound the grip of the whip again in the air.

As he released it, Tandy jumped in front of the woman and grabbed it in her bare hands. She jerked the whip to steady herself. Her wavering advantage pulled the startled overseer from his horse. As he fell, his rifle discharged. Some of the slaves scattered. They knew that the sound of a gunshot would summon help. The standing women still held their dresses high as the baby began to crown. Tandy let go of the whip and moved between the skirted curtains to aid the mother. She kneeled and gently pulled the baby out while its mother lost herself in the agony.

The overseer thrust his way through the standing women and with lightning speed stung Tandy's back with three quick strikes. Tandy screamed with both surprise and injury. Rockfield Stiles, the chief overseer, had responded to the gunshot with five other men. He arrived on the scene in time to witness what the driver had done to Tandy. He jumped from his horse and put the driver in a chokehold. Stiles berated him and asked him what was he thinking? He cursed him and said that these people belonged to Harris, not to him. He asked him, as he pushed him loose, what danger could a birthing event pose to his life? The driver offered nothing in his defense. His face glistened with sweat and was red from loss of breath and embarrassment.

Stiles told the other men to take Robbins and place him in the jail to cool off. He would deal with him later. Stiles said nothing to the women. He mounted his horse and drove off with his men and Robbins in tow.

Tandy finished the delivery and placed the bloody rags in her sack along with her tools. She asked some women to help carry Ibina and her new baby to the birthing cabin where she could care for her further. She thanked the rest for their help. As she walked, she felt the sticky welts on her lower back. Her right hand still stung when she blocked Robbins' whip. The marks were not deep. She pulled her hand to her face and saw the blood.

"Robbins", she remembered to herself.

The Cricket Cries, the Year Changes

Chapter 3

One evening, Sadie, one of Tandy's assistants rushed into the cabin. She told Tandy that she passed a white girl with two little white babies in a cart headed for the cabin. Sadie told her that the babies looked like they could be twins. Tandy immediately knew the purpose was to bring these babies to suckle at the black slaves' breasts. Tandy resented this intrusion as she had in the past. She recalled a new slave mother whose milk went dry from the hourly feedings of white babies and eventually could not feed her own. It did something to that mother's spirit, Tandy remembered. She was never the same after that.

Tandy was put-upon by the audacity of these white folks. "Is there anything we have that does not belong to them?" she mourned. She took a deep breath and bit her lip. She told Sadie to go meet with the woman with the babies and speak to her in a tongue that the girl would not understand. Make up something—— anything, she told Sadie. The white girl would not know the difference. Tandy told Sadie to motion to the girl in made-up babble to wheel the cart around to the back. The white girl obeyed Sadie's incoherent instructions, moved the cart, and left.

Tandy told Sadie to go work elsewhere in the fields and stay gone until she called for her. She cautioned her not to speak of these babies. Tandy did not know what she was going to do with them yet and was not going to implicate Sadie. Tandy went to the back of the cabin and removed the light blue cotton that covered the two sleeping babies. She looked at the tags that hung from their necks. It read: "Robbins Twins." Tandy suddenly realized that she did not have a dilemma after all.

She went to her room in the creche and mixed a powdered substance that she normally gave to mothers soon after birth to sedate them. She and Ngango had collaborated on the recipe. Tandy added warm water to the beige substance, stirred it, and placed it in a clay cup. With a very tiny spoon, she walked to the abandoned area by the goats. She pursed the lips of the slumbering infants and equally streamed the entire liquid into their mouths.

Tandy decided to visit Hamp.

It had become routine for Tandy to visit Hamp at the sugar mill. They had been seeing each other for over three months since they met. Their feelings had grown in leaps and bounds. He and Tandy walked to the perimeter of the plantation and made love in the thickets. When he first lay with her, Tandy was hesitant. He was surprised that she was still a virgin at forty-three years old.

She told him of her strict Catholic upbringing. The nuns had probably worked some kind of mojo on her that made her believe what the two of them had done was wrong. Tandy was ecstatic. Overwhelmed by the awakenings in her body and spirit, the newness caused her to lie still and savor the moment. Hamp was gentle with her and patient with his own lust. Tandy did not know if she wanted to thank the nuns first for intimidating her until she met Hamp or kill them for holding back the true essence of what it meant to be a woman.

The night was as black as a witch's cat. Hamp carried a small lantern so they could see to eat; Tandy had brought it from the Big House. The cooks fed Tandy daily. They knew she did not have time to prepare her own meals. They regarded her as a valuable asset. The basket was heavy with fresh fruit and vegetables. There was plenty of meat and bread for Hamp. Once a month, the butler would place a gourd of peach wine wrapped in a cloth napkin for the two of them. Everyone knew that Tandy and Hamp was an item.

That night he held her naked body in the envelope of intimacy with only the crickets as intruders. Hamp ran his hand down her back and felt the now-healed welts. Tandy felt him jerk as he moved his hand away quickly. He asked her if she had injured herself. Tandy told him about the overseer in the field when Ibina gave birth among the corn. Hamp, horrified, asked Tandy if she know what the overseer's name was. Tandy told him she did not. Hampton jumped up from the blanket and told her to put her clothes back on. He did the same.

He pulled her close to him and told her he loved her and he wanted Harris to allow them to jump the broom. She needed his protection. He stressed that it was important he asked her when they were both fully clothed. Tandy leaped into Hamp's arms and hugged him. She then told him laughingly that she would have to think about it.

Two days later, on a Sunday the two were married. Many slaves attended the ceremony. Little girls and boys that Tandy had brought into the world paraded around them. They sprinkled flowers and colorful weeds around the two of them as they sat on high wooden stools. Tandy was concerned there was no bible reading. Their marriage should be a sacred ceremony like the ones performed in Haiti, even among the blacks. A cook brought a pamphlet from the Big House for them to swear an oath upon not knowing that it was an almanac. Tandy laughed so hard she cried. She did not let on she knew what the item was.

#

That same week, the white girl came to the birthing cabin to retrieve the twins. This was the first time she had ever entered the creche. Tandy approached her and asked her what she was doing there. The girl, Suzanna, told her she had come to pick up the twins from the Big House that she had dropped off four days ago. Tandy told her she did not know what she was talking about. Puzzled, Suzanna told her another black woman had told her to push the cart to the back of the cabin. She pointed to the area where the goats were penned.

Again, Tandy emphasized she had no idea of who she was and what she wanted. She invited her to examine every crib in the nursery to find some white babies. Suzanna insisted she brought the babies to this place. She stomped her foot as she grew angry and fearful. She started toward the back of the cabin to point out to Tandy what she had done as instructed by the other girl. She told Tandy to follow her.

When Suzanna reached the area about thirty yards from the creche, her eyes beheld the tattered cotton blankets that had covered the babies. Two ashen bodies lay side to side, their eyes plucked out by buzzards. The vultures had fed upon their tiny corpses. There were numerous insect bites upon their skin. Flies by the hundreds had hatched from the maggots and buzzed the summer afternoon with intensity.

The stench was unyielding. Rotting flesh and human waste baked in the heat.

Both Tandy and Suzanna screamed in horror and rushed back into the cabin. Tandy covered her face with her apron and wailed. When she no longer heard Suzanna's dry heaves, she removed her cover of deceit long enough to see her run for her life toward the mansion.

#

Robbins and his wife, Master Harris, Suzanna and Stiles arrived at the birthing cabin in a huff. Robbins' wife was trembling and unsteady. Tandy was in her room. She was rocking two babies to sleep. She was no longer agitated at the way the rocker had moved in the past. The two books, *Gulliver's Travels* and *Oliver Twist* had served their purpose well. Tandy had read both books growing up in Haiti. She began to call her little babies "Lilliputians," being reminded of the Jonathan Swift novel.

The doulas and other assistants were shaken with the grisly discovery of the babies at the back of the cabin where no one ventured. They huddled together as they wrung their hands, moaned, and clicked their teeth. They dared not bother Tandy. She was holed up in her room probably just as upset as they were, they concluded. They knew how much she loved babies.

Robbins and his wife were inconsolable. His wife eventually fainted when he would not let her touch the cart that bore the remains. Harris and Stiles looked upon the twins with shock, pity, and anger. They walked with heavy boots into Tandy's room. Harris asked her to tell him how this could have happened. Tandy told him it was just as much of a surprise to her as it was to the rest of them. She never knew those babies were outside at all. She added that no one told her of a delivery for nursing. She hung her head in sadness.

Harris asked Suzanna if she gave the babies to Tandy personally. Suzanna said she never gave anything to Tandy; a different girl told her to place the cart way out back. He questioned if she could recognize the girl if she saw her again. She plaintively answered that she could. Suzanna said she could identify her if she could hear her speak because she talked in a different way. It was not English. Robbins and his wife had made their way into Tandy's sanctuary. His face went white when he recognized Tandy.

The Cricket Cries, the Year Changes

Harris continued his probe. He asked Suzanna what she meant when she said the woman she gave the babies to did not speak English. She began to cry. With growing impatience, Harris told her to walk among the women who stood in the cabin to search their faces for the one who spoke to her. Suzanna tentatively walked among the glaring eyes of the slaves and then bravely told Harris none of them resembled the girl.

Suzanna said she thought that the unidentified woman told her to take the cart to the back of the cabin because she pointed in that direction. With her eyes now swollen and her nose reddened, Suzanna started to shout that it was all her fault. She kept repeating it. She ran out the door and stumbled toward the mansion. She shouted to the skies that she had killed the babies.

Robbins stood over Tandy and with clenched fists and accused her of murdering his kids because he had whipped her nigger ass in the fields. Harris was startled by his claim. Stiles told Harris that Robbins had struck Tandy a while ago when she attempted to deliver Ibina's baby. Robbins's wife looked at her husband in disbelief.

Tandy said to Robbins she never saw the babies placed in the back of the cabin. She continued that no one goes behind the birthing house except the kids that fed the goats. The babies were too far away for her to tell the difference between the bleat of a goat and a baby. The birthing cabin and nursery are always very busy and loud, she said, as she reinforced her argument. She insisted that she could not possibly know that they were Robbins' children. Robbins said she could know because they had his name strung on a card around their necks.

Tandy defiantly asked him when she had learned how to read. She continued to rock and coo to the little babies she held in her arms. They had become agitated with the loud voices and had awakened and cried furiously. She stood and carried the babies toward one of the women to calm. She returned to her room with her arms folded defiantly across her chest. Tandy went into a rant. She faced Harris and said that he knew how much she loved children; she had birthed hundreds of them on this plantation alone. She reminded Harris that she took care of all babies——black and white, and for Robbins to accuse her of that kind of neglect demanded an apology.

Tears dotted her cheeks. She slumped into the rocker. Tandy lay back into the chair. Robbins noticed that the runners had stopped moving immediately blocked by books. He moved toward them and picked them up. He shoved them in Tandy's face and asked her if she could not read why did she have them?

Harris grabbed the novels from Robbins and examined the embossed Harris seal on the inside page. He angrily asked Tandy where she got the books. She explained the problem with the rocking chair and said one of the little boys in the Big House told her she could use them to steady her chair. He gave them to her when she picked up cloth from Kaffie.

Harris apologized to Robbins and his wife. He said all of this seemed to be a big mistake, a tragic misunderstanding. He said he could not hold Tandy responsible for someone else's fatal error. He promised Robbins that he would not rest until he found this mystery woman. Robbins cursed Harris as he exited to retrieve his dead sons for burial. He cried openly. His wife, with swollen eyes and wringing hands looked at Tandy. She was not sure that Tandy was innocent.

Tandy stood and returned her look with a stare of her own and inwardly quoted from *Oliver Twist*: "Kiss your baby goodbye with cold, white lips".

The Cricket Cries, the Year Changes

Chapter 4

One early morning, Tandy walked barefoot toward the thickets. She planned to collect leaves and roots to grind for tea. A misty green lay over the ground shrubs dotted with dew. She thought about Hamp. She had not seen him for two weeks. The last time they had met he had given her cane stalk remnants for the pregnant women and the help to eat.

He always said funny things to her that lightened their conversations after being apart from one another. One time he snickered that donkeys were smarter than horses. Hamp told Tandy that he had replaced the horses with donkeys to port the cane stalks to the sugar mill. He said donkeys could stand the stress, strain, and heat better than a horse. They could get used to abuse and not being fed at the same time or not at all. He said donkeys were just like slaves! Tandy had slapped her thigh with laughter.

Tandy promised herself she would go to the mill late that night just to look at Hamp. She missed him. She walked back to the crèche. The work bell had not rung yet to arouse the slaves. She heard the hoofs of a horse that slowly plodded the thick grass. She turned in the direction of the sound and saw Robbins. He began to speed up in her direction. Tandy panicked and ran toward the trees, rocks, and shrub border that she knew the horse would not be able to navigate. She did not want to go deep into the heavy brush. Robbins might follow her on foot.

About six feet into the forest, Tandy stopped and stood behind a tree. Robbins hollered into the dense area. He called her a nigger witch and promised that come next time she would not be able to run away from him so quickly. Then he rode off.

\#

At noon in the birthing house, one of the doulas told Tandy that Harris had come inside and took three newborn babies with him to the Big House. She told Tandy that he took the whitest looking babies outside to a wagon where Robbins' wife sat and examined them in the sunlight. Out of the three, she chose two. Oftentimes, some of those white features of newborns could disappear as early as six months. The once blue eyes could turn brown and the straight hair could get downright nappy! They would still be raised in the mansion because of their light complexions——but as mulatto slaves.

The black mothers, who had given birth to those babies, were outside of themselves with grief. Tandy comforted them and told them that nothing could be done about what had just happened. She reminded them that those births were a result of rapes——not of love. Tandy gave those mothers a root mixture that made them lethargic and weak. She did it to allow them more time to rest and grieve before returning to the fields.

#

During the twenty-minute rest break in the fields, nursing mothers would run to the crèche to breastfeed their children. Harris sent a driver to round some of them up and bring them to the Big House to suckle the white babies. He no longer trusted sending white infants to the birthing cabin. Tandy hailed the driver and told him to tell Harris that some of the women's milk was unclean. Many of them had fevers. She said there was an infection in the cabin. She told the driver to tell Harris she could not advise against using them because she could not tell the master what to do.

The new black mothers were not summoned to the Big House for a long time.

Tandy walked on the moonlit field that night toward the sugar mill. She could see the fires that illuminated the steam that dashed into the dark air. As she approached it, she felt the heat and humidity. It was thick. She removed her headscarf that exposed her shorn head. She saw Hamp as he climbed down from a ladder on the roof. Tandy walked toward him with food in her basket and a smile. The weary worker was glad to see her but told her he could not walk away with her just yet. That was a term he used for laying her down. Tandy told him she just wanted to see him. She gave him a big hug. Hamp gave a quick response in return.

The light from the roof torches revealed the dried red paste on Tandy's body. Hamp asked her what had happened. She told him this ritual calmed her spirit when she was in Haiti. She told him it protected her from the evil one that wanted to see her dead. She told him she was very afraid.

Hamp sighed deeply and told her to tell him what had happened.

Tandy apologized for lying to him about not knowing who the overseer was that whipped her in the field. She knew he would be upset. She told him the entire episode about the white twins that were brought to the nursery. She omitted her part in the tragedy. She told Hamp that Robbins threatened her at the time of the incident. He had chased her early this morning on his horse when she walked near the thickets. He called her names. She cried that she was afraid of him. She leaned into Hamp for comfort and almost unbalanced, moved slightly to the left of him to recover her stance. He steadied her.

Suddenly, Tandy dropped the basket of food on the ground. She told Hamp she was sorry to have bothered him. She ran back to her cabin. She shouted back to him that she loved him. Tandy burned incense throughout the night. The pungent smells filled the cabin. She rocked herself to sleep in the chair. The next morning Tandy found herself facing in the opposite direction from which she had originally sat. A rooster stood in her doorstep and crowed in the mist.

Cynthia Harris-Allen

Chapter 5

The following day, the ladies of the Big House held a luncheon for the Society of Southern Antiques. About twenty women from homesteads and farms attended. Some of the guests had not been there before and relished the opportunity to dine with real southern gentry, like Luvinia Harris. She was pleased to flaunt her wealth. Some had asked for a tour of the mansion. Exclamations of awe resounded throughout the finely furnished house as guests moved from room to room.

When they traipsed into the library, Luvinia made a point to tell them that she had found some antique books at a quaint shop in Savannah and had them shipped home. With her voice an octave higher, she asked the group if they cared to see them. The women, with gloved hands, ran their fingers over the hundreds of shelved tomes. Some in attendance did not know how to read. They mimicked the comments of those who did.

Before Luvinia could lead them to her newest find, one of her guests spotted the leather-bound novel, *Gulliver's Travels*. She grabbed the book and held it to her chest as if it were a treasure. She swooned and said how much she loved the story. She said Ole Gulliver reminded her of her father who was quite big and burly but gentle. His Lilliputian friends were so cute.

She examined the outside cover and saw a well-worn dent down the middle of it that was about four inches long. Before she could point out the flaw to Luvinia, a young slave girl that had just finished sweeping the corner of the library stopped working. She hollered to the other house help in the drawing room that a woman just said the same name that Tandy called the little babies: "Lilly Pootins."

Laurel Robbins heard what the slave girl had said. She hurried into the room. She grabbed the girl by the arm and asked her to repeat what she had just said. The slave girl hesitated. Laurel slapped her. The girl began to cry. Luvinia rushed into the room when she heard the commotion. She pulled Laurel aside and asked her if she was feeling well. Laurel told her what the slave girl had said. Luvinia, not to raise a fuss, gently pulled the girl aside and ordered the girl to answer Miss Laurel.

The Cricket Cries, the Year Changes

The young woman said that when she had her baby in the birthing house, Tandy had told them that she had read about "Mr. Gullibles" when she was young. She told us that the "Lilly Pootins" people always stood up for themselves. Laurel felt faint. She balanced herself on the table. She hurriedly left the mansion to look for her husband. She lifted her taffeta skirts and ran toward the fields as she screamed his name.

Luvinia apologized to her guests for Laurel's behavior. She told them she knew that most of them had learned how Laurel's twin babies had died in a horrible way. Some days she was still not right, Luvinia explained.

Laurel realized when she stopped to catch her breath that it was Sunday and Robbins did not have a post in the fields. She called some slave boys over and told them to go find the driver at once and tell him to come to the mansion as soon as he could.

Three days passed without a sign of Robbins. Laurel pleaded for Master Harris to send out the patrollers to find him. She said something had happened to him. Harris knew that both parents had suffered greatly with the death of their babies. He had hoped that the two babies from the nursery that Laurel had picked out ten months ago had helped them both with their grief.

By night, he had his overseers put the hounds on Robbins' scent as they sniffed his shirts and hat. It was unusual that Robbins did not have his hat with him, Harris thought. Torchlights scaled the darkness. The bleating dogs signaled their inability to keep a solid trail because Robbins traveled throughout the fields. The slaves were pleased that Robbins was missing. He was one of the meanest drivers on the land. They did not talk much about his disappearance. They sent the news by way of drumbeats. Tandy did not understand the coded noises and asked one of her doulas what the drums said. They interpreted the codes for her.

#

The cane harvest was over and new cane was stored or shipped. Forcing or reaping was not going to occur for another year in those fields. Now was the layover time for Hamp. He resumed a normal schedule. He even visited Tandy in the crèche. She had constructed a lean-to with a blanket thrown over it in the room she shared. The angled sanctuary was their refuge when they slept together.

A conch shell blew the dawn into pieces and awakened everyone. Many knew it was not yet time for them to rise. It continued to blare with such ferocity and urgency. The large bell on the plantation porch began to ring also. The blasting duet frightened the slaves and the residents of the Big House. Master Harris had called everyone to the porch. An overseer stood next to him and held two torchlights. The crowds slowly merged toward the house. Harris and Luvinia held Laurel Robbins between them as they stood. She was sobbing softly. Her head held down. She shifted back and forth on her feet.

Harris yelled over the din of the shuffling feet in the dark that someone on the plantation had killed Robbins. A huge cheer came from the throng of slaves who knew their reactions were anonymous in the dingy dawn. Harris pulled his pistol and shot it into the air to quiet them. He told them that everyone was a suspect and come daylight, he was going to get answers. Meanwhile, he ordered the slaves to sit on the ground for the rest of the night. The slaves huddled together in the chilly air because the damp ground was too wet. Soft murmurings and loud complaints continued until dawn.

The Cricket Cries, the Year Changes

Chapter 6

The thickets hid Robbins's decomposing body. A Cypress tree held it tightly to its bloody bark. Its head could not be found. Harris and his men surmised that the decapitation had to come from a powerfully strong man. The cut was so clean and deliberate that the blood had coagulated at the opening. What little that was left of it began to seep out when his body was loosed from the crude crucifix. Their minds immediately went to the cane cutters. They were among the strongest men on the plantation. Harris decided to begin his inquest by questioning Hamp. Hamp denied knowing anyone who would do such a thing.

He told Harris his crew was still very tired and sore from the work just completed at the sugar mill. They did not have time to kill anyone. He added there were no altercations at all at the mill that involved Robbins. The whites scoured the plantation for information. None was forthcoming. They eventually gave up.

#

Months later, Laurel Robbins prepared to move from the plantation back to South Carolina with her parents. Harris had given her a sizeable amount of money as compensation for the loss of her babies and her husband. When the footmen had helped Laurel and the adopted babies into the carriage, Harris stepped inside for one last word of consolation and comfort.

Laurel numbed by all the rhetoric, told Harris to go to hell. She said he knew all along who had killed her babies and her husband. It was Tandy and Hamp together, she revealed. She asked Harris how he felt about having a nigger on his plantation that could read better than most whites he knew. She recalled for him the conversation with the young black girl at Luvinia's party.

Laurel told Harris that she would ruin him. She knew it was the law in the state of Georgia that prohibited slaves from learning to read. If a slave was purchased from someone else and the new owner knew they could read, the fine would be a stiff one, she warned. She sneered that he could not pay her enough money to keep her quiet. He had allowed that nigger wench to ruin her life. She then asked him politely to please remove himself from her wagon.

With his face as red as pepper, Harris exited the carriage. As he stepped out, Laurel threw a brass bracelet at him. She told him that the young boy that worked in the Big House recognized it and said that Tandy had given it to him when he gave her those books. His momma made him return it to her. She broke down and cried to Harris that Tandy's bracelet was found trapped in the hem of her dead husband's blood-soaked trousers.

\#

Tandy was to be hanged on a Sunday.

Harris had had enough of her lies and manipulations. He clearly believed that she had killed the Robbins' babies. All motives pointed to her. He was devastated at the thought that Hamp was involved in this murder. He had him whipped constantly in the yard. He threatened him with castration by his own machete if he did not confess.

For days, Hamp still maintained his innocence. He asked Harris to allow him to talk with Tandy who was now the lone prisoner in the jail. Harris felt that he owed one of his most trusted and skilled workers a chance. He told Hamp he would allow him to talk with Tandy but he was going to be listening in the next cell.

Tandy screamed and reached for Hamp when she saw him. The guards pushed him inside her cell and then departed. She was chained to the walls of the cell with her hands behind her. She leaned towards Hamp; her angled, stinking body searched his face for signs that he still loved her.

He sat at the opposite end of the cell, glad to be able to rest his feet. Only his hands were loosely bound in front of him. Tandy told Hamp how sorry she was for all that she had done. She said she had been a prisoner in this country since she left Haiti. Being a doula was the only thing that settled her. The nuns in the convent had loved her. They did not treat her like a piece of property. She began to rant incoherently as her sobs overcame her pleadings.

The Cricket Cries, the Year Changes

Hamp motioned to Tandy with his eyes that someone was in the next cell. He moved close to her. They became silent for a very long time. Harris could hear the sounds of the two of them breathing, sighing, and crying. No words were exchanged between the two of them. Finally, chains started to rattle as Harris heard Hamp pace the graveled floor.

Tandy told him that she had to take him with her at her death so she could be complete on the other side. Hamp retorted that he could not dare love her where she was going. He then stood up and hollered for Harris to come get him. Hamp shouted to Tandy that he was not going to die on the same day that she would hang. He wanted no association with her in death he spewed.

Harris stayed put and continued to listen.

Tandy started to tremble and then whispered one word. Hamp could not hear what she said. He asked her to repeat what she had said. Harris moved closer to the common wall on the other side of the cell. Tandy whispered again. Exasperated, Hamp then told her she was going to hell for lying. Just then, Tandy yelled the name "Ibina". She shouted that she and Ibina had killed Robbins.

Harris jolted on the cot. He had just sold Ibina three days ago!

Tandy said that the two of them got Robbins drunk and promised him that they would lay with him in the thickets. She wiped the spittle from her mouth onto the sleeve of her tattered blouse and laughed that he was such a whore and easily bought their invitation. She told Hamp that the two babies that Laurel picked from the nursery were her own husband's slave-born children.

Harris winced.

Robbins was too drunk to fight them off, she continued. They attacked him when he went to pee by the tree. Tandy confessed that she had buried Hamp's machete in the thicket and she already had a rope. Ibina had brought a stool to stand on to kill him but she was such a weakling. She could not even hold the long knife. Tandy boasted that she took care of that fool by herself.

Hamp burst into tears. Harris escorted him from the jail.

Cynthia Harris-Allen

Tandy was the first and last woman hanged by Harris. He hung her because she could read. The slaves watched as the sound of her beads on her matted hair rattled against one another seemingly in protest and then fell silent.

Do you want to know what actually happened?

Hamp actually killed Robbins. He knew before he had met Tandy that Robbins had whipped a midwife in the fields. He had heard it from the father of Ibina's baby who worked with him. When Tandy told him of Robbins' recent taunts and threats, Hamp reacted.

Tandy had dropped the basket of food and ran away that night from the mill because the sight of a headless body on the ground behind Hamp frightened her. He had moved sideways when Tandy had hugged him. The corpse was no longer obscured by his height. She walked toward it and bent down close to examine it but could not recognize who it could be. Her bracelet fell on the body. Hamp started to explain but she ran away as fast as she could.

Hamp had lured Robbins to the sugar mill that night and murdered him. He threw his severed head into one of the boiling vats. Most of Robbins blood spilled from the open cavity while his body was straddled to a donkey that Hamp steered into the thickets. He tied Robbins to a tree. He made it appear that he was slain there. He tossed Robbins' hat far from the mill. Someone had retrieved it and placed it on the mansion porch.

Tandy and Hamp made an agreement the night that Harris had announced Robbins's murder that if they were implicated, she would spin a tale that would free them both from conviction. All Hamp had to do was to convince Harris that he could make her confess. It was all Tandy's idea. She made Hamp promise her to go along with her story no matter what he heard her say. They said goodbye to one another in the jail cell. They made fervent love while the master leaned toward the puzzling silence as he sat in the adjoining cell.

Robbins was actually the father of Laurel's surrogate babies.

Tandy could no longer live with the guilt of killing those little white Lilliputians. Her words spoken inside the jail had set Hamp free. Her mock confession did likewise for her. She just wanted to go home.

Kaffie needed time to reconcile her feelings about Tandy. In her mind's eye, Tandy had been a benefit to so many slaves. She became a victim of her own revenge. Kaffie used fabric from one of the draw-stringed bags saved for the corpses of the stillborn babies to honor Tandy's contribution.

Cynthia Harris-Allen

LUGE

Chapter 1

Luge was the self-appointed Christian minister for the slaves. He had been counselor and adviser to them for thirteen years. He grew up on the Harris-Jones plantation. His parents worked in the onion fields. As an only child, his mother dragged him to Sunday services down by the riverside. As a teen, Luge looked forward to attending the white church.

Blacks were only allowed to sit in the balcony of the small church that they visited on the Wilson's homestead that was near the plantation perimeter. The black women wore their coarse blue dresses to church along with makeshift "fancy hats". Children were bathed in the river the night before. It was difficult to remove the ingrained stench from the bodies that labored constantly but they tried their best. Few black men attended. They did not trust the whites or their white savior. They balked at sacrificing their sole day of rest to an unworthy cause. They paid homage to their own gods in their own way.

Luge felt he was called by God to lead his own people. He begged Master Harris to allow him to work with the slaves. He said he could keep them from wanting to run away and doing harm to the crops. Harris welcomed Luge's request. It was a rare occasion when he could get a slave to oversee his own people in that regard. He told Luge as long as he did not rile the slaves up, he could roam the entire plantation to save souls to their master's favor not necessarily to God's.

Luge could not read. He memorized the sermons which on many occasions were repetitive. The white minister from the neighboring farmstead gave him a bible. There were many pages missing. The ragged leather-bound covering could not keep the remaining epistles intact. Luge used it as a convincing prop. He preached to the blacks on Sundays as he flipped the thin worn sheets not knowing what they read. He held some of the pages upside down.

One day under the tent, Luge approached Kaffie and asked her if she would make him a robe to wear on Sundays. She had heard Harris had given him permission to evangelize. She took his full body measurements and noted the length from his shoulders to his ankles. He was quite short and slight in stature.

He roamed the plantation in his new frock as he began his ministerial duties of seeking and saving the lost. Most of the women embraced with pride that one of their own taught the lessons from the bible to them and their children. The black men however, believed in their rooted traditions of multiple gods and pagan worship. They resented Luge's Christian intrusions. After all, he was an African, too. This black, self-ordained slave preached to the others about the white God. He tried to merge their gods with this Jesus person. He wanted to convince the African descendants to support the colonial religious precepts.

Luge was the only person of considerable religious influence among them. He had few real friends and held no interest in finding a wife. His parents were sold down river long ago. Many of the young boys made fun of him. They stood next to his spare size and teased him relentlessly. They taunted him while they asked him when was he going to grow up. Luge's soft voice and mannerisms did not add any heft to his supposed position of leadership.

Some slaves had agreed to be baptized by Luge and found the experience harmless. However, none of them spoke of an experienced and true conversion. He often preached to the slaves that they had to view their bondage as a fence. He said it could either confine them or protect them. They had to "make do" with their struggle. Luge was steeled by his belief in the Christian god. His resolve was based upon what he had heard from the whites. He patiently rode out the cruel swipes from his own people.

Chapter 2

Gabriel adjusted the knapsack that hung from his stout, burly six-foot frame. It contained a canteen, some beef jerky, flint for a fire, some dried berries, and his bible. A fiddle hung from his shoulder in a worn brown case. He had run out of soap about forty miles back.

His reddish-blonde hair was thick and curly. His stark bulging blue eyes were set in a very large head. His hairy stubble was the testament of a weary traveler. Dust from the sandy red clay sprayed his full-length leather coat with its first Georgia welcome. He was terribly uncomfortable while he wore the burdensome coat. It had warmed him from his northern start to southern Tennessee.

He was not tanned. He was ruddy and splotched despite his long days in the sun. His yellowed teeth rivaled the daylilies and the sunflowers that grew wild along his path. His boots were worn, damp, and wrinkled by the elements. It did not alter the three-foot strides he took toward the Harris-Jones plantation.

Gabriel knew he should be there soon, if not already on the property. It was after all the largest plantation in Georgia. He had hitched by wagon and rail way car to Georgia from his home in Jefferson County, West Virginia. When the roads ended, he camped out to rest. He rinsed the dust from his hairy skin and awaited a lone wagon to appear in the dust.

He was a son of Dutch-German immigrants. He had given himself over to God at the age of thirteen years old. He was not willing to persevere in the salt mines of his hometown. He never married, had no children, and felt that his quest to be the cry from the wilderness was best served if he had neither.

Preaching to the unsaved had become a very lucrative profession for him. It was aided by the rise of the abolitionists who used the bible to site slavery as being evil and ungodly. Gabriel preached the opposite to gain favor with the plantation owners. He told the Africans who received his messages that the bible had a redemption promise if they obeyed their masters. His profession seeded many opportunities on the spaced out homesteads. He seized them all with the full freight of being a minister as his credentials.

The Cricket Cries, the Year Changes

Gabriel sang church hymns to pass the time. His thundering baritone voice frightened many of the animals and routed birds from the trees. The fields echoed his bellows from hill to angled dale, to valley low. They struggled to maintain balance and peace. He also played his fiddle.

#

One purple and orange sunset found Gabriel seated at the root of a giant Sycamore tree. He had nodded off while reading his bible. He was awakened by a wagonneer who asked him where he was headed. He told him that he was looking for the main house on the Harris-Jones plantation. He was seeking permission from the owner to talk to the blacks on the plantation about God. The driver informed him that he had indeed been on the plantation maybe for four days now and that the owner lived in the center of the plantation.

The driver was in the employ of Master Harris. He was just returning home from posting packages in Fulton County. He told Gabriel the planter might not be too sure if what he wanted to do was in the best interest of his slaves. Harris did not favor any type of religious conversions. Most times it put the winds of freedom at their backs, the driver joked.

Gabriel told him he was a Baptist minister and all he wanted to do was to tell the slaves about the Good News. He furthered that he had developed the ability to communicate with other slaves on many plantations with his unique style of evangelical preaching and baptisms. He would tell Harris that he was more than happy to oblige him with recommendations, if requested.

#

The Master gave Gabriel free access to the slaves on the weekends and in the evenings to see how things would go. He told Gabriel his slaves could choose whether they would give up their free time to listen to him. Most slave women were receptive and attentive to what Gabriel had to say; however, some did not clearly understand the messages he preached. They were confused about the role he was to play in their lives.

Harris thought it not necessary to check references of itinerant preachers because too much time was involved. Mail delivery had become slower and slower. He could not keep up with auctions schedules, the news about the abolitionists, and the valuation of his crops let alone follow up on a stranger's endorsements.

The Haitian slave, Ngango kept a watchful, distrustful eye on Gabriel from day one.

Chapter 3

Luge was infuriated that Master Harris allowed a white man to usurp his religious authority over the blacks. Who better than one of your own could lead them to the throne of heaven, he scoffed angrily.

Gabriel had introduced himself to Luge when they were both at the riverbank. This was the first face-to-face meeting between the two of them. He grabbed Luge's hand with both of his and shook it vigorously. Luge's hand disappeared completely inside of his grasp. He towered over him. His imposing frame blocked the sun from Luge's view. This ruddy Goliath intimidated Luge. He was surprised to learn that many of his followers were curious about this trespassing messenger. Now he had two adversaries to deal with, Ngango and Gabriel.

#

As months passed, Gabriel had postured himself as a baptizer. He met with a lot of resistance from the majority of the slaves who wanted nothing to do with going under water. Their own purification rituals were above ground. They used fire and hallucinogens to dispel spirits or to become empowered. None of that involved deep immersion into a river. They did not pay much attention to Gabriel's baptismal invitations. To warm to them, Gabriel had taught them new hymns to sing while he played his fiddle. He preached mostly from the Gospel according to St. John, but most churchgoers continued to seek Luge on Sunday mornings.

There was a fiddler on the plantation named Hank. He played his instrument all day long. At times he was invited to the Big House to play on the porch when Harris had guests. He was well liked. Hank felt that although Gabriel played a fiddle well, he played a different kind of music than he did. Soon Hank resented his own tried-and-true melodies being compared by the slaves to the newness of Gabriel's.

On the other hand, Gabriel sensed the slaves' preference and allegiance to Hank. He did not want Hank or anyone else to garner more attention than he did. He needed to establish trust among the slaves as the only true messenger of the Word with reinforcing hymns. On a Sunday afternoon at the riverbank, Hank challenged Gabriel to a fiddling contest. Gabriel apologized that he had not brought his violin with him that day, but promised they would have one the next Sunday. Rumors spread that the two men would engage in a musical duel.

The slaves converged in the middle of the fields and sat with anticipation on the warming grasslands. The women still had on their "Sunday Blues," the coarse cotton color of their church dresses. Gabriel placed his violin under his chin. He started with a song played long and slow. The slaves listened, but were not impressed. Some grew bored.

Hank used an upbeat tune that soon had the slaves clapping their hands and slapping their thighs with the rhythm. Some had started to dance. Hank played for a long time as he held Gabriel's next turn at bay. He held his fiddle on his lap and played. Hank fiddled for hours. The children brought him water and food. His clothing was drenched with sweat. He kept a broad toothy smile on his face while he stared at Gabriel throughout his renditions.

Soon the horsehairs on his bow started to unravel. When he saw that he could no longer play his fiddle that way, he threw the bow to the ground and began plucking the strings with his fingers. The crowd went wild with his mastery and applauded him loudly. They began to shout his name. Young boys lifted Hank from his chair and carried him off to his cabin while he still strummed the instrument.

When Gabriel stepped into the circle to best Hank's skills, the tired crowd disbursed as they hoarsely praised Hank's abilities.

#

Gabriel deposed Luge as the sole baptizer with a pair of binoculars. One day when the two of them were alone by the banks of the river, he asked Luge to look into the larger lens. Luge was fascinated that he could see the far-away pine forests on the plantation appear so close to him! He continued to hold the binoculars as he reached out with one hand to see if he could actually touch the trees.

Gabriel then asked him to look through the smaller lens. Luge could hardly make out the distant scene he had viewed earlier when he looked through the larger lens. His mouth was agape and his eyes widened as he exhorted Gabriel for an explanation. Gabriel told him that he, Gabriel, had the power to make him small as a gnat just by looking upon him through the binoculars if he did not do what he told him.

Gabriel told Luge if he acknowledged to the slaves that he was now the chief baptizer and minister, he would train the larger lens upon him and make him the biggest and strongest black on the plantation. Luge eagerly accepted the opportunity to co-operate. His first voluntary act of demotion was to give Gabriel his robe to display to the slaves. Luge told Gabriel that his followers would know immediately that he had ceded his position to him. Gabriel's status as the new courier of the Word now came with Luge's blessing.

Chapter 4

With unchecked oversight given to him by Master Harris, and the bloodless coup of the former baptizer Luge, Gabriel was now ready to engage in his deliberate acts. On Sundays, Gabriel preached, sang, and danced among the slaves. He held the women and children close to him. The baritone beseeched them to abandon their savage rituals and join him in serving the one true Lord.

Soon, many slaves allowed Gabriel to baptize them. He won them over with his strength and size. He promised them that he would not let them loose in the deep waters. Luge watched from the riverbank. He nodded his approval to the slaves who cooperated with Gabriel as he coveted his future reward.

The children complained to Luge that the big red man had touched them in their sacred places when he put them under the water. Some of the younger girls and women had mentioned to Luge that Gabriel had groped them and asked him was that part of the ritual. Luge told them that Gabriel did what he did in the eyes of God and the name of Jesus. He cautioned them not to say anything to their husbands and fathers. Secretly, Luge was enraged by the widespread molestation to women and children committed by Gabriel. Nevertheless, he told no one. He secretly savored the possibility of becoming the largest man on the plantation; then he would kill Gabriel.

Gabriel preached to the men separately. He told them that God put man above the woman and she should obey him. Most were able to grasp that concept although some argued that in certain villages in Africa, the women were equal to men. He showed the men pictures in the bible that accompanied the chapters. The drawings depicted Jesus with children around him all the time.

Gabriel quoted from the bible what Jesus said: "Suffer the little children to come unto me". The slaves interpreted the passage as meaning that they would suffer, perhaps by the whip, if they did not let Gabriel have access to their children. Additionally, other pictures in the bible and Gabriel's explanation of them confounded the slaves.

The Cricket Cries, the Year Changes

#

After the continued increase of baptisms on Sundays, Gabriel lay in the cabin that the master assigned him near the slaves. He relived the euphoria that gripped him under his robe as he recalled how he stood in the warm waters and baptized the black beauties, the little nymphs, and the pure children. Gabriel touched them wherever he wanted to. He thought of the personal heaven he had created for himself. He needed no God.

He had arranged, with the Master's permission, to have Kaffie make him two longer robes out of osnaburg, a heavy coarse cloth. When he baptized the women and children, he wore nothing under his robe. He grew so cocksure with his sway over the slaves that he no longer preached conversion. He bellowed to the slaves that the will of God had sent him to save them.

Gabriel celebrated his new life on this plantation. In his mind he was the only one that was truly redeemed. He grabbed his member in the dark of night and cried.

Chapter 5

The male slaves thumbed through Gabriel's abandoned bible. They looked at the fading inked pictures and talked among themselves about the possible meanings. Gabriel had grown a beard. His reddish-blond curly hair grew long enough to reach his shoulders. He parted it down the center of his head. He began to assume the stance in the Jesus pictures as he held out his arms to welcome all slaves unto him. Several slaves began to consider if Gabriel was indeed Jesus.

The Africans became confused with the language that Gabriel used repeatedly especially when he quoted John 14:6. *I am the way, the truth and the life and no man comes to the Father but by me.* Was Gabriel the "I" and the "Me"?, they pondered. Was Gabriel talking about himself or was he preaching about this Jesus? There were debates that found its way into the night whispers inside the cabins only to rehash whenever there was a free moment in the fields. The men argued daily. They grew agitated.

Soon Gabriel shared with them how Jesus died so that they might live. He showed the men a cross in the bible. He told them about the sword that pierced the savior's side. He said the Romans kept Jesus alive so he would suffer longer. They gave him a potion called "hyssop" that was administered to him while he hung on the cross. It was placed on a rag attached to the top of a long branch to reach his lips, he taught. Gabriel kept reminding them that Jesus never cried out until the very end.

Soon, Gabriel had ordered the slaves to construct a large oak cross and erect it high on a hill in the distance. It took seven men to haul it to its place. To look upon it daily from any field position on the plantation would move them toward a complete conversion to Christ, Gabriel said.

As he began to baptize more and more, Gabriel insisted that the slave men cover their nakedness when entering the water with him. He mandated that the women and children be stark naked so their sins could be purified, again, and again. With his earlier convincing argument to the men that they were superior to women and children, they reinforced Gabriel's instruction.

The Cricket Cries, the Year Changes

Master Harris was proud of Gabriel. He had brought about a new form of spirituality in the slaves. He surmised that many were more pliant and docile. Their songs of hard labor and woe were replaced with ones such as *Swing Low, Sweet Chariot* and *Shall We Gather at the River*. In truth, however, they had never been more baffled and confused in their lives about which gods to worship.

At harvest time, the slaves had to work on Sundays because crops that year had surpassed any year that the master could recall. Harris wondered if this had anything to do with God blessing him, because he allowed Gabriel on his plantation to preach the gospel. He thought it was an omen that this minister's name was Gabriel. He had certainly blown his horn of plenty onto his land.

#

Baptisms ceased during the long harvest. Gabriel grew tired of waiting for the opportunity to avail itself to be with the women and children. The temperatures dipped low during many nights that leaned toward winter. Gabriel asked the owner if it was possible that children and young women could be brought to his cabin to keep him warm as he slept. Of course, the master complied; he wanted his spring planting season to be just as harmonious as the fall harvest had been.

Gabriel acted out his fantasies with his night visitors and told them how proud of them the master was. He rewarded them with candy and some of his foodstuffs before he slid closer to them as they slept.

#

Late one night, Hank sat on the stoop of his cabin and softly played his fiddle. Even the crickets were soothed by the melodies. His daughter, Sissy, came out of the cabin and stood behind her father and placed her arms around his neck. Hank dropped his bow, pulled Sissy to the front of him, and returned the gesture. He asked her why she was not asleep. She told him that she hurt between her legs. He summoned his wife to the porch. There, the two of them learned from Sissy of the vile acts that Gabriel had committed upon the children.

Cynthia Harris-Allen

At first Hank thought that the muffled cries from his wife reflected the pain she felt for Sissy and the others until she told him that she, too, was violated as well during her purifications. She told him many women had this shared experience. Gabriel threatened them with damnation if they broke their silence.

Hank looked off into the distant darkness. His jawbones twitched as he clenched his teeth. He cursed Gabriel. He told his wife and Sissy not to tell anyone what was shared with him. They would be safe from retaliation if they remained quiet. Hank knew that Gabriel was a much larger man then he; but he was going to take care of him.

The Cricket Cries, the Year Changes

Chapter 6

Luge had second thoughts about Gabriel and his promise to him. He had done what he was supposed to do. He had influenced much of the slave populace to follow the teachings of Gabriel.

He was sought out when they could not locate Gabriel; and then it was about small matters, like blessing a newborn baby or settling a family dispute. It had been over a year now and Gabriel had not come to him with the binoculars that would change his size.

Luge sat on the riverbank and stared at the sprouting bulrushes by the shore. Along the banks the bare trees, not yet in bloom, reflected upside down in the still, slate gray waters. Luge felt remorse. He had committed one of the seven deadly sins——pride. He gave up his soul for a promise that was not delivered. He knew that he could not overpower Gabriel. He prayed for forgiveness——and a solution.

\#

With the advent of the early spring planting season, Sundays were again used for baptisms. Gabriel morphed into John the Baptizer, as he begged the lost to become the found. He gathered the black men around him again for their private lessons and talked about the resurrection. He read to them about the many people who loved Jesus and followed him wherever he went. He told them the story of how Jesus fed five thousand people with just one basket of bread and two fish. Gabriel looked skyward to heaven as he preached and cried.

The male slaves remained confounded with the pictures throughout the bible.

Luge found the courage to confront Gabriel. He visited his cabin and timidly asked him when he was going to use the binoculars on him. Gabriel apologized profusely to Luge. He walked toward him and placed his strong arms on Luge's diminutive shoulders. He said he had completely forgotten his promise to him. He asked him to forgive him. He walked over to his sack and pulled out the glasses.

He told Luge that because evening was upon them, the binoculars might not work so well without much daylight. He warned him that he only had one opportunity to make this happen. He asked Luge if he wanted to come back in the morning or did he choose to do it now. Luge was inspired that Gabriel still intended to make him the largest man on the plantation, grinned from ear to ear. He did not want to wait another minute to be transformed. He thanked Gabriel and told him to change him that very moment.

Gabriel obliged, but warned him that it was not going to be an instant change; it probably would not happen until two to three full days. Luge trembled with excitement and told Gabriel to do it. They walked out into the dusk. Luge stood up straight, pushed his shoulders back, and placed his feet close together. Gabriel looked through the lens and told Luge to stand perfectly still.

An entire week went by. Luge had held huge ideas about what he would be able to do when he became the largest man on the plantation. He would be able to best the strongest cane cutter, carry the most lumber, not as a job but to show a strength that could not be rivaled. He would be larger than Scipio! Most of all, he would be feared and respected by everyone——including Gabriel and that damned witch doctor, Ngango.

Gabriel's promise was eminent. Luge was overjoyed. Each morning that he awoke, he hoped that long muscled legs would extend beyond his woven mat where he slept. He harbored grand expectations of his robe being torn through by his transformed colossal frame. Gabriel had warned him that it might not work in the dark; but he was so anxious that he allowed him to perform it anyway. Gabriel had warned him that the act could not be repeated.

After a long tortuous month of great expectations, Luge cried. He now realized that he was tricked. The only person that could help him avenge this ruse was Ngango, but he was afraid to go near him.

#

Gabriel stood among the Cypress trees and preached to the crowd. His sermon was about forgiveness. He told the slaves that if they could not forgive one another, they would not see the kingdom of God. The people nodded in agreement as some fanned the insects away. Many of the children fidgeted. It was a long sermon and they were growing restless.

As Gabriel called for heads to bow with the benediction, a huge rock fell on his head from the top of the trees. It cut a sizeable gash in the middle of his head. He fell to the ground on his stomach, unconscious. Women screamed. Children scattered. The men approached Gabriel and turned him over. One slave put his head to his chest and said that he was still alive. They sent others to get a wagon to port him. They could not carry him all the way to the Big House to get help.

Just then, Hank had made his way down from the Cypress tree. He walked to Gabriel's large immobile frame on the ground, and spat in his face. The slaves were puzzled by Hank's motive. While they waited for the wagon, Hank told the men what Gabriel had done to his wife and child and assured them that the same thing was still going on with their women. The men looked at their wives for confirmation of Hank's story. None, out of fear of Gabriel and shame among their people, came forward.

The wagons arrived with the overseers aboard. The whites were angered by the assault on Gabriel. They knew he was highly favored by Master Harris. When they questioned what had happened, Hank boldly stepped forward and confessed that he had dropped the boulder on Gabriel. Before he could continue, one overseer said that it was because Gabriel was a much better fiddler than Hank and he tried to murder him. Hank attempted to rebuke that reasoning but the whites had subdued him and placed him in the wagon.

He was chained in the yard and whipped for three days. Eventually the drivers used the "buck and gag" method of punishment on him. He sat on the cinnamon ground with his hands tied and his feet bound. His knees were drawn up to his chin and a rod was inserted under them and then over his arms. Everything was held together very tightly. Then they beat him again.

Hank's daughter, Sissy, leaned on the fence posts and cried. She talked to her father every day and every night. By now, Hank could not hear a word she said. He was severely injured. The prolonged beatings had rendered him unconscious. On his sixth day in the yards there was a thunderstorm. Sissy and her mother stood in the chilling rain and shouted above the torrents to Hank that they loved him.

No one was outside except the three of them and a hog that had gotten out of the pen. Suddenly, lightning struck the pole held by Hank's knees. His family saw the wavy chartreuse streak as it coursed the length of the metal. Hank's face was lit up like a ghost. His eyes were struck shut by the wavy pattern of intense light. He made not a sound. He no longer felt the pain. His bound body shook and fell angled to one side in the mud.

The slaves held a nice funeral for Hank. Sissy would not allow them to bury his fiddle with him. At the following Sunday service the slaves decided to forgive Hank since that was the message that Gabriel had preached the day when Hank dropped the rock upon his head.

Gabriel was recovering in his cabin, emboldened by the outcome and strengthened with unbridled support from his followers.

The Cricket Cries, the Year Changes

Chapter 7

Master Harris had attended a meeting in Watkinsville, Georgia. He had been gone for about a month to negotiate with the planters. He wanted to lease more field slaves should the coming fall yield prove to be more than his prior record crop. He promised his family he would return home in time for Easter Sunday. He had instructed his chief overseer, Rockfield Stiles, to distribute hams to the slave families as a reward for the previous fall harvest.

While he dined with his peers, Harris caught up on the latest news that affected his business interests. It included the Underground Railroad, a former slave named Frederick Douglass, and a couple of major slave uprisings in Virginia. Additionally, new territories were admitted to the Union designated as free or slave states. It was a lot to digest.

From a more personal standpoint, he learned how effective the Fugitive Slave Act had become and was grateful that runaways and those that abetted their escape would both be severely punished. He was widely respected as the largest slaveholder in the state of Georgia and for the many unique business enterprises that had made him a wealthy man. Harris certainly had a reputation for knowing how to pick the right nigger, his colleagues told him.

On the last day of his stay, he went to a saloon to have his favorite drink of rye with a few friends and a good game of poker before he headed home the next morning. He had been gone now for about six weeks, longer than he had expected. He had missed the Easter holiday with his family.

He sat and studied the bulletins that were posted on the walls that featured runaway slaves and outlaws. He was glad that none of them were his own. He continued to scan the handbills and was shocked to see an artist's rendering of Gabriel who was wanted in three states for child molestation and rape of young girls, both black and white. His real name was Cole Epperhardt.

Harris did not let on to his card-playing friends what he had just discovered. He was glad that he was leaving in the morning. He privately cautioned himself not to use the telegraph to inform his family and overseers about what he had just learned. Word could get out through open communication that he had harbored a fugitive. More personally, he did not want a white man to sire babies by his slaves on his plantation. He could not let this get out.

He lit a cigar and anted up.

#

On a Thursday night, the slaves sang *Meet Me at the River of Jordan*. It was their code to converge at the banks in secret. The men and women decided that they had to give Gabriel what he deserved. They hollered in agreement and raised petitioning hands to the sky. Several men met with Ngango in his hut at dayclean on Friday.

On a hill far away on the Harris-Jones plantation, Gabriel hung naked from the very cross that was erected on the plantation by his orders for all slaves to see. The blacks made crude jokes about his small private parts. Earlier, the throngs of blacks had walked ahead of the cross-carrying Gabriel. They mimicked Palm Sunday and used fronds from the Windmill palm trees to line the path toward the crucifixion site.

They could not hoist Gabriel's nearly dead and heavily sedated body weight upon a donkey to reenact the pictures in Gabriel's bible of Jesus' ride through the village. Instead the cross was returned to its original place on the hill by the whipped and spat-upon itinerant preacher. The base of the dragged cross dug a deep furrow into the clay: it was deep enough to bury a rabbit, but not deep enough to bury the shame of the molested women who finally came forth.

The slaves had beaten him along the way, just as Jesus had been scourged. They retrieved long nails from Scipio. They would use them to secure Gabriel's feet and hands to the cross once they climbed the hill.

Gabriel's pain-filled shrills disturbed an otherwise perfect Friday morning. The strongest slaves on the plantation raised the upright post with the battered, bloodied body attached to it. They had dug a deeper hole into the ground to support Gabriel's weight. They were puzzled by the fact that Gabriel screamed his lungs out though he had taught them that Jesus never cried out until the end.

The Cricket Cries, the Year Changes

The women gladly fashioned a crown of thorns from the thistles that had grown along the riverbank. The spiked adornment stabbed his head with a ring of piercings. The blood dripped into Gabriel's eyes and ears and created competing streams of beet red. It fell to his burly chest between his pinioned arms. His body was rife with evidence of a savage beating. Large blue mottled markings and broken skin attested to the deeds of his well-intentioned congregation.

The witch doctor had prepared a sedative from the powdered hemlock plant that would only sedate Gabriel at first but would eventually kill him. The rag-soaked liquid wrapped around a long willow branch was extended to his bloody swollen and bruised lips just as the bible read. Gabriel would suffer long. He had taught the slaves that this is what happened to Jesus on his cross. However, Gabriel's screams came early from infinity.

A young black had pierced Gabriel's side with a knife but the blood and water did not run out as the bible said it would. He then pierced his other side with a longer blade and a stronger thrust and it happened. He smiled. Gabriel did not scream any last words as Jesus had, they agreed. His swollen head slumped to his chest. With a small gasp, he expired.

#

The slaves were so proud of themselves that they were able to follow Gabriel's instructions and teachings. They held a celebration on Sunday in the high-noon sun with plenty of food, drink, and dance. They beat their chests with pride as their final understanding of the Good News was made whole.

Luge watched the festivities from afar. He misunderstood his own thoughts that Gabriel was going to become a greater man to the slaves in death than in life. That possibility would make it harder for him to reposition himself as their religious leader. However, his other side celebrated with them. The wicked man was dead; his cabin was burned to the ground. The slave women and girls did not want to pass that den of iniquity and be reminded of the red preacher's betrayal.

#

Two days later, the slaves returned to the hill to retrieve Gabriel's body. The flies and maggots had begun to emerge from his open wounds. Vultures circled high above. Their patient, expansive wings cast shadows on the noise below as they awaited a needed meal. The obedient slaves had followed Gabriel's teachings: "When peace surpasseth all understanding". They readied themselves for the next phase of their operation.

Master Harris would dare not treat them as runaways, they agreed. They were doing the work of the bible. They understood now. Their hearts were no longer troubled. The men wrapped Gabriel's body in his two white robes and drove him in the back of a wagon with a large blanket thrown over him. The stench was quelled somewhat by the garlic cloves they sprinkled around him, and placed in their nostrils.

The wagon with Gabriel's massive body, wobbled on the red clay as it trudged slowly to the northeast; the six slaves rode in silence. They took Gabriel's body to the perimeters of Stone Mountain which was about thirty miles away from the plantation. It took them four days to get there. Luckily, no one passed them on their route. It was Easter weekend and many whites were on a full-week holiday.

The males dragged the hemp-strapped body up the side of the mountain. They struggled to find the ascent with the least incline. Their unified grunts aided the strength to pull the huge carcass up the mountain. It slammed on crags and points of the rocks as it left pieces of flesh and blood as unintended dangling markers. The path created small dust storms and snapped twigs and branches along the way.

Soon they found a cave opening and hastily laid Gabriel to rest inside of it. It took many back and forth trips to gather enough small rocks to equal the one giant stone likeness in the picture from Gabriel's bible to seal the cave opening. The six rested and quenched thirsts before they headed back to the plantation. They were bruised, exhausted but proud that they "made do" with what they had to re-enact the "crufikshun".

Chapter 8

Luge had learned earlier what the slaves intended to do. He did not participate. The majority of the slaves had shunned Luge when he tried to explain to them that Gabriel was not Jesus Christ. They threatened his life if he continued to interfere with their Christian mission delegated to them by Gabriel himself. They made Luge swear not to tell Master Harris. Luge feared that he would be whipped or hung by the overseers who might hold him responsible for Gabriel's demise.

The overseers did not pay close attention to the slaves on their free Sundays. They allowed them to gallivant. None of them even questioned their activities on that fateful Friday.

Luge had stayed back particularly to search Gabriel's charred cabin for the binoculars. To his chagrin he discovered the lenses shattered at both ends. Only gaping holes remained in the perceived power-rendering portals.

He sought out Ngango for a powder to cure his constant headaches. The witch doctor reluctantly gave him a gauze bag of ground roots. He told him that the opiate should last for a week. He chided Luge for his overall weaknesses. He called him a "rabbit".

Luge was shamed by the same ill regard shown to him by his own people as before. He repented his willingness to sell his soul for a covetous impotent idol. He did not wait for a Sunday morning to drown himself in the baptismal river. The sun shone brightly on his balding head as it descended into the cool, reflecting waters. His last bubbly supplication was an indistinct cry to his god for forgiveness.

He had a simple funeral.

#

Upon his return to his homestead, Master Harris was relieved to hear that Gabriel had decided to evangelize elsewhere.

To the slaves' unfulfilled expectations, there was no resurrection.

Cynthia Harris-Allen

Kaffie stored a piece from Luge's white cotton-slubbed robe for her quilt.

The Cricket Cries, the Year Changes

Chapter 1

Patrice, a mulatto of intense beauty, was the daughter of an African enslaved mother. Her father, a Spaniard took residence on a plantation in Louisiana to oversee his business of exporting sugarcane abroad to Europe. It was there in 1833 that he met and fell in love with her mother, Caroline.

Jacinto Ruiz doted upon his daughter. As Patrice grew older and her gift for singing became obvious, Ruiz honed it further. He hired voice and elocution coaches to raise the level of her innate skills into an amazing talent. He took her to riverboat shows where she was exposed to all genres of music, song, and people. Her insular life and sensitive demeanor had not prepared her for the city life.

She found many people crass, disrespectful, and vulgar. Culture shock had splintered her placid slow-moving Louisiana plantation life into pieces. These new surroundings troubled her spirit.

She traveled with her father to many auctions and became distressed by the bidding wars and the crude and violating inspections of black people. Those scenes singed a place within her that she never knew existed. These eye-witnessed events revealed to Patrice part of her mother's history. Things her mother had never revealed to her presented themselves front and center.

Though Patrice grew up on a plantation, she never considered the dynamics that drove the hosted institution of slavery. Ruiz said to her that he wanted to expose her to real-life situations that would build up her confidence to handle the notoriety that was certainly destined for her. He often told her how much he loved her, in Spanish and in English. He smiled each time he said "te amo". He promised "when Fate availed herself", he would take her to Spain with him for good.

Patrice was abandoned at sixteen years old on that sugar cane plantation on a Monday. That day, her father had purchased her mother. He was taking her to Spain to marry her. She was never close to her mother; but Patrice was the apple of her father's eye. The only person that she loved had robbed her heart of hopes and dreams. She was petrified with the prospect of being away from her father.

Before Ruiz set sail for Spain with her mother, he gave her a cameo that contained Patrice's profiled silhouette. It was set in a raised black ivory relief and strung through a silver chain. Patrice accepted it as her only inheritance. Ruiz cried with his daughter and through his tears said his father had died. As his sole survivor, he needed to settle his large estate. He had to seize this opportunity to legitimize, through marriage, his love for her mother. He also had to ensure Patrice's birthright.

He said it was acceptable in Spain to marry whomever one wanted. If they stayed in the States with Caroline as his wife it would be a detriment to his livelihood and perhaps their lives. He told her about the Nat Turner rebellion in Virginia and its consequences to blacks who had participated in the insurrection. He feared that the rising tide of dissent for and against slavery was making a dangerous turn in the United States.

Ruiz placed a kiss in the middle of Patrice's forehead and as his habit, softly placed his palm over it to seal it. On the dock her mother gestured a detached wave of "Goodbye" accompanied by a faint smile. She grabbed Jacinto's hand and drew his crying eyes away from his daughter as they walked toward the plank to board the ship.

The *Lafayette* was lost at sea two weeks later, claimed by a hurricane.

Patrice mourned for her parents twice in the same month: once for deserting her, and secondly, for making her an orphan in one fell swoop.

The Cricket Cries, the Year Changes

Chapter 2

Harris-Jones heard Patrice sing at soirees in Charleston, South Carolina. He was moved by her performances. He had attended a rice planters' convention to learn if production of this crop in the Georgia lowlands was feasible and saw her again. When he learned of the death of her former owner, he purchased her from the estate for three thousand dollars. She was twenty years old.

Patrice was a professional singer——an opera singer. Her father's investment had successfully mined her natural ability. She was a quick study of both the Italian and Spanish genres. She sang arias from the operas of *Cinderella,* written by Rossini. Bellini's *The Capulets and the Montagues* fueled Patrice's passion to sing about the two lovers, Romeo and Juliet. She always sang a Capella. Her voice swelled to octaves with long held notes and riffs that beguiled her audiences. They were amazed at such talent——for a black woman.

Her beauty was undeniable. Her smooth skin was the color of a chestnut. Thick feathery lashes that gently opened and closed as they protected the onyx gems, fringed her huge liquid black eyes. Her tiny nose topped thin, wide lips. When she smiled, their corners touched the edges of the high cheekbones that accented her sculpted face. Her waist-length hair culled its ebony tresses from her Spanish roots and its wavy texture from African shores. She was tall and thin like her mother. She was well mannered, and refined.

The convergence of loveliness, grace, and talent offered Patrice a blessed refuge. A cocoon-like existence vacillated between public displays and private hopes. Neither one brought her peace. Her spirit remained unsettled.

Patrice dressed in the same quality of clothing as the better sort of the white gentry wore. She donned silk and charmeuse dresses with matching shoes of peau de soie, lace shawls, goatskin gloves, and petite arm bags.

On the Harris-Jones plantation, she had formed a relationship with Kaffie who sewed Patrice's entire wardrobe. Patrice's favorite dress was made from blue and white plaid taffeta. The design detail of the dress drew a lot of attention. Kaffie had kept pace with the fashion trends. She studied haute couture design details from catalogs that Tillie Harris had collected on her many shopping trips. After her death, her daughter Luvinia continued to covet the brochures.

Patrice spent lots of time in the attic with Kaffie. She learned about the plantations' slave environment. She never tired of personal stories related second-hand via Kaffie's visits under the tents. Their one-to-one relationship provided a sense of belonging for Patrice. Kaffie had figuratively adopted her. She counseled Patrice. The seamstress's own lifestyle limited her ability to understand some of the things that Patrice discussed with her. Kaffie welcomed the personal interaction. It had been a long time since her relationship with Luvinia had ended. She missed being a friend to someone.

Patrice longed to be loved by a man as much as she remembered how much her father loved her mother. She wanted children but she wanted a husband first. She knew if she had a child she would love it with all of her heart and soul. The strength of their bond would balance the scales of her abandonment. Patrice told Kaffie that she had never felt she was a slave given her upbringing by a Spanish parent. The fact that she never performed manual labor of any sort added to that particular point.

She likened her type of bondage to an ornament—— inanimate, and incidental. Blessed and humbled by her station in life, she realized that she needed to sing. She was as bound to her arias as the shackled slaves were with hard and enduring work. She told Kaffie that unlike them she was a *willing* prisoner of her own voice. Her talent allowed her to be free and healed. Inwardly, it placed her above the pains of her circumstances. The impassioned words written by these revered composers were her friends. She corroborated with them to present the musical lamentations that clearly matched her own.

Patrice traveled to slave actions with Master Harris and his entourage. She sang arias on the upper floors of the stucco buildings where the whites dined and were entertained. Harris charged a hefty admission to the planters and their families. Often he brought his own cooks with him to make the occasion a complete dinner theater.

The Cricket Cries, the Year Changes

Varied mixtures of cigar smoke competed with scents of overpowering perfumes from the quasi-aristocrats. Those two elements combined with the incessant swishing of evening gowns, trite chatter, and pretentious cultural awareness served as the perennial backdrop for most of her performances.

Patrice's quiet eyes, like limpid water, came to life as her first inhale released the words of the songs. Mentally, she had elevated her spirit high above the audience. She had chosen a dearer plaintive crowd to soothe with her voice—— the slaves who awaited their fate in the sweltering cells below.

As they stood in the beginning soft rains, the slaves believed that their eyes had deceived them. The black faces pressed against the bars as they shoved the livestock that shared the pens with them aside. They saw Patrice's umbrella escort to the top floors. Dressed in finery from head to toe, she gazed toward them and offered a closed kind smile. Many shouted in their native tongues words that she could not understand; but the apparent tone was one of awe and almost regal respect.

Privately, her heart was heavy as she walked lightly towards the stairs that took her to the fancy rooms and parlors. The overpowering foul smells of the captured below lessened with each step that she took towards the free climate of the assembled audience.

It was a confounding but common backdrop. Her voice drew many people to the auctions just to hear her sing. She added a spiritual in the Yoruban language. In her youth, a Nigerian slave had taught it to her and interpreted the meaning. She set the words to her own original melody. The song entertained the white audience. It was rendered in a language unknown to many of them, yet they appreciated the beauty in its haunting linguistic expression and delivery.

The words breathed new life into old memories of the black waiters and cooks who went about their business of food service and preparation. The footmen, porters, and grooms were grateful to be at rest; they listened from the stone pathways below the chambers above. Some recognized the words from their homelands and hung heads low in reflection and regret.

Cynthia Harris-Allen

The expressive African song imbued a calming effect among the majority of the weeping chattel in the lower quarters. The guards witnessed the somewhat sweeping silencing of the slaves when Patrice sang. The blacks stood motionless as they listened with eyes lifted swelled with rain-mingled tears. The ringing chains quieted. The holding cells could not prevent their whimpered whines from escaping into the free air. They arced toward the upstairs and yearned to join hands with Patrice's gift to them. They held their shackled arms upwards as they reached for the beautiful African who called out to them in the language of their villages.

When Patrice sang that song, she sang for a lost tomorrow. It was her wandering, wondering, and woeful pleas for the rescue of the enslaved——that also included her.

At a certain auction, Patrice eyed a slave awaiting purchase. He stood on an auction block, head held high and proud. She hoped that her master would buy him; she could tell that he was of mixed breeding. There was something elusive about him that piqued her interest. Master Harris saw the silent exchange and began to consider the slave. Harris would do almost anything to please Patrice. She made a lot of money for him and was no trouble at all.

He contemplated the potential of their ability to produce light-skinned children that would present a more acceptable representation of the help in the big house. Luvinia, his daughter, would appreciate that fact. His ever-present business mindset recalled that those children always fetched a higher price when sold. Harris checked the auction bill that described the skills, background, and demeanor of this slave before he proceeded to purchase him. He found nothing untoward. The slave was physically fit, and appeared to be composed. Harris motioned to the auctioneer to place his bidding number around the slave's neck pre-auction as an interested buyer.

Branding irons filled the air with the smell of seared flesh. The purchased blacks received insignias of new ownership burned over the original ones aboard the slave ships. Wild screams of pain from the orange-hot irons offered no apologies to the blue-sky gathering of the buyers. It added to the clamorous bidding process. The division of slave families and friends pricked the souls of the Africans.

The whites shouted as they over-talked one another. Their dollars competed and jousted to get the best of the lot. The humid hot afternoon accented the gamy smells from the fort that lethargically hung in the air. Chafed by their yokes, the slaves were greased to appear healthy. They longed to walk to an auction block alone to finally stand upright and untouched. The eminent future did not matter to them at that very moment. They wanted to breathe on their own and feel their own fear-filled heartbeats.

Harris purchased Saikou, the mulatto slave. Patrice wished she could ride in the slave box train with Saikou back to the plantation. It would give her time to claim him before anyone else could. However, she had an engagement in Florida and she would be going by way of steamboat.

As the boat surged northeastward, Patrice stood at the aft and held onto the patina brass rails. She studied the frothy knitted lace trails left by the rudders in the water. Her heart was lifted with possibilities. Her mind swayed with hope in three-four time with the waves. During her concert in Jacksonville, Patrice performed light-hearted and comedic arias. She did not want to be sad that day. In addition, her twenty-fifth birthday was tomorrow.

Cynthia Harris-Allen

Chapter 3

Saikou was the name of Patrice's destiny. He had been a cattle herder on the island of Jamaica by way of the Ivory Coast. He was captured at the age of six. His ancestral tribe was the Fulani, an Islamic people. These nomads avoided pagan worship. Many of them thought they were superior to other Africans who practiced idol worship and worshipped many gods. The Fulani's one god was Allah.

In his native country, Saikou was the son of a judge who himself, had managed to escape capture. Now thirty-one years old, Saikou was a skilled cattle herder. Other enslaved Fulanis who pastured their ancestral knowledge on the open meadows on the islands taught him the fundamentals. The daily rituals of praying on mats toward the sun continued on the plantations in Jamaica. The majority of Christian whites did not trouble to convert the Muslim slaves. They felt because their numbers in the islands were so small it did not pose a threat to their missionary outreach.

Saikou was an adept herder. He knew the body language of the cattle. He kept them at peace without aid from a shepherd dog. He studied their boundaries or flight points and avoided invading their space which could cause them to panic. In the late evenings, he peaceably steered them back into the enclosed fences on the Harris-Jones plantation using only a long thin stick and a calming voice. He gave Master Harris updates on the condition of the herd be it disease issues, birthing matters or grazing relocations.

He quietly refused to assist in the branding of the cattle. He feigned lack of knowledge and not having a steady hand. He remembered his own branding event when he was just six years old; now the most recent one had added to his angering avoidance. It was against his religion to have any sort of tattoos on the body. He was met with no resistance to his claim of disqualification.

Herding was a lonely, all day process. Cattle grazed from peach dawn to dove gray dusk to fill their collective stomachs. Saikou liked the solitude this job warranted. It enabled him to pray five times a day uninterrupted. He followed the positioning of the sun to stay on schedule. From time to time he would ask for assistance to round up the

The Cricket Cries, the Year Changes

cattle when their numbers grew. The help came from very young boys who frolicked far from the standing herd. Saikou would interrupt the merriment and summon them to help redirect the variegated brown animals back to the pens.

Saikou slept among the other slaves sometimes. He exercised the strict dietary laws of his religion. He engaged in general conversation; many considered him standoffish yet non-threatening. Just like the cattle he herded, Saikou zealously guarded his space.

One evening after prayer, called *Isha,* Saikou heard the same voice that had enchanted him with song five months earlier. It came from the direction of the mansion. He rolled up the new woven mat and walked toward the huge porch where a crowd had gathered to hear this songbird.

Master Harris had given a party to celebrate the beginning of what would be one of the most bountiful harvests he could remember. Crop and animal production were both high which pleased Harris to no end. Bales of dark blond hay circled the expansive landscape. Soon it would be unfurled to fill mattresses in the cabins, line the floors of barns, and top off the animals' feeding stations. During this fete the slaves were allotted their ration of new clothing and a brand new pair of shoes, called "brogans."

Saikou saw Patrice, dressed casually in a robin's egg-blue dress. The simple off-shouldered garment appeared to create an aura around Patrice. In addition to the slaves, the overseers, drivers, and indentured servants were in attendance at the evening celebration. Saikou was awestruck by the number of inhabitants that were solely under Harris' authority. His solitary duties as a herder placed him in remote pastures. He never considered the enormity of this place.

Patrice had ended a song and urged the other slaves to begin to sing with her. Soon, she stepped from the porch to walk among them——a rare occasion for her. She grabbed the hands extended to her in friendship. Young slave girls hugged her with admiration. She was moved by the gestures. She came to a clearing in the crowd. Patrice stood still and faced Saikou. He held his mat and his eyes were still transfixed on the crowd; his senses drew in the smells, sounds, and sights of the event.

Her shadowed movement averted his attention toward the woman in the blue dress. The words from his mouth were a stuttered "Hello, Ma'am". Patrice, delighted to see him extended her hand to him. They walked away from the crowd towards the open grounds. Saikou opened his mat and spread it upon a small grassy hill. He extended his hand to invite Patrice to sit under an oak tree. He leaned against it and studied this miracle as she sat and twirled a blade of grass.

The Spanish moss, in its dusty quiet grace, moved slightly over the golden silence. Saikou was the first to speak. A dumbfounded and flummoxed Patrice just stared up at him. Her loss for words crippled her well-rehearsed plans of how she would first greet him. Saikou said that he never knew that she lived on this plantation. He asked her if she was a free slave. Patrice told him that she was a slave and pointed to the same overbrand on her upper arm. She then gave him her history.

She cited her itinerant April to September social schedule as the reason they might not have crossed paths earlier. She added that she would be on the plantation for about six weeks before the year-end holidays would have her on the circuits again.

Saikou told her how beautiful she was.

Patrice shyly thanked him.

Saikou told her that he was a Muslim.

Patrice told him that she had no god.

Saikou told Patrice that he respected women but women had to be submissive to him as was his culture and religious tradition.

Patrice replied that she had been submissive all of her life.

Saikou asked if she would submit to a kiss from him.

Patrice said "No", but she would surrender her all to him if that was what he wanted. That evening Master Harris allowed them to marry; it was his intention all along. The added celebration intensified the revelry.

That night in their new cabin, Saikou kissed Patrice in the middle of her forehead. He placed his palm over the kiss to seal it.

Patrice wept.

The Cricket Cries, the Year Changes

Chapter 4

Six months later, to sweeten a huge deal on a rice-planting co-operative with one of the other plantation owners, Master Harris acceded to the wishes of the slaveholder's young son, Phillips. He was smitten with Patrice and wanted to father her children. The agreement met with feelings of betrayal and anger towards Master Harris by a shocked and mortified Patrice. Master Harris had warned Saikou that he had no say in the matter and threatened to sell him "down river" should he buck him in any way. Saikou prayed to Allah to unburden him and his wife from this horror.

Phillips made sure that he flaunted his random access to Saikou's wife. He scoffed to the cattle herder that he was just "slave-married" to Patrice. Phillips brazenly visited their cabin whenever she was home from tour and took her any way he wanted to. Saikou took to leaving the cabin when he saw that Phillips's wagon had made the turn onto the graveled plantation driveway. He stayed through the night on the range with the cattle; sometimes he stayed for days.

\#

Patrice cited her shame and helplessness in letters written to Saikou, through Kaffie, who read them to him when Patrice was away. In some posts, she had placed her own handkerchief scented with the fresh sassafras chips she carried as breath freshener. At times she included a pressed flower. Kaffie read the secret code words that only Patrice and he understood. It urged the sanctity of their love for one another to remain true.

Saikou prayed on his mat in the fields and smelled the handkerchiefs. He placed them inside his shirt collar to preserve the scent for as long as it held. He would get word to Kaffie and asked for another opportunity to meet her in the tent to hear Patrice's same words read again until he had them memorized.

When Phillips lay with Patrice, he was put off by the way she immediately moved her mind to another place when he touched her. She did not respond in any manner. Her only reaction was a muffled sigh of relief from her when he withdrew from her dispassionate body.

Patrice was irritable and agitated throughout her pregnancies. She could not fend off Phillips's repeated rapes. Each child could possibly be Saikou's. She did not want to abort for that one major fact; but at times she was tempted. When she made love with Saikou, Patrice called upon her father in her heart to make it right for her, for Saikou——for good.

Saikou's angry, anguished mind fringed his distress when he entered Patrice. Many times he thought of running away from this whore, this unclean woman. Once he thought of hurting her badly to bring about a miscarriage. He was frightened by his own alien and vicious new nature. He blamed the vile visitor who took his wife at will and breached his own vengeful thoughts.

He hated to be with Patrice when she was in the final months of her pregnancies. With each maternal episode the anticipation of who actually fathered each child created a heavy heightened suspense between them; it often caused heated and hurtful exchanges. Patrice and Saikou's opposing wills were not collectively strong enough to crumble the opposition.

Kaffie worked day into night as she made larger sized dresses for Patrice. She still had to sing, to feel free, and to get away from the hell that had taken over her life. When she tried to sleep, exhausted from the concert tours, the growing baby moved in her womb. It brought on nightmarish dreams and suicidal thoughts.

Each time Patrice bore a child by Phillips, it was taken from her and raised and suckled on his plantation. She never saw them again. In three years she had given birth to three children by him. Saikou began to think that he was unable to father a child with his wife.

Phillips did not visit Patrice for over two years after the birth of the last baby. Still under the pall of the fatal influence of this funereal ordeal, Patrice continued to sing. She hoped to rehabilitate her soul. She added musical tragedies to her repertoire. To sing them was effortless, unforced, and fluid.

When she could be with Saikou during her performance breaks at home, the two treasured their time together. He did everything to lift her depressed spirits. He remained positive and expectant despite being emotionally pockmarked. He felt deep remorse for the selfish way he treated her throughout her trials. His acts of contrition were overwhelming and served to bolster her spirits. Most times, they were able to suppress any discussion that could re-open wounds that remained fresh in their bleeding hearts.

They only had one major argument. Patrice asked Saikou to consult with Ngango to seek a cure for his infertility. Saikou adamantly refused.

In the spring, Patrice was pregnant with Saikou's child. She continued her tours. She still sent love letters to him. She sang to the baby inside as she impatiently anticipated its birth. Fortunately, the baby was born when Patrice was at home. Saikou wept openly as Patrice presented him with a son.

Ngango danced naked in the rain with rooster feathers on his head. He shook a rattle made from a hollowed-out broom handle. It was filled with nutshells whose powder he had given to Patrice to increase Saikou's fertility. Slave drums signaled that Patrice and Saikou were made whole.

#

When he heard the news that Patrice had had Saikou's child, Phillips was inflamed. He felt that he should be her sole breeder. Phillips had loved Patrice from the moment he laid eyes upon her. He was obsessed with her. Marrying a slave would have been out of the question due to his status. Having children by her was an acceptable practice though it was an illegal act as defined by the Slave Codes.

Phillips was now a plantation owner himself. His father had passed on and he now wielded considerable influence with Master Harris and others. On a Sunday morning, Phillips met with Harris. He petitioned him to sell Patrice to him outright. He offered him a large political contribution. Phillips said that he would allow her to bring her nigger baby with her to keep the peace.

Patrice begged her master not to sell her and her baby to Phillips. Master Harris dismissively ignored her. He ordered her to sing at that evening's soiree; he said they would talk about it in the morning. Harris' attitude had changed toward Patrice. He did not appreciate the advantage that Phillips had inserted into their business dealings.

The evening's dinner meeting discussion was about a possible run for office by Master Harris.

Many wanted to hear Patrice's performance.

That afternoon, Patrice ran frantically to find Saikou in the herding fields. Clutching the baby boy not yet named, she found her husband and fell into his arms. She gave him the news of Phillips's reappearance and his unbelievable demands.

Saikou almost fainted. He lay on his mat, prayed, and cried. He stood up, ripped the mat into shreds and scattered it onto the grass. He held his family close to his heaving chest and assured Patrice that she and his son was not going anywhere. They held long glances. Feelings of hopelessness fell with a heavy hush between the two of them. The unspoken crippled thoughts pierced through the heat unable to find a reasonable time to be heard. Their angst collided in mid-air wrapped in feeble yellowed attempts to make sense of what lie ahead.

Saikou outlined his son's face with his fingers. With an impassioned moan, he kissed Patrice's sweaty cheeks and told her not to worry.

Patrice walked in a trance towards the mansion. Saikou was powerless to help her and her baby in any way, she thought. She consulted the witch doctor. After she begged him to give her a way out, he administered a potion that temporarily rendered her speechless with no other physical side effects. She was unable to perform that evening.

Harris, infuriated by her impertinent deliberate retaliation, set the sale of Patrice and her baby to Phillips before word could get out that she could no longer speak, let alone sing. The trip to the Phillips' plantation in Macon, Georgia to deliver Patrice with the baby was set for Tuesday morning. He ordered her to pack her things.

The Cricket Cries, the Year Changes

Chapter 5

Monday evening, Patrice dressed in one of the finest silk dresses she owned. She plaited her hair in a style high above her head and held the braids together with a huge amber comb. She put on full makeup.

She walked into the fresh coal black night air. She passed slaves still working the fields; she received their knowing, pitied glances. Softly placed pats of sympathy touched her shoulders. Slave drums had already messaged her visit with Ngango and the resulting consequence to her voice. Saikou was still herding cattle. He had heard the drum codes but did not know what they meant. The slaves beat out news so often, he thought; he could not tell a warning from a piece of gossip.

Patrice deliberately walked towards the bridge she had traveled over repeatedly. She smiled sadly as she held her big-brown-eyed baby boy. She twisted his hair around her finger forming temporary coils. She hoarsely whispered parts of a song to him on the two and a half miles she had walked. ".. and I just can't keep from crying——sometimes; most days my soul is dying——sometimes."

She stooped to abandon her high-heeled shoes at the wide turn in the road; they freed her aching feet. She turned to see a cloud of dust that formed in the distance. It signaled that someone was coming towards her on horseback. The background din of a Yoruban song that the slaves had begun to sing in unison accompanied the sighting. Patrice had taught it to them.

Hound dogs with bleating barks ran alongside the horseman. A nebula of red dirt was illuminated by a lantern that swayed back and forth; the rider on the animal held it high. He pressed its ribs with his spurs to increase its speed.

It was now pitch black on a star-filled night that offered no ground illumination. Patrice continued her walk to the bridge with hurried steps. Her pace quickened with the swishing of her green and white plaid taffeta dress. The prolonged high-pitched wails of the slaves' voices gradually melted into the distance. Crickets held their usual choir rehearsal and fireflies danced to their songs. The rising smells from the Georgia pines wafted toward Patrice. It indicated she should soon reach the river bridge.

Patrice plaintively sang to her son from a Bellini opera. The wistful song of consolation was to protect her son and quell her own fears:

> *Little butterfly, wait, O, wait.*
> *Don't fly away so quickly.*
> *I don't mean to harm you.*
> *Stop and fulfill my wish!*
> *I want to kiss you and to feed you,*
> *to save you from danger.*
> *You shall have a crystal room,*
> *and will always live in peace.*

The sound of the river's lazy flow signaled Patrice's arrival at the bridge. The cool breeze was not able to dry her unbroken tears. She stood with her feet together, dusted by the russet Georgia clay that had torn holes in her silk stockings. She stopped and took one long deep breath punctuated by a hesitant sob. Her coiffed hair now dismantled by dirt, wind, and perspiration was now upon her shoulders. She pushed it back out of her face and tucked it into the high back part of her dress.

The pursuer had not yet reached her; but she discerned that the lantern loomed brighter, bigger, and closer. She was glad that her escape was eminent.

Her toes gripped the smoothed oak rails of the bridge. Her left hand reached for the vertical posts. She hoisted herself to a standing position. She precariously balanced her footing. She hugged her son close to her breast with the other arm. Patrice whispered Yoruban words to him: *"temi ife"* (my son). With both arms she encircled him.

The yelping, tired dogs had lost the scent of her tracks at the post. They began to lunge at her feet atop the high fence.

Patrice took flight as a kiss from her lips glued itself to her child's forehead. Her billowy silk dress with the many white crinoline slips underneath resembled a butterfly misplaced in the night. Just as the rider jumped from his horse to grab her, a piece of the green tartan-plaid garment was caught in the barbed wire of the bridge.

The trapped hem of her clothing pulled her back for an instant. The recoil redirected her flight pattern. It caused her to lose hold of her baby as the dress ripped apart. The sudden return of her voice emitted a wretched scream. Her arms flogged the air. It grasped for any part of the little boy to rescue him from a life that she did not want him to endure. She wanted to gift the both of them with death.

The baby, frightened by the free fall, gasped for breath. His thin swaddling cloth opened in the breeze as he floated towards the ground. A tall Georgia pine caught the crying baby in its middle branches and held him, not swayed by its tender weight.

Patrice's face cracked into pieces when she hit the jutting rocks in the river. Her long tresses shielded her gory features. Her silk dress shrank immediately, shocked by the cold water's embrace as it temporarily attempted to dye it blood red.

\#

Saikou cremated Patrice's body and angrily tossed her ashes with abandon throughout their cabin. He placed her cameo necklace around his collar.

Philips took his own life when he learned of Patrice's suicide. His wife, disgraced and humiliated all those years by her husband's blatant, overt disregard for their marriage, sold his three children by Patrice down river for one dollar each.

A week later, a thunderous roar awakened Master Harris and others who slept in the mansion. It increased in intensity as it stormed towards the mansion.

The bolting frightened occupants ran towards the windows. The earth quaked under their feet. The entire structure shook. The residents in the house were terrorized as three hundred-plus cattle bore down on the mansion. The beasts burst through doors and windows. They splintered furniture, shattered china, and demolished everything in its wake. The bellows and bawls of the livestock drowned out the screams of the tenants who ran wildly for their lives. Some would not escape the horrific groundswell of fury and frenzy.

When the last cattle had exited through the back walls of the mansion, the trail of ruin had weakened its beams. The captain's porch lay fractured on the living room floors. The entire left side of the mansion had fallen in on itself.

Saikou had placed his son, Shawq, meaning "longing" in Arabic at the end of one of the meadows to await his return from his last cattle drive. He picked him from the bowed branch of a bough, studied his sleeping face and began to walk northward.

A new praying mat hung from his shoulder.

Kaffie suffered deeply at the loss of her dear friend, Patrice. She sent a slave to the bridge to retrieve the piece of plaid fabric rumored to be ensnared in the barbed wire fence. It would become the centerpiece of her quilt.

The Cricket Cries, the Year Changes

AMIDOU AND NGANGO

Chapter 1

Amidou was a griot, a West African word for a storyteller. He toured the plantation and summoned children and young adults to come and hear his stories on Saturday evenings and all day Sunday. His proverbs and parables spoke to pride, self-confidence, and patience. He carved symbolic words on his wooden teaching stick. He slackened the stubborn hard clay with a rake and drew figurative marks upon the persimmon ground. Sometimes he placed stones in formation to make his point. To offer an unexpected treat to his audience, Amidou would do an interpretive dance.

When he learned of pending family separations, due to Master Harris' constant dealings, he ran to that group to comfort them and offer words of encouragement and strength. He drew illustrations on the cabin doors of those who were in mourning for others to see. He asked them to act on their feelings of community. It was a privilege for many children to vie to be participants in Amidou's storytelling. He used them in masquerades or dressed them in costumes to bring the animals that he depicted in certain fables to life.

Amidou was captured when he was a young Ghanaian slave. He was sold on the island of St. Simon just off the Georgia coastline. The captured walked in lines called "coffles" toward the big ship. On the island of St. Simon, he stood in deep rows in barricoons the cells that simultaneously housed both slaves and livestock. His arms lay crossed behind him by his captors, bound securely behind him with dried ivy strands of rope. Circled collars of thorny twigs were placed around the necks of most young males to stave off revolt.

He was auctioned off in Savannah, Georgia and purchased by Master Harris. Amidou arrived on the plantation at thirty-five years old. The slave drivers and overseers noticed right away that Amidou did not do any work in the fields——no matter what the crop. He instead, moved among the workers and made their burdens lighter. He recited African folklore, doled out proverbs or made them laugh. He had a natural talent.

Harris saw that he did not present a threat and allowed Amidou to do what he did the best; he calmed down the slaves. Soon, Amidou asked Harris for a single cabin for himself. He wanted to be able to meditate and reflect without being interrupted or disturbed. He added that he wanted to receive slaves in their free time that needed comforting and solace. Harris agreed for Amidou to be the sole tenant of one cabin for a trial period of three months after which time he would re-evaluate the situation.

The griot stressed to the slaves that they should know the planation landscape better than any white person around. Physically it looked very much like their homeland. He urged them to pay more attention to sound than to sight. He mimicked the noises made by animals and the calls of certain birds. He asked them to familiarize themselves with the ruckus of the forest denizens.

He cautioned the slaves to heed the tone of the voices of the overseers and gauge their attitudes toward them by how they spoke. Amidou told them to give full ears to the drummed codes. If he had a pressing message he would change the words in the Sunday songs belted out on the riverbank to communicate its urgency. He hand painted designs on his shirts. They revealed colorful silent messages to some slaves who still understood the Yoruban symbols. They in turn, would pass it on.

#

Amidou served the slaves at cross-purposes with Ngango. Many referred to Ngango's powers as being supernatural. Amidou dismissed their speculations. Nevertheless, when he saw the positive effects of Ngango's medicinal treatments, he understood the reverence they gave to his position. Ngango firmly entrenched on the plantation for decades, was feared by most whites. He wielded power and influence over the slaves. He had an extensive knowledge of poisons. Ngango could incite a riot at his will. In spite of this, Master Harris had given him free reign. He saw how useful he was at healing the slaves, both physically and spiritually.

Ngango would tell the slaves that listened to Amidou's parables that the road to freedom and respect was not wrapped up in words, particularly when those words were calls for submission and bowed heads.

Amidou countered and recalled ancestral tales of triumphs by those who learned as they lived and lived by what they had learned. He stressed that stupidity may not kill you, but it can certainly make you feel the whip.

Soon, Ngango issued warnings that the slaves could no longer wear the messages that Amidou painted on their bodies. He banned the women from wearing their head wraps in certain ways that sent veiled messages from Amidou. They immediately obeyed him.

#

One afternoon Amidou counseled a slave family that had learned through gossip trails that two of their members were going to be sold down river the next week. Amidou spoke comforting words to the family about strength, endurance, and hope. The affected family was distressed. A slave driver stood by the window opening of the cabin undetected and observed. He saw the huddled crying group shake their heads collectively as they heeded Amidou's words.

Before the week was out, the entire family had escaped from the plantation. Coondogs were let loose in all directions. It appeared that the escapees had chosen different paths to flee to complicate their capture. Harris immediately assumed that Amidou had aided them, based on the report of his overseer. The master had Amidou chained in the yard for two days. He did not protest. His silence sent mixed messages to the slaves. Was he involved or not?

Harris removed Amidou's privilege of being the sole occupant in his cabin. He had violated his trust. Ngango was pleased that Amidou hid his embarrassment with a cloak of silence. It restored his full sway over the slaves. He seized this opportunity to convince the blacks that Amidou's teachings were flawed. The master's actions altered Amidou's reputation among the slaves.

Released, sunburned, and dehydrated, Amidou returned to his cabin in the evening to find that eight other slaves that included three children lived there, too. Amidou took Harris' decision in stride. He spied his personal belongings that the new arrivals had respectively stacked in a corner. He claimed a small space as his permanent area. He sat on his short woven mat in meditation.

As was his nature, he soon started to engage with the little children. Some of them smiled shyly. Others slowly withdrew toward their parents. They eyed the stinky man in the strange clothing with fear. One young woman named Lucy stared boldly at Amidou. When she had arrested his attention, she showed every ivory tooth in her mouth. Amidou did not know how to react.

He turned his back to the wall and moaned loudly as he sat stretched out on the mat. He welcomed the opportunity to lay flat on the ground after being chained in the yard. He was very tired and sore. The small fire inside the cabin projected his shadow on the wall he faced. He saw that it made him appear larger than he really was. The forms of the little children that danced and played while they defied sleep were superimposed upon his silhouette.

Amidou grinned slightly. The gods had given him a sign that his role as a guide and counselor was still intact. He lay down and closed his eyes with thoughts of tomorrow being Sunday. It was his opportunity to rest, bathe, and speak with the slaves. The crickets cried and lulled him to sleep.

The Cricket Cries, the Year Changes

Chapter 2

Lucy was infatuated with Amidou. She made sure she garnered the majority of his free time in the cabin using her endless chatter and threatening stares that fended off the other tenants. Even if a hard day's labor of hoeing in the field had exhausted her, she was determined to be with him. Amidou treated her with indifference. He was not looking for companionship or a wife.

Amidou had trained several slave women as griottes. He carefully selected the storytellers based on his perception of their commitment and care toward the children. Lucy decided to join the ranks of the griottes and asked Amidou to include her. He reacted negatively to her sly request. He knew that Lucy wanted to be around him more often to sit alone at his feet like the others he had trained, but with an entirely different motive.

She had become annoyingly irritating to him. She frequently brought him food, asked to wash his clothes by the river, and swept his mat clear of crawlers. During Amidou's lesson to the children one Sunday, she stood next to him as he sat on the ground and boldly wiped the sweat from his brow with the bottom of her cotton skirt. The hem lingered upon his lips. Amidou was embarrassed. The griottes were shocked at her behavior especially around the young girls. The women looked inquisitively at Amidou and searched his face for signs of complicity in this brazen display. Amidou halted the storytelling and dismissed the crowd.

That night in the cabin, Lucy skulked over to his mat and lay next to him. She lightly touched his back and shoulders. When that did not awaken him, she began to rub his neck and head with both hands while she blew into his ear. All the while she moved her body closer and closer to his. When she decided to mount him, Amidou, startled, picked up the large flat stone that he kept for protection. He hit her in the face with it.

Her loud shrills awakened the other families in the cabin. Through the darkness they could not make out what had happened but knew by her continued wails that it was not good. They did not move toward the commotion. Lucy, in excruciating pain, felt the warm red liquid as it flooded down to her neck. It soon became sticky. Her eyes stung and her forehead throbbed. Her nose was numbed. Her jaw was frozen. The screams stifled to hoarse grunts; she could no longer open her mouth.

Amidou gripped the massive stone in his hand, jolted by what he had done. He never looked at Lucy. He did not speak a word. He sighed deeply and moved toward a corner. He sat in a crouched position with his head bowed. He rocked backward and forward and waited for dayclean.

Lucy had made her way out of the cabin assisted by Buttah, one of the occupants of the cabin. They both sat on the stoop of the splintering planked porch. Buttah placed a coarse blanket around Lucy's shoulders. The two swayed with the sounds of the night. Soon the chilly cloudy morning cast a greenish-gray shroud over the sleeping plantation. Amidou had fractured Lucy's face. The blood, now crusted and brown, had dried in the cracked lines and created a labyrinth of disconnections. Her clothing bore pasty splotches of her red injuries.

From her forehead down to just above her chin, the damage from the circled stone's imposing dent in her face was prominent in the pending daylight. Buttah began to scream toward the skies in her native tongue. She rubbed her own forehead and jaw and then pointed to Lucy's injuries while she babbled incantations into the void. Lucy began to shudder at the obvious damage to her face. She was in a lot of pain.

The young girl guided her on the long walk to Ngango's hut. Ngango sedated Lucy. He knew early on that he could not do anything to repair her face. She would be able to see and talk, but her face was permanently smashed in. To him, her face looked as if a large animal had set one deliberate foot upon it.

Gossip spread like the plague. The inhabitants of the cabin said that Amidou had attacked her during the night. The griottes that knew of Lucy's behavior toward Amidou cast doubts upon her claims. Lucy told those that would listen that Amidou was upset with her because she would not lay with him. She said he restrained her on the cabin floor and overpowered her. Then he threatened her to say nothing about what had happened. Lucy said she swore to him that she would tell everyone and that was when he hit her with a rock.

The women ceased their storytelling and did not want to have anything to do with Amidou. Many slaves questioned their allegiance to him. The women kept their children away from Amidou, mainly their young daughters.

Amidou wanted to kill himself. Ngango celebrated.

#

Two months later, during the allotment of clothing under the tent, Kaffie confronted Lucy. She pulled her aside and asked her about her injury. Kaffie had already heard of the incident but wanted to hear it from Lucy. She repeated verbatim the lie she had perpetrated so many times. Kaffie told Lucy she did not believe her. Kaffie told her she had known Amidou for a very long time. She asked Lucy why a man of almost fifty years old, with no wife or children would do what she claimed he did. What moved him to commit such an act?

She asked Lucy to consider what kind of man Amidou was. He had a strong character and discipline. He was unselfish and dedicated, she declared. Kaffie told her the children and young adults needed him; even Harris saw the value in him. That is why, in the beginning, he had given him a cabin of his own to receive slaves privately and help them.

She looked Lucy in the eye and asked what other slave on the plantation once had had use of their own singular cabin sanctioned by Harris. She told her Amidou was special. She told Lucy that she had to love him as the rest of the slaves did. He was not meant to belong to any one person.

Lucy was silent. She knew how many people respected Kaffie. Now this face-to-face conversation revealed to her why. Lucy buried her face into her own hands and cried. She asked Kaffie if she ever loved anyone so much that it made you a different person. She confessed she needed Amidou to belong to just her and no one else. She admitted that now his life was ruined and so was her face.

A young girl overheard the entire conversation and ran to her parents.

\#

Many bonfires burned on Sunday. Amidou was restored to his position among the slaves as counselor and storyteller. There was a celebration.

Pleas for Amidou's forgiveness from the slaves were plentiful. The children decorated his space in the cabin with flowers and fruits. Someone replaced his bloodied mat with a newer, much longer one. The other tenants agreed to leave the cabin anytime Amidou needed privacy. Lucy moved out.

Lucy continued to work in the fields. Most slaves shunned her. During the fall harvest, she suffered a mental breakdown. She was removed from planting and harvesting duties. Her new job was to beat the dust from the carpets that hung from the poles at the back of the mansion. Her violent swings with a rugbeater that consisted of rattan switches wrapped around an iron handle highlighted her wrath and frustration with her circumstances. She beat the choking dirt into oblivion each day. She screamed until she was croaky. She impatiently awaited the next piece to fall victim to her rage.

The Cricket Cries, the Year Changes

Chapter 3

On a snail's-pace summer afternoon when the beige corn was not as high as it should be and the almond cotton had not burst through its boll, Amidou entertained a group of slaves with his stories. This was the layby. Harvest time was approaching. There was little fieldwork. The slaves were kept busy but not as busy as usual. The normal reverberating hoes, picks, and machetes lay idle in the sheds.

Grunts from heavy lifting, groans from wearied backs, and the gritty calloused hands of the labor force were absent. The overseers' whips were relaxed except for minor incidents of slave "back talk" or idled disobedience.

During this time Amidou had the opportunity to increase his storytelling. He told the group a story about a mouse. He and his troupe acted out a tale about a huge cat that tried to catch it. The tiny little creature was able to elude the cat's paws and pounces because he knew that a hole was nearby. Amidou explained to the onlookers that unless one has a place of safety and protection that they can quickly find, do not act like a fool out in the open. Many slaves acknowledged the meaning of his words.

He was an expressive memory maker. His tales fascinated children and adults alike. Twig and branch-filled bonfires crackled and snapped around the watchful crowd while he told them of their storied past. He said their ancestral glories gave them the strength to survive. Once he wore a black hat similar to the one Harris owned and pretended to be him. Amidou acted as if he was old, decrepit, and mean-spirited. He imitated the Master's inability to mount a horse on the first try. The crowd applauded the exacting impression Amidou rendered. They slapped their thighs with laughter and clicked their teeth.

Amidou would ask them whom did they want to be: a proud person in temporary bondage or an old white man who would not live long enough to spend all of the money he had made off of their backs?

#

Harvest time was now in full swing. The pendulum of lull and laziness had swung totally to the right and the plantation field workers were now fully involved. Wagonloads of crops were ported to their next processes: the corn to shucking, the chaff to separation from the wheat, the animals to slaughter, and cane to the sugar mill.

One day, Harris had several business colleagues accompany him on horseback to tour his large plantation. He wanted to impress them with the size of his bounty. When he arrived at the fields, many of the slaves turned their backs to him and stopped working until he had left the area. The same dramatics were repeated like the ebb and flow of the tide until he returned to the mansion embarrassed and angered.

An overseer whispered in his ear at dinner that a while back he had witnessed Amidou's impression of him complete with the black hat to a crowd of slaves. He continued that the nigger had led those blacks into some kind of wild excitement that Sunday night.

Harris had Amidou taken to the open yards. He was chained and beaten for three days. He went without food or water for four additional days. Slaves were threatened with the whip if they attempted to feed him. Amidou never learned the reason for the punishment. Drumbeats throughout the plantation dispatched the news of Amidou's plight. Harris, tired of the incessant noise, had all the drums confiscated and burned next to Amidou in the yards. The slaves began to pound their own bodies. Some had their backs beat upon by other slaves to continue their communication throughout the homestead. They used sticks to strike trees in rhythmic beats. They clapped rocks and other solid objects to convey their messages.

The codes encouraged the slaves to "gold brick," a term that meant "work stoppage" or "resistance". They destroyed tools, poisoned the harvested fruit, and did anything else that lessened the progress of the yield. The slaves pulled fences down that freed the penned animals to roam aimlessly. The blacks cracked all the eggs that had been collected that week and spilled the contents upon the ground.

Harris would not give in. He was not going to release Amidou. He ceased whipping him and moved him to the jail instead. He posted three guards around the building. He ordered thirty lit oil lamps to hang from the wrought iron perimeter of the jail to make sure Amidou could not be set free.

Three poisonous darts met the targeted necks of the sentries. Instantly, they fell dead to the ground. The bodies, with the aid of the excess illumination were removed, weighed down, and thrown into a freshly dug grave in the Ole Field. Harris limited the punishments to the slaves that he thought were responsible for the disappearances and assumed deaths of the guards. He was not going to sabotage his own harvest. He needed every able-bodied hand to complete it.

He ordered his drivers to pour brine salt and turpentine on the open whipped welts of the beaten for every slave to see and think twice before they continued the vandalism. In response some slaves self-mutilated to get out of work. The washerwomen purposely left fragments of lye soap in the wet clothing of the whites when they hung them out to dry. It caused rashes and severe irritations to their skin. Vexed by the prevailing dissension, Harris harbored mixed feelings about the effects of the continued imprisonment of Amidou. If he freed him he could still cause trouble and use his release as a victory over him.

He and Rockfield Stiles went into the tent to visit Kaffie. She told Harris she did not keep up with the goings-on of the plantation. However, she told him she had heard nothing but positive things about Amidou. She asked Harris politely that he not put her in the uncomfortable position as a snitch; it made her very uncomfortable. She said she was in good standing with the slaves. She began to cry. Stiles bowed his head down.

Harris looked into the grey eyes of this mulatto. Her face was dotted with soft brown freckles. Her light brown hair rested on her shoulders. He had never studied her before. He wondered to himself who was her father. He comforted Kaffie with a pat on her shoulder and told her to forget that they had ever had this conversation.

Harris freed Amidou with clamorous opposition from his employees. An overseer attempted to bribe little children with sweet stuffs if they let him know about Amidou's future activities. Harris was desperate for any information. For weeks, the kids ate candy and were sickened by the excess. Nothing they said to the overseer made sense.

The Cricket Cries, the Year Changes

Chapter 4

Efforts to salvage the harvest after all the events were further hampered by severe storms. It ravaged the plantation for a week. Heavy chilling rains fell onto the furrowed crops. It swept away many of the plants that clung helplessly to the saturated ground. Tubers, such as potatoes and radishes were lifted to the surface by the downpour. The auburn clay turned into ginger brown puddles of streaming water. The torrents raised the level of the river. The swollen tides coursed toward the slaves' quarters at the back of the homestead and flooded most of them.

Harris, daunted by the latest events, moved as many black males as he could into the jail he had built on his property. The crowds brimmed over the cells. They fought for a space where they could stand. They raised their fists in anger and shouted epithets at the whites. Other groups of blacks were chained in the open yards. The drivers stood around them in the rain and discharged firearms into the air to quiet the throngs that resented the incarceration. That task grew more cumbersome as the rain wet the gunpowder. Soon, the overseers walked away to seek shelter.

On Harris' orders, his workers pitched tents on the huge mansion porch to house the women and children who had fled the high waters. They huddled in the cold damp downpour. Slaves questioned why most of the elderly and infirmed were left to fend for themselves in the flooded cabins. They were frightened for them. They knew that the high surges brought forth snakes.

At daybreak, Harris promised the tented, chained, and jailed slaves he would still make certain they were fed and relieved of their wet clothing. He emphasized to them he was not punishing them but protecting all from the rising river. After four days of continuous rain, slaves in the tents became sick from the cold and dampness. Harris lost about fifteen slaves——three were children.

Luvinia Harris, sickened by the stench just outside the mansion door, argued with her father about the difficulties and inconveniences he was causing by sheltering these niggers at her front door. She told him that their own food storage was diminishing. There was no dry wood to cook or to

311

build fires. The house slaves were not working fast enough, she grumbled. She wanted the water rats that had taken over the drawing room flushed out by somebody——anybody.

Harris told her emphatically that he had to preserve the slaves. Without them the entire plantation would be ruined and along with it, his legacy and her future. He reminded her that he had already lost a lot of his crops and animals before the storm because of the latest incidents. Luvinia continued to complain.

Harris, with an angry bang on the dining room table with his cane, interrupted her. He hollered that he questioned her ability to run the plantation after he was gone. He said she did not possess an ounce of business sense nor the civility to be respected as an heir. With that, he ordered her to have the cooks prepare food to refill the cauldrons and troughs stationed at opposite ends of the porch. They had to make haste before the cloud-filled daylight rains began again to feed the masses.

He did not want lamps burned throughout the night. He wanted only one lamp per person in the mansion. The oil supply had dwindled considerably. There were no deliveries to this plantation situated in the valley. The roads were impassable.

#

After his release, Amidou had stayed behind in the cabins, and rounded up most of the old slaves. He carried them one by one toward drier cabins at a higher elevation at the end of the row. He placed the crippled and infirmed slaves on the wooden chairs he had taken from other cabins. He covered their shivering, aching, and ashy bodies with dry blankets or clothing that had hung from the walls. Amidou told them he was going to get food and water for them. Some laughed weakly when he told them not to run off.

As he walked towards the Big House, his brogans sloshed in the flattened grass and heavy mud. On the way, he heard the jailed and boisterous males that still protested their detention. His lamp lit his path. It illuminated remnants of food: peach pits, chicken bones and the like littered the ground below the jailhouse windows. He was relieved that at least the slaves were being fed.

The Cricket Cries, the Year Changes

He arrived at the mansion porch. The smells of urine and feces mingled with that of steaming soup, ham, corn pones, and chicken. He swallowed hard and tried not to vomit. The drenched gray tents glistened in the pre-dawn night. The sounds of disconsolate slaves drifted into the dank despair.

An overseer named Simmons stood in Amidou's path not recognizing him at first. He asked him where he had come from. The overseer knew that most of the black men were jailed or chained in the yards. Amidou identified himself and asked Simmmons to allow him to get food for the elderly people that were left behind. Simmons called Stiles to where they stood and informed him of Amidou's request. Stiles saw no problem with it and thanked Amidou for his help.

He told the overseer to fetch some of the younger females from the tent to help port food and water to the area. Simmons took it a step further to ensure that the slaves would return to the tents and not try to run off. The plantation watch detail was not at full force. He told the women to gather the staples and stand in a certain area and wait.

As dawn broke, a flushed and breathless overseer returned with five hound dogs tethered to a single leash. The dogs were trained to track their prey with speed. The frisky, barking dogs sniffed at the heels of the women. Two of the dogs lunged toward the food that one of the young girls held. The girl screamed to the top of her lungs, petrified with fear. She clung to the food as she ran faster toward the cabins. The two dogs pursued her. They pulled the entire pack along with them. Their deep chests breathed power into long strides. Their combined weight broke the hold of the overseer.

The women and girls began to spill out from the portable shelters. They had heard the barking dogs and the wailing girl. It was now daybreak. The tents collapsed with the calamitous flight of the slaves. Their bare feet splashed in the dirty debris-filled puddles. They ran towards the child and shouted for the overseer to reign in the animals. Simmons stood dumbfounded in his muddy tracks.

Harris, moved to the porch by the clamor, saw the crowd of running women. He rang the bell on the porch three times that summoned all hands to the mansion. The jailed blacks climbed over each other's backs to investigate the noise. What they saw was a bunch of zealous dogs that chased a small girl. The women from the porch tents suddenly came into their view. The men shouted to them as they thrust muscled arms through the bars of the window. They begged for information.

The pursued little girl slipped in the mud and rolled onto the ground onto her back. She covered her face with the trembling hands that had dropped the plate. At first, the dogs fought over the food that the child had held. However, they were trained to subdue their running prey. They viciously bit the child. The sharp incisors below their pointy snouts began to yank the flesh from the slave. The girl screamed in unendurable agony until her last breath.

The crowd of women arrived at the spot where she lay on the ground with the dogs on top of her. They had disemboweled her still-twisting torso. The slaves began to throw rocks and stones at the dogs. The slippery objects missed the mark most of the time. It took several women to hold the main cord that tethered the dogs. The animals continued to spiral themselves free.

Soon, other women arrived with rakes, hoes, and hatchets and brutally beat the dogs. The slaves cried, cursed, and wailed with each blow. The dogs' painful yelps added to the pandemonium. Some had managed to bite some of the slaves. A slew of overseers and drivers on horseback came onto the scene. Stiles shot a rifle into the air and ordered the women to stand still.

Simmons, who had gathered the dogs in the first place, finally gave a whistled signal that immediately interrupted the continued attack of just one dog. The other four were killed by the women.

The rain had stopped.

The Cricket Cries, the Year Changes

Chapter 5

Ngango treated the slaves' injuries in the hut that Harris allowed him to build long ago. The thatched roof domicile was not damaged by the floods. He had built it upon stilts. His products, potions, and pomades were spared from the deluge.

While he applied the healing ointments to the skins of the bitten slaves, he asked each one why Amidou was at the root of all bad things that had happened recently on the plantation. Ngango said Amidou destroyed the accord that Harris had with them. Their disabled communication was slowly being rebuilt but that griot was responsible for the destruction of the drums.

They were never put on watch in tents on a porch during a rainstorm before, Ngango pointed out. Their young men did not deserve to be crowded in a jail or chained in the yards. Ngango begged his patients to consider these things when Amidou wanted to talk with them again about patience and love. He spat on the floor in disgust. Simmons, who used the hound dogs, was not even punished for his stupidity by Harris, Ngango continued. Another dead slave girl was sent to the Ole Field because of a white man's ignorance, he said bitterly.

As he ministered to the wounded, Ngango asked each one of them to go back to the fields, riverbanks and cabins and consider why Amidou still deserved their high praise.

#

Amidou continued to tell stories to whomever would listen. He noticed that the ranks had diminished considerably. In the fall, the slaves lined up for their winter allotment of clothing under the tent. Amidou told Kaffie he did not need sleeves sewn on his shirts as before. The slaves no longer read his shirts. He told her he had fallen out of favor with them. Amidou told her he only wanted his parables to make his people think. He just wanted consideration for his messages.

Kaffie never knew the symbols he painted on his shirts meant something. She was able to connect the reason for Master Harris' inquiry. He had had suspicions about Amidou. In a way she was glad she no longer had to alter his tunics.

Kaffie gently urged Amidou to move along. She had many more people to tend to. Amidou thanked her for her friendship and told her one day she too, would be forced to put her own reflections into action.

#

One evening, over a hundred bales of hay were set afire near the barn. The rolling smoke made it necessary to evacuate the livestock in nearby pens along with the horses and mules in the barn. Master Harris was vexed by the numerous incidents of insurrections that had occurred on his plantation. His relationship with his slaves was tenuous. He feared sometimes for his own life and that of his daughter and employees. The slaves outnumbered them twenty-five to one.

He called a meeting with all the whites that also included the indentured servants. He expressed concern over the growing dissent of the slaves and reminded them not to let their guard down nor travel the grounds alone. He assured them he did not have any specific information about any pending dangerous activities, but he was sorely disturbed by the increasing unrest among the slaves. Harris told them that if they noticed or heard anything unusual or threatening, they should bring it to him first. He did not want anyone to act on his own.

#

Harris walked toward the back of the mansion with his dog, Buck in tow. He was smoking a long cigar. It was an oppressively humid afternoon.

Lucy beat the carpets as they hung from the lines. She talked to herself as usual. She swung the carpet rods towards their targets. She did a semi-curtsy to Harris and tried to grin. She flexed; she had forgotten that her smile had morphed into a grimace long ago. She had heard Harris' warnings to the people who had attended the meeting, through the windows. Lucy told Harris she knew who was behind the hay burning. It was Amidou.

Harris told her to talk with him. Lucy leaned against one of the sawhorses. She held her head down and told Harris she did not want him to look her in her face because she was no longer proud of it. Harris obliged without even asking her about her deformity. Lucy told him Amidou painted symbols on the light-skinned blacks' arms, shoulders, and backs that showed the slaves what he wanted them to do for him.

She said the latest inked designs had the symbol of fire on it. Soon after that the hay fire happened. She told Harris that Amidou also wore codes on his shirts that he drew himself. The slaves from the same tribe as him would read the markings and inform others of his plans. Harris, shocked and angered, sat up straight. He was not fully convinced but it could be a very clever method of communication since he had ordered the burning of the drums.

He warned Lucy that she better come to him in the future with any information that linked Amidou to something that would cause hurt, harm or danger on his plantation. Lucy curtsied and returned to her carpets.

Harris did not realize how long he had thought about what Lucy had revealed to him, bit down hard on the stump of his cigar.

#

Lucy found Ngango near the perimeter of the plantation. He had pulled roots from the ground and rolled them in his hands. He placed the exposed bunch to his nose and nodded in approval. He then placed them in the sack that he always wore over his shoulder. He looked at her and remembered the broken face he tried to patch up a while ago.

Lucy told Ngango they both had an opportunity to get rid of Amidou for good. She told him she knew he was angry that Amidou was stealing some of his power. She said she would give him something that belonged to Amidou to place a hex upon it. She relayed to Ngango what she had told Harris and invited the witch doctor to join her to destroy Amidou. In her mind, she was prepared to set Amidou on fire if she had to.

Lucy told Ngango that her plan was to walk into the mansion as she always did when she replaced the cleaned carpets and retrieved the dirt-filled ones. However, this time she was going to enter Luvinia Harris' bedroom and steal all of her ball gowns. She would roll them up in the rug from her floor and carry them outside. She decided to add two of Luvinia's wigs just for kicks and giggles. She would place the gowns by the slaves' cabins. She knew that the black women would fight over such a collection of finery. They would think that a member of the Big House no longer wanted the items.

The act would serve a two-fold purpose. Lucy hated Luvinia. That cow bossed her about every hour of every day, Lucy complained to herself. She slapped her often for no reason at all. Both Luvinia and Amidou deserved to get what was coming to them.

Three days later, Lucy ran to Harris with the news that Amidou had painted colorful long dresses on his shirt and walked slowly among the slaves in the fields. She swore to Harris she had seen it with her own eyes but she did not know what it meant.

The Cricket Cries, the Year Changes

Chapter 6

Ngango had snatched one of Amidou's shirts from his porch. He could not wait for Lucy to bring him something else of his as she had promised. He spread it out in front of him on the floor as he kneeled upon his mat. In his hut, he burned incense and began to chant. He smoked one of Harris' cigars that Lucy had stolen and given to him. He had placed the oiled cloth over his door opening that signified to others that he was not to be disturbed. Soon he would be rid of Amidou by the master's own hands, he thought.

He threw the roots that he had dug up by the bulrushes into the center of the shirt. It was faded with muted colors that collided into each other and formed a muddled mass of meaningless messages. He drew a long puff from the cigar and let the wispy trails escape from his mouth and nostrils on its own. Ngango then chewed on the dried plant that hung from the top of his hut. The intoxicant put him to sleep. The glowing cigar fell by his side.

#

Lucy placed the pile of dresses in a heap in the laundry area near the river. The slave women washed clothes two to three times a day. Lucy was certain that the gowns would be discovered early.

Black men, who had returned from their early morning fishing chores, came upon the dresses. They knew at once that the wardrobe belonged to Luvinia Harris. They had seen her prancing and dancing when they worked near the mansion. They hated her. They placed each dress separately on the ground. The men peed and defecated several times on each one. They cursed Luvinia while they relieved themselves. Two of the slaves placed the coiled wigs

on their heads. They danced with one another and mimicked how the whites moved in a funny fashion during the parties. They laughed themselves into exhaustion. The fish abandoned on the grounds began to smell.

Cynthia Harris-Allen

The slave women had just tied their head wraps on and counted the clothespins in their apron pockets. They headed toward the washing area. The sight of the male slaves in such a festive mood surprised them. The females eyed the dresses on the ground and stopped short of stepping closer. The gowns smelled. Flies laid in the waste. They covered their mouths to muffle their sounds. Some of them laughed at the two slaves who still donned the wigs. At the same time that the women stifled their voices, a fully loaded scream rocked the mansion.

Luvinia had opened her armoire to find empty hangers still on the poles and on the floor. Her prized ball gowns were stolen! She ran to her father, already awakened and armed. She pulled him to her room to show him the carnage. That act was the last straw for Harris. Intruders had dared come into his home. They all could have been murdered!

He gathered his men and rode on horseback to the cabins near the end of the farm. They passed the washerwomen. Harris stopped his horse and viewed the gowns on the ground——ruined.

With guns and whips in hand, the men raided the cabins. They kicked every black male awake until they found Amidou asleep. He had stayed up late last night to counsel a grieving family whose elderly mother and father had died on the same day. He did not know why he was dragged from the cabin. He was taken to the open yards, stripped naked, and beaten severely.

Meanwhile, Luvinia rode in a wagon at top speed accompanied by two armed overseers. She saw her gowns as they curled in the wind on the ground. Some could not move due to the entrapped amount of waste heaped upon them. She swore to herself she had also seen her blondish wig in the fields but did not want to pursue it. She stood on the hard clay ground and looked at the desecration with her arms folded tightly across her chest. Harris moved to console her. She rebuffed his comforting hands.

#

The Cricket Cries, the Year Changes

Harris rang the porch bell. It awakened the entire plantation. When the slaves slowly assembled near the porch, Harris ordered those to come forward who knew that Amidou had sent out a message to steal his daughter's clothing. None answered the call. Lucy had placed herself inconspicuously among the onlookers. Her entire plan had gone awry. Nevertheless, she celebrated this outcome as the better one.

Harris had the slaves dig a fresh grave in the Ole Field. He had Amidou dragged to the site and thrown into the hole. Amidou begged for his life. He swore to Harris that he did not know why he was being punished. He repeatedly shouted to him to tell him what he had done. He begged for a covering for his nakedness. Harris obliged him. He had his men throw Luvinia's soiled gowns upon Amidou's body. Then they poured buckets of lamp oil on the dresses and lit it with a torch. The slaves turned their backs on the pending gore. Amidou roared as the silk, charmeuse, and taffeta fabrics quickly melted into his skin. The cotton pieces burned longer. Harris in his continued rage ordered his men to bring him a bale of hay to keep the fire going. With contempt, he asked the dead and charred body how he felt about hay now.

Lucy stood by the grave in the hot afternoon and lamented all of her dirty deeds. The intense sun caused wavy images to form over Amidou's body. The hay fire continued. The burning golden straw turned to wispy spirals as the scant breeze moved it lengthwise across the grounds. The chocking jackrabbit gray smoke burned her eyes. She still loved Amidou and believed that Kaffie was correct in her evaluation of him. He was a kind man. He really did care about his people. Lucy bowed her head in shame and whispered a plea to Amidou to forgive her. She joined him in the funeral pyre.

\#

Ngango still felt the full effects of his inhalants. He awakened and put on Amidou's shirt. He exited the hut and stretched. He saw a large fire down in the valley near the slaves' graveyard. He staggered toward it.

The same overseer who had brought his hound dogs to the tented porch stood guard by a tree. He saw a tall man who walked with a large stick over his shoulder. He heard his ceaseless incoherent babbling. He walked passed Simmons. His yellowing bulbous eyes stared menacingly at him. Simmons was frightened. He cocked his rifle and shot the drunken slave in the back of the head. He fell to the ground, killed instantly.

The slave who wore the painted shirts was the griot that Harris warned them about, thought the

shooter. Simmons was proud of his actions; he could be placed in Harris' good graces once again, he gloated. He walked over to kick the dead storyteller over onto his back. His face paled with incredulity when he discovered his grave error.

Fearing for his life, Simmons ran far away from the plantation with the embedded memory of Ngango's twisted facial expression as a constant reminder of his mindless act.

The pilfered cigar incinerated the hut of the Master Healer.

The Cricket Cries, the Year Changes

Chapter 7

The largest homegoing for any slave on the plantation was held for Ngango. Generations of slaves owed their health, both physical and spiritual to this powerful man. Conflicted with the death of this practitioner, Harris allowed a work stoppage for a week. Ngango had been a valuable asset but was also a man who struck fear in all who he thought would cross him.

Ngango had lived on this homestead for fifty-four years. He was eighty-six. The slaves buried Ngango in a six-foot hollow of a trunk of a giant Cypress tree. This was a traditional custom of extreme reverence. His apprentices prepared his body. They greased him heavily with special ointments that retarded the onslaught of flies and other insects.

Asters, Thimbleberries, Firewheels, and Dogwood from the meadows were colorfully stuffed all around his body. They filled the cavity behind him with Spanish moss. A laurel wreath of Black-eyed Susan and Buttercup was placed upon his head. Large pieces of marble from the quarry were placed in his eye sockets. To prevent birds and animals from feeding upon the dead body, bells, chimes, and rocks were strung from the tree branches with remnants from the leather lashes. Their movement in the breeze frightened the would-be feeders away.

When Ngango's body began to rot a month or so later, the slaves cremated him. They took tiny bits of his ashes and spread them everywhere over the plantation. They wanted his presence felt wherever they walked. Some rubbed his ashes onto their heads. Others swallowed bits of it. Ngango was mourned for a very long time. An uncertain fragile calm hung ominously in the air on the Harris-Jones plantation for many years.

#

Cynthia Harris-Allen

Kaffie felt part of her soul was pulled out when she learned of this valuable man's mysterious death. She retrieved Ngango's gunnysack that had held his roots and herbs. It had leaned against a tree near his burned-to-the ground hut. She would wash it and insert a remnant from it into her quilt.

Later, she cut a smaller piece of the cotton fabric that she had used to make sleeves for Amidou's painted tunic. In retrospect she thought that he was a good man in his own way.

The Cricket Cries, the Year Changes

SCIPIO

Chapter 1

Scipio raised his sledgehammer high into the steamy air. He pounded the iron pieces that soon would be forged into axes, knifes and machetes. The high-pitched sound of each strike resounded throughout the plantation. It paced the stop, stoop, and stepped movements of the planters in the fields. The flattened hot pieces hissed when they met the murky cold waters, steamed by its submersion. The apprentices that assisted Scipio kept a watchful eye on the lesson he was teaching that day.

Scipio was the plantation blacksmith. He was a "salt water negro" a term the whites used that identified him as an African- born slave. Scipio was from Gambia. His tribe, the Maninkas was renowned as blacksmiths as well as other artisans. His mother was a potter. His father was a celebrated blacksmith. Unlike Scipio, who made horseshoes and planting tools, he fabricated ornamental ironworks.

Along with other villagers in his native Gambia, Scipio was captured when he was a young man of seventeen. He was taken to the island of Barbados. His parents were sold apart from him at the initial auction. He was enslaved on a small farmstead in Beaufort, South Carolina where he worked for thirteen years. Harris bought Scipio when his former white forger died.

He was taught to shape and design iron by his father but his blacksmithing was limited to the agricultural and mechanical demands of the Harris plantation. As his contribution to the dead slaves' families, Scipio usually made symbolic wrought iron markers for the graves in the blacks' cemetery that was called the "Ole Field." The more of an impact the deceased's life had had on the plantation the greater his piecework revered them. That was the only time Scipio used his otherwise arrested imagination and innate talents.

Scipio's physique was intimidating. At thirty-six years old his strength was the envy and marvel of many. He could carry an eighty-pound anvil in one hand while he lightly swung three to four hammers strung from a thick leather tie in the other as if all of it was a mere ball of feathers.

Cynthia Harris-Allen

Harris respected him above all of his slaves. Of particular interest to him was Scipio's growing knowledge of forging horseshoes. He had mastered the process. Many horses throughout the northern Georgia counties were shod with Scipio's work. As a farrier, he made Harris an awful lot of money. When the armies had arrived to move the Cherokee and Chickasaw west of the Mississippi, the forges met the needs of the Calvary. The incessant clanging of tools guaranteed a restless sleep for the entire plantation but it filled the master's coffers tenfold.

#

Harris wanted Scipio to breed with the slave women who were tall, strong, and young. Scipio resented being used like an animal and he told Harris so. He entreated him to allow him to distance himself from these women once they bore his children. He even asked that the women be blindfolded and brought to him in a random cabin and not his own living space.

He told him it was against the will of his gods to have sexual relations the night before a huge smelt. The forging would not go well if he did. Harris, not convinced that he told the truth, allowed Scipio to have his way. He did not want to waste time, money or material on something that might go awry.

Scipio fathered eleven children. The women did not know who had sired their children——all except one. A slave named Darling, a Nigerian, knew in her heart that Scipio was the father of her son. She had named him Abidemi that in Yoruban translates to "born during the absence of the father". As the boy grew, many slaves had noticed his remarkable resemblance to Scipio; not only the physical attributes but also the way the boy carried himself and spoke, as well.

At sixteen years old, an overseer placed Abidemi in the forge to assist the blacksmith and his apprenticed help. When his tall strapping dark body shadowed the entrance, the eyes of the workers darted back and forth between father and son in amazement. Scipio told one of his helpers to assign the young man to the tasks of hammering the light axes and knives. He never spoke directly to Abidemi.

At nightfall, the other workers left for their quarters while Abidemi sat on the floor among the shards of iron and scraps of wood. Scipio told him that he could go to his cabin now. The boy told him his mother had died that morning and he no longer had a home. He told Scipio that his mother told him he was his father. Scipio studied his own mirror image with bewilderment. He had not formed close relationships with anyone since his capture. He did not want to love anyone or anything. Harris had tried to give him a dog but he refused it. Separation from his own family in Gambia pulled the life out of him. He placed all of his energy and strength into pounding his hate, hurt, and disappointment into the tools he made. The wall around his heart was fortified with iron.

He allowed Abidemi to sleep in his cabin that night. He told him he had to wait and see if he would like him or not.

#

Over the course of two months, Scipio was taken aback by the natural skills of his son. Whatever he taught him was absorbed like the sun's rays. When Scipio thought that Abidemi was somewhere else on the plantation on Saturday and Sundays, he was actually working in the forge. During the week, Abidemi would secure his body across the rafters high in the barn and watch every move that his father made when he wrought horseshoes. He rolled them out pretty fast, his son thought. How proud he was of his father's strength and boundless energy. He was saddened that his father had neither a wife nor a friend.

That same night he saw his father fall to the floor on his knees and pray. He called out in a language that Abidemi had not heard before. After about half an hour later, Scipio grew still and silent. Abidemi silently navigated his brogan shoes down the layered rafters but he landed on the floor with a thud that alarmed Scipio. Before he could say a word to his son, Abidemi walked over to him and knelt next to him. He asked him to teach him how to pray like him. He asked Scipio if he could just touch his hand.

Scipio became a father at age fifty-three.

#

For the first time since his arrival to the Harris-Jones plantation Scipio took off work on Saturdays and Sundays unless there was a job that demanded a full-time effort. He and Abidemi spent entire days together. Their favorite pastime was fishing. Scipio taught him how to make spearheads that could penetrate the scales of the bigger fish in the deeper parts of the river.

He told his son about life in Africa. Abidemi told him his mother had told him about her village as well. Scipio told him that hundreds of thousands of villages exist in Africa; many of them had their own distinct customs. Scipio told Abidemi his grandfather was regarded as supernatural because he could fashion something from nothing. The Maninkas felt his forging powers came from on high. His family was greatly respected in the village. He described the wrought iron ornamental objects his father had made. They ranged from large fences to small intricately sculpted faces that the royals gave to visitors to carry. It granted the bearers safe passage back to their villages.

Scipio spoke of the limited time he himself had to make decorative markers for the graveyard. He said he was afraid he would lose entirely the talent to make them since he did not do it on a regular basis.

Abidemi responded that his mother always told him that one cannot "unlearn" something. Scipio laughed. He asked his father to teach him, out of respect for his grandfather, how to inscribe designs in the metal. One day he would pass it on to his own son, he assured him.

The Cricket Cries, the Year Changes

Chapter 2

One morning Harris sent Rockfield Stiles to tell Scipio to pack his essential tools and clothing. He was needed at the eastern porch of Big House. Scipio asked Stiles if his son could accompany him to the mansion. Stiles told him it would be okay. The three rode their horses to see Harris. They found him perched on the steps of the side porch.

Harris told Scipio that he had signed a contract to lease his skills for one year in the state of Louisiana. He was to travel there with a colleague of his named Randmont Fuqua who had moved his family south from Boston. Fuqua had known about Scipio's skill as an ornamental blacksmith. On a tour of the Harris-Jones plantation, he insisted that Harris allow him to dismount by the Ole Field when he spied the wrought iron arched entrance and the unique individual markers on some graves.

Awed by the near-genius replication of design and style, Fuqua wanted Scipio to assist in the creation and production of wrought iron balconies, archways, and fences at a major hotel in New Orleans.

Scipio was upset. This place was his home. He knew nothing about New Orleans except that it was a bad place for a slave to be. When Harris threatened the slaves in the field that he was going to sell them "down river", he was referring to that terrible place. He had overheard one of the overseers talking to a new driver that had just relocated to this plantation from Louisiana. He described the place as heaven and hell, mostly hell.

He asked if he could take his son with him. Harris told him he was making Abidemi a primary worker in the forge. He told him a year would fly by so fast and additionally, Louisiana was not that far away. He added Abidemi was now a grown man. He could take care of himself. He told Scipio to leave his tools with the driver to be packed. Abidemi mounted his horse and angrily rode back to their cabin. He cried until evening.

Harris' friend had paid him ten thousand dollars for Scipio to work for him. Harris knew in his sleep that he could not pass up that offer. Scipio left the meeting with Harris and paced his horse to the river. He knelt on the bank and prayed for protection for him and his son. He left the plantation in the morning.

#

A darting preview of the heavily populated and clamorous city of New Orleans was an eye-opening event for Scipio. It agitated him.

Heretofore, his life was steeped in a slow-paced agrarian environment that was encased in routine and simplicity. The frenetic pace of this gulf city heightened his curiosity. There were many more slaves in service in one place than he could ever imagine. The local gentries were dressed in their finest. Sailors and stevedores, auctioneers and entertainers filled the center of town with their varied purposes.

The business climate of New Orleans was a healthy one in 1850. It was second to Charleston, South Carolina in the size of its slave trade. Many fugitive slaves mingled in. They had run away from their owners in the low country to find their families that had separated by sale or flight.

The gulf shores teemed with trade activity. Sugar cane and cotton were the major exports. Other imports were comprised of many items that sustained New Orleans' business interests as a viable city. The chief commodity brought to her shores was slaves. Many northern slaveholders had sold their slaves to New Orleans buyers. Here, they fetched a higher price because the demand for industrial, farming and any other type of smithing had increased in the southern states.

Scipio saw blended hues of blackness clothed in glad rags. He saw copper-toned, light-skinned or midnight-black people. He concluded that they must be free folk because no one was chasing them. Moreover, he noticed that many of them had smiles on their faces. Slaves on the Harris-Jones plantation smiled too, but not that long and not that easily, he noted. He saw dapper black men in suits, and fashionable Negro women on the arms of white men. He recognized some Indians as well who walked the streets with familiarity.

On the selling blocks, the loud and fast voices of the auctioneers cracked the air over the competing bids of the buyers. Slaves were beaten and chastised in the streets by their masters who were not pleased with their slothful approach to their duties. Trollops and shameless women flaunted their partially clad bodies from the upper windows of saloons and hotels. They beckoned below to would-be customers with inappropriate words and gestures.

Scipio wondered what kind of place this was. It really must be where heaven met hell, he concluded.

He asked Fuqua for a much-needed day to rest from the trip before he saw the plans of the builder. He added that this city was unlike anything he had ever seen. He wished to see more of it before he started his work. Fuqua, a liberal northerner, did not object at all to Scipio's request. In fact, he told his driver to give Scipio a tour and make sure that he did not take him to the "back of the city" which Fuqua knew was the unseemly side of New Orleans. He told the driver to point out the hotel to Scipio where he would do his best work. This grand hotel held the largest slave auctions in the country. One of the owners had commissioned Scipio, through Fuqua, to build the wrought iron structures.

The horse-driven carriage ambled along the congested main streets of the city. The wagon wheels struck those of other carriages as they vied for forward-moving space. The circular frames were soaked in feces, mud, and trash. It had no choice but to trample through the sludge along with the hundreds of others.

Scipio looked at the bacon pink stucco buildings and the alabaster white steeples of the churches. He saw many small shoppes on either side of the street. Though he could not read, he knew by the goods displayed in the open air, what types of items were offered for sale. The smell of coffee, tobacco, ham, and molasses were a few aromas that he could discern. There was however, no mistaking the stench of labor and animals that at downwind, was odious.

As they entered the residential areas, Scipio saw many small two-story houses for the first time in his life. They stood close together and near the street. Very little land separated them. The carriage progressed up the hill. Huge mansions complete with gables and captain's porches stood regally on high expansive lawns. Scores of acres kissed with green cordoned them off.

The carriage driver told him that very rich people lived in this area. Most of them had made their generational monies from slaves, cane, and cotton, he added. Scipio was fatigued by both the long trip and the excitement of his Christopher Columbus-like reveal of a big city. He soon fell asleep before the carriage reached Fuqua's home.

#

Fuqua allowed Scipio to sleep as long as he wanted. The blacksmith finally awakened refreshed, rested, and hungry. He sat up in the middle-sized bed in this private room and ran his fingers over the cotton sheets and lightweight comforter. He had never slept upon something this grand. His eyes studied the furnishings in the room.

A porcelain pitcher and a water basin were on the small mahogany table next to his bed. The carpeting spread wall-to-wall. The drapes were suspended from floor to ceiling. There was netting on the headboard pulled over him as he slept. It kept the "no-see-ums", the bugs that bite in the night, away. Scipio knew nothing about these things. He had never entered the mansion on the Harris-Jones plantation.

Fuqua knocked on his door and entered. He was glad to find Scipio awake. He told him to get dressed and join him for breakfast. They had quite a day ahead of them. Scipio moved tentatively around the room to fetch his clothing, afraid that he would break something or look at objects he was not supposed to see. He was completely out of his element and totally intrigued by his surroundings.

He thought of Abidemi and breathed a silent prayer for him. He missed him terribly.

The Cricket Cries, the Year Changes

Chapter 3

Nine months had passed since Abidemi saw his father. He blandly assumed his duties in the forge as he produced the pieces to fill the orders. Harris was pleased with his work. Abidemi made his first graveyard marker for a slave burned in an accident at the sugar mill. The blacks complimented him on his work. They likened its quality to his father's versions of unique and original artwork.

Abidemi asked Harris many times if he had any news about his father. Harris told him he had none but he should not worry. He comforted him with words that indicated he would see his father in three months. He had no concept of what that meant and asked Harris to tell him how many new moons that was. Harris told him three.

Abidemi placed three small rocks next to his mattress in the cabin he shared with his father.

#

Instead of removing stones with the advent of a new moon, Abidemi added thirteen more. He grew agitated, distant, and melancholy with the continued absence of his father. Harris had grown tired of his daily inquiries about Scipio and ordered him not to ask him again. However, Harris, too, was quite concerned that Scipio had not returned as specified by the contract between him and Fuqua. He tried to communicate with Fuqua after Scipio had been gone for over a year beyond the contract specifications.

Harris' telegraphs went unanswered. He consulted his attorney, Allen Wilkes. He told Harris he would make it a priority to find them both. Wilkes decided to post a fugitive slave bill to New Orleans. He used Harris' description of Scipio. He added that he was last seen in the company of Randmont Fuqua, formerly of Boston, Massachusetts, but currently a property owner in St. Bernard Parish, New Orleans.

He also sent an inquiry to the builder that had contracted with Fuqua. The reward for Scipio was three thousand dollars. About four weeks later, Wilkes received a response. The owner of the hotel that hired Fuqua to design the ornamental wrought iron structures responded. He had seen the posted warrant.

In the letter, the owner revealed that the work was completed on time much to his satisfaction a little over eight months ago. He stated as far as he knew, the slave called "Scipio" was still with Fuqua. He continued that when he settled with him, he asked him how long this talented black would be with him. The owner said that Fuqua told him there was another job to do in Texas. Fuqua had shown him the copy of the contract between him and Harris that stipulated he had the services of his slave Scipio for four years.

The attorney was enraged that Fuqua had changed the number one in the contract to a number four. Fuqua had committed fraud with this deceitful tactic and Wilkes was hell-bent on retribution. After consulting with his duped client, Wilkes told Harris that he was also posting a bill for the arrest of Fuqua on charges of kidnapping, forgery, and trickery. He would extend the communication to include the state of Texas.

Harris however, was not sold on a long drawn-out search for Scipio. He called upon his own patrollers to search for him. He wanted Scipio captured alive. He believed he was not part of this ruse and deserved his leniency.

\#

Abidemi's spirit was dislocated as he surveyed the rocks that now bordered his woven mat. He vowed not to place another one. He had heard the house slaves speak of Scipio as kidnapped by Fuqua and taken to a place called "New Orleans".

He had ceased personal communications with Harris as ordered. He walked the plantation alone having worked in the forge long after others had left; he hammered his grief into the blackness.

He slept at the riverbank some nights. He had hoped to relive the times he and his father had spent together but his angst for a resolution fended off any peaceful memories. Often on the nights of the new moon, he would curse the lunar sphere for the faith he had placed in it. He long ago had counted on this monthly event to foretell his father's return.

Abidemi grew perplexed at the prospect of running away to find Scipio. He worried that if he left the homestead and his father returned to it, they would not be reunited; but if he stayed on the grounds and his father never showed his face again, he could not live without him either.

The Cricket Cries, the Year Changes

One afternoon a slave working in the fields pointed out the direction of New Orleans to Abidemi. He was seized by patrollers and returned two days after his runaway attempt. Harris had him whipped and jailed him for a week. A month later, Abidemi ran away again. This time Harris had him hobbled, a painful punishment wherein he was placed on his back and a railroad tie was situated between his feet. The driver used one of Abidemi's own sledgehammers to knock each foot toward the wooden board. Abidemi's anklebones were smashed in different directions.

In the months to come, one ankle healed enough for his full weight to be placed upon it. The other one never fully supported his right foot again. Abidemi dragged the millstone-like appendage behind him as he walked. He created furrows in the dry red dirt.

He was a crippled man——inside and out.

#

As a reward for secretly supplying long knives and axes to some field workers, Abidemi included himself in yet another attempt to run away. This time the young men had gained access to a crude map that showed a route in pictures and symbols to travel to Jacksonville, Florida. One of them knew that from that location it would be easy to run to New Orleans.

Abidemi fearing the group might leave him behind asked the leader if he would abandon him if he proved to be too much trouble. The young man told him his father was the one who had lost his life in the sugar mill accident. He knew it was Abidemi who had made the wrought iron symbol for his grave. He gave him his word that even if he had to carry him, he would see the trip through, with the five of them.

For a good while the drivers did not realize that these men had run away. The only one that had bounty papers re-issued by Harris was Abidemi. He reduced the reward for the crippled slave to five hundred dollars. Many fugitive hunters searched for infirmed slaves; to them it was an easy pursuit.

#

In the fields, the fugitives had worn light-colored clothing the day of the escape only to dye them at the river in the evening with bark and roots to a mud brown camouflage. They used a third of their traveling time to double back on their tracks; then they would proceed in the opposite direction. They salted their footsteps to confuse the coondogs. It bought them more time and distance.

Abidemi was able to keep up most of the time. He could lift his leg to step over fallen branches and rocks as long as he paced himself. If the group felt that they needed to pick up more time, his large frame was supported by two of the escapees.

One hot afternoon they came upon a white man who drove an empty wagon. He did not appear to be a patroller or a bounty hunter. A runaway had spotted him high from a tree he had spent the night in. The man traveled in their direction.

One slave had stashed a high-quality men's jacket in his sack along with a book that he could not read. He had stolen both items from the mansion's porch bench. He donned the jacket and placed the book in his hand. He told the other runaways not to speak a word. They pretended that the driver frightened them as he came upon them. They cowered. Soon they realized that he was just a clodhopper.

The driver stepped from his wagon and approached the light-skinned man of the group. He asked him to state his name and his business. The man did not wield a whip or a gun. The mulatto stepped forward and in a brazen mimic of a British accent, told the man that his name was "Oswald" (recalling a name of an overseer on the plantation) and that he and his "boys" were traveling to New Orleans when suddenly a band of thugs attacked them. He said they had stolen his clothes, his money, and his wagon.

"Oswald" stood with one hand in his tailored jacket pocket that touched the concealed knife. He ran the other hand over the visor of his cap as he couched the book in his elbow. He pretended to be annoyed by the pesky flies as he whisked them away. He held his nose slightly in the air. The other slaves held their heads down in the perfunctory slave position. One of them almost gave the scheme away as he struggled to conceal his laughter.

After the mulatto had conned the white man with his tale of woe, the waggoneer finally spoke. He addressed the speaker, believing that he was white and said they were only ten miles from Jacksonville, Florida where he lived. He said he would be more than happy to have company the rest of the way home. He pointed out to him the treeless horizon that signaled that they were in Florida, one of the flattest landmasses he knew about. He pointed southwestward as the direction to travel to get to New Orleans.

The speaker thanked the driver profusely. Then they tied him to a tree with his own rope. They left him with a blanket and some water. One of the slaves gave him a biscuit. The driver was too dumbfounded to speak. He uttered one word: "Damn".

Chapter 4

After two and a half years of hopscotching through Texas and Louisiana, Fuqua returned to his home base in New Orleans with Scipio. Scipio found Texas as dry as an African desert. The land was flat and useless he thought. Many people were renegades and outlaws. There were many battles between the Texans and the Mexicans with both of them against the natives. It paled in comparison to New Orleans and for the most part, the Harris-Jones place as well, he thought.

Fuqua had made thousands of dollars from Scipio's work. At times, he was concerned that Scipio had never asked him when he could return home. The white ironworkers could not believe this black was capable of smelting such decorative artwork. They resented that he did not offer drawn formalized plans they could follow or use for their own future projects.

Scipio drew his patterns in the sand with hot liquid candle wax. He would get design critique from the builder and make adjustments. From there, he memorized the template he had created. He then started to work. Each forged piece was laid upon the ground. He asked the white assistants to solder the pieces together with his supervision. Even if the wrought iron configuration repeated itself every fifteen feet, Scipio was able to duplicate it without hesitation. When the item was complete, he oversaw the final installation.

The whites did not like taking orders from a nigger. Actually, neither did some of the slaves who worked as laborers. To add saltwater to their already open racist wounds, Fuqua insisted that Scipio dine with them. Fuqua never let him out of his sight.

One night at dinner, with too many drinks and too many lies exchanged all around, Fuqua spied a lovely young Creole girl. She batted her wide eyes at him from under her large feathered hat. Fuqua grabbed a cigar from his pocket and excused himself as he told the group he had ordered another round for them.

Scipio, who never drank, stood up to follow Fuqua. One man pushed him down into his chair and told him that though he looked like a shadow, Fuqua had his own. Another man pulled a knife out and placed it close to Scipio's neck. He asked his cohort to pour a drink for the nigger unless Scipio thought that he was too good to drink with them.

Scipio refused at first until the blade was moved closer. Then he opened his mouth. The whiskey burned his throat and caused him to cough violently. The white men kept the drinks coming. They laughed and gloated at their first opportunity to retaliate. Scipio held his hands tightly together under the table. After several drinks were forcibly dispensed, the man withdrew his knife. He started to replace it into its sheath. Scipio grabbed it and stabbed him deeply in the heart. Only the handle of the weapon was visible. The other men began to assault Scipio.

As in most saloons, one fracas could ignite another. Soon men were fighting everywhere. The women-of-the-night screamed and scattered. Scipio ran outside toward the back of the tavern. Fuqua's party pursued him. They left the dead man on the table. One of them had broken a bottle over Scipio's head. He fell to the ground. The five of them kicked and punched Scipio repeatedly. They beat him continuously with boards and iron sticks discarded as trash behind the building. They pummeled him with their boots. They beat him unconscious.

#

Fuqua had returned to the saloon after sashaying with the young girl to find the furnishings destroyed. He was frightened by the gory site of his associate who had bled out on the dinner table. He could not find Scipio and feared for his life. Fuqua was steered to the back alley by slave boys who were cleaning up after the melee. He found Scipio lying in the debris.

Scipio lay in his bed at Fuqua's rented home. The servants tended to his injuries. The next day when he could not move at all, Fuqua summoned a doctor. After his examination, the doctor told Fuqua Scipio had suffered head injuries that were not life threatening. He had sustained several broken ribs. He had a fractured knee and a broken left ankle. It would take several months for him to heal.

Fuqua really liked Scipio not just as journeyman, but as a person with a good heart. However, he was of no use to him now if he were to be out of commission for a long time. He could not send him home to Harris in this condition. There was enough bad blood between the two of them. The altered contract that used Scipio for his own personal gain had already sealed his doom.

When Scipio recovered enough to walk on his own, Fuqua abandoned him in the back of the city where not only slaves but outlaws, thieves, and gangs lived. He told Scipio it was for his own protection from the men who had beaten him. He promised that he would come for him in a few months.

#

Scipio was repulsed by the quarters that he lived in. The contrast went from day to night as he compared this squalor to the many years of comfort he had lived alongside Fuqua. He refused to sleep in the vermin-infested houses. He recoiled at the size of the water rats that were as big as cats. Many strange insects flew around. He had not seen their kind, even in Africa.

Daily fights ensued over women, whiskey, contraband, and even a place to sleep. Nefarious deals of all types were haggled and hashed out throughout the day and night in the shacks in the streets. Scipio slept outside even when it rained. His bones reacted to the weather as they had never done before. He now walked with a limp.

He thought of killing himself. He knew nothing of Abidemi's fate and it pained him deeply. Scipio's face had taken on a lackluster expression devoid of any hope or purpose.

The Cricket Cries, the Year Changes

Chapter 5

Abidemi sat in a crowded jail cell in St. Bernard's parish. He and his friends had arrived in New Orleans weeks ago. The group he had escaped with, had abandoned him soon after. They told him they had fulfilled their promise to bring him to New Orleans but their intentions in this city called for more mobility than he could muster.

He leaned against the worn concrete wall of the jail. He finished eating the corn pone bread and slimy grits that was the one daily meal. This prison served as a detention center only. It held indentured servants as well as slaves. The holding cells separately housed the men and some women as advertised in posters or wanted slave bills. They awaited release to their masters or to the state that held jurisdiction.

Abidemi resisted the patroller's assertion that he was his father. He told him his name was Abidemi. The bounty hunter however, was assured by the description that he had the right black. The name on the bill sought a slave named "Scipio" who was wanted in Georgia. Buoyed by the fact that Scipio could be in New Orleans, Abidemi relented and extended his arms as he welcomed the cuffs. He felt his father's presence. He was jailed in his place.

#

One humid gray-blue August day the skies darkened. Thunder and lightning approached from a distance. The gulf waters had begun to rise and soon spilled over into the city of New Orleans. Trumpets sounded to warn the residents of the pending storm. Stores closed early. Additional tethers were attached to the anchored large boats. Animals were herded into barns. The New Orleans natives knew a hurricane was approaching.

Hotels boarded up their windows and placed sandbags near the foundations. The slaves toiled well into the early evening and stopped when the skies turned greenish black and the winds increased. They took off and ran toward their homes on the other side of town. Many whites moved inward to seek higher ground. The poor whites located themselves near the back of the city where the ground was higher. They knew of its reputation and came heavily armed. The wealthy had posted sentries around their mansions to ward off looters.

The concrete and wrought iron jail was the most secure building in the city. The only threat to it was the rising tide. The prisoners, most of who were not from the area, looked fearfully through the bars as the coastal waters' angry surge came into view. They shouted as they inserted their feet onto the rungs of the bars of the cells to climb toward the ceiling. Others locked arms as if to form a human chain of desperate survival.

The gale force winds churned the carbon black seas. It screamed like a woman. Its incessant eerie noise was like a tornadic whistle. It blared through the tallest of trees and lifted buildings from their foundations. Debris filled the streets. Winds pushed stray dogs and mules along the land. Several people who had felt the storm would not have a great impact upon the city, soon joined the wayward animal variety as they were swept into fences, wagons, and storefronts.

The storm raged for three to four days, if you included the eye of the storm that passed over only to bring up the rear with its circled vengeance. The wealthy who lived high up in the inland hills had survived the heavy wind and watery onslaught. However, the metropolis of New Orleans was decimated.

Looters had stormed the business district. Police and soldiers struggled to stave off the thieves and restore order. The coalition formed rescue and recovery parties. They arrested looters but many were not jailed due to the levels of insurgency against limited space. The elite frantically waved dollars high into the air and boisterously offered to pay handsomely for transportation out of the city. Many structures were wracked masses of brick, wood, and glass. Merchants struggled to re-open their stores and salvage their wares. People scoured the area for clean water and food. Slaves and free alike roamed the streets. They temporarily abandoned the caste system and substituted survival in its stead.

The patrollers however, seized this moment to round up more fugitives from justice and runaways forced from their hideouts by the storm. The enforcers walked around the city with wet and wind-blown slave bulletins and wanted posters in hand and studied the crowds for prospects. One patroller named Hawkings, had compared the slave bill that held the description of Abidemi and studied the tall dark man that limped toward him. He appeared much older than the warrant stated. Hawkings motioned to his partner to grab this large runaway from behind so they could both tie him up.

Scipio, too tired and weak to offer any resistance, asked them who they thought he was. The patroller did not answer. Scipio told them his name. Hawkings searched him for his freedom papers. Scipio told him that he had none. He was on loan by his master from Georgia to work with a white man on a smithing job.

Hawkings asked Scipio who was his employer. Scipio responded, Randmont Fuqua. The bounty hunter was puzzled. He knew that he had jailed a "Scipio"-named person already in the last month. The wanted poster also mentioned Fuqua. He stepped back from Scipio and eyed him from head to toe.

He then asked him who a nigger called "Abidemi" was. Scipio came to life and looked straight into Hawkings' eyes, and told him he was his son. Hawkings turned his back to Scipio and laughed heartily as he slapped his thigh.

He pulled his associate aside and told him they had gotten themselves a "two-fer." With Scipio's reward and Abidemi's posted price, the men had just made three thousand five hundred dollars. The good thing about it, he bragged, was that Harris had already dispatched a team of men to recover Abidemi. They would be paid for the both of them at the same time. The two celebrated.

Scipio was mystified but heartened by the conversation that Hawkings held with his partner. He eagerly rode to the holding center. He climbed in the wagon and wondered why the patroller had mentioned his son's name.

#

Scipio received dry clothing and lots of food and water in the jail. The inmates were well cared for by their captors; the profiteers protected their prey. Two weeks later, a wagon from the Harris-Jones plantation pulled up to the jail that was as large as a fort. Three drivers stood in the rain at the door with the proper paperwork and money from Harris. They asked for two slaves. They gave them the names of Scipio and Abidemi.

The patrollers were paid. The detention center officials were satisfied with the documents that the drivers presented. They were familiar with Harris' seal that was used on prior occasions. The guards went to two different cells in this huge prison. Over the incessant noise, they shouted out the name of Abidemi. Abidemi limped to the front of the bars. Upon his release his hands were chained behind him.

Scipio heard them shout out Abidemi's name. He pounded on the wrought iron rails with his fists and roared his son's name. The drivers accompanied the jailers to the place where Scipio was held. They called for the nigger Scipio to show his face. Scipio screamed his location to the men.

The two enslaved blacksmiths stood outside in the rain shackled together in body and soul. Father and son knelt upon the muddied ground and thanked their gods for divine intervention. The guards removed their chains. As they stood to walk toward the wagons, they recoiled at the similarities of their infirmaries. The ride back to the plantation was not long enough for father and son to re-align their life stories. They volleyed their near four-year ordeals as they held rough hands together for most of the trip.

The drivers considered the captives as slaves, not fugitives. Upon orders from Harris, he wanted them both rehabilitated with rest and food, fully able to resume their duties on the plantation the very day they arrived.

#

It was time for the cane harvest. Upon their return, the slaves feted father and son. They had cleaned out their cabin and replaced the weather-beaten woven mats with new ones. They had thrown away the stones that had fringed Abidemi's makeshift bed. Master Harris was delighted to have his master artisan back and able to work.

It took Scipio a long time to catch up on the past incidents and events on the plantation. He was sorely vexed to hear about Ngango's death. The witch doctor had been his friend. Scipio immediately began to think about his iron memorial for the empty grave. With tears, Kaffie hugged Scipio under the tent. She kissed Abidemi on the cheek as she welcomed him back, also. Scipio was glad to see her soft smiling face.

Kaffie mourned the fact that both men were crippled.

The Cricket Cries, the Year Changes

Chapter 6

Scipio had not forgiven Harris for Abidemi's broken ankle. He shelved for now, thoughts of avenging that act and plunged into forging tools for the harvest.

One morning, drumbeats messaged that the man who had stolen Scipio away was in the mansion with Harris. Harris had Fuqua brought to him when he learned he had tried to return to Boston to begin a new life under an assumed name. The frail thief sat at the table with Harris and begged for his forgiveness. Harris demanded the full refund of his money and an additional sum for his loss of the work of one of his prized slaves.

Fuqua told Harris he was penniless. He lost most of his money on speculating and his wife took the remainder when she divorced him. An apathetic Harris told Fuqua he would be an indentured servant. He would work next to the niggers until the time came that he, Harris, thought that his debt was paid. He told Fuqua to make himself familiar with the plantation grounds for he would be there for quite a while.

His ankles were chained together. He did odd laborious jobs on the plantation. For the first six months he was able to get drunk on stolen liquor from the drivers. He did not want to realize his fate. He knew he was going to die on this homestead of old age.

Scipio never acknowledged Fuqua whenever he saw him on the grounds. Abidemi had told his father to consider the irony from their gods toward Fuqua's condition. Each of his manacled ankles represented one of theirs. Scipio was no longer surprised by his son's deep, reflective thoughts.

#

Scipio had finally made the marker for Ngango's grave. It was a long-stemmed rod that had leaves, trees, and roots placed on either side. The objects spiraled high toward the top of the wrought iron where an exact replica of Ngango's thatched hut was fashioned. The etchings were intricate and detailed. It was Scipio's best work.

On Sunday, the slaves held another memorial service for Ngango. Many still mourned his death. The dedication reopened the grief and loss. Kaffie attended the service along with Grafton and Meriday. Scipio approached Kaffie. She stood off from the crowd and wept as if Ngango had died the day before. He limped toward her and held her hand to comfort her. He told her that the slaves' collective mourning divided the pain into small bearable pieces. That is what Ngango had purposed for them. His words soothed her.

Then Scipio asked her if she could write a word on a piece of paper for him. Kaffie asked him what word he wished to see. Scipio answered, "Thief." She told Scipio that she would have someone bring it to him later in secret.

#

At night in the forge, Scipio pounded out the letters to form the word that Kaffie had made known to him. He had made a wax pattern on the red clay to stage each letter. Every time he fashioned a letter, it appeared backwards or upside down when he soldered them together on the metal bar. He repeated the process several times; each one resulted in the same outcome. Exasperated, Scipio threw his sledgehammer to the ground and limped to the riverbank. He had not forged a long-lettered brand before and was unfamiliar with the process.

The next morning, he found Abidemi on the ground in the forge with the cold iron letters in his hand. He asked his father what they meant. Scipio told him. He also told him of his dilemma when he tried to reproduce the symbols. Abidemi flipped the letters in his hands while he contemplated a solution. The symbol for the letter "F" fell to a spot on the ground and faced backwards. Scipio was ecstatic! He knelt to the ground with Abidemi and turned the remaining letters over upside down. Then they matched it in the order that Kaffie had written on the paper. Scipio sighed deeply.

Now the blacksmiths could forge the design correctly.

He burned Kaffie's note.

#

On a still navy-blue night Scipio and Abidemi found Fuqua in his usual remote spot in the fields. His chained feet rested on the ground while he laid his head against a tree trunk. He was in a drunken slumber. The smell of alcohol and his rancid, unkempt body presented a stark contrast to his earlier lifestyle of pomp and circumstance. The two men quickly chained his wrists on his outspread arms. They placed stakes in the ground that held him down. He lay crucified on the hard clay. Fuqua opened his eyes with horror.

Scipio had carried a small-handled pot that housed the molten smelt. He seared the word "thief" on Fuqua's chest while Abidemi held the lamp to illuminate the branding iron. The moment that Fuqua began to scream, they stuffed Spanish moss into his mouth. A rag was tied over his lips and painfully knotted to the back of his neck. Fuqua's suppressed howls continued as the two of them disrobed him. The acrid smell of burning flesh overpowered his rum-soaked body. He was branded on his torso, arms and legs many times over. The permanent markings were Scipio's gift to all whose lives were torn asunder by Fuqua's greed.

Abidemi met his father's raging eyes and gently pulled the branding iron from his hands. Abidemi seared the word "thief" on Fuqua's forehead. He had stolen the only family he had. Fuqua had held his life in a purgatory of uncertainty for many years.

The drivers found Fuqua's body the next day. He was literally branded to death. Additionally, Master Harris' horse was blackened three times with the same word.

#

Scipio and Abidemi had stolen away from the plantation that same night. In the distance they could see the flames that engulfed the forge. The angry arsonists' conflagration breathed a fiery final life into the many tools that had defined their art. The incandescent orange grew smaller as Scipio and Abidemi continued their northward trek.

The blacksmiths limped alongside one another; the good left leg complemented the good right leg of the other partner. The crickets compensated their singular crippled loss with a balanced song.

The men walked in unison as they inhaled freedom and held it for as long as they could.

They were never found. Harris abandoned his unrelenting pursuit of them after two years.

Kaffie pulled Scipio's shirt that he had worn during Ngango's memorial from the pile of discarded items in his abandoned cabin.

He was deserving of a place in her heart and in her quilt.

GRAFTON AND MERIDAY

Chapter 1

Grafton changed his uniform at the end of his workday to disguise his job as a butler in the Big House. He donned ordinary clothing. He trudged the hard red clay toward his mother's cabin and waited for her. He spied Sarah as she slowly plodded with the rest of the rice planters toward temporary relief. She was bent over and gaunt. She looked as if she was a woman of seventy years old instead of thirty-nine. No matter how often he witnessed this scene, his heart was torn asunder.

Many West Africans were accomplished rice farmers in their native lands. Some were enslaved in Barbados before they were auctioned to the States. Sarah, with her two sisters and father, was among those first shipped from Barbados to South Carolina before Harris purchased them. He parsed them out to other plantations, leaving only Sarah behind.

Grafton routinely brought his mother the leftover food from the dinners that he and the head butler had served. She gratefully accepted items that she would never have had access to as a slave——especially the sweets. She looked forward to seeing her son. He was the only light in her life. She was grateful that he did not literally follow her example as a worker in the rice fields.

Her calloused palms and fingers scratched him as she caressed his face. He lifted her and carried her to their usual place at the back of her cabin. Sarah's chapped peeling lips placed a rough "hello" kiss on his neck. Tears filled Grafton's eyes while he held his almost weightless treasure. He had brought browned rice flour from the kitchen to apply to the many mosquito bites she suffered while working daily in the wet shallow lowlands. Grafton quickly associated the irony that the powder that soothed her injuries had come from the source that caused them. He clicked his teeth in loathing.

The Cricket Cries, the Year Changes

Sarah's feet were blistered, swollen and water-filled from the constant standing in the rice fields. She had many marks on her legs and arms inflicted by the prickly rice leaves and insect bites. Grafton slathered her body with palm oil and other pomades. Sometimes, animal feces made its way into the stagnant water and Sarah often became ill from various bacterial infections. Ngango's apprentice gave Grafton powders for his mother to ingest that induced vomiting and diarrhea.

The rice planters slept separately from the rest of the slaves in designated cabins near the fields. Most were too weak and infirmed to run away. When Grafton did not have to hurry back, he would tell his mother of the goings-on in the Big House. Her weak eyes would show surprise when her son told her about the slave uprisings and said that maybe freedom was coming to get them. She slowly moaned from her injuries but sighed with delight with her reaction to his news. He fed her the wonderful warm food while he teasingly held dessert for last.

Grafton was her only child. She bore him when she was fifteen. She did not know who the father was. As a young slave who first worked in the cotton fields, she was tethered by chains in a cabin of ten to twelve people. She did not have the strength to fight off her midnight rapist. She could not identify him come dayclean. They were all black. They all shared the same stench. His sizeable strength had subdued her in an instant.

She blamed herself for her son's speech condition at birth. She connected it to her inability to scream when her attacker painfully deposited him into her fertile womb. The virginal rape coupled with the future absence of any man was appeased by her son's love for her. She concluded that somehow Fate had evened the score. Sarah never complained. The only lively thing about her was the smile that Grafton inherited but refused to use. She became the mute in his place. That was all she had to give to him. Her love protected his secret. He began to speak around the age of seven but continued the ruse as a mute. He used his "deafness" to protect and shield him in certain situations.

Cynthia Harris-Allen

When it was time to leave, Grafton lay Sarah gingerly down upon her thin worn blanket and placed his own cover from the Big House on top of her; he hid the newspapers that Kaffie and others gave to him that he would read during future visits. He would burn them after he had committed to memory all of the details. He kissed Sarah three times and said "There, now." He stepped over the already sleeping slaves as he exited the cabin.

The two butlers who served dinner in the mansion were Grafton and Meriday. Meriday was aged and had been on the plantation since a boy. He was around seventy-five years old. Grafton helped him serve the meals and drinks. By all accounts on the plantation, Grafton was a mute. He was born with a condition that rendered him speechless. He only spoke to people whom he trusted. Those included Ngango and Abraham, both deceased.

Ngango had had earlier ulterior motives to acquaint himself with Grafton when he first met him. He wanted to find out if Grafton possessed powers that were superior to his own. He thought that Grafton acted strangely. Soon, Ngango realized that he like some of the other slaves just had an "infirmary." The two of them soon formed a symbiotic relationship. Grafton would bring him information from the Big House; in turn, Ngango supplied herbs and balms for his mother.

Kaffie became the soft refuge for Grafton. He trusted her to know that he was not a mute. His coarse hair was tamed with the daily saturation of oil that Kaffie had administered since he first came into the house as a boy. Her slow supportive strokes of the brush to his hair sealed a silent mutual caring between the two of them. She talked to him and paced her words to assure herself that he could understand what she said.

He was brought into the mansion as a footman at the age of six. He placed stools by the wagons for the passengers to board or disembark. Later, his chores expanded to filling the guestroom water pitchers and face basins. He hauled wood for the fires.

Grafton stood erect and proud at six feet tall even as a teen. His eyes were small and discerning. They projected a sense of wonder and curiosity toward the world around him. His ivory teeth flashed grins on occasion but did not bless the day with the smile that could lift hearts. As he grew older, Master Harris became impressed with his work ethic and demeanor. He was far too serious to be as young as he was, he thought. Additionally, Grafton was a good-looking black, Harris surmised, aside from being deaf and dumb. Harris inserted him as Meriday's apprentice when he was just twenty-four years old.

These days, Kaffie always ended their visits with a lint brush that removed the stray hairs from his white shirt. She assisted him with his butler's coat. She gave him three pats upon his shoulders accompanied by the words "There now". That gesture first wrapped him in security when he was seven years old.

Kaffie secretly taught him how to read and write. He also became a student of all of the information shared at the dinner table. He quickly absorbed it and had more questions after each event. At fifteen, Grafton began to read the newspapers that Betsey the artist slave had brought back from Ripley, Ohio. She wrapped glass and china for use in the Big House inside the publications.

One afternoon, she found Grafton as he sat under the Cypress trees where she set up her easels. He was reading a newspaper. His brows furrowed as his eyes quickly darted back and forth over the print. Betsey looked at him and was startled. Grafton's eyes held her stare. She told no one of her discovery. From then on, she included more news items intended for him disguised as wrapping material. Kaffie passed them on to Grafton.

Grafton had to stand at-the-ready if any of the whites needed their drinks refilled or plates removed, etc. In full butler regalia, he stood at attention on his feet for seven hours straight. His hands remained crossed behind his back while he awaited the next summons. He listened to everything with a distant inattentive look in his eyes that supported the belief of his master and the many guests that he was harmless.

He memorized conversations about the slave "question". He witnessed the impassioned arguments that favored slavery. He heard the most disdainful comments about his people. His soul flinched at the graphic mockeries that were derisively exchanged among the attendees. It included the rape and molestation of black women and children. They all agreed that examples of castrations and hangings kept the male "monkeys" who planned to run away docile and in check. They laughingly raised their wine glasses in agreement.

Grafton trained himself to brace his reactions against loud or sudden noises. He placed his mind in remote places and would "come to" when Meriday would tap his arm or his back to bring him back to attention. His heart quickened when he heard talk of abolitionists from the North and the infamous speeches from freed southern slaves. Many times out of feigned respect, Grafton would keep his eyes shut and his head held down.

He placed asterisks in his brain on words such as the Underground Railroad. He had to look into that thoroughly. Did the rail ways actually travel under the earth?

Meriday was brought into the Harris mansion when he was forty-seven years old though he continued to be called "boy". A white butler, Scanlon Hines, who was forced to death by pneumonia, trained him. Hines' health involuntarily surrendered the tight-fisted manner in which he ran the kitchen, dining, and guest operations. By default and because of long employ, these duties were ceded to Meriday.

As the head butler, Meriday would recite his "I remembah" stories to the black staff who obliged him. They knew that to ignore him would result in duties that no one wanted to perform. They scurried around as they prepared the house for one of Master's soirees. Once again, Meriday stood in the center of the huge kitchen and told them about the Zong Massacre.

He recounted how the guests at a past dinner had laughed at the story of a captain of a ship who threw one hundred forty-two slaves overboard. He had miscalculated how long it would take his ship to reach its destination. He did not have enough supplies or water to sustain the entire black cargo. Therefore, he decided to lighten the load. Meriday told that story every Thanksgiving because he said it happened near that time. He added that the invitees began to expand on the tale with horrible jokes that raised the level of laughter even higher.

The staff tired of hearing Meriday, who oftentimes embellished the story and exaggerated the responses of the whites. The blacks rolled their eyes towards the ceiling with heavy sighs that mingled with the aromas from the kitchen.

Meriday became head butler the same year the city of Savannah became the first capital of Georgia. Harris made him wear the white gloves that used to belong to Hines. Meriday only spoke to whites when spoken to. He often bribed the help with time off if they did his bidding. He wanted to continue to appear competent as head butler. He was too old to be parsed out to the fields.

He would run like a rabbit as he flitted between tables and soup tureens. He grinned like the man in the moon. He always bowed to Harris whenever the Master entered or left the room. By the time each course was served and the guests moved to the drawing room, Meriday's clothing was drenched in sweat.

His semi-balding head reflected the small oval flames from the candelabra. It created such an exaggerated caricature that was ecstatic to breathlessly return to his position in the corner. He held his head down while he clasped his gloved fingers behind his back and silently begged for rest.

Grafton abhorred this step-and-fetch-it show called "Meriday" but never showed it. He never verbally communicated with him. He knew that Meriday was an old-fashioned house nigger that cow-towed and catered to every white man——especially Harris. Meriday's stature reminded Grafton a lot of the old slave, Abraham. Grafton had had frequent open arguments with the now deceased broom maker about survival as a slave. That was the first and only time, outside of Kaffie, Grafton revealed that he could hear and speak. He really did not trust Abraham but his archaic views irked him to the point of reveal.

Meriday wanted desperately for Grafton to step into his shoes——and soon. He was seventy-one years old. He was tired of being the chief apple polisher.

Chapter 2

The slaves prepared an elaborate dinner party for over fifty guests. The night before, many slave children had tracked red dirt into the mansion on the just-waxed wooden floors. They had ported additional pans and cauldrons from storage and wine barrels from the cellars. By morning, the mud had dried. Meriday ordered the youth to sweep the dirt away and then remove the dirt from the huge planked porch. Their reddened nappy hair attested to the fact that most of the grit was gone when they spied the caravan of wagons that approached the house.

Weeks earlier, Harris had ordered Kaffie to make new butlers' jackets for Grafton and Meriday. He included instructions for fresh aprons and caps for the cooks. Kaffie, with her head apprentice, Fanna, worked through the night to embroider the Harris-Jones monogram on the white crinoline apron pockets.

Fanna brought the new pieces into the kitchen; she smiled at Grafton. Her infatuation for him created bubbles in her stomach and it showed in her eyes. Grafton knew that she liked him. He liked her also; but he was not going to marry her and live inside this hellhole, he thought. He always greeted Fanna with a "I-know-what-you-thinkin'" grin. She had no idea that he could hear or speak. His deafness did not matter to her.

He helped her with the uniforms with a nod that acknowledged their shared admiration.

#

The high-level politicians began to arrive in the hot afternoon. The mansion grounds were spotless. It was Sunday.

Harris had the slaves gather by each side of the porch and sing for his arriving guests even though it was their rest day. He promised them the leftover scraps from the dinner for their time. Inside, the cooks had prepared turtle soup, brook trout fried in butter, baked potatoes, roasted ham, wild turkey stuffed with walnuts, corn pones, and biscuits. The vegetables included rice, asparagus, and green beans. For dessert, pecan pie and peach cobbler, each complemented with sweet cream, was served.

The Cricket Cries, the Year Changes

Harris provided Madeira wine for his colleagues. He also made sure that there would be plenty of cigars and entertainment in the drawing room. Slaves had already hauled wood to the massive fireplace in case an evening chill would cool the spacious room.

Grafton and Meriday, in full butler attire, attended to the needs of the dinner guests. Both wore the mask of servitude while they made sure that Harris would be pleased with their works.

All of the information shared at the table stunned Grafton. The times were really changing. Slaves no longer were afraid to rise up and fight. He heard many stories of riots and insurrections on the southern plantations; the most brutal ones had occurred in the Caribbean islands. He was dismayed to hear that even free slaves in South Carolina had to wear distinctive identification tags. The Georgia legislature planned to adopt the same Slave Codes. He also learned that many trails led to freedom in a country named Canada where blacks were treated as equals by the British.

He made up his mind that night that soon, he was going to have to make his move northward. His biggest concern would be what would happen to his mother should he escape and how he could convince Fanna to run away with him.

#

The guests soon retreated to the parlor and drawing rooms. Grafton returned to the dining area to clean. He glanced into the chambers and saw the whites. They sat and chatted before the recital; some were already drunk. The dresses of the women were reflected in the mirrored walls as prisms of many colors. The alcohol or the amber glow of the candles softened the earlier dinner-table vitriol of the privileged gentry, he observed.

Luvinia Harris strolled over to the empty seat next to Rockfield Stiles, the chief overseer. Grafton noted that on other occasions she always wanted to sit next to him. At an earlier party, she asked a guest to trade places with her. Of course they obliged; she was the daughter of the host.

This time, she pulled out her pleated fan with the peacocks on it and daintily fanned herself as she coyly smiled at Stiles. She extended her gloved hand for him to kiss. He did not follow through but instead just nodded at her.

She folded the fan and placed it in her left hand. With one fluid motion, her right hand reached across the velvet chair and touched Stiles' hand. She let it linger there. He carefully lifted it away and gave her a stern look. Her reddened face rivaled the crimson taffeta gown she wore.

Grafton noted that encounter.

#

Grafton had befriended three of the black carriage drivers on the plantation. He formed a great alliance with Cooper Midday, the youngest of the three. He and Midday took long walks together while the dinner guests were being entertained. Midday at first, attempted to use awkward gestures to communicate with Grafton. After a couple of years of familiarity, Grafton stopped him the evening of the grand party and finally spoke to him. Midday cried and hugged Grafton. He said he had always wished that he could speak and hear.

Soon after, Midday elevated his communications to Grafton with relevant information that he gleaned from conversations heard aboard the carriages. As he drove the passengers, Midday pretended to be more interested in the gaudy yellow outfit he was forced to wear by the pretentious Luvinia Harris.

Grafton returned to the Big House after his break. He walked into the dining room where Meriday was stacking newspapers that the guests had brought to the dinner. He heard Harris order Meriday to burn the papers. He bowed to him and gave his perfunctory "Yes, Marse" response. He shuffled to the back of the mansion where barrels were used to burn papers and other items and made a quick right turn. He found Cooper Midday, his great-grandson, cleaning cigar stubs and other debris from his carriage. He told him to give the papers to Grafton.

The Cricket Cries, the Year Changes

Chapter 3

Grafton sometimes carried the slave allotment clothing to the place they referred to as "under the tent" in the open yards. In that space, Kaffie would pass out the next season's garments and shoes to the slaves. He nodded to the slaves and hugged some young men that he came to recognize because of this practice. The slaves knew that he could not speak. They motioned gestures of respect toward him.

As the afternoon turned to dusk, Rockfield Stiles entered the tent. Most of the clothing had been rationed. He approached Kaffie and asked her how she was doing. He offered his help to carry things back into the house. Kaffie was not surprised by this gesture. Stiles visited her often.

That evening, he told her about new fabric shops he had observed on his last trip to Boston. He made a promise to take her with him to pick out some holiday fabrics during the fall layby. She was elated! She had not traveled outside the plantation except to alter ball gowns or tailored jackets on nearby homesteads. She clasped her hands to her heart and graciously thanked Stiles.

Grafton heard the conversation and was puzzled by Stiles' past and present overtures toward Kaffie. Luvinia stood near the window seat that overlooked the back of the mansion and witnessed the exchange. She pursed her lips when she saw Stiles place both his hands on Kaffie's shoulders. He grinned at Kaffie with a smile that would never be meant for her.

Later at dinner, Luvinia, now head mistress of the household, informed her father that she wanted to go to Boston to shop and maybe see a play. She added she knew it would be much colder up there this time of year but she could get Kaffie to make her a new wardrobe in no time. Harris responded that Stiles had already planned a trip to Boston in three weeks and she could accompany him and the rest of his party.

Stiles played with his food for a while and then let his fork drop to the bone china plate. With all eyes on him, he told Harris that this trip was his only vacation. He had made plans for himself only. He promised his friends in

Massachusetts he would lodge with them, do some hunting and poker playing. He would not have time to look after Luvinia.

Luvinia rose from her chair and sat on her father's lap. Like a child, she put her arms around his neck and begged him to let her ride with Rockfield to Boston. She could always stay with the Wileys or Smythes that Harris knew very well. Through fake tears, she looked at Stiles and said she crossed her heart and hoped to die she would not be any trouble on the trip. Why, he would not even know that she was there, she cooed.

Harris told Stiles he did not see a problem. Luvinia planted a kiss on her father's ear, resumed her seat, and stared victoriously at Stiles. Stiles abruptly rose from the table. He threw his napkin into his plate and left the dining area.

Harris found Stiles in the drawing room. Stiles had lit a cigar that sent spiteful puffs of smoke into the air. Harris asked Stiles if he wanted to talk to him about anything. Stiles told Harris about the many times that Luvinia had approached him in awkward, off-putting ways. He asked Harris when he planned to reveal to that spoiled brat that she was his half-sister. He recalled the latest incident at the dinner party where she forced him to embarrass her. He continued that Harris' wife Tillie was dead now for a very long time. He respected that Harris wanted to protect her from knowing that he had had a child out of wedlock.

Rockfield reminded him he was now over fifty years old and Luvinia was in her forties. He asked his father how much longer he was going to deny him his birthright. He said making him the chief overseer and paying him great wages through the years was no longer sufficient. He emphasized to Harris that he was his sole male heir. He then moved from the chair and stood near his father face-to-face. Stiles told him how much he loved him and how proud he was to be his son. With tears rimming his eyes, he asked him was his love and loyalty not enough to be acknowledged openly to everyone. Harris stood silent.

Stiles stormed out of the room, hot under the collar and disappointed by the lack of a response from Harris.

The Cricket Cries, the Year Changes

Neither of them noticed that Grafton had stood motionless in the far corner of the drawing room where he had stopped stacking chairs when Stiles entered.

#

Luvinia climbed the attic stairs to Kaffie's room. She had not done that in many years. As she entered the sun-lit area, she was immediately taken back to the time when she insisted to her parents that Kaffie become her playmate. Over the years, Luvinia had spent many a night in the attic with the cook and Kaffie.

The walls were painted robin's egg blue. There were plants everywhere that grew toward the light. The brilliant white lace-trimmed curtains kissed the wooden oval window sills. Luvinia immediately thought drapes like this would be well-suited for her own bedroom. She viewed the shelves that held the bolts of fabric that Kaffie used. Everything was neat, orderly, and color-coordinated. On Kaffie's bed were many pillows and two dolls. Woven mats dyed in every color warmed the otherwise cold rough flooring.

Well-used treadle machines stood on the opposite wall; each had a garment under the needle. She was surprised that the picture the two of them had drawn together on brown butcher paper as best friends still hung on the wall. That day long ago, they had a contest to see how long it would take them to fill the paper with every color of the wildflowers in the meadows. The memory moved her.

Kaffie had noticed Luvinia when she first entered her room. She stood behind the dressing screen. She watched Luvinia as she examined her living area and ran her fingers along her quilted bed. She walked into her sight puzzled by her visit. Luvinia, not knowing how long Kaffie had watched her movements, quickly snapped to the present and assumed her role as the mistress of the house who gave orders to all the niggers.

Luvinia sauntered over to the cheval mirror and admired herself front and back. She moved closer to examine a small pimple that had settled in the middle of her forehead. She caught her breath in disgust. She spoke in distant tones without once looking at her. She told Kaffie about the necessity of needing a completely new wardrobe sewn within the next three weeks. She caught Kaffie's blank expression in the reflection. She told her she wanted swatches brought to her early the next morning. She needed to see more loud colors than subdued ones and cloth that was suitable to the cooler weather up north. As Luvinia exited, she turned to face Kaffie and said in a haughty tone that Rockfield Stiles was taking her to Boston.

#

Midday prepared for the journey to the rail way station for the trip to Boston via his carriage. The black boys had footstools at the ready for the travelers.

Kaffie would carry but one carpetbag. She had completed the wardrobe for Luvinia earlier than she had expected. She made Luvinia's dresses from gowns that she had on standby from the same swatches. All she needed to do was make minor alterations. She had awakened early that morning and watched the new dawn as it colored her room in a soft apricot. She reminded herself once more that she had not dreamed she was actually going up North.

Midday helped Kaffie with the same pomp and circumstance that he gave to the white women. He took her hand and steered her to the double seat where she would not have to ride backwards for three hours. With a smile and a wink, he welcomed her aboard. Stiles boarded next. He sat across from Kaffie. He greeted her with an "I told you so" smile and asked her if she was excited. She could hardly whisper "Yes". They both waited impatiently for Luvinia.

Fifteen minutes later, after Stiles had sent one of the boys to the butler to summon Luvinia, she showed up, giddy, and over-perfumed. She expected Stiles to get out and lend her a hand. He made her wait until she understood that that was not going to happen. Once she entered the carriage, aided by a nonchalant Midday, her first step inside let loose a barrage of high-pitched coquettish reasons why she was so terribly late. The sight of Kaffie, who sat *inside* of the carriage no less, blunted the chatter. Luvinia looked at Stiles puzzled. He did not utter a sound.

Kaffie addressed her as "Miss Luvinia" and said "Good morning". Luvinia said nothing. She scowled at her. Then she bulldozed her way to the front-facing seat and diminished most of the comfortable room Kaffie had taken. Midday shouted "All aboard" and clicked the team of horses into action toward the rail way station.

Chapter 4

They rode through the open countryside beyond the places unfamiliar to Kaffie. Stiles pointed out different landmarks, mountains, and rivers. She saw a herd of deer that nested in a thicket. She saw Indians who rode bareback just outside her window. She was frightened but Stiles assured her they were not in any danger.

Kaffie felt relaxed and unburdened. The wind was in her hair. A new sun shone on her freckles. Her hands no longer rested in a tailor's position. The rhythmic turns of the carriage wheels were as happy as she was. Was this freedom? Is this what whites felt every single day of their life?, she wondered. She leaned back to rest after having shoved herself forward for so long so as not to miss one moment of glory.

Luvinia decided not to participate in this carnival. When they reached Boston, her first moment alone with Rockfield Stiles would set him straight as to who was really Kaffie's owner.

\#

On the train, a disgusted and disgruntled Luvinia had decided to ride in another car. Stiles and Kaffie sat next to each other in the open seats. Stiles had seen to it that Kaffie had traveling papers should they separate.

Kaffie thought the train ride would have been the ultimate dream; but when she walked the cobblestoned grounds of Boston, her eyes ached from trying to take everything in at once. The teeming pace of a large city certainly impressed Kaffie. There were people everywhere and large buildings! She heard church bells ring on the hour. The horse and carriage traffic was enormous.

She walked the streets of Beacon Hill and Charles. She purchased sweet treats at the confectioners. She looked at

Stiles and smiled. She pressed her face in wonder to gaze at the haute-coutured mannequins in the store windows. Her breath left a temporary wide-grinned vapor print. She laughed and beamed at him in total appreciation.

After Stiles checked the three of them in at the hotel in adjoining rooms, they refreshed themselves and agreed to meet in the lobby. Kaffie quickly changed her clothes and sat on the high four-poster bed. She swung her stockinged legs that could not touch the floor. She awaited Stiles' knock on her door to join him.

Kaffie heard an urgent rapping on Stiles' door, then the voice of Luvinia. She stepped in and slammed the entry. She asked Stiles who in the hell he thought he was. She reminded him that she was the daughter of one of the richest planters in Georgia, and next in line to assume full authority and responsibility over <u>everything</u> her father owned.

She accused him of being an old man who lusted after black meat. She recalled for him the many times she saw him under the tent talking with Kaffie. She said even though Kaffie was a mulatto, she was still a nigger——<u>her</u> nigger. She chided that even her fine brown hair and grey eyes gave little reason to believe that a white man would want her more than they would a woman of her own wealth and breeding.

She ranted to Stiles that she grew up with that now squeaky-clean bitch. She was the one who pulled her out of the fields as a bag of dirt and lice. No one even knew who her mammy was. No one has ever come forward to claim her, she hollered.

Stiles clenched his fists.

Luvinia then took a deep breath as she waited for a response or at least an interruption from Stiles. She calmed down and slowly walked over to him and buried her face in his chest. She asked him almost in a whisper, what was wrong with her that he rejected her advances many times since she had become a young woman. She wondered aloud to him what man would not want the status, prestige, and respect she had handed to him. Stiles gently pushed her away from him.

Defeated, Luvinia stood back from him and angrily told him that when they returned to the plantation, she would no longer allow him to have any further contact with Kaffie. She assured him her father would enforce her wishes.

The Cricket Cries, the Year Changes

Stiles told Luvinia that he loved Kaffie.

Luvinia, shocked and startled, dared him to repeat what he had just said. Rockfield Stiles told Luvinia that Kaffie was his daughter.

Luvinia screamed.

Kaffie fainted.

Chapter 5

It was now the layby on the Harris-Jones plantation. All awaited the full harvest of cotton and corn to affirm the toil, sweat and sometimes loss of life that contributed to its yield. The slave labor force focused on repairs to cabins, barns, and other maintenance issues. Silos were reinforced and more underground cellars were dug that would house dried meat and wines. Spanish moss was pulled from the trees and dried. It was used as replacement stuffing for the makeshift mattresses of the slaves.

Harris was away for two weeks in Savannah. He usually left around this twice-a-year harvest to visit with friends. Inside the Big House, routine cleanups were minimized. The cooks, butlers, and carriage drivers were almost idle. They did not complain about the opportunity to do virtually nothing. Most pretended to be hard at work.

One afternoon, Meriday motioned to Grafton to come into the library. Grafton hesitantly followed him into the room. It smelled of ink and leather. Pipe and cigar smoke lingered long after its users had departed.

Meriday lifted a long key chain from his vest pocket and unlocked the rifle cabinet. The dark glistening cherry wood cabinet held Master Harris' prized rifles, pistols, and derringers. Grafton stood away as he tried to determine what Meriday had planned to do. Meriday spoke to him and told him he was going to teach him how to shoot a gun. He revealed to him he knew he was not a mute. He had known it for a very long time.

Abraham the broom maker, now dead, had told him about their endless debates in the barn about slavery. Meriday revealed that Abraham had befriended him as a young man. He told Grafton that long ago he had known that Betsey had brought him papers back from Ripley, Ohio. Meriday confessed that the articles that Midday gave to him at the last big party came from him, despite the fact that Harris wanted them burned.

Meriday told Grafton Midday was his great-grandson. His last name was a version of his name that got lost when passed on to the third generation of his family. Grafton, startled by these revelations, turned aside from Meriday and hung his head. All those times he had disrespected the old man caused him to become very upset. A lone tear streamed down his cheek. Meriday walked toward him and placed comforting gloved hands on his shoulders. He assured him that he was not going to betray him. He steered Grafton back towards the kitchen.

He whispered to Grafton to meet him at sunrise by the back of the mansion. He wanted to show Grafton how to use the guns. He told him to wear his butler outfit. Meriday insisted that they wear the suits. They could not be mistaken for the field hands who could not bear arms. Should they be stopped and questioned, the plan was to say they were shooting geese and mallards for dinner. He added that he and Grafton should act and talk like the most ignorant indentured servants on the plantation. If the drivers laughed at them, they would know they had convinced them.

#

The two men walked toward the fringes of the plantation at dayclean. Meriday carried both rifles. Grafton carried two pistols. Ammunition was plentiful. They ambled along past the deserted fields. Grafton started to apologize to Meriday. Meriday told him it was not necessary. He told Grafton he had been humiliated all his life on this plantation.

He spoke of his wife and granddaughters who were raped. Midday's father had been part of a Hanging Party on the Wilcox's plantation. He had committed no crime. He was chosen to swing in the wind——just for fun because they wanted an even number of niggers. Meriday said it was only time and place that separated their different attitudes. His generation could not seek change in groups. They ran away alone. He called Grafton the biggest threat to these slave-holding folks. He asked Grafton if he knew that blacks who could read and write were called "double-headed niggers" by whites. Grafton laughed aloud for the first time around Meriday; it softened their hearts toward one another.

Grafton took a serious look at Meriday and asked him why he chose to do this for him. Meriday told him he could see the fire in his eyes and he did not want it to dim. He said he wanted to see him make a difference in his lifetime. He, himself did not have many years left. Had he not been a butler, he concluded he would have died a long time ago because his body always served him poorly.

They began to shoot at empty tin cans and thin strips of wood called "scabbard" that leaned against trees and rocks. Meriday praised Grafton on his first lesson.

#

At dusk, the two of them made their way back to the Big House with no quarry in hand. The sound of urgent drumbeats became louder and louder. They quickened their steps. Meriday stealthily took the guns back to the cabinets. Grafton walked to the huge front porch of the mansion and stood among the crowd of gathered slaves and overseers. Down in the valley by the rice fields rows of slave cabins were burning.

Mary, the cook, turned to tell Grafton that with "the vengeance of de Lawd" the malaria had broken out in the last four days. Slaves from the main plantation were not allowed in that area. Harris long ago had ordered the overseers to burn the cabins, fields, and the rice slaves if that dreaded disease found its way onto his land. Mary complained that some of the rice slaves probably were not even sick.

Grafton, panic-stricken exited out the back door of the mansion and raced toward the rice fields. He had seen his mother early that week. She had not appeared to be any sicker than she always was. He knew nothing about praying to African gods or the white folks' god. He did not believe in either one.

His feet pounded the russet red clay towards the lowlands. He wished he could call on someone to ease his unavoidable pain. He threw off his jacket, a bow tie, and pulled his shirttails outside of his pants——anything that could get him to his mother quickly. Tears ran roughshod over his sweating face.

Thick black and gray smoke from the burning buildings spiraled defiantly into the air like small tornados. There was no breeze. The hand of death was silent but unrelenting in its destruction. Some cabins were completely gutted save for the chimneys that no longer served a purpose.

The Cricket Cries, the Year Changes

Grafton ran to his mother's cabin and to his horror found partially charred unidentifiable bodies that lay on top of one another. Others evidenced mortal gunshot wounds from the drivers who heeded Harris's orders. Lines of smoke trailed each other as they relayed towards the open skies. The smell of burned flesh subdued the smoldering wood and clothing.

He retreated to an open spot and vomited. He could not clear the acid in his stomach. He vomited again. He screamed to the top of his voice. It allowed more smoke to infiltrate his stinging lungs. His chest pained him like never before. He ran to the riverbank and washed his eyes. One swallow of water seared his throat as if it was the fire itself. He remained prostrate on the ground. He cried more tears than the river had water and the sky let fall.

Thunder began to roll.

Come morning, a rain-soaked Grafton awakened to a more extensive view of the carnage. Buzzards were nowhere to be seen. There was nothing left to feed upon. Everything was gray and gone.

Chapter 6

On the railway, Stiles told Kaffie about her mother. She had loved horses. Harris bought her at an auction. She carded cotton for the weavers. Stiles told Kaffie they fell in love at once. She was a beautiful woman. When she was around seventeen she was pregnant with his child. She had a miserable pregnancy. She was always sickly and bed-ridden. She died in childbirth. Stiles quickly added that she presented him with a pretty baby girl that was she.

He told her no one knew he was her father. At that time for reasons that he would tell her soon, he could not have risked her life with this confession. That is how Kaffie came to be an orphaned slave——safe among many. Stiles said he watched over her. He was her daily guardian. He told Kaffie he wanted to tell Harris first before Luvinia came back from Boston. Luvinia had decided to stay in Boston until the day her father returned home from Savannah.

He promised Kaffie he would give her freedom papers and make sure she wanted for nothing for the rest of her life. Kaffie asked him how he could do that. Stiles said there was one more piece to the puzzle that had to be brought to light in due time. He clasped her hands in his and told her to enjoy the ride home. Inwardly, Kaffie said the word "freedom" to herself. Tears flooded her freckles.

#

The ashes of the dead bodies were buried in the Ole Field in a common hole. Meriday tried his best to console Grafton.

After he had calmed him, Meriday whispered to him that guns were also hidden in the pantry and the stairwell. He prodded Grafton to make his move before Harris came back. He told him to be the man he knew he was. He added that he could cry all the way to Boston if he chose to but he needed to get away from here——and soon.

In the middle of the night, the carriage had returned Stiles and Kaffie to the mansion. Grafton heard the rustle of Kaffie's dress as she climbed the stairs. He ran to Kaffie's room. She turned to him with extended arms. He fell into them heartbroken and desolate. She had learned from Midday of the fire at the rice fields. She held Grafton as he was on his knees with his face buried in her lap.

Fanna placed a blanket over Grafton and rested her hand on his back. This was the first time she heard a sound come from his mouth and the first time she ever touched him. She was both moved and confused. Kaffie gave her a look that cautioned her to say nothing. She told Fanna to have Cook make some sassafras tea and bring it upstairs for Grafton.

While Fanna was downstairs, Kaffie soothed Grafton as she told him about the North. She had brought back maps of the Underground Railroad locations. They were trails shown by river and road landmarks that led to homes of sympathizers who hid the escaped blacks. She told him how much better he would fit in the northern society. She told him it was time for him to make a move. Nothing held him back now.

Grafton told her that he loved Fanna. He made Kaffie promise him she would share information he would send to her with Fanna. He told her that he would use the name "Sarah" when he signed the letters. He had several friends that lived on the plantation who would be able to get his correspondence to her.

Over the years, the few slaves who could read and write, unbeknownst to the whites, pulled the mail from the perimeter posts and separated Kaffie's letters before Harris and his people saw them.

Kaffie said she already knew about their feelings for one another. She then asked him when he was planning to leave. Grafton answered, "Tonight".

Fanna had listened to their conversation from the top step to Kaffie's room. Both hands pressed the porcelain cup tightly as her dreams vaporized with the rising steam. She had heard Grafton's voice. The sound of it was riveted in her soul.

Cynthia Harris-Allen

Chapter 7

Harris had put his "coondogs" on Grafton's trail after he learned that he had escaped from the grounds three days earlier before he was actually missed. He sent two patrollers after him and posted the cursory slave runaway notice. The description included that Grafton was deaf and dumb. He knew that those restrictions would have him caught in no time.

Weeks later, the bodies of the patrollers were returned to the plantation with mortal gunshot wounds in their heads and chests. One of Harris' own pistols was in the waistband of one of the dead. The other murdered man wore Grafton's butler coat. Harris wanted to know how Grafton got hold of his guns. His first thoughts were directed towards Meriday.

Some overseers told Harris that not too long ago they had spotted the two of them as they shot guns by the thickets. The butlers had told them they were hunting duck for dinner. They told Harris it was a hilarious scene. They jokingly said that between the two of them, if they did not miss a target by a minute, they missed it by a mile. Harris was not amused.

He called for the old butler to come into the parlor. Meriday slowly moved into the room. Meriday balanced himself along the wainscotted walls to steady himself. Harris demanded the keys to the gun cabinet. Meriday obliged. Harris struck Meriday and knocked him to the floor. Meriday cowered and screamed.

Black members of the household help ran to investigate the commotion. Harris ordered them to get back to what they were doing. Meriday signaled to them with a gloved finger that he was all right. The slaves answered Harris with a unified glare of defiance. It frightened him, but they slowly left the room. They exited while walking backwards. They kept their eyes on Meriday.

Harris had him chained and whipped in the yards for all to see. The old man hollered and laughed at the same time. Tears gleefully met the infrequent smile lines on the old man's face. He taunted Harris and called him names. He told him he did not have a clue about what was happening on his own place. He motioned for Harris to come closer to him or be damned.

The Cricket Cries, the Year Changes

Harris took two steps toward Meriday and looked with rage into his face. Meriday told Harris he was held too high and mighty by most folks but he knew the secrets he had kept through the years. On that threat, Harris cleared the stunned crowd that had gathered.

With spittle falling between his missing teeth, he told Harris he knew he had poisoned his own wife; he saw him put the powder in her teacup. He warned Harris "Even after you kills me, other folk already knows yo deeds", because I told 'em."

He begged Harris to kill him. Harris, startled by Meriday's expose, told him he was going to do just that. Meriday began to cough from the exhaustion and hollering. He spat toward Harris' direction. When he returned from the mansion with his pistol, Meriday asked him to do him one last favor. Harris thought this nigger had truly lost his mind if he expected him to accommodate him in any way.

Before he could answer him, Meriday said "never mind" in a very high-pitched teasing voice. He began to pull the bloodied gloves off his hands finger by finger. His trembling hands struggled; he begged Harris to help him to remove them. Meriday panted into the air that he was not going to go to see his daddy with Scanlon Hines' shackles upon his body.

Harris began to shoot at Meriday as if it was target practice. He used a rifle and a pistol. He pumped at least six shots into his torso and chest. Mouse gray smoke discharged into the air. The sound of the shots brought many slaves back to the area. All the while, Meriday with jerked movements, strained to remove the gloves. When the last shot killed him, the bloodied and dirt-filled gloves lay on the persimmon ground. Meriday's body swayed limp against the chains.

Kaffie chose fabric from one-half of Grafton's butler shirt and one-half of Meriday's butler jacket for her quilt. She now had twenty pieces. She did not wish to collect any more.

KAFFIE

Chapter 1

Master Harris isolated himself from any plantation business for about two weeks after the Meriday and Grafton incidents. He had yet to hear of any updates on Grafton's whereabouts from his patrollers.

He was tired, weary, and worn through. He had been on the road most of the past year and was ready for a much lighter schedule. Though his doctor had found him to be in reasonably good health for a man at seventy-nine years old, Harris just wanted to go fishing.

He paced his bedroom and grew nostalgic for times past. He reminisced about Tillie, long deceased and worried if Meriday had actually taken to spreading the word that he had murdered his own wife. Harris surmised that Meriday could have been present in the Big House on that fateful day. Tillie had become a nagging vindictive bitch to him. She interfered with his business decisions. She maimed slave children. They had not been intimate for decades. She did not respect him at all.

He rubbed his forehead as he looked at his image in the mirror. His wrinkled face with obvious jowls and deep furrows stared back at him in silence. He studied the sideways view of his thin frame. The bay-window belly and the sparse grey hairs on a sunken chest signaled that the years had impounded his youthfulness. The age spots on his arms and legs supplanted the freckles that were almost invisible on his weather-beaten face.

Harris sighed. He accepted his condition and regretted nothing he had done in the past. It was now time to settle the dangling questions that both Luvinia and Rocky (the nickname that he had secretly called Rockfield as a child) had burdened him with lately. Luvinia had left countless notes under her father's door. She had requested that he meet with her privately. Her solicitations turned to pleadings that morphed into quasi-demands.

Harris summoned Luvinia and Stiles to his private study on a Sunday. When they entered he greeted them and told them to help themselves to the fresh peach tea or liquor

The Cricket Cries, the Year Changes

that the butler had brought into the chamber. Stiles declined. Luvinia to Harris' surprise, asked for a shot of rye whiskey.

As she sat and sipped her drink, she wondered to herself why in the hell was Rockfield here with her father, too. She thought that perhaps Rockfield had revealed the truth about Kaffie to Harris and wanted to usurp her ownership of the mulatto in person.

Harris began the conversation by going down memory lane. He started with the simple start of this homestead with twenty-five slaves that had expanded over the years to over three hundred. He bragged about his wealth, his political ties, the reputation of the Harris-Jones plantation and lastly his legacy. He continued it was time for him to pass the torch of new leadership on the plantation though the monies and properties would not flow through until after his death.

Luvinia sat up straight; her piercing brown eyes were focused on Stiles. They softened when she turned toward her father as she readied herself for the pending coronation. Rockfield, not threatened by her intimidating glances, held his peace.

Harris unlocked the side drawer of his walnut desk. He laid two separate documents in the center of it. He sipped his whiskey and cleared his throat. He then girded himself for Luvinia's reaction to what he was about to say. He told them that he would cede his day-to-day authority over the plantation's business to the new majority owner, Rockfield Stiles. He said that upon his death Stiles would inherit sixty-percent ownership and Luvinia forty percent.

Luvinia grew faint. Her fingers clutched the English-embroidered antique lace napkin that rested upon her lap. With a reddened face and a rise in her body temperature, she asked her father if he knew what he was doing. She angrily pointed at Stiles, the man who had repeatedly rejected her advances, and asked her father why. Harris told Luvinia that Rockfield was his son. He told her he would make no apologies for an indiscretion committed over half a century ago. He said he was getting older and he needed to settle things before he died.

She threw the whiskey tumbler toward the curio and shattered it into pieces. Shards of glass peppered the hardwood floor. One of the butlers ran in to see if everything was all right and was quickly dismissed by Harris.

Luvinia went to pieces and begged her father to reconsider his last will and testament. She said she knew that not many women ran plantations as large as this—— then she stopped short. She clutched her blouse. She turned to Stlies, cried loudly, and said to him, "You are my brother"! Then she plaintively questioned him with disbelief, "My brother?" Rockfield said nothing. She began to stomp and shout and scream and holler. Her reactions confirmed to her father that she was still the impetuous child, the spoiled brat, and a manipulator like her mother.

He was glad that he had bequeathed just forty percent of his life's work to this spinster. He cautioned her to sit down and compose herself or he would have to postpone the meeting until she could act more like an adult.

Luvinia started to pull books from the shelves and hurled some at Rockfield. She directed a few at Harris as well. She asked her father with a snippy tone if he knew Kaffie was Rockfield's daughter. Harris leaned toward her in his chair, his face reddened in disbelief. She threw yet another vase to the floor when she asked Harris how he felt about being a grandfather to a nigger. The expensive piece met the hardwood floor the same time that the word "nigger" did.

She laughed in his face and sneered that his life was a total lie. The highly respected rich Mr. Harris was an adulterer with a damn-near-white nigger for a grandchild, she scoffed. She mocked the fact that his bastard son knowingly allowed him to bring his bastard daughter into the mansion as if she was entitled to a better life.

She shrieked to her father that Kaffie was his granddaughter——her niece. Luvinia stammered while she caught her own words before she could complete her rant. She slouched on the couch and remembered the day that she insisted that Kaffie be her friend. There was something about her, Luvinia reflected. Now that bitch was at the root of all things bad that had happened to her, she rued.

Harris slumped back into his chair. He was in shock. He spoke not a word. His eyes glazed over. He stared blankly into nothingness. Time stood still in the study. He motioned to the two of them to go away; but they moved quickly toward him and thought that he was having a heart attack or apoplexy. Tears streamed down his leathery face. He ordered them to leave him be.

Rockfield, jolted by the entire scene, told his father that he wanted to explain his past actions. Harris called him "Son" for the first time. He waved him off and bowed his head. He murmured that now was not the time. He ordered them out of the room.

Half brother and sister reluctantly left the study; they looked at one another with extreme hostility. Stiles quietly closed the door with a backwards pitying glance towards his father and hoped that everything would be all right. He sat outside upon the floor with his back against the wall and waited. Luvinia's rustling taffeta dress announced the haste with which she flew upstairs to her room.

Harris poured himself a tall drink.

"A granddaughter," he said with pride. "Kaffie is my granddaughter," he repeated to himself. He had often wondered what white man had fathered Kaffie. He had studied her grey eyes and her freckled face from the day Luvinia pulled her from the rows in the field.

Tillie had also regarded Kaffie's features with suspicion on many occasions while she grew up in the Big House. Among her many tirades during their marriage, she had damned Harris for openly welcoming his bastard child into their lives. He always thought that she was speaking of Rockfield.

Kaffie was Harris' Balm from Gilead. She was a lovely woman well into her forties now. She was kind in spirit and deeds. This revelation sealed his intention to make his son master of the plantation.

Harris rose feebly from his chair. He had to see Kaffie before Luvinia's acidic words could hurt her terribly.

Cynthia Harris-Allen

Chapter 2

Harris' climb to the attic was a slow one. He had not used the muscles required for such a feat in a very long time. It was a telling experience. He knocked on Kaffie's door. Kaffie thought it was one of her apprentices and quickly answered the door. She looked down when she saw it was Master Harris. She motioned for him to come in and called him "Sir".

Harris, out of breath, asked Kaffie if he could sit down. She nodded and offered him a drink of water from the porcelain pitcher. As he walked toward the tufted chintz seat, he stopped and grabbed her and hugged her. Kaffie grew afraid and struggled to free herself from his arms. He asked her to forgive him for he did not mean to frighten her.

Harris sat and drew a long breath. He told Kaffie that he was her grandfather; he cried that he had just found out. He said she probably already knew that she was Rockfield's daughter. He judged it by the recent incessant hounding from Luvinia for a private conversation of the "utmost importance" after the three of them had traveled to Boston.

However, he said, he was sure she did not know as he didn't, until now, that she was his granddaughter. Kaffie dropped her sewing pieces and slumped to her knees on the woven mats on the floor. She covered her face from the impact of the news. She pondered the facts just presented to her. She had just learned a few weeks ago that Stiles was her father. But, the master of the largest homestead in Georgia was her grandfather! That made Luvinia her auntie!

Harris managed to stoop beside Kaffie and hold her. Still on her knees, she began to cry as she did when Stiles told her he was going to set her free. Now she knew why he could have promised it with such authority and resolve.

Luvinia burst into the attic room with a revolver in her hand. She sarcastically asked the two of them if they were not a pretty picture of love——or not. With her unsteady hands she pointed the weapon downwards toward Kaffie and discharged it. It missed her but grazed Harris in the shoulder.

Kaffie screamed.

The Cricket Cries, the Year Changes

Fanna ran from her bedroom towards Kaffie. She pushed open the door. It hit Luvinia in the back. Luvinia moved forward and attempted to cock the gun again. Fanna surprised her by wresting it from her grip. Luvinia turned and cursed her. Fanna hit Luvinia on the side of her face with the butt of the pistol. Luvinia fell over the cutting tables to the floor.

Harris writhed in pain on the floor. The gunshot wound was accompanied by a heart attack.

Kaffie continued to hide her face in her hands.

The entire mansion populace, freed and slave alike, stampeded toward the attic steps.

Cynthia Harris-Allen

Chapter 3

Spring, the Music of the Earth, had arrived. She danced and sang as usual, freshly arrayed with budding trees and perennials. The plants had broken their underground gestation to greet the world. They said "Hello" to their neighboring evergreen shrubs that would provide them the cool shade in the summer when their colors dared to peak.

Insect eggs by the thousands lay upon each other like a bowl of burnt rice. They quickly hatched; the tiny trails of marching bugs angled their paths toward pre-destined prey. Wrens and swallows sang songs of welcome to their newborn babies. The patriarchal flights to catch the early worms were accented by the dutiful attention of the nesting new mothers that feathered their young.

Sluggish rivers, though never frozen, seemed to move faster as the warming breeze decried its winter slothfulness. With the aid of animal feet and other mysterious traffic, seeds and pods from the giant trees that dotted the thicket in the fall, had taken root in the softer ground. They stretched to rival the heights of those whose fruits they were proud to represent.

The results of the off-season efforts during the lay-by that repaired the fences, renovated the mansion, added tubby to the slave cabins, and dug new wells were evident. The longer light of day allowed more than a cursory examination of the extensive work completed by the slaves.

The Harris-Jones plantation was alive, prepared, and ready for the first sowing week. The master wanted it to begin on a Sunday, usually the rest day for the slaves; but they, too, wanted to welcome the advent of newness with their own incantations to their gods of harvest and plenty.

They would pray for a bountiful reaping. They supposed it would somehow benefit their plight or slacken the crude cruel conditions of their lives. The shepherds readied themselves for their vigilant watch over the sheep and the goats. They might get three outfits this year to wear instead of two, they reckoned. Whether the quality of care for the cows was prayed over remained a mystery. Their life-sustaining milk was also the source of the whip.

The Cricket Cries, the Year Changes

Rockfield Stiles was now the master of the plantation. Master Harris had died of a heart attack ten years ago. He had suffered for a long while. He struggled to make sure that his wishes were carried out. He pleaded with Death to allow him time for the litany of lawyers to arrive from various parts of the North to set his pathway straight.

His skeletal figure lay in repose in the mansion drawing room. His body was viewed for three days. Hundreds of planters came to pay respect to this little giant. They spoke to his business insight. They remembered Harris' self-sufficiency that sustained the many industries that thrived on this huge homestead.

Luvinia, as counterfeit as usual, received the guests while dressed in all black. The outfit included the big hat and dense veil that hid her artificial despair. She began to appear palatable to the many suitors who coveted her wealth. She accepted their attention as well deserved and would not consider that her money was their only motive.

She was now sixty years old. She was still thin. The sunken right broken cheekbone cracked by the hands of Fanna, accented a gaunt facial appearance. Fleshy bits hung from her neck like the wattle of a turkey. Her thinning hair struggled to support the huge fake chignon circle that perched atop her head anchored by dozens of hairpins. She rarely looked at herself in the mirror. She preferred to hear from her male suitors how attractive she was.

When the last of the guests had left the funeral services, Kaffie tiptoed into the drawing room. It smelled of cigar smoke, perfume, flowers, and goodbyes. She walked over to the closed casket and lifted the partitioned top. She leaned in to kiss Harris on the forehead for far too many reasons to list here. She placed a pieced remnant from the dress she had worn the day he told her how pleased he was to be her grandfather under his cold stiff hand.

Later, most of the slaves sang their loud version of a funeral dirge. The casket rested in a horse-drawn carriage that was driven to the white graveyard. There, Master Nealy Sewell Harris was laid to rest in the family plot.

#

Cynthia Harris-Allen

Rockfield Stiles, already liked and respected by the gentry, humbly presented himself as the new master to his slaves. He had plans for the future of the plantation that would have to wait for another time to disclose. Now in his late seventies, he had slowed down his aggressive approach to running the farmstead alone. He paid handsomely for trusted able-bodied young men to keep him apprised of all-important situations. He had a new generation of drivers and overseers who followed his example.

His relationship with Luvinia remained strained. Oftentimes, he would chuckle to himself that once she was so enamored of him before she found out he was her half-brother. He figured the only attraction that he lost was his availability.

Kaffie voluntarily remained behind the scenes. She was grateful for the time she had spent with her grandfather. Harris revealed things to Kaffie about his upbringing that he had never told anyone. Before he became infirmed, the two of them would ride in a wagon together toward the slave quarters where Kaffie oversaw the seasonal allotment of clothing. It became a special time that the two of them looked forward to sharing.

Harris bragged to the slaves that Kaffie was his granddaughter. None were surprised except for the new arrivals. Many had said that they knew when that "chile" was snatched to the Big House, that Stiles had claimed his baby girl. The old slaves had known her mother. Nevertheless, they gave no credit to Stiles for Kaffie's looks. They clicked their teeth collectively and declared that the matching sets of grey eyes and freckles were evidence enough for them.

Harris saw how much the slaves loved Kaffie. They thanked her for the articles as if she was the source of the cotton itself. Under the tent they often presented her with gifts of beads, trinkets, and pottery. He had her manumission papers drawn up, underwritten and witnessed by Luvinia and Rockfield. She was free to leave the plantation anytime she wished. Harris also established a bank account for Kaffie. It held a great deal of money.

Luvinia was agitated and stressed by the entire process.

The Cricket Cries, the Year Changes

Luvinia assumed the role as mistress of the mansion. She continued to hold parties, soirees, and picnics. The only thing that she required was easy access to the funds that sustained her high living and expensive taste.

Kaffie oversaw the mass sewing of the clothing for the entire plantation. She no longer participated in the day-to-day operation. Fanna, her assistant now for many years, had assumed that position. With no deadlines to meet for the first time in her life, an aging Kaffie began to quilt blankets that could hang from a wall or adorn a bed. Fanna supplied her with scraps and remnants that were far too small to make anything to wear out of them.

One afternoon, Kaffie hung her quilts outside after laundering them for the first time after completion. The five pieces moved briskly in the sunny day breeze. The flapping pieces of vivid color attracted a lot of attention from the slaves. They stood and marveled at the large creations while Luvinia sipped her tea and looked on from the back mansion window.

She remembered the first quilt that Kaffie had made, the one that had excited her mother so much. She made a mental note to find out what had happened to it. Luvinia's friends had told her about the quilting bees that took place in Atlanta and Charleston and smaller towns. They told her several plantation mistresses had entered the quilts made by their women, free or slave, in the contests.

The slave owners received the prize money and the recognition. The indentured servants, who sewed the piece, could receive a small pittance from their employers if it received an honorable mention. Luvinia, always interested in enjoying the spotlight, decided to call a truce with Kaffie.

The two of them were on very thin speaking terms since the disclosure of the familial ties. They never socialized. They spoke when necessary with carefully guarded words devoid of warmth and emotion. In fact, Kaffie had referred Luvinia to Fanna for her dressmaking needs. Luvinia was forced to accept the young woman's sewing skills which were well above all the others.

Luvinia approached Kaffie with news of the contests. She encouraged her to enter the first quilt that her mother,

Tillie, was so taken with. Kaffie replied that she did not know where that quilt was and it probably had rotted away.

She jumped at the opportunity to continue the conversation. She asked Kaffie if she could take one of her quilts that she saw hanging from the line the other day as an entry into a contest. She swore that she would give Kaffie the credit for making it. She asked Kaffie to agree that it would be nice for the Harris-Jones' reputation to be further enhanced by showing its excellent new products. Kaffie thought about it but did not answer.

Luvinia reminded Kaffie that she was a free black now and she could travel the circuits if she so desired. She furthered that it would not bother her if Kaffie used Harris as her last name. Most white folks knew that even free niggers took the surnames of their masters. She told her to never ever say to anyone that they were blood relatives.

Kaffie was unwilling to travel with Luvinia period. She did not trust her. She gave Luvinia permission to take along a couple of her quilts, enter them herself, and tell her how it fared with the competition when she returned.

Luvinia agreed. She added personal stops along the circuits to her itinerary. Sometimes she would be gone for months. Kaffie told Fanna of Luvinia's request. Fanna said she was thankful that Kaffie's beautiful quilting skills would be seen and appreciated beyond the plantation borders, but she called to Kaffie's memory Luvinia's self-serving ways.

Kaffie decided to complete her own personal quilt with the remnants she had saved from too many slaves whom she had cared for deeply. It came to her one night that she should use the dark green twill fabric from the clothing that Harris wore most of the time for the backing of her quilt. It was heavy and double woven.

Though the twenty pieces represented the lives of Abigail, Lewis and all, Harris was the dominant factor that had brought them all together. He certainly was important to her. Had it not been for him, she would not exist. She did not feel she was betraying the memories of her friends by using his fabric. There would be a barrier of batting between them. He could no longer touch them. To bind the entire piece together at the border, she would use her father's shirt fabric of beige twill.

The Cricket Cries, the Year Changes

With these decisions made, Kaffie was persuaded to finish this long ago project. To her, it had meaning and purpose more than it ever had before.

Chapter 3

Kaffie continued to receive letters from Grafton under the pen name of "Sarah". In those letters, he described the political and social climate of Boston, Massachusetts, and living up north as a whole. He added that he was truly free to move about. He worked in a print shop as a typesetter.

Once, he and two white friends traveled to Ohio to hear the abolitionists William Lloyd Garrison and Frederick Douglass speak. He wrote he thought that their names might go down in history. He told her more about the Underground Railroad in his communications. He asked her to tell Fanna he loved her and that he had written her name twenty times on a separate piece of paper contained in the letter. He promised her they would be together soon.

As usual, Kaffie burned the letters except for the special insertion. Fanna asked her many times to repeat what he had written. She took his promises to bed with her along with his twenty affirmations.

\#

A long, soft rain fell on the Harris-Jones grounds. There was little work in the fields. It was the layby. The drops fell on the attic roof like the tiny pins that populated Kaffie's many cushions. A sudden gust of wind would change their numbers to the thousands and dwindle again.

Kaffie had pulled a chair to the side of her bed and sat on it. She examined the layout of her quilt pieces and was finally pleased with the scheme. She had placed Kalulu's yellowing remnant next to Mathilde's marigold piece. Barbury's brown shirt was placed to the right of Helder's ecru denim strip. She had spent days auditioning the quilt sections until she was pleased with the arrangement. She positioned them in rows of four across and five down.

She touched the individual portions and could not help but recall their personal histories. She was saddened when she thought about their struggles to be free. Here she was, free as a bird, and did not choose to leave. Even as a slave, she did not suffer like a true bondswoman in the fields. Though she was intrigued and excited about her Boston trip long ago, Kaffie felt that she could not live on her own. She chided herself for being weak. Besides, she had the love of her father, Rockfield Stiles-Harris. She had loved her grandfather; and then there was Fanna.

Kaffie adored Fanna. She was the exact opposite of her. Fanna was strong, resilient, feisty, and afraid of no one. She protected Kaffie and cared for her when she was ill. She denied others access to her services when she felt they were taking advantage of Kaffie's benevolence.

Soon Kaffie began to baste the pieces together. Tears moistened her cheeks as she drew Boway's silk thread from back to front. She connected the torments of Luge, Ngango, Betsey, and Patrice. Distracted by her grief, she pierced her finger with the needle. While she sucked the tiny red pinprick clean, she suddenly found a way to liberate the owners of these pieces.

Kaffie was going to allow Luvinia to enter her private quilt into the competitions. Abigail, Jelani, Scipio, and her dear Grafton remained as the living tributes within the quilt. They were free. She knew in her soul that they were well. Now, the ones who had died would also be able to breathe the free air, she concluded. They could travel beyond their chained existences away from the riverbanks and the hanging trees. Finally, they could be free of this abysmal red clay, she rejoiced. Their lives would be immortalized by this journey. Their souls would be lifted by the winds.

Kaffie called for Fanna to join with her to finish the piecing.

#

Luvinia told Kaffie that she was glad about winning second prize for one of her quilts that she had pulled from the clothesline. She told her that if she could embellish that same design in a new piece, she might consider taking it with her on the next tour. Kaffie was startled. Luvinia had never revealed to her that her work had garnered an award. She asked her why she had never told her. Fanna pointed a knowing figure in Luvinia's face and smirked.

In the attic, Luvinia studied the new quilt that Kaffie had started. She argued with Kaffie and Fanna over tea about the unconventional methods and fabrics that she had used to construct her special piece. She told Kaffie she had seen hundreds of quilts in Tennessee, Alabama, Florida, and Georgia combined. This latest project would not even fetch an honorable mention. She cited the Victorian crazy quilts that were comprised of random piecing of silks and velvets that were beautiful. Luvinia said that the homespun farmwomen made the same type of pattern, but with cheap cotton fabrics. They were not as pretty as the silk ones and were never chosen.

Before she could continue, Fanna interrupted her.

Fanna called Luvinia a bitch. She told her that Kaffie was a free woman. She did not need Luvinia to represent her at a quilt fair or anywhere else. Fanna folded her arms across her chest and told Luvinia she was no expert on quilting or anything that had to do with yard goods. She reproached her use of big words that she had heard someone else use. She scolded that everyone knew that she was an educated fool.

Luvinia, reddened by the remarks, stood up to leave.

Kaffie put her hand up to stop Fanna's verbal onslaught. Fanna gently pushed it down and held it to the tablecloth. Fanna told Kaffie to draw up traveling papers for her. She would travel with her as her attendant. They did not need Luvinia. They would take the quilt to the exhibits themselves and see what the tree would shake out.

#

From March to July, Kaffie and Fanna traveled by rail way or carriage to many quilt fairs. It was a new world for Fanna. She was as happy as she could be. Sometimes, Kaffie had to have talks with her about holding her temper and her tongue but otherwise, she was glad that Fanna had convinced her to show her own quilt.

Fanna was surprised when they visited Monroe, Louisiana to learn that two cities could have the same name. While they were there she told anyone that would listen she was from Monroe, Georgia with the emphasis on Georgia. Observations like these endeared her even more to Kaffie. Fanna was both a strong woman and a young child, she thought. She made sure she would mention her words to Grafton in her next letter to him.

The Cricket Cries, the Year Changes

I got an honorable mention at its first showing, a second place at the fair in Memphis, Tennessee and first prize in Bessemer, Alabama! There were many quilts sewn by abolitionists among the southern-made ones. That surprised Kaffie. She soon realized that the common denominator was the women and their craft. Very little politicizing was witnessed at these exhibitions.

In Atlanta, streams of women gathered around me in the morning. Many quilts were covered by noon so that the hot sun would not accelerate the fading process. I was among them. The judges appraised me several times before I was finally covered up. Then they took their seats to consult.

They marveled at the quality of Kaffie's work. The blanket stitches and French knots were perfect. They had never before seen the other types of patterned quilting that she had used and were intrigued by its origin. There were other clusters of raised threads throughout the piece. The whole cloths used in my assembly were a refreshing distraction from the countless piecing and scrapping that were displayed in the others. Each of my pieces stood on its own. From my wide wale corduroy to my silk taffeta insertions, the judges were awed by my simplicity and beauty!

Earlier that morning, one of the competitors had pointed out to the judges that I did not move in the breeze like the others. She wanted to know what had weighted me down. She accused me of not being in compliance with the rules of submission. The judges examined me both front and back and scrutinized my binding. They felt my soft stuffing and concluded it was pliant enough to roll between their fingers like the others. They dismissed the entrant's veiled assertions.

While the judges deliberated, Kaffie and Fanna sat at a table and drank iced tea with some quilters from up North. On future trips the two would eat and socialize with the abolitionists.

Cynthia Harris-Allen

Kaffie told Fanna that she was glad to be returning home in the morning. Fanna agreed with her and expressed hope that letters from Grafton would be waiting for them.

In the late afternoon, Kaffie's quilt was awarded the Grand Prize. She was surprised and elated. Fanna jumped up and down and screamed for way too long. The prize was five hundred dollars! Fanna told Kaffie that was how much her mother said she was sold for. That comment jerked Kaffie back to reality.

The Cricket Cries, the Year Changes

Chapter 4

Luvinia received word about Kaffie's celebrated quilt long before the two women would return to the plantation. She was outdone. No credit was given to her. She still resented Kaffie's position on the plantation. Surely she would receive Rockfield's sixty-percent share at his death. She could even evict me from my own home if she cared to, shuddered Luvinia. Nevertheless, she decided to worry about that later.

After about two weeks of shuttered silence between the two of them, Luvinia decided to break the ice. She visited Kaffie in the attic under the pretense of talking to her about designing a gown for an upcoming ball. Kaffie told her that her measurements remained the same and it was not necessary to make a new muslin template. Kaffie dismissively told her to go to Fanna to choose her fabric. Luvinia looked closely at Kaffie and asked her if she were well. She told her she looked sickly. Kaffie answered that she was just tired from her journey and that rest would be the best tonic.

Luvinia told her she would have Cook bring her some soup and tea. She need not run the stairs in her condition. Kaffie thanked her but told her that Fanna took care of her needs. Luvinia left the room and closed the door slowly as she spied Kaffie moving weakly toward her bed.

#

Kaffie had pneumonia. Fanna slept in her room for two weeks until she showed signs of making a full recovery. In her feverish delirium, Kaffie had called out some of the names of the slaves that were represented in my quilt. Her sweaty renditions of how they died or escaped were blurred and convoluted as she cried in her sleep. It hurt Fanna deeply. She never mentioned it to Kaffie when she recovered.

Fanna told Kaffie that she allowed Luvinia to take me to the largest quilt exhibition held in the south in Savannah. She asked for Kaffie's forgiveness and said that she wanted it to get its due respect. Kaffie nodded and told her it was fine. She asked Fanna to bring her the mail that she had not read.

Cynthia Harris-Allen

Letters from Grafton were full of hope. He told Kaffie that the grounds had shaken up all over the North with anti-slavery protests and debates. He asked her if she had heard of Abraham Lincoln. He might be the next president. He informed her that Great Britain had ceased their slave trade and was actively seizing other slave ships in route to the islands and the Americas and freeing its slaves by the thousands.

He wrote that Fanna should know that it was time that he made plans for her to come to Boston to marry him. The package contained a book called *Uncle Tom's Cabin*. Grafton urged Kaffie to read it to Fanna. She was elated that Grafton was ready to receive her but she would not leave Kaffie. She knew Kaffie had not written Grafton about her health. She never recovered fully from pneumonia. Any sign of dampness or moisture would send her straight to bed.

She asked Kaffie to tell Grafton she would be ready in a little while to see him. As Kaffie wrote the note, their eyes met and sealed their common thoughts of separation.

Fanna signed her name for the first time to the letter.

\#

Kaffie gave permission to Luvinia to continue to exhibit her quilt. She could no longer travel. In her condition it was too strenuous for her. Stiles-Harris had visited her with more regularity than usual. He wanted her to be well and told her if she needed anything to let him know. He constantly reminded her how much he loved her. He told her every day he could look into her face and be reminded of his father and by her spirit, he knew her mother again.

He had already chosen the best doctor in Atlanta to care for her. He made monthly visits and assured Stiles-Harris that he would come whenever he need be.

Luvinia had a blue-ribbon wall in the locked library that celebrated my notoriety. Framed certificates and commendations from various sewing societies were displayed. She had convinced the organizations that Kaffie was a slave on her plantation that she had commissioned to sew the quilt. She took credit for my design. Fanna resented Luvinia's trophy room. She had learned of it from the house help. She told Luvinia it was a bold-faced misrepresentation of her blackened heart. She never told Kaffie about the audacity of Luvinia's claims.

Fanna immediately retrieved the quilt once Luvinia brought me back from the competitions. She wrapped me in a large muslin sheet, placed it in a box, and slid it under Kaffie's bed for safekeeping.

One sunny afternoon, Luvinia had entered Kaffie's room to look for me. Kaffie and Fanna were under the tent with the slaves. She had received a notification of an important exhibition in Milledgeville, the capital city of Georgia. Luvinia pulled me from the box and spread me over Kaffie's bed. She ran her bony fingers over me, still puzzled by the fact that I did not move on the clotheslines when I was presented.

As she touched the different pieces to study the design details up close, the sun went out. It was quickly covered by a dark cloud that took its time moving out of the way. Suddenly, the attic room grew dark. Luvinia was alarmed. She ran to the back window and peered outside. She looked for the direction of a pending storm. Children still played in the yards. The field labor continued. No one was looking up at the sky.

Just then, Fanna entered the room. She had come to retrieve Kaffie's sewing tools to make some alterations. She said nothing to Luvinia. She moved toward me, folded me up, and replaced me under the bed.

She pointed to the door with tight lips closed. Luvinia walked out. The sunshine returned.

#

A month later, the doctor told Stiles-Harris and Fanna that Kaffie was very sick. He was sorry to say that she was slipping away. He told them that he had sedated her. All they could do was keep her warm. He said she was totally blind.

Fanna ran to the empty tent. She cried for hours. Kaffie was not an old woman, she said to herself. The only sign of aging that was noticeable was the slight hunch in her back from bending forward for years at the treadles. What was she going to do without Kaffie?, she mourned. A hand placed on Fanna's shoulder caused her to jerk. It was Stiles-Harris. He cried with Fanna. He thanked her for her years of dedication to Kaffie. He told her that Kaffie had asked him to grant her freedom in the event something happened to her and book her passage to Boston, Massachusetts.

Fanna consoled Stiles-Harris by saying everyone knew how much he loved Kaffie. She was glad that she was going to be free but she had to take care of Kaffie first. She hugged him and told him Kaffie was alone and needed her. She told him she would send word to him if Kaffie's condition changed.

Fanna had spread me out upon Kaffie's frail dying body. When she was coherent, she lovingly spread her hands over me as she felt my familiar weaves and knots. A few times her breathing became shallow faint pants and it frightened Fanna. One morning she could not feel that Kaffie barely breathed at all. She called for Stiles. Kaffie was still alive the doctor told them, but it was time to say goodbye.

Meanwhile, Luvinia had begged Fanna to let her take the quilt to Milledgeville. Fanna refused. Kaffie needed to be with her friends when she died, she insisted to herself. Luvinia inserted herself as the authority figure who could now issue orders to Fanna. Kaffie could not defend her. Luvinia demanded that Fanna wash the smell of liniment from me and pack me for an exhibition in Macon. From there, she would take me to the capital city. She threatened to have Fanna whipped. Fanna stuffed old clothing in muslin and gave the roped box to one of the footmen to place inside Luvinia's carriage.

#

Kaffie died that night. She had mouthed "Thank You" to Fanna and touched her own heart as a sign of love. Her hands clutched the purple caftan remnant of Abigail. Fanna did not cry. She had shed all of her tears under the tent. She breathed a sigh of relief that her friend no longer suffered. She called for Stiles-Harris. He knew what the summons meant. Never before had Fanna seen a grown man cry aloud with the grief and loss that Kaffie's father did.

Stiles-Harris lifted her frail body from the bed and held her in his lap. He kissed her hair. He moved his fingers gently over her grandfather's freckles. He asked Fanna to leave him alone with her for one last time.

Fanna covered all the mirrors in the room.

Chapter 5

The slaves hated the weekly sunrises, but loved the ones on Sundays. What a lovely day to pay tribute to Kaffie! The plantation was on a virtual shutdown. There were no games played. The washerwomen abandoned their personal tasks at the river. On orders from the master, the entire day was devoted to saying goodbye to Kaffie. He told them to rest, reflect, and rejoice for a life well lived.

The slaves were distraught, especially the ones who had known Kaffie for decades. They were at a loss. There was no Ngango to pray to the gods for them. Scipio wasn't there to create an ironed tribute to his dear friend. Cecelia could not array her in freshly dyed cotton.

The entire roof of the allotment tent was covered with fresh flowers. Floral wreaths hung from Kaffie's attic windows. Many young slave girls used bark paint to dot their faces with brown freckles in remembrance. All the males wore the white shirts that were sewn at Kaffie's feet. The slave women were attired in the brightest outfits that Kaffie had made for them. Skirts, dresses, and turbans of every color in the spectrum, were on display that afternoon. From above, the entire homestead looked like a thousand carousels of dyes that turned, spun, and twirled. Each movement seemed to catapult Kaffie closer to the heavens that already knew her name.

Generations of white women, whom Kaffie had clothed over the years, paid their respects. The blacks carried her coffin overhead while they solemnly walked to the cemetery. The entire plantation was still except for the long sighs and the silent tears of Kaffie's people. One could hear a pin drop.

Stiles-Harris was inconsolable. He could not hold in his sorrow when they lowered Kaffie's body into the ground. She was buried in a cloth covered wooden casket and lowered into the Harris family plot next to her grandfather.

Fanna lay in Kaffie's bed in the attic. She would not emerge for a week. She had a white servant place the word "deceased" on the letters from "Sarah" and "return to sender" to notify Grafton of their loss.

The Cricket Cries, the Year Changes

Luvinia chose to keep a low profile. She knew that the slaves disliked her immensely and any crafted gestures of grief on her part would not be tolerated. She feared a hostile response to her charade.

#

Luvinia took me to Milledgeville. I was chosen by the governor's wife to hang in the new rotunda of the capitol!

Many of the carpenters, masons, laborers, and blacksmiths who were black built this structure. The huge marbled pavilion featured art and sculpture gathered by the governor's wife from all over the world. The light from the large Greek-style windows illuminated the frescoed ceilings.

The governor's wife knew of my reputation as Kaffie's quilt. She chose me because of my beauty and because I represented work done by native Georgians. She praised Luvinia for her donation. Luvinia was one of the honored guests to occupy the dais on the day of the dedication.

I was draped fifteen feet above the floor from wrought iron dowels inserted in my muslin hems. The embedded cloths of my slaves had a front row view of the governor's grounds. We hung high above everyone else for miles around.

I was suspended above the large-scaled fireplace that was front and center when one entered the room. Now we were able to look down upon a white person. They all appeared small and common. To the left of me on the wall was a brass plaque that thanked Luvinia Harris of the Harris-Jones plantation for the gift. Luvinia was happy that she had finally secured her place in Georgia's history.

As she moved closer to me, Luvinia looked up and discovered that the letters "KH" lay embedded all over me in different sewn positions and sizes. To her defense, others had not discerned it as well. They thought it was part of my threaded pattern. Kaffie had bent the discipline when she made me. Her work was more of a rhythmic quality that challenged the repetition and rigidity of this spatial craft. Her work answered the needs of its occupants.

#

Cynthia Harris-Allen

That night, Luvinia laid out the dress and accessories that she would wear to the dedication. No longer burdened with the presence of Kaffie in her life, she slept with a smile of confidence and assurance upon her face. She was glad that tomorrow was her birthday.

At six-thirty on the evening of the next day, the politicians and their well-connected friends gathered in the courtyard of the capitol building. They awaited the arrival of the rest of the invitees. They were to enter at the same time per instruction from the governor's wife.

Two gloved butlers opened the large mahogany doors of the mansion and the crowd began to climb the granite stairs. The governor, his wife, and their guests were the first to enter the huge foyer. Their voices echoed off the oyster stoned walls and the immaculate battleship gray reflecting floors. The more people that filled the large room, the louder the voices resounded.

The doors opened to the huge rotunda. Those at the front of the crowd suddenly fell silent. I had pulled myself from the wall and lay in a heap on the floor. The iron dowels were loosed from its casings. The force from one of them had cut a huge gash in the stone fireplace. The dry concrete plaster formed a dusty perimeter around me. I was not even soiled.

More guests filed in; the sight rocked them. Many attributed it to vandalism. The governor's wife was flummoxed. Luvinia was thrown into a panic. She was escorted through the burgeoning crowd to the outside grounds to recover from the experience.

Because the reason for the dinner was my installation, the people were feted anyway. The hosts did not want to offend their highly placed friends. They chose to have dinner and drinks served in the yard that had been prepared for the occasion. Luvinia did not bring me back to the Harris-Jones plantation.

The Cricket Cries, the Year Changes

One of the drivers had returned to the capitol to retrieve me. He hid me in the back of the wagon as an ordinary parcel. He notified the other blacks to deliver the package to Fanna directly.

Fanna had learned what had happened in Milledgeville from the carriage drivers. They told her Luvinia was visibly spooked by what had happened in the rotunda. They added that she was drunk and agitated during the entire ride home. Fanna held her head low and thought of Kaffie. She smiled.

She had moved into Kaffie's room. She slept over me, Kaffie's quilt, still boxed under the bed. Somehow, I granted Fanna peace. She no longer worried about Luvinia. Stiles-Harris had freed her and removed any authority over her from Luvinia. He had taken her to the bank and opened an account in her name. He deposited eight thousand dollars and told her she had access to it whenever she wished.

Upon his orders, an indentured servant began to teach her how to read even though Kaffie had done so long ago.

Late into the evening, Fanna walked to the deserted riverbank. The grounds were quiet and empty. She carried a large glass jar of buttons that Kaffie had collected over her lifetime from clothing that had worn through.

Fanna's bare feet met the dry red clay that steadily moistened the closer she came to the water. An almost tropical breeze fanned her skirt. The night was warm. The licorice sky held sterling silver dots that took turns animating the blackness. The half-moon was bright enough to guide her soft rabbit-like steps.

Fanna sat on the bank and threw the buttons by the handfuls into the streams that rippled toward the Oconee River. She knew one day that this water would take her to Grafton. However, she could not leave now. She would join the northern women that she had met many times at the fairs as a quilter herself.

Cynthia Harris-Allen

They had shown her the secret language that depicted the freedom routes sewn into their quilts. Fanna would make sure that the Harris-Jones plantation slaves could understand the cyphers and use them to liberate themselves.

She carried the empty jar back toward the Big House. Along the way, she playfully tried to catch the fireflies and place them inside of it.

The crickets laughed at her humorous attempts.

The End